Dancer, lover, drinker – never knew which one to pick,
'Til I found them all in one girl and I called her Superchick

JIMMY COLLINS

Superchick

STEPHEN J. MARTIN

MERCIER PRESS

MERCIER PRESS
Douglas Village, Cork
www.mercierpress.ie

Trade enquiries to COLUMBA MERCIER DISTRIBUTION,
55a Spruce Avenue, Stillorgan Industrial Park, Blackrock, Dublin

1 85635 464 4

10 9 8 7 6 5 4 3 2 1

 Mercier Press receives financial assistance from the
Arts Council/An Chomhairle Ealaíon

Superchick is a work of fiction. All the characters and situations are entirely
imaginary and bear no relation to any real person or actual happening.

Printed in England by J. H. Haynes

FOR
RUTH

Four bags of peanuts, three pints of Guinness, two Hamlet cigars, and a fairly dodgy glass of red. All in one trip. Without even using a tray. Not bad for a Sicilian, thought Marco, as he put the glasses down onto the table with a small flourish and looked around at the lads with a wry grin. They weren't even looking at him. Not two weeks ago, in this very pub, he'd gotten a big cheer and a round of applause for doing the very same thing. And tonight? Nothing. Not a bloody sausage. They hadn't even noticed the deft footwork and sprightly pirouette he'd had to use to avoid the old guy who'd stumbled out of the toilet right in front of him and nearly upended the lot. He sat down with a sigh and took the peanuts from his breast pocket, passing them around.

'Cheers Marco,' said Jimmy.

'Good man Marco,' said Norman.

'*Arrivederci mon Frauline*,' said Aesop.

Jimmy, Norman and Aesop all took the top two inches off their pints and put them down. Marco took only the smallest sip of his red but managed, as always, to look like John Wayne while doing it. It was the only reason the lads didn't take the piss out of him for drinking wine in the first place – he was a cool bastard. It wasn't that he didn't like Guinness; it was the volume of the stuff that you were expected to consume, in any given session, with which he took issue. He'd even tried going the whole hog – twelve pints of the stuff – one night soon after he arrived in Dublin eighteen months previously, but that had been a mistake. He rose first thing the next morning for what was to be his customary sunrise wee-wee but quickly found his need more pressing. The ensuing thirty minutes put many aspects of Marco's life into perspective for him. It was that long before he was able to emerge from the bathroom and stagger back to bed, ashen-faced and shaken. He curled up with his fists tucked into his belly, waiting for Death to take him, and decided then and there that no amount of acceptance from your peers was worth whatever had happened to his insides during the night. If that cast an aspersion on his manhood around here, then that was just the way it was going to have to be. He'd wear a bloody dress before he'd do that to himself again.

Jimmy had asked him about the whole John Wayne thing. How did he manage to look so cool, drinking wine out of a stupid little glass like that? Marco had shrugged in that Medi-terranean way and pouted.

'I am Italian. I drink wine.'

That didn't help Jimmy much, but he had to admit that Marco looked the absolute business – pinkie up in the air and all – and so he tried it himself one night. His little experi-ment in Latin sophistication ended, however, when Aesop told him to cop fucking on and get himself a pint before he turned the place into a bleedin' homo's bar.

Tonight they were there for Jimmy. Not that they wouldn't have been there anyway. It was Sunday and they often went for a pint on a Sunday night. But it was different this time. Jimmy was having a bit of trouble with Sandra and they were all there to show some solidarity. Basically, she'd dumped him.

'Four years,' said Jimmy, shaking his head once everyone was comfortably munching nuts. 'Four bleedin' years and then she goes and shags that bastard Beano. Bastard! And he's a crap bass player. Always was. Didn't I say that from the beginning? Didn't I, Aesop?'

Aesop nodded. Jimmy needed to get it all out of his system. He'd be grand once he calmed down a bit.

'Yeah, Jimmy. We all said it.'

'I said it first, but, didn't I? Bass players ... you'd swear it was the hardest thing in the world. The face on him, like he's trying to do long division in his head instead of just playing the same four bleedin' notes over and over again all night. And sure, he couldn't even do that properly, could he Aesop?'

'He was brutal, Jimmy.'

'I mean Aesop, you had to try and keep time with the fool. He was all over the gaff. I'd be standing there, trying to remember the lyrics of a new song and trying to keep me shades from falling off from the sweat and getting meself geared up for a solo and just trying to concentrate on everything, y'know, and still look cool, and in the back of me mind I'd be thinking "Any minute now, Beano's going to change key or drop his pick or go arse about tit off the fucking stage or something." It was very distracting so it was.'

'Ah, don't be talking to me Jimmy,' said Aesop, in his most soothing voice. Marco and Norman were just sitting there quietly, looking into their glasses. They were leaving this one to Aesop.

'And he couldn't sing for shit, could he?' said Jimmy, swallowing a mouthful of beer and looking around. '"We should put harmonies on that" he'd say, like he was Simon and Garfunkel all of a sudden. "That'd be deadly." Harmonies?! He wasn't able to sing *Happy Birthday* without forgetting the words. "Why don't we do *Bohemian Rhapsody?*" he says to me one day, the muppet. "I can do the opera parts with you." Opera! Jaysis, I can hear him now.' Jimmy started singing, 'Mama, just killed a song ...'

He paused to take another slug of his beer. Norman and Marco looked quickly at Aesop, hoping he'd say something to lighten things up a bit, but there was no time. Jimmy was on a roll.

'And that wagon Sandra. She'd be there going spare in McGuigans any time some young one gave me a little smile or something up on the stage, like it's my fault I look the

9

bollocks in me leather pants. I'd be tiptoeing around her all day every Sunday trying to tell her it was nothing and her there the whole time giving Beano a portion, the fuckin' little … you know what she says to me last night? You know what the stupid bleedin' cow says to me last night? Listen to this. "I just feel like we don't understand each other anymore," she says. "What's that s'posed to mean?" I says. "There you go," she says. "See? You don't even understand me now." And I'm looking at her. "What are you bleedin' talking about? How am I meant to understand you when you won't tell me what's wrong with you?" "You should know, Jimmy. You should just know," she says. Now. There you go. I should just know. That's women's logic for yiz, lads. "Oh, right," I says, "Well sorry I'm not fuckin' Uri Gellar, y'know Sandra?" It's … I'm telling yiz lads, it's bleedin' …'

Jimmy stopped and looked at them, out of breath. They all looked into their glasses again, not knowing what to say. Jimmy shook his head and took another drink. It was Norman who'd finally had enough. He didn't like it when his friends were upset and a pint on a Sunday evening with the lads was something he looked forward to all week. Women. Nothing but trouble. He looked around. There wasn't even a woman within ten feet of the table and they were still messing up his evening.

'Ah, feck … feckin … feck her, Jimmy. The cow,' he said out loud and immediately went red.

They all stared at him and then Jimmy burst out laughing.

'Exactly! Thanks, Norman. Feck her is right. Feck them all. All women are bastards.'

The rest of them all started to laugh too, happy that Jimmy had finally been distracted more than anything.

'You do not need this trouble Jimmy,' said Marco. 'You can do better than Sandra.'

'Yeah,' said Aesop. 'Nice looking bloke like yourself.

Good job. Plays guitar. A bloke like you could probably get, I don't know, someone special. A stripper or something. Big sticky-up tits and legs up to her armpits. A girl like that would understand a performer like yourself. We might even get her up on the stage near the end of our second set for a bit of a twirl. That'd raise a few eyebrows in McGuigans, wouldn't it? They wouldn't all be hooring it out the door to catch the last bus if your bird was pencilled in for a guest appearance with the oul' nipple-tassels, would they? Down to her scanties and doing the Mashed Potato.' He was standing up now, rubbing his chest and wiggling his hips.

'Yeah,' said Jimmy, laughing. 'We'd never be short a gig.'

Norman was looking at them all laughing.

'What's up with you?' said Aesop, when he saw that he wasn't joining in.

'Hmm? Nothing. Nothing at all,' said Norman, quickly picking up his beer.

'There is. What's wrong?'

The rest of them were looking at him now. He glanced around at them uneasily and cleared his throat.

'Well, it's ... it's just that ... y'know, having your own girl-friend on the stage, like, and she taking off her clothes. It's a bit, y'know, it's a bit bad, like, isn't it? Everyone would see her, sure.'

'That's what strippers are for Norman, yeah?' said Aesop, giving Marco and Jimmy a quick wink. 'You look at them. Anyway, what's wrong with having a beautiful girlfriend and wanting to show her off?'

'But, God, you could show her off when she's wearing clothes,' said Norman. 'You could do that, couldn't you? Everyone looking at her like that, in the nude. It's not on. It just isn't.' But Norman was speaking to Aesop's back, which was disappearing in the direction of the toilet. He was good and red now, the glass to his lips. This always happened to Norman. He was so easy to get a rise out of that sometimes it

11

was just too difficult for the lads not to do it. Even Marco could wind him up, and he'd only recently been introduced to the concept of 'slagging'. He hadn't been able to see the point at first but was now a true believer. There was something strangely satisfying about targeting one of your friends for an entire evening of verbal abuse, ultimately tormenting him to the point of apoplexy. The more people that could be called upon to participate, the more fun everybody would have. Marco couldn't explain the cruel pleasure in it all, and he was sure that he'd be knifed in Palermo for trying it, but it was all part of the 'craic' here. An Irish thing, seemingly.

He took over in Aesop's absence.

'My old girlfriend at home used to be a model,' he said to Norman. 'She posed for artists. So, this is bad?'

'No, Marco. That's different. That's art, y'see?' said Norman.

'But dancing, it is also art, no?' said Marco, pretending to be confused.

'Well ... it depends on the dancing, doesn't it? Being in the nip just for the sake of it ...'

'But the body is a beautiful thing, yes?' said Marco. He was exaggerating his accent now, doing the hands and everything. 'And art is a celebration of beauty. I don't think my girlfriend was a slut just because she posed nude.'

'I never said she was a slut, Marco. I was just ...'

'You did,' said Marco. 'You called my girlfriend a slut.'

'I did not! I just said that ...'

'I think we are friends, Norman. But you say this things and I am hurt. You do not know Lucia and still you say this things. She was a beautiful girl. Before the accident. And you say this horrible words to her. So, now you think I am some kind of pervert, yes? And what about Jennifer? You think she is also a slut? Because she is now my girlfriend? Hey,' he said, looking around as Aesop returned to the table, 'Norman he says Jennifer is a slut.'

'What did you call my sister?' said Aesop, standing over Norman.

'I didn't call her anything!' said Norman. 'Good God, I'd never say that about Jennifer. We were just talking about art and Marco got a bit confused, that's all.'

'Oh, so now I am stupid,' said Marco. 'I am stupid and my girlfriend is a slut bitch. Thank you, Norman. Ha. My good Irish friend Norman. I sheet on your country and I sheet on this cheap sheet wine.' He put down his glass, stood up and grabbed his coat. 'Fuck you Norman,' he said and marched off, muttering something in Italian.

'You really did it that time,' said Jimmy, looking at Norman and shaking his head.

'I didn't say anything! He's gone mad. Jimmy, you heard what I said. Christ, talk to him. Go and run after him.' Norman was cherry-coloured now and sweating. He was half out of his chair himself when Aesop put a hand on his arm.

'So you think Jennifer's a tart, then?' he said, scratching his chin. 'You might be right, there.'

'I never mentioned ... What?! ... That's a terrible thing to say about your sister!' said Norman, swinging around, scandalised.

'Did you never have a jant on her, but? Everyone else did. She always said she'd love to shag you.'

'Wha ... that's ... Jennifer isn't ... Aesop, we were just talking about models and posing and the next thing Marco was talking about Jennifer, and ... and ... God, poor Jennifer ... I'd never, ever ... you're shocking, Aesop, the things you say about your sister. You should be ashamed of yourself. God, and your poor mother ...' he stopped and looked around. Jimmy was laughing opposite him. He turned in his seat. Marco had come back and was standing behind him, one hand on his hip and the other wagging a finger at Aesop over Norman's head. They were all laughing at him now.

'And I s'pose ye all think that was hilarious,' said Norman, turning back around and folding his arms.

They tried to stop giggling.

'C'mon Norman,' said Aesop. 'We're trying to cheer Jimmy up. I was only messing about Jennifer.'

'Well, that's something anyway,' said Norman, opening another button on his shirt to let some air in.

'Of course I was,' said Aesop, grinning. 'She never said anything about wanting to shag you.' That started them all off again.

'Aren't ye the feckin' gas men, hah? It's the three feckin' Stooges I have with me this evening,' said Norman, and made for the toilet.

'Nice one,' said Jimmy to Marco, high-fiving him.

'Ah, Jimmy. Bleeding deadly, no?' said Marco, beaming. He was a natural.

Marco Fellini was thirty-two years old. When he left home to try and see if the Celtic Tiger had anything left to offer this particular EU passport-holder, before it gave up the ghost completely, the only thing his mother seemed to be pleased about was that if he did meet a girl, the chances were she would be Catholic. This was good, but it wasn't brilliant. Brilliant would have been Marco's immediate ordination into the Priesthood, but she was pretty much resigned to that never happening. Next best thing would have been to have her son married and living next door, producing a good half-dozen offspring and escorting her to Mass on Sunday mornings. She'd actually been reasonably confident on that one but, again, her little boy had other ideas. Thus it was that she found her tissue-clad fingers being pried away from her son's backpack so that he could escape through the security check and board his flight to Rome. She might not have been able to make him stay, but she could make bloody sure that the last thing he heard from her was the pain of her heartbreak

14

through the frosted glass barrier as Marco's Dad led her, wailing, to the airport café.

Sitting on the plane at last and seeing to the teary patch on his shirt with a napkin, Marco thought about what he was about to do. He knew no one in Ireland. The weather was terrible, right? And his English wasn't as good as he liked to pretend. He forced himself to concentrate on the good points. He had a degree and good experience working for Olivetti. Everyone knew Dublin was booming, despite the recent downturns. He might get to fly to England to see some of the Premiership games live. Maybe even Glasgow. Celtic and Rangers. The derby games up there were legendary. Anyway, he could always go home if it didn't work out, right? What was the worst thing that could happen? He'd have to eat potatoes all the time? He was reasonably sure that that wouldn't kill him.

He stayed in a hostel at first. It made him feel adventurous, shopping day to day and washing his own underwear, but he found it completely useless for making friends. For one thing, few of the people he met were Irish and if he was going to be living here, then they were the ones he'd have to get to know. For another thing, no one was hanging around. Germans, Dutch, Brits, Aussies ... everyone was just passing through. Hoping for a break in the weather before they cycled to Donegal, or some other unreasonably far-off corner of the country, and then giving up the wait and doing it anyway in the rain. Marco also gave up. He bought a raincoat and took the DART to Howth and Bray on opposite sides of Dublin Bay. He walked around the city a dozen times to get a feel for the place. A few weeks later he found a one-bedroom flat in the north of the city, near the new university, and started talking to headhunters. The following Tuesday, he found himself walking to his new desk in the Eirotech Solutions headquarters. The Tiger, it seemed, had a life or two left in it yet.

He checked that everyone else had done the same and

then he took off his jacket, hung it over the back of his chair and sat down.

'Howzit going?' said a voice behind him. He looked around and stood up. The voice went on, 'I'm Jimmy Collins. And that's my desk you're sitting at.'

Marco immediately went red.

'Oh. I am sorry. Please excuse. The girl, she told me to sit here,' he said, pointing towards the large desk in the corner where the secretary sat.

'Eileen? Christ, don't mind her. If she had a brain she'd be dangerous. We had a move at the weekend and I'm here now. You're Marco, right? C'mon, I'll show you where to go.'

Jimmy Collins strode away, leaving Marco to grab his jacket and trot after him.

'Excuse me, Mr Collins?' he said.

'Yeah?'

'Did I talk on the phone with you last week?'

'Me? Nah. You're thinking of Jim Carson. Don't mind him either. He's an arsehole.'

Marco didn't know much about Ireland, and almost nothing about Eirotech Solutions, but he was sure of one thing. The last person in this country, or company, that he wanted anything to do with was Jimmy Collins.

'By the way,' said Jimmy, looking over his shoulder. 'I'm your new boss. Call me Sir.'

'Eh, yes ... Sir ...' said Marco, gulping. Oh God, what was he doing in this awful place.

'I was joking. Relax the head, will ye, for fuck sake?' said Jimmy, raising his eyes to the ceiling and shaking his head.

'You're not my boss?' said Marco, hopefully.

'No. I am your boss. But don't call me Sir. At least not in front of people. Here's your desk. Look, I've got some stuff to take care of, so I'll talk to you in a bit. Put your gear down here and go back and talk to Eileen. She'll get you pens and pads and all that.' He looked back over his shoulder at her. 'If she can remember where she bleedin' put them, that is,' he said. Then he turned back around.

'C'mere. Do you like jazz?'

'Jazz?' said Marco. 'Eh ... music?'

Jimmy nodded.

'Eh, it is not my favourite ... eh ...'

'Good,' said Jimmy. He turned and left without another word. Marco nearly did the very same. Instead he looked at Jimmy moving up the aisle and then turned to the desk. Eventually he sat down and pulled his shiny new shirt away from his soaking back.

'*Bastardo* ...' he muttered.

'So, Norman, who would be your ideal mot?' said Jimmy. Norman had come back from the Gents and was sitting there quietly. The lads knew not to keep at him. You could only get so much mileage out of Norman on any given night. After that you were asking for a slap in the ear that you'd never see coming. He'd let on that it was all part of the fun, but it was no fun at all getting a slap in the ear from Norman Kelly. He'd spent ten years in the army and had hands like roof tiles.

'What do you mean?' he said, squinting sideways at Jimmy.

'Nothing,' said Jimmy. 'Just, y'know, what kind of bird would you be into? If you could pick anyone, I mean.'

The others all hushed. Women and Norman. This should be good.

Norman cleared his throat.

'Well ... she'd have to have a nice face of course. And be a bit of craic. And quiet. Less of the oul' chat, y'know? Not like these women that are always yapping the whole time, wouldn't give you a minute's peace. Eh, if she liked the country that would be good. Y'know, we could go home and she'd enjoy herself, like.'

Norman was originally from Cork. You could take the

man out of the bog, but you certainly could not take the bog of out Norman. Aesop and Jimmy had been trying to do that for the best part of twenty fruitless years. When Norman said home, he was still talking about a farm that was halfway up a goatshit-clad mountain on the other side of the country.

'Anything else?' said Jimmy.

'Well, she'd have to have, y'know ...'

'Big tits?' said Aesop, who was ripping up a beermat and flicking the pieces into an empty glass.

'Ah stop, would you? I was going to say that she'd have to like me as well. There's no point in being with someone who doesn't want to be with you, is there?'

Jimmy nodded.

'Okay. Aesop?'

'Big tits. Definitely.'

'Besides that.'

'Eh, a real goer in the sack, obviously. And loads of dosh. Has to like Black Sabbath, or there'd be no point. That's it. Oh, she'd have to be able to drive. And have a car. That way I could have a few pints when we go out. Yeah. That's it. No, hang on, she'd have to like Deep Purple as well. And Zeppelin.'

'Right. Marco?'

'Well, Jimmy, I want to have many children. My ideal woman has to love children, yes? She must be able to cook all the proper food. Not only potatoes and meat. And of course she must be beautiful. Yes. That is all.'

Jimmy nodded again.

'Okay. So Aesop wants a rich, tone-deaf slag with a clean licence, Marco wants to marry his Mammy and Norman doesn't care, once her name is Biddy and there's a smell of cattle off her. Ye spas. I was being serious. That's the best you could come up with? One girl. The woman of your dreams and that's all you can think of?'

'Well what about you then?' said Aesop. 'Who's the sad

cow has to look at your bendy nose for all eternity?'

Jimmy said nothing. He just started wiping the condensation down the side of his glass with two fingers. He was thinking about Sandra again. He honestly thought that the two of them would go all the way. Four years. He'd be thirty-one in March. His Mam already had two kids at that age. That was supposed to be him too. But now look at him. And even if he'd stayed with Sandra – forgetting the whole Beano thing for the moment – would they just have been settling for one another, or did they really love each other? How did you know anyway? He didn't want to just settle for someone. Forever? Nah. No way.

'I don't know,' he said, at last. 'That's the problem.'

Aesop snorted.

'What's the problem?' he said. 'You were always the same, Jimmy. Get out there and get your end away, for Jaysis sake. You'll be grand. A few sessions with the baldy fella and you won't even remember what Sandra looks like. I'm telling you. It was the same with me and Loretta. I was flying once I was out there doing the business again.'

'You went out with Loretta when you were fifteen, Aesop. For six weeks. It's not the same, right? You haven't had a steady girlfriend for about fifteen years and you've been up on every tart you met since. So stop telling me I'll be grand. What I had with Sandra was an actual relationship. Adults have them, Aesop, so I wouldn't expect you to know what it feels like.'

Aesop looked at Norman and Marco and jerked a thumb back in Jimmy's direction.

'Will you listen to this homo, will ye?' He turned back to Jimmy. 'Relationship?! Have you been at Cosmo again?'

'Ah fuck off Aesop, yeah?' Jimmy sighed. 'We were together a long time, right? I think I'm allowed be a bit pissed off about it.'

'Jaysis. Touchy, touchy.'

Norman was watching all this. He'd seen Jimmy a hundred times on the stage. Cool. Talented. Audience in the palm of his hand. Singing when he wanted them to. Clapping when he said so. Girls coming up to him afterwards, wanting to talk to him. So confident. Norman could never do any of that. He'd be mortified. But he looked at Jimmy now. Hearing him talk like this gave Norman heart. If Jimmy Collins could be unsure about himself, then anyone could. He put down his pint.

'Seriously Jimmy,' he said. 'Don't mind that eejit. Who would you choose?'

'Let me think a minute,' said Jimmy.

Aesop stood up, exasperated.

'Oh for fuck sake. I'm going up to the bar. Do you want to give me a hand, Marco? Or are you part of this bleedin' Tupperware party as well?'

'I'm coming. Anyway, I already have Jennifer.'

'Yeah, ye do. Poor bastard.'

They left Norman and Jimmy to it, Jimmy with his eyes closed in concentration and Norman watching him.

'She should be good looking, I suppose,' said Jimmy eventually. 'I mean, I knew Sandra was good looking, but after a while you don't really see that any more, do you? So maybe it's not so important. In the long run, I mean.'

He opened his eyes and smiled at Norman. 'It's not easy, is it? Picking one girl that has everything?'

'Nobody has everything Jimmy,' said Norman. 'Your perfect girl wouldn't be mine. Mine wouldn't be Marco's. And no one else would touch Aesop's with a feckin' barge pole.'

'Yeah, you're right. Still but ...' Jimmy was thinking again when there was a yell from the bar.

'Jimmy! Hey, Jimmy! Phone call ...'

He looked over. Aesop was pointing behind the bar. 'Phone call for you.'

'Who is it?' Jimmy called.

'It's the Avon Lady,' Aesop shouted back. 'Wants to know what time she should call around tomorrow.'

Jimmy went red. Half the bar was looking at him now, laughing. He gave Aesop the finger and turned back around, picking up his pint quickly.

'Bastard.'

The lads came back with the drinks and sat down. Aesop was still laughing.

'I told her eleven would be fine.'

'Thanks.'

'No problem.'

Jimmy frowned. Something else was on his mind.

'What's the matter, Jimmy?' said Norman.

'Hmm? Oh. Eh, I'm just thinking of something. A song.' He was looking to one side. Not at anything in particular, it was just the way he held his head when he was trying to grab onto an idea before it left him.

'Which one?' said Norman.

'A new one. Something I might write.'

'What's it about?' said Aesop. He was suddenly all ears. Music was one of the few things that Aesop took seriously. He and Jimmy had been playing together since they were kids. Mostly just messing about, but the latest incarnation of their band, The Grove, was really starting to do well. Until Beano started shagging Sandra, that is. They hadn't had time to sort out what to do about that yet.

'It's about a woman,' said Jimmy. 'The perfect woman.' He was smiling now. 'The most perfect bird you ever did meet.'

Aesop nodded at him to go on. The others just watched. They'd never seen the creative process in action before – not that they were aware anyway – and weren't sure what to make of it.

'She's perfect,' said Jimmy. 'She's beautiful. Everyone wants her.' He was getting excited now. Humming and tapping two beer mats off the table as he talked. 'She's ... she's Girlfriend Lite – a chick without all the crap that's bad for you. Yeah, that's it. She's eh ... she's ...'

'She's what?' said Aesop.

'Superchick!' said Jimmy.

'Superchick?' said Aesop. He was rubbing his chin and looking at Jimmy.

'Superchick,' said Jimmy again, nodding.

'Jimmy,' said Aesop, 'That's a bit, y'know, it's a bit juvenile, isn't it?'

'Oh, it's juvenile, is it? Aesop, tell the lads the name of the last song you gave me lyrics for.'

'What? Ah no ...'

'Go on. Tell them. I'll tell them, will I? Lads, Aesop Mc-Shakespeare here came to me with lyrics for a new song for the band. You know what it's called? It's called *Meatloaf's Underpants*.' He turned back to Aesop. 'So fuck off. The song is called *Superchick*, right?'

'Grand, yeah, whatever ...' said Aesop, grabbing up his pint and looking away.

'I'll have it ready for the drum parts on Wednesday,' said Jimmy, nodding again at the glass in his hand. 'Definitely.'

They all picked up their new pints.

'Marco, what happened to her?' said Norman.

'Who?' said Marco.

'Lucia.'

'Lucia?'

'Your girlfriend in Italy. The model? The one who had the accident? What happ ... ?'

He stopped, closed his eyes. His ears were tingling red before the others even had a chance to laugh. He managed a small smile.

'I'll get me coat ...'

Jimmy was sitting in his bedroom the next evening. His acoustic guitar was beside him on the bed, next to a writing pad. He loved this. The start of a new song. Looking at a blank piece of paper and wondering how it would look when he was finished. Well, he knew how it would look. It would be a bloody awful mess, it always was, but on it would be a little piece of magic. Something new. Something that no one had ever seen or heard before. Something that, for now, was all his. This time he even had a title. *Superchick* was written on the top of the front page and underlined twice. So far, so good.

Jimmy had studied physics in college and had a great job with Eirotech Solutions, but this was where his heart was. He knew, now on the slippers and cardigan side of thirty and with reality being a fairly insistent bastard, that he'd probably never be a rockstar, but he knew too that he could always be an artist and that would do. He made music and that made him different. Jimmy knew it was good music too. It was unfortunate that the world at large would probably never get to find out just how good, but Jimmy could live with that. In the six years he'd worked at Eirotech Solutions – and they had been six pretty successful years by anyone's standards – nothing he'd done there had come close to giving him the same satisfaction he always got from writing a song, playing it for an audience and seeing people move to it. The first time Jimmy looked down from the stage to see three girls he didn't know singing along with him on the chorus of one of his own songs, he was so chuffed with himself that his jaw ached at the end of the night from the hours of non-stop grinning. It had probably been the highlight of his life.

He took the pen out of his mouth and picked up the pad.

Sometimes the lyrics came first, sometimes it was the music. This time it would have to be the lyrics. He already knew what the song was about. Gripping the pen in his fingers and his bottom lip in his teeth, he started to doodle an elaborate exclamation mark beside the title as he tried to get the thoughts flashing past to slow down enough for him to get them into some kind of order. He smiled, remembering the first song he'd ever written. *The Plague of the Exploding Haemorrhoids*. A jaunty little blues boogie with a Paganini-inspired guitar solo. Beautiful, daring, cheeky. He was sixteen and felt that pop music had become too wishy-washy. That Kylie Minogue was Number One just about said it all. He sat listening to her processed warblings on *Top of the Pops* and thought to himself that if there was one person on the planet who shouldn't be so lucky lucky lucky, it was that squealing little pop tart. What the world needed was emotion, energy, life. Jimmy Collins, in other words.

The Plague wasn't actually a bad tune. Even Jimmy had to admit that the lyrics were a bit silly, but silly was okay. Where was it written that art couldn't be a bit of a laugh? Later he even forgave Kylie and her ilk for polluting a generation of youngsters, although Paul Weller would remain in his bad books for another few years still – at least until Jimmy could come up with a reasonable explanation for the Style Council. He eventually settled on Paul having gone a bit mental there for a while, and moved on. In general, though, he opted for a live and let live attitude to music. He might not like some genres himself, but it was all entertainment and it had its place. He differed in that from Aesop, who took most modern pop music as a personal insult. The only exception that Jimmy made in his newfound largesse was jazz, which he still thought was pure shite no matter how many times he gave it a try.

Performance. That was an art too and Jimmy was an avid student. Mick Jagger, Freddie Mercury, Phil Lynott. Even

Frank Sinatra. Jimmy didn't have much time for that kind of music, but he'd seen Sinatra mesmerise audiences and he wanted to know how he did it. With the others, it was obvious. With Jagger it was the way moved his arms and his arse. With Freddie it was the way he arched his back and threw his hair around in the early days. Phillo had the leather pants and the wry smirk. But with Frank it was all in the eyebrows. Jimmy watched, enthralled, as the old fart finally gave up his secret. *Frank's Birthday Special* or something was on the telly, and Jimmy sat looking at it with his parents. Sinatra's eyebrows. They changed from song to song, even from verse to chorus. Their slightest movement altered his whole demeanour and the song would follow, leading the crowd wherever he wanted to bring them. It was amazing.

He tried to be all of those people, but of course that was a disaster. Once he stopped trying, it just seemed to fall into place. Suddenly, he was Jimmy Collins without even thinking about it. The first time he saw himself on video – his Mam had the new camcorder out at his cousin's wedding and Jimmy, eight pints on board, had gotten up with the band – he was stunned. What was all that with the right hand in the air? Why did he keep bending his knees? And his tongue flicking across his teeth during solos? He had no idea that he did any of that, but there it was in front of him. Was it really him up there? Yeah, he decided, it must be. Jimmy Collins. Rockstar. It was only a matter of time. Jimmy smiled again, as he sat in his bedroom with the pad on his lap. Only a matter of time. His cousin's wedding had been twelve years ago.

He mentally slapped himself in the face. He was drifting. Focus, Jimmy. Superchick. He needed to decide the tone of the song. She's the perfect bird ... whatever that meant. Does he have her already, or is he looking for her? Looking for her, probably. Or maybe he used to have her and now she's gone.

Why did she go? Because he messed around? Nah. That wasn't Jimmy. Oh. So we're talking about *Jimmy's* Superchick now? Eh ... yeah. Well then, is she real? Has he met her? Yes. And no. She's real, but Jimmy doesn't know who she is. Yeah. That's the point. Where is she? Don't know. Where do you look? Eh ... everywhere. Could it be that he's met her already, but hasn't recognised her as Superchick? Maybe. Hang on, that would mean ...

It was getting complicated. Jimmy threw the pen down and stood up. This was a tough one. Lyrics weren't normally this hard. He couldn't even get started. Usually he just started scribbling away and the song pretty much wrote itself, but that wasn't working. He knew what the problem was. This wasn't just a song. He really wanted to believe that she was out there somewhere, waiting for him. Sandra doing the dirt and leaving him for Beano had shaken him up. Other people split. Not Sandra and Jimmy. Shit! How was he supposed to concentrate on the song with this stuff going on in his mind? He walked back to the bed and tried again. And again.

An hour later he only had four lines done and he sat staring at them, scratching his chin with the chewed-up end of the pen:

> I've loved a lot of women in my time on this blue ball
> Some cute, some smart, some sexy – didn't matter, loved
>   them all
> Dancer, lover, drinker, never knew which one to pick
> 'Til I found them all in one girl, and I called her Superchick.

He sighed. The page was already full of crossed-out lines and inky blotches. What about the tone? He wasn't sure. Wasn't exactly going to have them reaching for their hankies, was it? He was so sure about the title, but ... maybe Aesop was right about the juvenile thing. The way it was going it would end up being one of those pop-punk songs that are all over the radio these days and he wasn't sure that that was what he was after. He'd written a few of those already. Throwaway tunes with a catchy riff. This one was supposed to be different, but Jimmy knew that if he served up those lyrics to Aesop, the mad bastard would turn the whole thing into a Ramones song. Then again, that was Aesop. Give him a Whitney Houston song and ten minutes later, if you didn't keep an eye on him, he'd be thumping out the Stiff Little Fingers version.

Jimmy was about to lean forward over the pad again, when he heard a key slide into the lock on the front door downstairs. He cursed to himself and stood up in a panic. He wasn't supposed to be here tonight. Sandra was coming round to collect her stuff. Once he started writing he completely lost track of time. It wasn't unusual for him to stagger into the office, bleary-eyed and stiff, having only gotten two hours sleep because he'd been working on something new. Being focused could be a real pain in the arse sometimes.

He heard her voice and ... what ... was that Beano? Downstairs in his house? Oh bollocks, he thought. He needed this like a hole in the head.

Aesop was also at home, in his bedroom, and focused. In Aesop's case, however, his concentration was centred on the glowing end of the huge spliff that was sending twirling wisps of smoke up his nose. All the doors and windows were shut. Not because he didn't want anyone to smell the weed, but because he didn't want any of it going to waste. When the joint was too small to hold in his gold-plated tweezers, he reluctantly put it down on a saucer and stood on the bed with his nose in the air, sucking noisily as he followed the haze that drifted about overhead.

Aesop lived at home, but wasn't unduly worried about his father coming in and catching him smoking the stuff. His Dad hadn't set foot in the room since 1987; the year Aesop finally saved enough money to buy his own stereo. It was also the year that Mr Murray gave up and accepted that his son was destined to forever be the messiest and noisiest little so-and-so in Dublin. He still put down as the biggest mistake of his life the drum kit he'd bought for Aesop on his twelfth birthday.

Aesop decided that if there was anything left of the joint floating around the room, it would just have to seep through his skin and so he took off his clothes and lay down on the bed in his blue underpants to give it a chance. Occasionally he waved his bare arms languidly out over his chest to keep the currents moving. Aesop had no job and didn't want one, but he was extremely conscientious in the pursuit of his pleasures, which numbered just four – music, women, beer and a nice big smoke after his tea. He was about to follow an unscheduled train of thought to some unlikely terminus, as was his wont during the absorption phase of a spliff, when the door burst open and Jennifer walked in.

'Paul, Marco told me about Jimmy and Sandra ...' She paused. 'Good God, the smell in this place.'

'Shut the door, quick,' said Aesop, his eyes still closed.

Jennifer shut the door.

'Dad's just downstairs, you know.'

'On the couch? Watching the news? God, you just never know what he's going to do next, do you? Do you think blue suits me?'

Jennifer found his jeans on the floor and flung them at him.

'Will you put them on? I want to talk to you and I can't if you're lying there in those awful things. God, the mess in here ...' She started to push the mounds of dirty clothes that were scattered around the floor into one big pile with her foot, as Aesop struggled with his jeans on the bed. He seemed to have more hands and legs than he was used to.

'Ah, leave the window down Jennifer,' he said. Jennifer

already had it open and was sitting down next to it on his drum stool.

'I'm driving to Marco's later, Paul, and I'm not doing it with a head full of that stuff.'

'Jennifer, you're spoiling me smoke. What do you want?'

'Jimmy and Sandra. I want to know what happened.'

'She dumped him.'

'I know that, Paul. Why?'

''Cos of Beano. She's riding Beano now.'

'How long is all this going on?'

'Eh, since Saturday I think.'

'Paul, Marco told me that Sandra and Beano are moving in together. It's only Monday night. I think it must have been going on longer than two days.'

'Ah Jennifer, you're talking to the wrong bloke. All I know is that Sandra gave Jimmy the bullet and now she's with Beano. She told him on Saturday night. He told me yesterday. Will you shut the window now? I'm getting cold.'

'No.' She picked up a T-shirt from the floor and threw it at him. 'I want to know what happened. Think, Paul.'

'Think?' said Aesop, lifting his head up and trying to focus on her. 'Think? In case you hadn't noticed, Jennifer, I'm having trouble just lying here without holding on. You'll have to think for both of us.'

'You bloody useless fool. You've been hanging around with Jimmy for twenty years and you haven't got a clue what's happening, do you? Is Jimmy okay?'

'He's grand, he's grand. He was grand last night anyway. Rotten, we were.'

'Paul, being drunk doesn't mean being okay.'

'Jennifer, will you make me some chips?'

'What? You just had your tea.'

'Yeah, but, y'know ... after the smoke ...'

'Feck off, Paul. Jimmy's okay? You're sure?'

'Ah Jennifer, he's fine. He's Jimmy, isn't he? He's not

going to go out and top himself over some mot, is he?'

'Paul.'

'What?'

'Look at me.'

Aesop lifted his head again and peered at her.

'There's two of you.'

'Well, listen to both of us. You're a gobshite.'

Jennifer walked out of the room, leaving Aesop giggling to himself on his bed. She was worried about Jimmy. She'd been mad about him, secretly, since she was a little girl and even though she was delighted with how things were going with Marco, the thought of Jimmy being sad was upsetting her. She'd have done anything for him, but he was always her brother's pal first. He never seemed to see her as anything other than a kind of little sister of his own. When she was younger she'd often put on some smoochy George Michael songs and lie on her bed with her eyes closed and imagine Jimmy finally noticing her. But he never actually did. She'd invent and play through dramas in great detail in her head. Sometimes she cried. But that was then. Jimmy was brilliant and she loved him, but she knew she'd never have him. She'd worked that out when she was sixteen.

Jimmy was sitting on the armchair, looking at the muted telly. Beano was on the couch, looking at Jimmy. Sandra was upstairs in the bedroom, putting her stuff into a huge suitcase.

'Jimmy,' said Beano, his eyes jumping to the floor when Jimmy looked around. 'I'm sorry, y'know ... about everything. Sometimes these things just happen. And I wouldn't have come along tonight except that Sandra told me you wouldn't be here. Thanks for letting me in. Fair play to you, y'know? I hope we can get past all this stuff and ... eh ... be like ... y'know ... mates and all ... eh ... with the ... yoke, like, after ... y'know?'

'Jesus, did you practice that, Beano? Will you ever shut bleedin' up, you spa, before I start to cry?' said Jimmy, shaking his head.

'Right. Eh ... Jimmy ... I'm leaving the band.'

'Oh no! Don't say that. What'll we do without you? Only for you, we'd be shite. You're an arsehole, Beano. You can't leave the band, 'cos I'm fucking you out. I'm not even getting a replacement. I'm going to buy one of those bass machines. It can't replace a good bass player, but it can replace you. It'll stay in key, keep proper time and it won't wear fucking brown cardigans on stage. We won't know ourselves.'

'That's not nice, Jimmy.'

'Ah, ask my arse Beano,' said Jimmy, picking up the paper.

Beano was about to say something but Sandra was coming down the stairs, so he just sat back and looked over at the telly again.

'Okay,' she said, coming into the living-room. 'I've got everything. Except the CDs. Will I come back for them?'

'No,' said Jimmy. 'Can you not just take them now?'

'It'll take a while.'

'It won't. Just take anything with a female vocalist. That's all yours. Except for Blondie. The other stuff ... Texas, Sheryl Crow, Natalie what's her face, yer woman with the hair, 10,000 Maniacs, Indigo Girls, The Corrs, all that shite. Just take it and go, right?'

'Jimmy, I hoped we could be friends, you know?' said Sandra.

'Tough.'

'Jimmy ...'

'Sandra, just fucking take them and go, will ye?' Jimmy was starting to lose it. He stood up and started towards the kitchen before turning back.

'I wasn't planning on being here tonight, right? I'm not in the mood for group therapy, if that's what you're hoping for, and I'm not talking to you in front of the fuckin' Rain

Man over there. Sorry I can't be more philosophical about things, but that's just the kind of unreasonable bastard I am, right?'

'Okay, Jimmy. Okay,' said Sandra, kneeling down to the CD case.

'Take it easy pal,' said Beano.

'Fuck off, Beano. This is my house. Don't tell me to take it easy. And I'm not your pal.' Jimmy went into the kitchen and sat at the table, looking at the back of a Weetabix box. How did this happen? Dealing with it all in his head was one thing, but he wasn't ready for having the pair of them call around for tea and fucking bikkies. He gave it ten minutes, and then stood in the doorway, watching them on their knees in the middle of a pile of CDs.

'Beano, the Aretha Franklin is mine. So is Bjork.'

'You said all the women singers ...'

'I meant all the shite ones.'

'Well, what's shite?'

'Yeah, I wouldn't expect you to know. Mary Black is shite. Why is she going back up on the shelf?'

'I bought you that for Christmas Jimmy,' said Sandra.

'Have you ever heard me playing it?'

Sandra took it and put it with one of her piles, saying nothing. She'd also bought him the Tori Amos collection, but took that too, without looking at him.

'I think that's everything.'

'Alanis,' said Jimmy.

'Jimmy, you like that album!' said Sandra.

'Yeah, well I think I'll be listening to different music for the next while. I'll listen to her again when she writes a fucking happy song. Are ye right? You have everything?'

Sandra stood up with her bags.

'Yes. That's it. Jimmy ...'

'Seeya Sandra.' Jimmy walked down the hall to the front door, and opened it.

'I'm sorry Jimmy,' said Sandra, her hand on his arm. 'Really.'

Jimmy just looked past her out into the garden. She walked out.

'Eh, seeya Jimmy,' said Beano, following her with the case.

'Fuck off Beano,' said Jimmy, without looking at him.

He shut the door behind them and walked back to the living-room. The CDs were in a mess so he started to tidy them up, to give himself something to do. The doorbell rang.

It was Sandra. Beano was putting the case in the car.

'I forgot to give you these.' She handed him the keys and looked at him. 'Take care, Jimmy. Please.'

He looked back at her and for the first time he felt no anger at all. He just felt sad. Sadder than he'd ever felt.

He didn't trust his voice, and so he just nodded back. She turned and started out to the car and he quickly shut the door.

'You too,' he said, as her footsteps faded down the drive-way.

He walked back to the mess on the floor and started to put the discs back in order. God, he felt crap. He'd have called Aesop to go out for a pint but he didn't feel like it tonight. Anyway, Aesop wasn't much good for this type of thing. He'd just sit there and nod and not know what to say. He always had some girl hanging around but he didn't get involved with them. That would be too complicated. As soon as a girl started to call around to Aesop's place or come up to him after a gig with the assumption that they were an item, then her hours were numbered. He'd tell her some big crap story about how they shouldn't keep seeing each other. It was usually an elaborate whopper involving terminal ill-ness or a fear of being hurt. No one could tell stories like Aesop. He'd been doing it for years. Even his Dad called him Aesop.

Jimmy left the CDs and went back upstairs. Maybe working on the song would help. He picked up his pad again. Sandra had left him a note.

Typical. A note was just her style. Nice and melodramatic. He glanced briefly at it. Lots of 'sorry' and 'move on' and 'always be special friends'. The next page on the pad was filled too. He laughed. Bollocks to this! This was ridiculous. He screwed both pages into a ball without properly reading them and threw them into the bin next to the bed. She wanted him to wallow and meditate on it all. She'd pretend she didn't, but that was exactly what she bloody wanted. It would appeal to her sense of the histrionic that he knew only too well.

No thanks, Sandra, he thought. We're over. I don't have to do that shit any more.

He picked up his pad again and opened it to a fresh page.

'Right, she's gone,' he said out loud, after scribbling *Super-chick* down again. 'Now, where are *you* hiding?'

Three

Jimmy's Dad looked up from his paper at Jimmy, did three or four double takes and finally managed to splutter something that would be very hard to spell. Jimmy grinned back at him.

'So do you like it, Da?' he said.

'Do I *like* it, Jimmy?' said Seán. 'Are you losing the feckin' small little bit you have? You look like a … a … bloody gobshite. You … ye … the feckin', the … ggh … fgh …' The English language and its alphabet often had difficulty accommodating Seán Collins when he was outraged or flustered. There weren't nearly enough consonants in it. Jimmy was delighted. He hadn't gotten a reaction this good since the days of the red skin-tight jeans when he was seventeen. Seán took a drink from the glass of water on the table in front of him and tried again.

'What about work, Jimmy? You can take out that feckin' girl's earring when you go into the office, but how are you going to hide the fact that your head looks like a bloody great big snowball? In the name of Jaysis, what were you thinking? I hope you got a receipt. You're lucky you didn't try that when you lived at home, I can tell you that for nothing. I'd have shaved your head myself … you … ngh.'

'Ah leave him alone,' said Peggy, from the sink. 'He's old enough now to do what he wants.' Jimmy's Mam would have hated the hair on anyone else in the world, but if her Jimmy had tattooed a penis on the end of his nose, she'd have said it suited him. Marco maintained that Italian mothers were protective of their sons, but Jimmy knew his Mam would batter Marco's Mam any day of the week.

'Oh, I'll leave him alone all right,' said Seán. 'I don't give a wag what he does. But he asked me what I thought of it and

I told him. I think he looks like a big feckin' eejit with white hair. Now. I've nothing more to say about it. Good luck to him. The fool.'

'Thanks,' said Jimmy. 'I'd have been more worried if you liked it. Y'see … I'm an artist, Da. You have to understand that.' He knew his father hated that kind of talk. He was a plumber.

'Ah, artist me arse. I know exactly what kind of artist you are,' said Seán, pointing at him. He turned to his wife. 'It's you has him this way, Peggy. With your elocution and your Irish dancing and that feckin' cat you always had in the house. He couldn't kick a football to save his life.'

Peggy Collins had heard it all before.

'Ah, will you give over and read your newspaper. Did it hurt Jimmy?'

'It did a bit, Ma. But it wasn't as bad as when I got me nipples pierced.' They both looked over as Seán's head immediately came out from behind the newspaper again, glasses threatening to fall off the end of his nose.

'Ngh …'

'Relax Da. I'm only joking … I only got the left one done.' Jimmy and his Mam laughed. His Dad muttered 'Gobshite', disappeared again and didn't say anything else until his cup of tea arrived.

Getting his hair bleached had hurt like buggery, and Jimmy nearly shat himself when the hairdresser turned his chair back to the mirror to show him the end result, but he was starting to get used to it. He usually dropped into his Mam's for dinner on Wednesdays before rehearsal. He was looking forward to surprising Aesop with the new look. He still wasn't even sure why he'd done it. It had cost the best part of a hundred euro and had burned the crap out of his scalp but Jimmy was a great believer in new beginnings and he knew that Sandra would have hated it. That was good enough for starters.

'So how are you, Jimmy?' asked his Mam later, when he finally put down his knife and fork and took a big gulp of milk to wash down the small mountain of spuds she'd kept trying to build on his plate. She'd been suspicious of Sandra at first, in the tradition of Irish Mammies, but she'd come around after a couple of years and loved her like a daughter now. Peggy was probably the one most upset by the whole thing at this stage. She'd put a lot of effort into teaching Sandra a thing or two about how to look after her son. And now this.

'I'm grand, Ma. No problem. Really,' said Jimmy.

'Are you sure? You two have been together for such a long time. I thought that you'd be the next ones to get married. Do you want to talk about it?'

Jimmy smiled. His Mam was brilliant. She might even be incredibly insightful and helpful at a time like this, but Jimmy wasn't about to find out. The last thing he needed was to talk to his mother, adult to adult, about relationships. That's not what Mam's were for. He'd sooner try and teach his Dad to play *Pretty Vacant* on the guitar.

'No, Ma. Nothing to talk about. Really. Things didn't work out. No big deal.'

'Sure, now?'

'Absolutely. Do you have your jam buns?'

'I do of course, love. Strawberry, blackberry or rhubarb?'

'Eh, can I have a rhubarb one?'

Peggy put a small mound in front of him and started filling a paper bag with fistfuls of hot ones from the oven.

'Take these home with you. And here's a few for poor Aesop.'

He'd been 'poor' Aesop since his mother had died twenty-five years ago. He was like one of her own now.

'Thanks, Ma. Look, I'd better go and meet him. I'm late.'

His mother looked at him and Jimmy immediately picked up a bun from the plate and stuck it in his mouth. In

Peggy's house you ate your buns when they were put in front of you.

'Okay, love. Well call if you need anything, won't you?'

'Yeah. Seeya Ma.' He kissed her cheek and turned around to his Dad. 'Good luck, Da.'

'Bye bye, Frosty the feckin' Snowman,' said Seán, without looking up from the paper.

'C'mere,' said Jimmy, 'Do you want the number of me stylist? He's brilliant. He could probably even do something with your head. If you went in early enough in the day, like, so he could take a run at it ...'

'I wouldn't have him cut the grass out the back,' said Seán looking up, 'never mind me hair. Look at the feckin' state of you. And c'mere, this barber of yours, is he insured? Because I'll tell you something for nothing, if that's what he does to people's heads then he'd want to be.'

Jimmy shook his head and waved a goodbye.

'Forget about it Da,' he said, as he went down the hall. 'I don't think you and Trent would get along.'

'Trent?! What kind of feckin' name is Trent ... the ... ngh.'

'Holy shit!' said Aesop, when he finally realised that it was Jimmy coming down the road towards him. He was outside the community centre having a smoke. 'I saw the guitar and thought the room was double-booked or something. The bleedin' state of you. Brilliant!'

They moved into the room that they'd been booking pretty much every Wednesday for years. There were a couple of old amps, a knackered drum kit and a lot of broken cables, mikes and mike stands. They set up the gear and Jimmy started tuning his guitar and adjusting the levels of his mike, while Aesop sat there throwing his drumsticks up in the air and catching them as he banged out the complicated rolls he used to get loosened up. He had one of Peggy's buns stuffed in his mouth.

Jimmy was ready.

'Y'right?' he said.

Aesop nodded, his cheeks bulging.

'Okay. *Teenage Kicks ...*'

Aesop counted them in, spitting crumbs, and they blazed through it. They could do that one in their sleep. Aesop was waiting for Jimmy to say something but he didn't. At the end of the fourth song he brought it up himself.

'Eh, Jimmy ... where's Beano?'

'Beano's gone, Aesop.' Jimmy made a gun out of his hand and pulled the trigger.

Aesop went pale and stared at Jimmy, his hands to his mouth.

'Christ, Jimmy, what have you done?' he whispered.

Jimmy looked back at him.

'I gave him the bullet, Aesop. From the band.' He did the hand again. 'See? The bullet. Jesus ...'

'Oh right. Oh, thank fuck. Me fuckin' heart. You hear stories, Jimmy, like y'know? Anyway, it still means we don't have a bass player. We're a three-piece. There can't be just the two of us on the stage. It'd sound shite and we'd look like a couple of spare pricks.'

'I know, I know. We'll find someone. I talked to John in McGuigans. They'll get someone else to cover for us this weekend. That gives us a bit of time.'

'Ah bollocks.' Aesop was pissed off. Playing live was one of the things he lived for.

'Can you think of anyone?' said Jimmy.

'What about Mikey Smith?'

'I called him. Carpetmuncher have a gig on Saturday, so he can't do it. And Rob Wrixon is away with his mot. There's no one else would be able to learn the set well enough in a few days. I was thinking of getting one of those machines that follows the guitar with bass lines. You know the ones, they ...'

'Ah Jimmy, I'm not into all that electronic shite. Beano was crap but at least he had a pulse. More or less.'

Jimmy nodded.

'Sorry, Aesop. What was I supposed to do?'

'Yeah. I know. Still, it's a pain in the hole. Him ridin' Sandra is after messing everything ... eh, sorry Jimmy. I just meant ...'

'We'll get someone, Aesop. It'll be grand.'

They kept playing through their regular set. Now that they'd talked about it, having no bass in their sound was glaringly obvious to both of them. They were brutal. Jimmy was getting frustrated and making mistakes. He was trying to add bass lines to the melody lines he was already playing, to compensate, and it wasn't working out too well. Aesop could see him starting to freak, so after about an hour he called a stop and stood up, pretending to stretch out his back.

'So, Jimmy, any sign of *Superchick?*' he said, grinning. They usually worked on new stuff for the second half of the session.

Jimmy looked embarrassed.

'Actually, no. I don't know what the problem is. I just couldn't get the lyrics down any way I liked.'

'What about the tune? We could work on that.'

'Eh, don't have one.'

'Right so.' Aesop was a bit taken aback. Maybe Jimmy couldn't always finish a whole song in three days but he never usually had a problem getting it started.

'Did you come up with anything?' said Jimmy. He did most of the writing, but he was fair about it. If someone else had a good idea he was always happy to hear it.

'Ah no, Jimmy. The way you were going on about this Superchick thing, I thought you wanted to do it on your own.'

Jimmy laughed.

'I was talking about *Meatloaf's Underpants*. Do you have any ideas for that?'

Aesop went red and looked down at his feet.

'C'mon, ye puff,' said Jimmy. 'It's your song. Did you have a riff in mind?'

'Eh, maybe a small one ...'

Aesop got up and took Jimmy's guitar. Jimmy sat at the drums. They did this the odd time. Aesop was a much better guitarist than Jimmy was a drummer, but they could get the bones of a song down this way. Jimmy tried to twirl the sticks as he waited for Aesop to begin and smiled as Aesop bent to adjust his effects unit on the floor, calling up a horrible growling wail that sounded a bit like a broken chainsaw.

They flew through the ideas that Aesop had for *Meatloaf's Underpants*. Jimmy loved it. It was an utterly stupid song but with the mood swings he'd been having since Saturday it was comforting to watch Aesop in action. He was one of life's constants. When they were done he looked at his guitar, slung down low around Aesop's crotch. It never ceased to amaze him how his beautiful instrument, the one he'd spent over a grand on and used to craft all manner of pure and evocative music, could sound so disturbing in Aesop's hands.

The song was about a man who kept making his son turn down the stereo. The son finds a book of spells in the attic and works some magic to condemn his father to a life of living inside Meatloaf's underpants. The last verse has Meatloaf on tour in India during a particularly hot summer and the father understandably seeing the error of his ways. His son lets him out during the last chorus and Daddy buys him a new guitar for a happy rock and roll ending.

'What do you think?' said Aesop. He wasn't very sure of himself as a songwriter and Jimmy's approval was important to him.

'Well, Aesop, it's better than *Swallow Every Drop of My Love* but I don't think it's as good as *The Sausage King*.'

'Okay. Yeah. Still, we're only getting started, right?'

'Yeah. Aesop ... eh ... where did you get the idea for it?'

'Ah, y'know Jimmy ...'

Jimmy looked at him.

'Not really, Aesop, no.'

'Well, I was watching a Meatloaf gig on the telly. He's a big lad, y'see? He looked pretty hot there, doing *Bat Out of Hell* in the tux and all, so I just kind of wondered what it must be like inside his jocks.'

'Right,' said Jimmy. 'Most people wouldn't think of that though, Aesop.'

Aesop shrugged. 'People are different, Jimmy.'

Jimmy nodded slowly at him. 'That's true.'

Aesop went on.

'Well, Jimmy, I would never have thought of someone like Superchick.'

'Why not?'

''Cos I don't think like that. I'm with some bird and she's Superchick. Simple. I'm with some other bird the next night and then *she's* Superchick. Y'see, Jimmy, I love ridin' women, right? That's me. Every girl I've ever been with is brilliant while I'm doing the business. No question. An angel, so she is. All of them. That's a lot of Superchicks, y'know? So, it's not the same kind of Superchick that you're thinking about, just 'cos you're a bit down in the mouth this weather. My Superchick is a more ... eh ... fleeting kind of thing, y'see?'

'Jesus, Aesop, I'm glad Norman's not here to hear this.'

'Well, there ye go. He knows as much about women, now, as my arse knows about throwing stones. He's the nicest bloke in the world but I betcha he's the one who ends up with a stupid fucking cow 'cos he'll fall in love with the first redneck he meets that lets him drop the hand on her.'

Jimmy squeezed his eyes shut and shook his head. Sometimes Aesop could be profoundly insightful, once you cleared away the weed-induced embellishments with which his observations usually came. Jimmy had been having some not dissimilar thoughts about Norman recently. He was too nice for his own good.

'Remind me to leave the room before you tell him that, will you?' said Jimmy. 'Especially if I'm wearing me beige shirt. So what about me then, Confucius?'

'Ah, you're only after getting dumped, Jimmy. Your problem is that you think all women are bastards. You said so yourself the other night.'

'I was only messing, Aesop.'

'Not at all, Jimmy. You just think you were. You were going out with Sandra for ages, she pisses off with Beano and now you feel shite. That's normal, but you can't write a song about the perfect woman when you're in that frame of mind. All you need is a session with some mad tart to sort you out. Then there's Marco. He's worse. He thinks Jennifer is the perfect woman for fuck sake. I grew up with Jennifer, Jimmy. If she's the perfect woman then, I'm telling you, we're all wasting our fuckin' time. We might as well all be Norman, and that's a long way to fall for me, Jimmy. A long, long way. A man could get hurt falling that far ...'

Jimmy shook his head and held up his hand to stop Aesop.

'Will you stop a minute, you bleedin' spacer? What about the song?' he said.

'I could take out the verse about the vindaloo if you think ...'

'*Superchick*, Aesop. We were talking about *Superchick*, remember? For fuck sake, how much did you have tonight?'

'Oh yeah. Eh, look, it's up to you, pal. If it's just another song then write about whatever you want. But if you're on some kind of mission then you'd better get your head in gear.' Aesop stopped re-tuning the guitar and looked over at Jimmy. 'This isn't about a song, but, is it?'

Jimmy stopped trying to spin the sticks and shrugged. God, for a man who spent a lot of his time in Happyland, Aesop could be a perceptive bastard.

'No. I s'pose it isn't. I was just thinking about breaking

43

up with Sandra, y'know? And wondering what I'm meant to do now. I was happy with her, Aesop. I thought we'd get hitched, do the whole bit. Eventually, like. And I was wrong. I mean, Christ, I wasn't even close, was I? Not only was she not going to marry me, she was screwing a bloke that I thought was me mate and planning to move in with him. And I didn't even see it coming. What does that mean?'

'It means Sandra's a trollop and Beano's a geebag. That's all it means.'

'No. For fuck sake, Aesop, it's not that simple. It means I haven't got a fucking clue about anything. That's why I can't write the song. Every time I sit down to try and get something on paper, I keep thinking that I'm full of shit and anything I write will be bollocks. Y'know what I mean?'

'Eh, kind of ... no.'

'Okay, I've written some songs that you might call "love songs", right?'

'Don't I bleedin' know it ... homo.'

'Right. Well, when I was writing them, I was doing it from experience. At least some of it was. It was personal anyway, okay? But now I'm thinking that I don't understand women and I don't understand relationships and I don't even understand me own thoughts on the subject. It takes a cheek to stand up in front of a crowd and start singing about something you don't understand, y'know?'

'Jimmy, I don't understand half the shite you write and I still get up and play it. What's the problem? You're getting mixed up. A song doesn't have to be meaningful. If it did then Oasis would be in jail, the spas. Their songs all sound like nursery rhymes. None of them mean anything and they're brutal and they're *still* fucking millionaires.'

Jimmy started raising his voice. Aesop was trying to simplify things again and Jimmy hated it when he did that. Artists were allowed be complicated sometimes.

'This isn't just music or a song, Aesop. This is life! I want to be able to think that I might come across the girl that's perfect for me and recognise her when I do. How am I going to do that when I don't even know what I fucking want?'

'I don't fucking know, do I?' Aesop shouted back. 'Talk to Norman or Marco or someone. I'm grand without all that shite.'

'You're not, y'know,' said Jimmy.

'Ah, don't fucking start that again Jimmy,' said Aesop.

'What?'

'That shite you always come out with. That I'm all unhappy deep down and I only *think* I enjoy ridin' loads of women. Is that what you're going to tell me now, is it? Well if I'm living in a dream world then don't wake me up 'cos I'm having a ball, so I am.'

'Okay, okay. So, what if you did come across her?'

'I'd clean it up.'

'Aesop. If you met Superchick, what would you do?'

'I'd tell her she has a stupid fucking name, Jimmy. Jesus, can we talk about something else?'

Jimmy laughed. This just wasn't Aesop's kind of chat.

'Okay. C'mon, we'll do your song again.'

'Right. But let me play the drums, will ye? You're all over the gaff. And I think this guitar might be broken. Sounds a bit girly.'

They swapped back. Jimmy knew the guitar parts to the song already. Aesop didn't write complicated stuff. Head down, volume up and hang on to your goolies. He'd find a reasonable setting on his effects unit for the song later. Something that wouldn't have the front row being rushed to the hospital with bleeding ear holes and loose teeth.

'Are you on for poker on Thursday night? Beano won't be there, but the four of us is enough.'

'Yeah, cool,' said Aesop.

'Grand. Okay. From the top,' said Jimmy. '*Meatloaf's Underpants*. In, eh ... G for the craic.'

Aesop counted them in and Jimmy smiled to himself. He had a plan for Thursday night.

Four

Marco was in his element. For over a year and a half he'd been the poor stupid foreigner in the office who didn't know his arse from his elbow. But that had all changed with the latest arrival in his section. Eirotech Solutions was trying to establish a relationship with Fujitsu in Japan, who had plans to launch a new type of mobile phone to compete with Ericsson and Nokia in Europe. Fujitsu wanted a local partner in the region, and in turn Eirotech Solutions wanted a foot in the door of the huge Japanese software market. Once the initial contacts and understandings had been made it was time to swap some expertise. Tony Fitzgerald from Marketing had gotten a six-month stint in Tokyo, the jammy bastard, and the reciprocal arrangement had seen the arrival of Marco's new pal, Shigenori Tsujita.

The Japanese guy had started working in Marco's team. Mostly just as an observer, but in the week since he arrived he'd already made some useful observations on their market research and projections. Marco had made it his personal mission to introduce Tsujita-san to everyone he knew in the office and practically fell over himself to help the new guy out with the little things, like the food in the canteen, with which he seemed to be having trouble. His English wasn't great but Marco had been there too and Tsujita-san couldn't have had a more patient guide. He also loved soccer and for Marco that alone could have made him a best friend. Jimmy would watch it but didn't really know anything about it, Aesop didn't seem to have any interest in sport whatsoever, bar 'ridin', and Norman only liked Gaelic football and hurling.

As far as Marco could tell, hurling involved thirty big men trying to kill each other with wooden shovels. He called it a martial art for farmers, but Norman would insist proudly that it was one of the safest sports around. So, by Norman's reckoning, that would make it the safest, the oldest *and* the fastest sport in the world, and generally much better than anything some bloody Italian could come up with, Marco often reflected with a sigh. Norman had brought him to Croke Park once to watch a game, but to Marco it just looked like some insane kind of aerial hockey played by people who badly needed a hug. He did however learn a lot of new swear words from one huge, beetroot-faced old guy who disapproved of someone down on the pitch to the point of having great clinging loops of spittle covering most of his face by half-time.

Jimmy had moved section about a year ago, so Marco went upstairs with Tsujita-san to find him and do the introductions. He was looking at his computer screen and tapping a pen against his nose when he saw Marco come through the door with some small oriental-looking bloke.

'Hey, Marco. What's the story?'

'Hello, Jimmy. Wow! What happened to your head?'

'Ah. I'll tell you later.'

Marco nodded with a concerned frown, and turned around. 'Tsujita-san, this is my friend Jimmy Collins. He used to work with us but now is the Head of Information Systems in Eirotech Solutions. Jimmy, this is Shigenori Tsujita. He is here from Fujitsu for a few months.'

Jimmy stood up and stuck out his hand. 'Nice to meet you ... eh ... Shi ... Shigy ... Sh ...'

Marco was in like a shot. He'd been doing this all week.

'You can call him "Tsujita-san", Jimmy. It means Mr Tsujita.'

They shook hands and Tsujita-san bowed low from the waist. Jimmy gave a little bow in return, looking around and feeling like a bit of a prat.

'Berry preased to meet you, Jimmy-san,' said Tsujita-san.

48

'Eh, right. So how long will you be here, Too … Soo … eh …'

'Tsujita. I stay Ireland sebben months, Jimmy-san. Sorry. Engrish not so good.'

'No, no. Your English is very good,' said Jimmy, who was looking at Marco holding seven fingers up behind Tsujita-san's back. 'Right. Good. Well, I hope you have a good time in Dublin. Marco here will be a great help. He'll be able to show you around.' He sat back down as he was talking. It was one of his favourite ways of getting people to go away.

'Tsujita-san likes jazz,' said Marco.

'Is that right?' said Jimmy, politely, looking at Tsujita-san.

'Ah, yes. I pray sax.'

'Good for you …'

Marco chirped up again, with a huge smile.

'Jimmy *hates* jazz. Don't you, Jimmy?'

'Well …'

'He hates it. He thinks people who like jazz are spas. Right Jimmy?' He was laughing now.

'Eh, well, I never said … y'know … eh … everyone has their own …'

Typical bloody Marco. When he got excited his mouth was far too fast for his brain. Christ only knew what he was like in Italian. Tsujita-san was looking at him now. Jimmy wasn't sure if he got Marco's gist so he tried to distract him before he did.

'I play the guitar,' he said, doing the actions with his hands.

'Ah. We pray toogezah?'

Yeah, right.

'Of course. Yeah. That'd be great. Love to … eh …' Jimmy glanced to his computer screen as if something critical needed his attention.

'Great! Sank you. Ah, nice, ah …' he was pointing at Jimmy's head.

'Oh, yeah. Me hair. Thanks. Not everyone likes it though,' he said, looking towards the closed door of his boss's office. 'Anyway, nice meeting you, Zucheeto-san.'

Tsujita-san bowed again and he and Marco continued off on their rounds.

'Fuck sake ...' Jimmy muttered to himself as he watched them disappear behind a partition. He wasn't having a great day. The first person he'd seen that morning had been Denise. She was on the network team, and happened to arrive at the front gate of the office at the same time he did.

'God, Jimmy. Did you get a fright or something?' she said, laughing.

'Do you like it?'

'Ask me later. It's a bit bright for this hour of the morning.'

In the three minutes it had taken him to get from the car park to his desk, he had been responsible for stopped conversations, dropped jaws and more than a few calls on the Holy Name. He just kept walking, blushing and trying to smile to hide it. It wasn't that big a deal he kept trying to tell himself, but then he'd catch a glimpse of his head in a glass door and realise how different he looked. Maybe white – or 'Brilliant Ash', as yer man had called it – spiky hair wasn't the way to go first time out. People actually seemed to get used to it fairly quickly, but Jimmy couldn't see it himself unless he looked in a mirror or something. Every time he went to the toilet he had to stop at the sink and stare at himself. It was supposed to be cool and punky but his scalp looked pink and raw and his hair was standing straight up on his head, like it was afraid of itself. He was thinking of being on the stage when he did it but had to admit that it was a bit out of place springing from the top of a man wearing a shirt and tie.

His phone rang at five past nine.

'Jimmy. Simon. Can you come in here a minute, please?'

Simon was his boss. Not a bad bloke. Even so, Jimmy got

up and started to walk across the floor feeling like he was heading to the principal's office.

He knocked and opened the door.

'Sit down, Jimmy.'

Jimmy sat.

Simon just looked at him, saying nothing.

'So,' said Jimmy, eventually. 'You're probably interested in my head this morning, right?'

Simon nodded.

'Well, blondes have more fun and I thought I could do with a bit of a laugh.'

'Jimmy.' Simon was being very calm. That wasn't necessarily a good sign. 'I was the one who insisted that you be considered for VP in this company. I did that because you work hard and I know you're able for the responsibilities that come with the job, even at your age. But Jimmy, I was counting on you to exercise good judgment in the role. And that,' he said, pointing at Jimmy's hair, 'does not look like the consequence of good judgment.'

'Simon ...'

'Hang on a minute Jimmy, I'm not finished. You're not just one of the grunts in here any more. You're in a position of considerable influence. You manage dozens of people and a huge budget. You're also one of our faces. One of the people who go out and represent the company to clients and prospective clients. I know you have your whole music side. I appreciate that. I even encourage it. I've seen you play and you're very good, if you like that sort of thing. But you need to get your priorities right. You're either a singer in a band, or you're an executive in this firm with stock options, a pension plan and a comfortable future. You can be both, Jimmy, but you need to be extremely careful how you mix them. Is that clear?'

Jimmy would have loved to jump up and tell Simon where to stick his pension plan. Throw his tie on the floor, give his boss the finger and quit his job. It would have been so rock and roll to storm out of the office, meet up with Aesop, record an album and become rich and famous. That would show the lot of them. Simon. His Dad. Sandra. They'd all rue the day they doubted him.

But of course he didn't do any of that. He might be a bit of a dreamer sometimes but he wasn't a complete fucking dope.

Besides, he knew that Simon was right. He still didn't know what had prompted the new hair-do. It was just supposed to be a bit of a laugh but he hadn't felt like laughing all morning. He'd felt self-conscious and awkward. So it looked like his Dad was right, too. As usual. How could the least cool person in the universe always be right?

'Jimmy? You want to tell me what's going on?' asked Simon.

'What? Nothing's going on.'

'Really? You know, when I was forty-five I bought a motorbike for myself. Always wanted one, but never got around to actually buying one. The wife was pissed off like you wouldn't believe. I was being irresponsible. I was being extravagant. I was trying to recapture my youth. Blah, blah, blah. She knew all about it. Called it the male menopause. I was adamant at first but of course I sold it a month later. Wasn't cut out for Easy Rider and all that, and herself fit to be tied. The thing is Jimmy, you're only thirty years old. That's a bit young for a mid-life crisis, isn't it? So what's going on? Is everything okay at home?'

God, this was getting more and more like the principal's office. Jimmy decided to just play along. Simon would be happy that he guessed correctly and maybe he'd chill out a bit.

'I broke up with my girlfriend at the weekend,' he said.

'Oh. I see. Sarah, wasn't it?'

'Sandra.'

'Right. Well Jimmy, I suppose that gives you an excuse to be a bit off. I won't pry into your personal life but I hope things work out. They usually do, you know.'

Jimmy tried to look sad and confused. That often did the trick on oul' fellas. Made them feel experienced and worldly.

'Does that wash out?' said Simon, gesturing in the general direction of Jimmy's shame.

Jimmy shook his head.

'Right. Well, I'll tell you what. It'll grow out, right? Will you do me a favour and not get it done again? And for God's sake comb the spikes down in the office ...'

'No problem,' said Jimmy. 'To be honest, that stuff they put on your hair hurts so bloody much I've no intention of ever doing it again anyway. I was nearly crying like a baby.'

Simon laughed.

'Okay. So we have a deal, then. And Jimmy, don't get too bogged down in the girlfriend thing, yeah? When you get to my age, you'll be looking back and laughing at all that. Really.'

'Yeah. Thanks, Simon.'

He stood up. Piece of cake. He didn't know what other courses of action Simon may have taken, but Jimmy's being stubborn and difficult about the hair would have been the worst way of finding out. This way, there wasn't going to be a big deal. When you grow up with someone like Aesop, you quickly learn how to deflect trouble. Now the important thing was to leave the office laughing. Everyone out there would be waiting for Jimmy to reappear. A bit of scandal. If he went out there looking chastised, and with his head down, the rumour mill would be churning out sliced pans by lunchtime. He could imagine the whispers already going around the room. 'Jimmy's been called into Simon's office.' 'Did you see that? He's fucked.' 'Serves him right. The head on him.'

'I don't suppose you play the bass, do you Simon?' asked Jimmy with a laugh, as he turned the handle on the door to go out.

'Me? God no,' said Simon. 'Are you stuck?'

'A bit, yeah.'

'Sorry. I'm no good to you. Unless you need someone to play *Twinkle Twinkle Little Star* on the tin whistle, that is.'

'Thanks. I'll keep that in mind.'

Simon laughed and Jimmy joined him with a loud roar as he swung open the door and headed back to his desk, eyes front. Nothing to see here, folks. Nothing to see here. Yiz nosy bastards.

Eirotech Solutions was one of the fastest-growing Irish software companies. In eight years, the workforce had doubled five times and the future looked like chocolate. Rather than concentrate on any one given aspect of technology, the company policy makers were unashamedly attracted to whatever was making money at that particular moment. Biotechnology? Yeah, we can write systems for that. Accounting? No problem. Smart cards? Sure, didn't we practically invent them? The result of all this 'specialisation' was that they were always busy. Busy writing software and busy pretending to the outside world that they were great at everything.

It worked too. Eirotech Solutions engineers were overworked and overpaid and none of them were complaining – it had become cool in Dublin to always look stressed. Jimmy's section alone had three current contracts out with big financial companies, another two with American telecommunications interests and six proposals out for various Irish and international projects. He had thirty engineers with five direct reports, a number of project managers on assorted assignments and some six or seven vendors to deal with on a day-to-day basis. His desk was almost completely obscured by paperwork and some of the deadlines were getting a bit too close for comfort. He sat there quietly, deep in thought, chewing his bottom lip.

Where the fuck was he going to get a bass player?

He sat there, looking at the *Hot Press* Website on his

computer. Sometimes you got lucky. Someone whose name you already knew would turn up, looking for a gig. He scanned down the list of ads but nothing was jumping out at him. There were only about four bass players based anywhere near them and Jimmy didn't know any of them. Ironically enough, there were about twenty keyboard players. If they'd been looking for a keyboard player then they would have been laughing. Unfortunately, even the idea of having keyboards in the band would have been too much for Aesop's heart. He'd have curled up and died at the merest suggestion.

Marco walked up.

'Jimmy.'

'Hiya Marco.'

'What do you think of Tsujita-san?'

'Yeah. Nice enough young fella.' Whatever.

'Not young. Jimmy, he is thirty-seven years old.'

'Really?' said Jimmy. That was a surprise. The guy didn't look a day over twenty-five. Jimmy made a mental note to eat more fish.

'So, you think he could play poker with us tomorrow?' asked Marco.

'Ah Marco. I don't know. We're playing for money, y'know? We don't even know the bloke. And his English isn't the best. The lads wouldn't be able to understand him. And he wouldn't have a fucking clue what Norman was talking about with his Cork accent. I have problems myself sometimes.'

Marco nodded once and hung his head. He really liked the guy and wanted his friends to like him too.

Jimmy felt like a bit of a prick, but poker with the lads the odd Thursday night was a special thing. You didn't just have anyone around. Did the bloke even know how to play poker? Would he be okay with losing fifty euro or more to Norman? Once you got to know him Norman was about as amiable as you could get without making people wonder about him, but sit him at a table with five cards in his hand and he was one ruthless bastard.

'Tell you what,' said Jimmy. 'We're all going in to McGuigans on Saturday night, to watch Slapper. Why don't you tell him to come along? They have a Chinese barman in there, the pair of them could have a chat.'

'Tsujita-san is Japanese, Jimmy. But okay. That's a great idea. I'll tell him. I think he is a bit lonely.' Marco was chuffed. McGuigans was even better than the poker. Tsujita-san would meet all the guys, have a few drinks. Marco could explain all the different beers to him like an expert. He might even drink beer himself to show off.

Marco gave Jimmy a big smile and practically skipped away and out the door. Jimmy looked after him, trying to picture it and grinning. Zucheeto-san in McGuigans. That could be interesting.

Five

Jimmy picked up his cards, glanced at them, stared at them and then looked over at Aesop, shaking his head in disbelief. Aesop smiled back nonchalantly. Jimmy turned to his left, knowing what to expect and wasn't disappointed. Norman was staring at what he'd been dealt with absolute horror. His mouth was open, jaw thrust out. He'd gone bright red, his eyes like flares sticking out of his head. He put the cards down and looked over at Aesop, who still had the big grin.

'Aesop! That's ... that's ... where in the name of God did you get those cards?'

'Do you like them, Norman?'

Norman picked up his cards again.

'Look at his langer! Aesop, that's, God, that's terrible. You can't play cards with them.'

'Why not? They're just cards with pictures on them.'

Norman looked at another card, squinting.

'Look where he's putting that! Ah stop the lights, Aesop. That's not on. Have you no proper cards? How can you concentrate with that going on?'

'Sorry Norman, they're the only cards I brought. C'mon. They're grand. Can anyone open?' he said, looking around. They all looked down again.

Marco sat with a cigar sticking out of the corner of his mouth. He didn't often smoke, but sometimes liked to suck on a stogie when they were playing poker. It added to the atmosphere and Jimmy didn't mind his stinking up the house, once it was only the odd time. Marco had one eyebrow halfway up his forehead and he kept alternating between looking at his cards from a distance and bringing them up close, for a better look. Jimmy's attention was focused on the golden retriever in his hand and the young lady who was ... holding him. Norman still looked dazed, but the cute Cork hoor instinct in him was taking over. He threw down fifty cent, saying nothing. The others did the same.

'So,' said Jimmy, once they'd all settled down and started playing, 'Where did you get the cards, Aesop? I didn't see them down the Spar.'

'A friend of Phil's was in Amsterdam for the weekend. I asked him to pick them up for me.'

Phil Murray was one of Aesop's big brothers. The other one was Andy. Everyone in the area knew them. Three good looking blokes, only two years between them, with no Mam and a Dad who was out working his arse off the whole time – the three Romeos had done more than their fair share of damage in the area during their teens. Unusually for brothers, they were all great mates and hung around together the whole time, even going so far as to swap around the girls they picked up at the local discos. At sixteen, the girls didn't mind – one brother was much the same as another. The lads felt the same way about them. They used to call it the Murray-Go-Round.

Phil and Andy were married now and well behaved, leaving Aesop to carry on the tradition on his own; an obligation he took very seriously.

Every time the lads played cards they took turns at being the host. Even though they almost always played in Jimmy's place, when it was your turn you'd bring the food, beer and cards. Aesop had two reasons for turning up with the Dutch cards and they were both to do with Norman. For starters, Norman always took money. Usually he took it from everyone, but Aesop was constantly being fleeced. He could read Norman like a book anytime he felt like it, except when it came to cards. Once the game was on, Norman could sit there for six hours and never change his expression once, even when he was collecting. It drove Aesop mad and he was hoping that the pictures would distract him and make him give himself away. The other reason was that the cards were particularly hard-core and Norman would freak – which was always good for a giggle.

Unfortunately for Aesop, two hours later it was clear that the plan wasn't working. He was down twenty euro to Norman and another twenty to the others. Marco was even and Jimmy was in for about ten euro to Norman.

Norman dealt and picked up his own cards. Excellent. The Jack of Diamonds, again. Norman thought he might be falling in love with her. He wasn't mad on her pose, which he felt was a bit too revealing in the bumhole department, but he thought she had a lovely face, what he could see of it behind the leek. And she'd go perfectly with the fine pair of nymphs on the Jack of Clubs that was also sitting there in his hand. They were gorgeous too, although they looked like sisters and Norman didn't think that sisters should be quite that close. He wasn't getting distracted at all. In fact, the girls and their various partners were having a great calming effect on him for some reason. Besides which, he knew what Aesop was up to. He'd be teaching Aesop a lesson before this night was up.

Norman's Mam, Mrs Kelly, was one of those people who didn't have a first name. Even the other oul' ones on the street called her Mrs Kelly and some of them were older than she was. His Dad had been in the air corps and had died when Norman was just a kid. It had been a coastal rescue job and the helicopter went down in a storm off the Clare coast. After a few years of trying to come to terms with her loss, and everyone around her constantly trying to help, Norman's Mam upped and sold the house in Cork, bid Norman's granny a tearful farewell and moved to Dublin where she thought she could get on with her life without the constant reminders. She was a hard woman who took no shite from anyone, least of all her son. Jimmy only had to look at Mrs Kelly to know why Norman was the way he was around women.

Jimmy and Aesop were always in trouble, and that's how they became friends with the huge culchie who appeared one day in their class a week after they started secondary school. Aesop was already going for the heavy metal look and Jimmy fancied himself for a brief period as a New Romantic, complete with pointy shoes and quiffy hair. They saw the big lad squeeze himself into a seat in the back of History, his face red, and didn't think anything of it. At lunchtime three guys from Second Year started to slag Jimmy and Aesop over their hair – 'Which one of yiz is the bloke?' – and took offence when Aesop replied, 'Your fat Ma.'

One minute they were being kicked all over the gravel behind the school hall, and the next they were lying there watching the new lad from Cork smacking the heads off their assailants with a vicious grin. The three Second Years eventually ran off, two crying, before the lads managed to stand up and walk towards their saviour.

'Eh, thanks,' said Jimmy.

'Wasn't fair. Three of them and only the pair of ye.'

'What's your name?' said Aesop.

'Robert Kelly.'

'I'm Aesop. And this is Jimmy.'

'Hello. What were they hitting ye for?'

'They didn't like our hair.'

Their new friend looked at their heads and nodded.

'Sure, I don't like it either but I'm not going to get in a fight over it.'

'I think you just did,' said Jimmy.

'Ah, sure that wasn't a fight. A few digs and they went off crying to their Mammies.'

Jimmy and Aesop looked at each other. It had looked like a fight from where they'd been lying. Robert Kelly had battered the shite out of three older lads on his own, calling them pansies and laughing as he did it.

They got to know him over the next few months as he quickly became something of a hero on the hurling field for the school, striking terror into the heart of any poor bastard who had to mark him. He had often felt at a loss since his move to Dublin but this was the one place where it all made sense. He was generally shy and awkward and uncomfortable with himself, but with a hurley in his hands his head was right back in Cork and no amount of intercession by the Sacred Heart was going to help the wee Dublin lads who fancied themselves against him. He played midfield and owned it.

With his mother running a B&B and with Robert being a bit of a psycho they decided to call him Norman, but not to his face. Years later, with Norman in the army and the first Gulf War on the telly, they were able to start calling him Stormin' Norman, which he loved, and finally just Norman, so it all worked out in the end and he never suspected where his nickname actually came from, which was probably a good thing. Slagging Norman's Mam, even indirectly, wouldn't be one of your healthier pastimes.

By half ten they were done. Jimmy was down twenty to Norman and Marco, Marco was up about ten, and Norman had almost cleaned out Aesop. He'd left him with a tenner out of pity. His mother always told him he was too soft.

'You're one lucky bastard Norman,' said Aesop.

'How's that, Aesop?'

'The cards you were getting. I've never seen anything like it. You're the jammiest bastard I've ever met.'

'Now Aesop,' said Norman, straight-faced. 'It's not luck. It's about skill and you don't have any. It's not your fault, you're just a very bad card player.'

'Piss off. The cards you had ...' Aesop started.

'The cards you thought I had. Aesop, half the time you didn't know what was in my hand.'

'I know you well enough, Norman, and ...'

'Aesop, Aesop, Aesop. Of course you do. That's why you've got a tenner in your pocket and I've got ninety in mine.'

'You cheeky bastard. C'mon and we'll see whose crap at cards. C'mon. One hand. A tenner.'

The other two looked at Norman and Aesop, smirking. This was going to be ugly. Aesop hadn't a hope.

Norman smiled at Aesop and nodded.

'Aesop, you're a terrible eejit.'

'Yeah, yeah. C'mon, ye bollocks, and we'll see.'

Jimmy dealt. Norman ended up with three eights. He looked at Aesop. Aesop had his chin in his hand, which meant he was bluffing. Norman had spotted that little trait twenty minutes into the first game of poker they'd ever played about ten years ago. It took less than ninety seconds. Norman let the tenner stick up out of his shirt pocket for the remainder of the night, where Aesop would see it.

The lads adjourned to the living-room for the stereo. They still had a couple of six packs to get through and tomorrow was Friday so it wouldn't be so bad if they felt a bit rough in the morning. Aesop was sulking a little but the agreement was that once they left the table then the game was over and no bitching was allowed. They'd had to introduce that policy a few years ago when Norman took the fifty quid off Aesop that he'd been saving to buy a new skin for his snare. Aesop had been none too impressed that night.

Jimmy sat in the corner on his armchair and picked up his acoustic guitar. It was usually either in his room or next to his chair. That way he could always pick it up if something came to him but he often did so anyway, like now, and just played away gently while he was talking or watching the telly. It was good practice for playing when there were distractions, like a fight in the crowd or Beano tripping over his guitar lead or something. If you could play without thinking when there were other things going on, it made you a better player. He looked over at Norman, grinning.

'Hey Norman, did you see any girls you liked in the pack?'

'Ah, sure they were only a bunch of scrubbers, Jimmy. A couple of nice ones, only. One of the Jacks wasn't bad. For a slapper, like.'

Jimmy nodded, smiling.

'I thought the Ace of Hearts was very talented,' he said.

'That'd be some party trick all right,' said Aesop, wistfully.

'I don't know what kind of parties you go to Aesop,' said Norman.

'The Queen of Spades was very beautiful,' said Marco.

'Eh Marco, the Queen of Spades was a bloke,' said Norman. He always watched the cards very closely, and it wasn't as though keeping track tonight had been all that difficult.

'No, no. I mean the Queen of Clubs.'

They all nodded in agreement. It was true. She had been spectacular.

'So, lads, did no one find their dream girl in there?' said Jimmy. He was looking at them carefully.

'Ah, no. No. Wouldn't be my type really,' said Norman, apologising in his mind to the Jack of Diamonds for his betrayal.

'No, Jimmy. I don't think so,' said Marco.

'Do I only get one?' said Aesop, picking up the pack and looking through it again.

Norman folded his arms and looked at him.

'You're a filthy bastard really, aren't you Aesop?' he said.

'Hey we all have our talents, right? I don't go around telling you how to plant turnips, do I? So don't be telling me how to treat the ladies.'

'Oh, it's ladies now, is it? Aesop you wouldn't know a

lady if she sat on your lap and did a big gick.'

'Oh right. Sorry, I didn't realise we were talking about Cork women, Norman. I usually only go for women who speak English.'

'Sure what difference would that make? You're hardly after them for their conversational skills, are you? As long as they have a hole in the right place, or close to it, then that's you happy.'

'At least I know what to do with a hole once I find it. You couldn't make a girl wet if you pissed on her.'

'That's what ye Dublin knackers do, is it? God, well, that would explain the smell of ye anyway.'

'Do ye hear this Marco? I'm getting hygiene lessons now from a man who owns two pairs of underpants. Norman, come and talk to me when you lose your virginity.'

'Okay so. And c'mere, you know you can always come to me if you're short your bus fare home,' said Norman, pulling the tenner a little higher out of his pocket.

They both took a swig from their beer.

Marco and Jimmy were watching all this. Jimmy was just grinning, doodling away on his guitar, but Marco had his face scrunched up in concentration. This back-and-forth type of slagging was something he was trying to work on but the lads' accents got stronger the more they got into it so it was difficult to follow. He got most of this one though and once he was sure it was over he sat back in his chair and shook his head in amazement.

The things they'd said. In Palermo there would have been a bloodbath.

Jimmy put down his guitar and stood up, disappearing into the kitchen. He came back with a bottle of Jameson and four glasses. The others looked at each other. Jimmy's Jemmy didn't come out that often. He poured a finger for everyone and sat back down.

Jimmy took the deck of cards from the coffee table in

front of Aesop and started to look through them.

'Well, lads,' he said, 'I think we proved one thing.'

'How do you mean?' said Aesop.

'Look at these women. Besides you being a scumbag, Aesop, there isn't one of them that we'd like to be going out with. All these shapes and sizes and nothing we want. That proves that we want more than just some tart that can do the splits and doesn't mind taking her tits out.'

'But Jimmy, sure I knew that already,' said Norman.

'That only means you know what you don't want, Norman. But do you know what you do want?'

'Oh Jaysis,' said Aesop with a moan. 'Here we fuckin' go again.'

'Shut up a minute, you. Lads, will you help me write the song? Y'know – *Superchick*.' He looked around. Aesop was slouched down on the couch, one hand over his eyes, the other holding his whiskey. Marco was looking doubtfully at the empty fireplace and Norman was looking at Jimmy like he didn't know who he was.

'I've never written a song Jimmy,' said Norman. 'I'm not very musical.'

'You don't have to be,' said Jimmy. 'I just want ideas. I asked you all before and you were crap. C'mon lads, who is she?'

Aesop opened his mouth to say something, but Jimmy cut him off.

'Aesop, I don't want to hear about her tits, okay?'

'So looks aren't important then?' said Aesop. 'She's s'posed to be this amazing, perfect woman but it's okay if she has a face on her like a hatful of arseholes?'

'You know what I mean. She can't just have nice tits. Although it would be a good start,' he said, smiling. 'If you went out there looking for her, what would you be looking for? Seriously.'

'Okay,' said Norman. 'For Aesop's benefit, let's just say she has to be pretty.'

'Right. That's a start,' said Jimmy, bending down to pick up a pen and notebook that was next to his chair and scribbling in it.

'Are you taking notes?' said Norman, alarmed.

'Of course I am,' said Jimmy. 'I want to remember this. Don't worry about it Norman, I won't put your name next to anything rude.'

'She has to like sex,' said Aesop.

Norman looked at him.

'What?' said Aesop. 'You live in Dublin now, Norman. People have sex up here, y'know? Not you, obviously, but other people do.'

'Okay, okay. She has to like sex,' said Jimmy, before the two of them started up again.

'Money. She can't be sponging off me the whole time,' said Aesop.

'Jesus, she'd want to be hard up,' said Norman.

'Clever,' said Marco. 'Stupid girls ... too ... too ... difficult.'

'Eh, not too clever but,' said Aesop. 'That can be a pain in the hole as well.'

'C'mon lads. Pretty, clever. Hardly groundbreaking, is it?' said Jimmy. He was getting excited now. This might work. 'What about her demeanour? How she carries herself?'

'She has to be self-confident,' said Norman. 'Not feminist.'

'Is that two things or one thing?' asked Marco, turning to look at him.

'Confident girls don't need feminism,' said Norman, quietly.

'How do you mean?'

'Ah, you can tell, sure. If you're slagging a girl about women being useless drivers or something, you can tell a lot about her by the way she reacts. If she's confident in herself, she'll just laugh and tell you to go and shite or something. It's the other ones that'd give you heartburn. They get all uppity straight away and tell you about how repressed they are. I was messing with this girl once and said something about women having the vote. Well, she nearly ate the face off me. I was only joking, sure! God, I was mortified. Only having a bit of a laugh so I was, and she hitting the roof. Going on about men causing all the wars in the world and how Thatcher didn't take any shite from anyone. Didn't mention the Falklands though, oh no. It's the same with that feckin' nonsense about women not taking their husband's name. All these poor kids going around with double-barrelled names just because their mothers didn't have the cop-on to go with the flow. "I'm me own person and I'll keep me own name" they say. Sure that's bollocks. The only ones who think like that are the ones who weren't sure they were their own person to begin with and have to make a big deal about it to convince themselves. "But Spanish women do this and Spanish women do that", they say. Sure they're not feckin' Spanish, are they? Feminism? Sure most of them don't even know what it means, they just get up on their high horse as soon as you open your gob. How many women do you know read Germaine Greer and all that stuff? Equality me hole. We're not meant to be the same. We're meant to comple- ment each other. Isn't it obvious, sure? They'll tell you that the likes of those playing cards are nothing but exploitation and an insult to women, and then they'll go off and read feckin' magazines, where they're being told that their clothes are all wrong and that they're too fat and that they should read this and listen to that and buy the other. That's feckin' exploitation if you ask me, paying young girls to be nearly anorexic so that normal women will feel like there's some- thing wrong with them and keep buying their magazines to check out the latest diet fads that don't even feckin' work. They think they're all liberated, and then they go and glue themselves to the telly to watch morons like J Lo and yer woman, Jessica thing Parker. What kind of role models are they? Pair of feckin' eejits. I've never seen such a ... a ... what are ye looking at?'

Everyone was staring at him.

'Eh, Norman,' said Jimmy, pointing at his pad. 'I have here "Not Feminist". Do you think that covers it?'

'It'll do, yeah,' said Norman, picking up his whiskey and taking a subdued sip.

'And Norman?' said Aesop. 'If you want to get something off your chest, don't be shy, okay?'

'Feck off you,' said a very puce Norman. He didn't know what happened. It had just all come out.

Jimmy coughed and kept going.

'Anything else?'

Marco spoke up. He'd been looking at Norman's lips move but had no idea what it was all about. It seemed to have been delivered in some strange Cork dialect.

'No more than ten pairs of shoes. That should be plenty for any woman.'

'Agreed,' said Jimmy. 'And if she has to shop, then she can't mind if you don't go with her.'

'Yeah,' said Aesop. 'And family. That's important. You have to be able to get on with her family. And her mates. There's nothing worse than meeting some bird's best mate or sister and she turns out to be an arsehole. Unless she has nice tits of course,' he added, looking at Norman.

They were all on their second whiskey now. Norman was heading for three.

'This is brilliant stuff lads,' said Jimmy. 'What else? We've covered the obvious stuff, and a bit about Feminism,' he said, with a sideways glance at Norman. 'There must be something unusual, though. Otherwise we'd all know her.'

The lads went quiet, thinking. They were starting to get into the idea, which was what Jimmy had been hoping for.

'She has to think you are wonderful,' said Marco.

'Yeah, and everyone who knows her will know how she feels,' said Norman.

'Lads, before we start going down that road, can I just say something quickly?' said Aesop, draining his glass and putting it down on the table next to the bottle. 'You're all fucking gay. Thank you.' He filled his own glass again and then Norman's.

They ignored him.

'Norman's right,' said Jimmy. 'It's as much about how she feels about you, as it is about how you feel about her. Cool.'

If Marco slouched any more, he'd have been lying on the floor. Norman had his feet up on the coffee table, with his eyes closed. They were both hammered and trying to form the words that would describe the kind of girl they wanted. Jimmy knew it was time. If he waited any longer, they'd be too drunk. He took a sup of his drink and put his head back theatrically.

'Ah lads, can you imagine it? The perfect bird. You know what? It's too important to just write a song about her. I think we should go out and look for her. Are yiz on?'

Norman and Marco looked over at him. Aesop was fingering his way through the CDs under the stereo, looking for something loud.

'Look for her where?' said Norman.

'Anywhere. In the pub. At gigs. In work. On the street. It'd be brilliant. One girl with everything and she's mad about you.'

Norman looked at him.

'I've been looking, Jimmy. She must be hiding on me.'

'Not at all. You just haven't been looking properly. C'mon, lads!' He sat up straight. 'We should do this. It's better than just settling for anyone, isn't it? Even if we can't find her, at least we'd know we tried. Marco. C'mon. Norman. Hey Aesop, you'd get to have perfect sex for the rest of your life.'

Aesop looked around.

'Someone mention my name?'

'Are yiz on? We could start this weekend.'

They were all grinning now, nodding at each other, pissed. Yeah, it'd be cool.

'Jimmy,' said Marco.

'Yeah?'

'Jennifer,' he said, simply.

'Marco, you've been going out with Jennifer for ages. Are you really getting the best out of one another? Are you even trying to? C'mon. Maybe Jennifer is the one, but you'll never find out if you don't really give each other everything. We only have one life, lads. Marco, maybe it's Jennifer and maybe it isn't ...'

'It fuckin' isn't, believe me,' said Aesop.

'... but your mission is to find out. That's all our missions. Say no to mediocrity, right? Yeah?'

'Okay,' said Marco, thoughtfully. 'Me and Jennifer ... maybe ...'

'I'm with you Jimmy,' said Norman. 'Maybe I'll get luckier hunting in a pack.'

'Aesop?' said Jimmy.

'Yeah. Whatever. You're telling me to meet more women? I think I can do that without breaking out in a rash.'

'Cool. So that's it. Saturday night in McGuigans we start. This is going to be brilliant. The lads are on the prowl,' said Jimmy, laughing.

They all giggled with him, Aesop rolling his eyes.

Jimmy watched them all wobble down the driveway about an hour later. It was half past two in the morning and he had to be up in five hours. He hadn't been this drunk in ages and he'd feel shite in work, but right now he was happy. He sat back down on the chair and looked at the notes he'd been taking. They were bollocks, he knew, but they weren't the point. The point was that he wasn't on his own any more.

The lads were in on it too. Ten minutes later he had another verse ...

> That chick was unbelievable, I swear she'd read my mind
> She knew exactly what I'd want, never bitched and never
> > whined
> She never dragged me shopping and I never met her folks
> But she always looked amazing and she laughed at all my jokes.

Jaysis, he thought, as he filled a pint glass with Ribena for his head, there might be a Grammy in this yet.

Six

Jimmy spent most of Saturday afternoon trying to work on the song, but he didn't really get anywhere. He'd even deliberately stayed in on Friday night so that he'd have a clear head. Sky were doing a *Simpsons* special for six hours and he watched it non-stop, eating pizza and drinking milk. After the whiskey and beer on Thursday, he'd been suffering all day and just wanted to plonk himself in front of the telly and do nothing. Six hours of his favourite show sounded perfect, but by the time he went to bed his brain had completely shut down. Even Jimmy could only take so much Homer.

By four on Saturday afternoon, he had given up on the song for the time being, and went to his wardrobe to get something to wear to the pub. Maybe something would need an emergency run under the iron.

Everything did, as it turned out. Superchick would have to be good at ironing, he decided absently, as he stood in only a T-shirt, seeing to his jocks on the ironing board and being careful not to burn his mickey. He always ironed his jocks. Not because he wanted them to be wrinkle-free and neat, but because there were very few things that could compare to the feeling of pulling on a fresh, clean pair of underpants that were roasting hot. It was hard to explain to someone who hadn't tried it. Boxers were okay, Y-fronts were pretty good, but to get the full effect, you needed to use cotton cycling shorts, Jimmy's undergarment of choice.

Slapper were playing McGuigans tonight. Jimmy knew the lads well. They were from the area and they'd all played the same venues before. They weren't usually free on Saturday nights but had an early college gig that day and so were available in the evening to take The Grove's slot. Jimmy was glad. They played similar enough music so that the band's regular crowd wouldn't be too pissed off, and anyway he'd get to see what they'd been up to recently.

He turned off the iron and stepped into his jocks, eyes closed and with a satisfied smile, and picked up the phone. He checked the clock on the wall. Five thirty. Norman answered.

'Hiya, Norman.'

'Jimmy. How's she cuttin'?'

'Grand. All set for tonight?'

'I suppose so. I'm a bit nervous, though. I feel like I'm fourteen and going to the school disco.'

'Ah, don't be worrying about it. We always had a good time at the school discos anyway, right?'

'You did, Jimmy. I usually just sat there and stared at me loafers all night, trying to get me hair to stop sticking up at the sides and scared of me shite in case some young one asked me out to dance.'

'Will you stop. Sure, d'ye remember snogging the head off Aisling what's-her-face behind the cloak room?'

'I do, Jimmy. And I remember her saying to me that she'd break my nose if I told anyone.'

They both laughed, remembering that night. Norman had been so excited that he immediately came back and told Jimmy and Aesop what had happened. Aisling saw him and came storming over to give him a box. Norman had to make up some story about finding a fiver that had fallen out of one of the coats and that's what he'd been telling the lads. When she demanded to see it, he'd only been able to produce three pounds fifty and a small packet of Jelly Tots.

'Norman, relax. All we're doing is keeping an eye out for someone a bit special. You don't have to do anything you don't want to. Just be yourself. If you're talking to someone and you need a bit of moral support, just give me a nod, okay?'

'Right so. She's bound to want me if you're sitting there next to her as well. Will you be wearing your leather pants?'

'Eh, maybe,' said Jimmy, looking at them hanging over the back of a kitchen chair, ready to go.

'Lovely. I might as well take me corduroy dungarees out of the attic so, for all the chance I have.'

'Norman, it's not a competition. We're just out to have a good time, and maybe meet a few nice girls. People do it all the time. Relax!'

'Ah, I'm only joking, Jimmy. I'll be grand. What time?'

'I'll be there around eight.'

'Okay, so. Seeya there.'

The funny thing, Jimmy knew, was that any girl would be lucky to have Norman. He was a bit shy and self-conscious but he had a heart of gold, there was no bullshit about him and he was built like a brick shithouse. Pull off his Aran jumper and stick a black T-shirt on him instead and he'd look like he should be swinging a sledgehammer on a poster in some teenage girl's bedroom. From the neck down anyway. His nose was broken from boxing in the army and his eyes were a bit menacing even when he smiled, but some girls liked the swarthy type, right? He just needed to chill out a bit. Girls like a bit of confidence and that's where Norman came up short. His mother had scared the poise out of him.

Jimmy went into the bathroom to brush his teeth and looked in the mirror. No problems with poise there. Jimmy was a bit of a pretty-boy. Even he had to admit that. He'd been told that he had natural charisma and charm, but he knew that there was nothing natural about it. He worked at how he looked and acted. It was all part of The Performance. Years ago he told himself that it was important because at any moment he might become a famous musician and image was all part of that lifestyle. He knew now that he didn't have that excuse any more, but he still thought that it was important to be a rockstar when he was on the stage, even if he wasn't really one. The crowd wanted a bit of a show at the weekend. If he looked and acted like a responsible software engineer up there, they wouldn't be interested. They saw shite like that all week. With Jimmy, though, it wasn't just when he was on the stage anymore. He couldn't really turn it off now except at work, where the routine of it all sapped his enthusiasm.

He called Aesop next.

'Aesop. Howya.'

'Howzit going, Jimmy. You're up early.'

'Aesop, it's nearly six o'clock. Are you in bed, ye lazy bastard?'

'Not in bed. On bed. Just relaxing a bit.'

'Let me guess. You're in your underpants, chasing smoke around the room.'

'Close enough. So what's up?'

'You all set for tonight?'

'Set how? We're only going to the pub, right?'

Aesop got a bit panicked. He never smoked before a gig and hoped he hadn't gone and forgotten that they were playing. He couldn't sit up straight when he was stoned, never mind play the drums.

'Tonight's the big night. We're going to start looking for the woman of our dreams, remember?'

'Oh that? Fuckin' hell, Jimmy, I thought that was just the drink talking the other night. What are we supposed to do again?'

'Okay Aesop, I'll make it easy for you. You have just one job to do tonight, right?'

'Yeah. What?'

'Don't screw the first girl you feel like screwing. Just wait and see if a better one comes along. Okay? Can you manage that?'

'Eh, I think so. But c'mere. What happens if someone else gets the first bird I want to screw while I'm pricking around with you, looking for some bird with a halo over her head and sunshine coming out the back of her jeans?'

'For fuck sake Aesop, you can go without it for one night, can't you? Offer it up for the Holy Souls or something. It won't kill you, will it?'

'All right, all right. And if I find her, what do I do? Stick a flag on her head so you'll know it's her?'

'Just talk to her, Aesop. It's not hard. Maybe you'll even like her enough not to want to shag her straight away.'

'Yeah, right. Whatever. Listen Jimmy, I have to go. I forgot to put a towel down and it's escaping out under the door on me.'

'Okay. Eight o'clock. Seeya. And Aesop?'

'Yeah?'

'Don't take the piss out of Norman too much tonight, will you? He's shy enough as it is, without you slagging him in front of some bird.'

'I'll try Jimmy, but it's hard sometimes, y'know? He asks for it.'

'Right, well just take it easy, okay? Seeya.'

'Good luck.'

Jimmy took up the iron again and checked it. It was cool enough to use on his best shirt; a cream granddad shirt with small brass buckles instead of buttons. It was Armani. Jimmy didn't normally go mad on expensive clothes, but this hundred quid shirt looked the bollocks with his leather pants. He ironed it carefully and went back upstairs. He barely even noticed his new hair any more, except to register that it looked pretty cool with the rest of his kit. He took a handful of gel and teased his wavy locks into a carefully arranged mess, wiping off the excess with some bog roll. He didn't like it sticking straight up in spikes any more – his scalp was still too raw-looking underneath.

Six thirty.

'Marco?'

'Hello, Jimmy.'

'All set for tonight? We're meeting down in McGuigans around eight o'clock.'

'Okay. But Jimmy, I will be a little late. I am meeting Tsujita-san at the office first, to show him the way.'

Jimmy groaned to himself. He'd forgotten all about the Jap.

'Eh, okay Marco. What time will you be there?'

'Nine?'

'That's grand. We'll keep a couple of seats. Listen, don't tell Zucheeto about the Superchick thing, right? This is just between the four of us. We don't want him feeling awkward or anything, yeah?'

'No problem, Jimmy. But Jimmy, I was thinking. I think it will be difficult to turn Jennifer into Superchick. She is, ah, independent, yes?'

'Yeah, I know Marco. Still. You never know 'til you try.' Marco was getting cold feet. 'Just remember, Marco, you're not trying to change her, you're trying to get the best out of your relationship. She'll appreciate that. Not that you'll be telling her anything, right?' he added quickly.

'No, no. I won't say anything to her. But, I don't know ...'

'It's grand, Marco. Just see what happens. Sure, you're the one with the steady girlfriend, right? You're the lucky one. It's us are the three sad bastards who can't find a decent bird.'

'Okay, Jimmy. Okay. See you later.'

'Seeya.'

Shit. Zucheeto was going to be there. His English was crap and he'd be hanging out of them, or at least Marco, all night. Maybe he'd just get drunk and go home early. He probably wasn't used to pints of Guinness and that's what Marco had in store for him. Still, if he stayed around all night talking about jazz, or whatever it was he was into, then Jimmy wouldn't be able to concentrate on the task at hand, would he? Bloody Marco, the friendly bastard.

He put it out of his mind and checked himself in the mirror in his bedroom again. Yeah, that would do nicely.

There was just time for a cup of tea and some bread and jam before he left, so he grabbed his Doc Marten's from the hall and polished them as he ate. He always wore Docs, except at work, because he'd wrecked his ankle doing a stage dive when he was young and stupid, and he liked to have the support. Grabbing his leather jacket as he passed, he went out the front door, slamming it behind him and humming to himself. It didn't matter about Zucheeto. Actually, it might work out well. A new face like that in the crowd. Might attract a bit more attention for them.

The sun was still up. Summer wasn't over just yet. He loved walking to the pub when it was still bright. It was better if he had his guitar with him but he knew he looked good even without it. They'd have a few pints, chat up a few girls, listen to the band. Maybe Ronnie from Slapper would even get him up to do a song or two. It would be interesting to see Norman trying to get a girl and Aesop trying not too.

Yeah. This was going to be great night.

Seven

He was first to arrive and grabbed one of the best tables, up on the left near the stage. The Sound Cellar in McGuigans was below the main lounge, which was at street level. It was a T-shaped room, fairly large, that could seat about eighty punters with space for another hundred and fifty standing. Maybe more if you stood people five deep at the bar and filled the small dance floor, which wasn't unusual. When Jimmy arrived there were about twenty people sitting around. Most people wouldn't come down from the lounge for another hour or so, when the band was due to go on, but they'd be standing all night. Aesop was probably up there now, supping a pint and looking around, trying to decide who he'd shag. It wasn't an easy one. There were some fine-looking women in McGuigans on a Saturday night, but the problem for Aesop wasn't in finding someone to ride, it was trying to remember if he'd already been there. He didn't like to repeat himself if he could help it, because he thought it might give the girl the wrong impression with regard to the commitment she could expect from him; something Jimmy very much doubted.

He nodded to a few people he recognised. Nearly everyone knew him of course, from being in The Grove. If they weren't sure, then the leather pants gave it away. He threw down his jacket and went to the bar to get a pint. Norman came in then and joined him. Jimmy called for another pint.

'Ye-hay, Norman! You took out the heavy artillery tonight, didn't you?' he said, looking at Norman's chinos and bright, tie-dyed denim shirt.

'Would you look who's talking? You're not even singing tonight and you look like feckin' Rod Stewart,' said Norman, laughing at him.

'Piss off. Rod Stewart had a huge arse!'

The two of them took their drinks and Jimmy led them to the table where there was room for about six people. On the way he saw Ronnie from Slapper come out from the toilet.

'Hey Ronnie. What's the story?'

'Ah, howya Jimmy. Jaysis, the head on you. Howsitgoin? Howya Norman. Listen, I heard about Beano and all. That's a bit shite pal,' said Ronnie. Beano had played with Slapper a couple of times.

'Ah, don't be talking to me,' said Jimmy. 'C'mere, thanks for doing the gig. If you couldn't do it John was going to call Bobby Gillespie.'

'Jaysis. Who wants to listen to that spa doing Duran Duran all night? Anyway, no problem. We were at DCU this afternoon for Rag Week, so we'll just do the same set. Will you get up for a song?'

'Ah no,' said Jimmy, delighted. 'Do you mind?'

'Not at all. We'll have a laugh. Is Aesop coming?'

'Yeah. He's probably upstairs.'

'Grand so. I'll give yiz a shout. There'll be a riot if the girls don't see him up there on the drums at some stage in the evening. Seeya later, right?'

Ronnie went off to get set up with the rest of the lads who were milling around the stage, plugging in cables and tuning up.

Aesop came in and wandered over to the table, looking guilty.

'Are you behaving yourself, Aesop?' said Jimmy.

'For fuck sake, Jimmy, I only got here ten minutes ago. Give me a bit of credit, will ye?'

'What did you do?'

'Nothing.'

'Aesop ...'

'Ah Jaysis, I just told this bird I might see her down here

later, right? That's all. Okay? Jaysis, ye'd swear I was sick in the head or something. Howya Norman.'

'How's the form, Aesop? Do you want a pint?'

Aesop looked down at his glass. 'Ah, sure go on. Thanks.'

Norman went to the bar and Aesop sat down with Jimmy.

'Now. I didn't say a word to him, did I? And the bleedin' state of that shirt. What's he trying to do? Catch butterflies?'

'Leave him alone, Aesop. He's excited about tonight.'

'Why? Jimmy, you're mad. Tonight's just like any other night. He'll sit down with some young one and ten minutes later she'll be gone off with her mates and he'll be sitting there on his own, trying to take his foot back out of his mouth. That's what always happens. It's pitiful.'

'Just leave him, right? He's bad enough without you winding him up, telling him he can always use his left hand and pretend it's someone else, or whatever.'

The three of them sat there chatting as the room filled up. Aesop was sitting at the next table so that they'd have two in case they needed the space. People were starting to get pissed off with that when Jennifer arrived with Maeve and Katie. That was grand. The girls could take the other table and the people standing around looking at it could fuck off and annoy someone else.

'Hi Jimmy. Nice hair,' said Jennifer, with a big smile. 'Hiya Norman. And how's my favourite waster of a brother?'

'Hiya Jen. What's the story?' said Jimmy.

'Ah, y'know. Out with the girls. Marco should be here soon. He's meeting that Japanese fella from work.'

The girls got comfortable and started talking about girl's stuff, and the lads got another round in.

Maeve was a lovely girl. A bit on the heavy side and her face seemed to have a few features too many, but she was a great laugh and a lot of fun to go out with. Katie was pretty enough, but she always had a bit of a sour pus on her around the lads. Jennifer didn't know it, but it was because Katie had spent the night with Aesop once, a couple of years earlier. First thing the next morning, he'd just said 'That was grand, love', and then he was out the door, like he was late for surgery or something. He'd never called her and had never mentioned it since. She always thought that the best way to get back at Aesop would be to seduce Jimmy, but it probably wouldn't have worked. Whatever unsavoury traits you might pin on Aesop, jealousy wasn't one of them. He was far too confident in his own prowess for something like that to bother him. And anyway, he was pissed that night and didn't remember shagging her.

'Jimmy?' said Jennifer, when it was just the two of them at the bar.

'Yep?'

'How are you? I mean, you know, after Sandra and all.'

'I'm grand, Jen. It was a bit, y'know, tough at first, but I'm just trying not to think about it. Anyway, don't I have Aesop to look out for me?'

'God help you. Well listen Jimmy, if you want someone to talk to or anything, just let me know, okay?' she said, touching his arm.

'Eh, right. Thanks.'

Jimmy looked at Jennifer out of the corner of his eye as they both picked up their drinks. She was a good-looking girl, no doubt about that. He always suspected that she had a small crush on him but just put it down to her being a teenage girl and himself being, well, himself. But she was in her late twenties now. He liked her. She liked him. She was a cracking-looking bird. Funny. Generous. Could she be ... ? Ah, hang on a fucking minute, Jimmy. What the hell was he doing? Jennifer was his best mate's sister and his other best mate's girlfriend. He breaks up with Sandra and a week later he's thinking inappropriate thoughts about the one girl in the world who he has no business thinking about at all! Jesus, he'd better be careful. This Superchick thing could get way out of hand. He walked back to the tables with her, reminding himself that Marco had a black belt in Tae Kwan Do and that Sicilians thought nothing of cutting your mickey off to settle a dispute.

Back at the table, Marco and Tsujita-san had arrived. Marco was beaming, introducing Tsujita-san to everyone and telling them everything he knew about him and Japan in general, which was a lot. He'd become quite the authority in the last couple of weeks.

'In Tokyo, Tsujita-san has to commute for an hour and a half to get to work,' he was saying to Norman. 'And the trains are so crowded that they have a man at the station to push you in the door, so everyone will fit!'

Norman was trying to picture that on the DART, and couldn't. It'd be a very brave man that started pushing commuters onto the 07.58 at Killester Station on a Monday morning. Norman had ten years' combat training and he wouldn't do it without a teargas grenade launcher and a couple of Rottweilers.

Tsujita-san just sat, nodding and looking earnest. The house system was on full blast now and it was hard enough to understand what people were saying without the disadvantage of not being a great English-speaker in the first place. He kept looking around in shock as he saw people coming from the bar with great big pints of black beer. In Japan you usually poured beer from a bottle on the table into a glass not a quarter the size of the small bucket that Marco had set down in front of him. He picked it up to taste but Marco stopped him.

'No no, Tsujita-san. You have to wait until it sets. See? It will go black, like Jimmy's.'

Tsujita-san looked up at Jimmy opposite him.

'You pray now?' he said, doing air guitar.

'No. Not tonight. Another band. Slapper,' said Jimmy.

'Srapp ... ?'

'A different band. Not me.' Jimmy leaned over the table so he could be heard.

'Jazz session?'

'Eh. No. Not really. Rock music. You know? U2?'

'Ah Yootsoo. I rike zat berry much.'

'Great,' said Jimmy, leaning back again and looking away. He wasn't going to spend the whole night yelling in this fucker's ear.

He did a quick scan of the room. All the seats were gone and the lounge crowd was starting to come in, queuing up to pay their fiver at the door. Normally he'd be mentally counting them, since the band took two euro per head, but tonight that dosh was going to Ronnie and the lads. Not to worry. It was only Aesop who actually needed the money. He didn't have a job and the money they got for gigs topped up his dole nicely. They averaged about ninety euro each per gig, and usually did at least one gig a week. Aesop would just have to cut down on his after-tea smoke, or maybe just his tea, until they got a bass player.

Around nine, Ronnie came out with the lads and started into *Teenage Dirtbag*. That was a no-brainer to get the crowd hopping. By the second chorus there were a couple of drunken eejits on the dance floor headbanging, and halfway through the next song the floor was mobbed. Jimmy was watching closely but trying not to look like he was. It was weird looking at another band playing. On one hand he enjoyed not having the pressure of doing the gig himself, but on the other hand he was itching to get up there. That pressure was what made him who he was. He winced at every dropped note and smiled when Ronnie cheated on a really high vocal line and sang an octave lower instead. He did that himself. Especially when he was doing two gigs in one day. He sat back and tried to enjoy the show but it wasn't easy. He badly wanted to be a rockstar tonight. He had his new hair and everything.

He glanced back over at Zucheeto who was listening intently to whatever Norman was saying to him. There was no way he'd be able to understand Norman, especially when the pints started kicking in a bit later. His Cork accent got stronger with alcohol. The poor bloke definitely seemed to be having trouble, with his face all screwed up and his ear nearly in Norman's mouth, but Jimmy knew it probably didn't matter anyway. He was probably only having the rules of hurling explained to him. That was Norman's favourite conversation starter when he was talking to anyone who wasn't Irish. Yeah, there it was. Norman had his hand out and was showing Zucheeto all the broken knuckles he had. Next thing, he'd be telling him how safe a sport it is. An hour or two of that and Zucheeto would probably leave the pub and go straight to the airport. Was there a direct flight from Dublin to Tokyo? Jimmy didn't know. He'd never been further than Torremolinos. He knew nothing about Tokyo, except for the fact that loads of people lived there and they were mad for fish. And that Japan had recently become part of Hong Kong again. Or something.

He looked around for Aesop and spotted him talking to a couple of girls that Jimmy didn't know at a table on the other side of the stage. They were laughing at whatever he was telling them. It could have been anything, Jimmy knew. Aesop didn't even try to ground his stories in reality. He could go from being a drummer, to an F1 driver, to a rat-catcher, in the space of ten minutes. It didn't make any difference; Aesop could entertain a woman at length on any topic that came to mind. And he'd been smoking earlier, so Christ only knew what it was this time. They were both fairly nice-looking. One of them in particular was having trouble keeping her breasts on the inside of her halter neck, which is probably what sucked Aesop over there in the first place. He decided to wander over. It had been years since he and Aesop had done this together. This could be just like old times. The two lads going to work on a couple of women.

'Jimmy!' said Aesop. 'Ladies, this is Jimmy Collins. He's in me band. Jimmy, this is Rhonda and this is Carol.'

Carol was the one with the set.

'Howya,' said Jimmy with his coolest smile, sitting down.

'We've seen you singing. You were here a couple of weeks ago, weren't you?' said Carol.

'Oh right, yeah. Thanks,' said Jimmy.

'What are you saying thanks for? I only said we saw you; I didn't say yiz were any good.'

'Yeah Carol,' said Rhonda. 'They're all the same, aren't they? Bleedin' love themselves up there. Your hair was normal as well. What did you do to it?'

Jimmy was bright red. He looked at Aesop, who had his face stuck in his pint.

'Eh. I just dyed it.'

'Jimmy has a stylist,' said Aesop, swallowing. 'Don't you, Jimmy?'

The girls screamed in laughter.

'A stylist?!' said Rhonda. 'And c'mere. Did he pick out your plastic trousers for you tonight, did he?'

Jimmy looked at Aesop again, who was now laughing as well the bastard.

'They're leather,' said Jimmy. He didn't know what else to say.

'Well, they look plastic,' said Carol. 'So, how come Aesop writes all the songs and you sing them? I thought the singer was supposed to write the songs.'

'I do write songs,' said Jimmy, quietly. His face was burning now.

'Ah, we're only messin' with you Jimmy,' said Carol. 'Rhonda here thinks you're gorgeous.'

'Fuck off you, I do not,' said Rhonda.

'Right, well sorry ladies, Jimmy ...' said Aesop. 'I've to go and talk to that bloke over there. I'll seeyiz later.' He got up and walked over to where Marco was explaining something about Guinness to Tsujita-san. Jimmy watched him go, hating his guts, and turned back around to the girls.

'He's a funny bloke, isn't he? Did he tell you about his fungal infection?'

Carol smiled at him. Rhonda didn't do anything. She just sat there, swaying slightly with the music.

'Do you like Slapper?' said Jimmy. He was desperate. He wanted to get away from them but he didn't want to be rude.

'They're all right, yeah,' said Carol. She was swaying now as well, looking over Jimmy's shoulder to the stage.

Jimmy turned and looked at the band himself. He couldn't think of anything – not one solitary syllable – to say to them. He got a poke on the shoulder from Carol.

'You're in me way. Can you move over a bit?'

Ah, bollocks to this! This wasn't like old times at all. A pair of women taking the piss out of him, Aesop landing him in it, him not being able to think of anything to say – was it really four years since he'd tried to chat someone up? It felt more like ten.

'Tell you what,' said Jimmy. 'I'm going to the bar. Do yiz want a drink?'

'Vodka tonic,' said Carol.

'Corona,' said Rhonda.

'Grand.' Jimmy stood up and went to the bar, ordering just a Guinness for himself. That pair of slags could piss off if they thought he was buying them drink. Plastic trousers me arse. He went back to his own table, watching to see how long they'd wait before they realised he wasn't coming back. He liked looking at a nice pair of tits as much as the next man but you had to have your pride.

'You're some bollocks,' he said to Aesop.

'Ah, I was only having a laugh. The state of you. "They're leather". For fuck sake, I thought you were going to cry. Anyway, I decided that they weren't what we're looking for, so there was no point in hanging around them, wasting time.

Amn't I good?'

'Yeah, you're brilliant,' said Jimmy. 'Since when did you write the songs, anyway? The only time we do any of your songs is if we're playing The Fiddler's Smig and most of the punters in there are E'd up to fuck. You could play Perry Como and they'd still be bouncing off the walls ...' He stopped. 'Hey, look at the head on Zucheeto. Is he okay?'

Aesop looked over. 'What do you mean?'

'The colour of his face ... fucking hell, he looks like his head is about to explode.'

'Jaysis, yeah.'

'Hey, Zucheeto. You okay?'

Tsujita-san turned away from Katie, who seemed to be having a laugh for once.

'*Nan da?*'

'You okay? Your face ...' Jimmy pointed to his own face and then Tsujita-san's. 'It's red.'

'Ah yes. Japanese people drink beer. Get berry red face. Okay *desu*.' He gave a thumbs up.

'Did you get that, Jimmy?' said Aesop.

'Not really. But I think he knows about it and he doesn't look too bothered. Fuck 'im.'

'Where's Norman?'

They looked around. He was up on the dance floor doing some kind of Twist to Slapper's version of *Johnny B Goode*. He was a big man to be doing a dance like that but the girl dancing opposite him didn't seem to mind.

'Oh Christ. Look at the state of him. When was the last time you saw Norman dance?' said Aesop.

'Jesus. At the U2 gig in Croker? When was that? He was hammered.'

'He was doing the Twist then as well, wasn't he?'

'I think so. Maybe it was big in Cork.'

'And that's what's going to reel in the woman he's been waiting all his life to meet, is it? He looks like there's a pound of butter up his arse and he's trying to shake it loose.'

'Aesop, remember not to slag him, right? He's probably dancing with her to give himself time to think up something to say.' Maybe he should have tried that, he thought, looking back over at Carol and Rhonda, who were still sitting there with no drinks in front of them. Nah. They weren't worth it. 'Anyway, at least he's making an effort. Look at Marco.'

Marco wasn't even talking to Jennifer. He was listening to Tsujita-san and Katie, butting in every few seconds.

'What's the story with him and that Japanese bloke?' said Aesop. 'He's all over him.'

'He's just showing off a bit. Usually he's the one sitting there trying to fit in with everyone, so this is his chance to be the big shot. Oh, by the way, Ronnie said he'd call us up later for a song.'

'Ah Jimmy, I've been smoking and drinking and all, y'know?'

'It's just one or two songs, Aesop. You'll be grand.'

'Right. Well, I better slow down on this then,' said Aesop, holding up his glass.

Jimmy smiled. Aesop would have made a brilliant professional drummer. It was the only thing he cared about enough to change his social habits for.

'Right,' said Aesop. 'I'm off again. The bar will be closing in a couple of hours and we're on a mission, right? Seeya later.'

Jimmy watched him go straight up to a girl who was leaning against a pillar on her own. He was a cheeky bastard, no doubt about it. Okay Jimmy, you can't just sit here all night. Get a move on. He still felt like an eejit after Carol and Rhonda, but decided that that had only happened because he was a bit rusty. There were a hundred other women in here and it was his sworn duty to check some of them out. He stood up, walked coolly towards the bar again and almost immediately tripped over a handbag, flying face-first into some-

89

one's arse and sending at least four drinks flying. He looked up from the ground and moaned.

He knew that arse.

Eight

'Jimmy! Are you all right?' said Sandra. She handed Beano her drink and bent down to help him up.

'I'm fine,' said Jimmy. He brushed her hand off his arm and stood up. He had been hoping to attract a bit of attention as he swaggered to the bar, bum tightly wrapped in leather, but not this way. He would have looked like a prat if it had been anyone else's handbag he had managed to get tangled up in, but the fact that it had been Sandra's had just made it all the more embarrassing. And that bastard Beano, grinning his head off.

'Drink, Jimmy?' said Beano.

Jimmy didn't answer. He was going to tell Beano where to stick his drink but he didn't want to do it in front of Sandra. He just glared at him and then nodded at Sandra, walking past her.

He kept going straight past the bar, knowing that they were both still looking at him and not wanting to stop. At this point there were only two places he could go without turning around and walking past them again, but he didn't know how to use the cigarette machine and he'd look even more stupid trying to make his way into the Ladies. Instead he executed an abrupt left and kept going, past the bouncer and up the stairs, until he found himself out on the wet street.

Nice one Jimmy, he told himself. Well handled.

He wasn't going to stand out here all night and get pissed on, so he turned around and headed back down the stairs. He was bound to bump into Beano and Sandra the odd time. Might as well get used to it.

He saw them talking to another couple at the bar and

walked past them, back to the table. Jennifer was watching him.

'Jimmy, I saw that. God, that was terrible.'

'Ah fuck it, Jen. It doesn't matter.'

'They shouldn't have come in. You were always going to be here.'

'It's a free country, I s'pose.'

'Ah no. That's not on. Are you okay?'

This was getting a bit repetitive.

'I'm fine, Jen. Really.' He wasn't really fine but he was getting ragged off with people asking him. He sat down next to her and leaned forward to Marco.

'Marco, your buddy there is starting to look a bit ropey.'

Tsujita-san had his head down on the table. Jimmy couldn't see most of his face, but his right ear and forehead were the same colour as the Cork jersey that Norman sometimes wore on Sundays.

'I think he is a little bit drunk Jimmy,' said Marco, who didn't quite look the picture of sprightliness himself.

Jimmy did a quick count. Marco must have had about five pints of Guinness. That was a lot of beer for Marco.

'How much has he had?'

'Only three pints. I think maybe he drinks less in Japan.'

Christ, it was only half ten.

Jimmy looked around for Norman and spotted him in a cosy embrace with the girl he'd been dancing with earlier. Well, that was a result. They were on their own at a small table, her hand inside his shirt and his arm around her shoulder, looking at the band. Jimmy caught his eye and got the biggest grin he'd seen in months. He smiled back. Well, even if everything else went to shite tonight, at least Norman got a snog. Another scan of the room revealed Aesop talking to three girls next to the stage. How many was that he'd gotten through so far?

Slapper were just starting their second set. Something

fast by Blink 182. Always good for a bop. Jimmy watched the crowd start to fill the floor again. Norman wisely stayed put with his bird.

The song finished and then Ronnie was speaking into the mike. Jimmy wasn't really listening but suddenly he heard his own name and then Aesop's. God, he'd forgotten about this. He stood up as the adrenaline burst through him. Marco and Jen and the girls were cheering around him. Even Tsujita-san managed a subdued 'Wayyyyy' through the arms that were folded around his head. He stepped between some tables and found himself on the stage next to Ronnie, who was taking off his guitar and handing it to him. Ronnie took up position at the bass player's mike with his spare guitar, while Aesop made himself comfortable on the drummer's stool. Jon, Slapper's drummer, took the opportunity to try and move in on the three girls that Aesop had been talking to. Must be a drummer thing, thought Jimmy, as he looked around and made sure everyone was ready.

He looked down from the stage. He could make out a few familiar faces at the front and under the bright lights at the bar, but the stage lights were in his eyes so most of the room was just a glare. Now. What to play? He'd have to keep it simple enough. The bass player and Ronnie would be winging it, so there was no point in going for one of his own tunes, or a Rush song or something. Anyway, this wasn't his gig. He'd have to do a crowd-pleaser. Okay. He had it. This would be good. *Nobody* would be expecting this one, he thought. They'd all be talking about it for weeks. Rumours. Scandal. Yeah, rock and roll.

He turned around to Aesop.

'Okay. *Still in Love With You*,' he shouted.

At the side of the stage, Jon stopped talking to Aesop's women and looked around in surprise. Aesop blinked and mouthed 'What?' Jimmy just nodded. Ronnie looked a bit puzzled but the bass player didn't know Jimmy very well so he just stood there and shrugged.

'The *Live and Dangerous* version. In A,' Jimmy said to everyone. And then he started it.

Still in Love With You was a ballad by Thin Lizzy and Jimmy didn't often play ballads, but it was an absolutely cracking song and the girls in the crowd would love him for it. The lads would all be looking at him playing the solo, each one wishing it was him up there being the guitar hero. It was a song full of emotion and tears and sadness at love lost. Jimmy could even do a fair impression of Phil Lynott by kind of blocking the back of his throat with his tongue to give his voice that nasally tone you might associate with heavy cocaine use. He closed his eyes and sang it like he meant every pitiful, miserable word. When he opened them occasionally, he looked towards the area where he'd last seen Sandra. This would really fuck up her evening.

He got through it, complete with a wailing, screaming, crying guitar solo, and stopped. There was a second of complete silence, and then the place went nuts. Jimmy smiled and tried to look like that song had been the most difficult song he'd ever played live. He stood there, guitar hanging low around his waist, and acted like he was physically and emotionally drained. There had been a few couples up dancing, but it was one of those songs where you want to just sit and watch and listen. Now that it was over, the spell was broken but Jimmy had done what he wanted to do. The girls in the crowd would think he was chocolate, everyone who knew the story of him and Sandra would be wondering what was going to happen next, Sandra would be feeling terrible that she'd hurt him so much, and, most importantly, there was absolutely no fucking chance at all of Beano having sex tonight.

'Thanks very much,' said Jimmy, when the crowd settled down. 'I haven't played that one in a while but I just had something on me mind. I s'pose you'd all like a bit of a dance now, yeah?' The crowd cheered again. 'Right. Well, we'd better do a fast one then, before Aesop walks out on us!'

He went into *Basket Case*, by Green Day. Within ten seconds the floor was a mosh pit. He looked back at Aesop, who was in his element. You couldn't get fast or loud enough for Aesop Murray. He wrapped up the song and gave a bow. The crowd was cheering like mad as he handed the guitar back to Ronnie.

'Ye fuckin' bollocks,' said Ronnie, smiling. 'What am I s'posed to play after that?'

'Do *Teen Spirit*,' said Jimmy, as he hopped off the stage. They were already starting it by the time Jimmy reached the table and started getting claps on the back from the lads. Jennifer was quiet.

'How was that, Jen?'

'Great, Jimmy. God, I was nearly crying for the first song. It was gorgeous. You meant it too, didn't you? You still love her.'

'Ah, Jen. It's just a song, right? I just did it to wind her up a bit. Did you see her?'

'She left when you were starting Green Day. I think her and Beano had a fight.'

'Really? Ah, that's terrible,' said Jimmy, with a huge smile.

'Jimmy Collins, I don't believe it! You're so bold!' said Jennifer, laughing.

'Only a little bit,' said Jimmy, taking a swig out of his flat pint. It was warm and thick, but it tasted just lovely.

'Hey, Jimmy. What the fuck was all that about?' Aesop was standing behind him.

'Just having a laugh, Aesop. Sandra was here earlier. Don't worry about it. Me heart will go on, y'know?'

'Thank fuck for that. You're lucky it was a Lizzy song. I don't bleedin' do ballads, right?'

'I know that, pal. Having any luck with the ladies?'

'Jesus, Jimmy, I've talked to about twenty birds. Believe me, there's no one special in this place tonight? Can I go and get me hole now? Please? Howya Jen.'

Jennifer just looked up at him. She shook her head and moved to join Marco at the other end of the table.

'Okay Aesop,' said Jimmy. 'You did your best. You've got half an hour to find a partner for the rest of the evening. Do you think that's enough?'

'Jimmy, in half an hour I could sort both of us out. I could probably even get someone to ride Norman, if he changed his shirt and promised not to say anything. Where is he, by the way?'

'I think he's scored already. Look at him over there.'

'Christ, she's a bit rough, isn't she?'

'For fuck sake, Aesop, you're never happy. He's delighted with himself. Look.'

'I am looking, Jimmy, and it's not a pretty sight. Anyway. I'm off. Talk to you later. C'mere, are you not on the prowl yourself? This was all your idea, remember?'

'I am. Just give me a minute to cool down.'

'All right. This is brilliant, but. Usually we're up there on the stage all night and all the decent women are gone by the time I'm ready for them. This way there's a much better selection.'

'Christ, Aesop, it's not like you're in the middle of a famine, is it?'

'God. Don't even say that Jimmy,' said Aesop, blessing himself, and was gone.

The Japanese bloke was asleep.

'Marco?' said Jimmy. Marco was talking to Jennifer and Katie and looked around.

'Are you going to do something about this?' Jimmy said, gesturing towards Tsujita-san.

'It is okay, Jimmy. I will get a taxi for him when we're leaving.'

'He's not dead or anything, is he?'

'I don't think so.' Marco punched Tsujita-san on the shoulder. 'Hey, Tsujita-san!' he shouted at him. 'Hey! Are you okay?'

'*Urasai yo!*' said Tsujita-san, lifting his head and wiping dribble from his chin. He was looking around the table with a very pissed-off expression.

Brilliant, thought Jimmy. I'm not staying here if this bloke's going to go mental and start doing Bruce Lee. He stood up again and started towards the bar. He was due a pint, and anyway he could get a better view of the talent from up there.

He was getting a lot of looks and smiles as he manoeuvred his way between chairs and people to get to the bar. This was more like it. John the manager saw him coming up and put a fresh pint in front him before he even asked for it, and then waved away the fiver Jimmy had in his hand.

'Good stuff, Jimmy. Haven't heard that one in ages. Takes me back to me smooching days.'

'Thanks, John.'

He took the beer and stood with his back to the bar to see what was on offer. A few of the girls who'd eyed him up as he was getting his drink were with blokes. Fuck that. Another few were with their mates. Jimmy still didn't feel confident enough to just sidle up to them and start talking. He used to be okay at it, but all that was a while ago. He'd been with Sandra so long that now he didn't think he could remember how to make himself sound interesting to anyone else. Besides, he kept telling everyone that he was grand but it had only been a week and it was going to take longer than that. It wasn't that he was pining for her, and most of the time he didn't even think about her, but sometimes he'd remember something and he'd feel it then. Like a burst of nerves or something.

He noticed that Tsujita-san was awake now, and talking

to Katie again. There was a pint of water in front of him and he was clutching onto it for dear life. Marco and Jennifer were having a snog next to them. Maeve was talking to some black fella with sparkling white teeth, and Norman was still with the same girl over at another table. They both looked pretty drunk. Whatever it takes, thought Jimmy. Aesop was standing next to the stage. Slapper were doing an AC/DC song that The Grove had thought of doing and Aesop was just seeing how Jon was handling the drum parts. There was a stunning blonde girl standing right behind Aesop, looking impatient with one hand on her hip. She was practically tapping her foot, probably not used to being upstaged by a heavy metal drummer with a big beard and green teeth.

Jimmy smiled to himself. He was the only one left on his own, and it was his bloody masterplan to dedicate the evening to meeting someone. He decided that he wasn't up for it. Not tonight. He'd been excited about the idea of the lads all going out and seeing what might be on the cards, but now that it was around the time in the evening for people to be pairing off, he knew that even if he did meet a nice girl it was too late to do anything about it. All anyone wanted now that last orders had been called was another drink. Possibly a shag. Jimmy turned back to the bar and nodded at John again. Another drink would be less complicated.

They all left shortly afterwards in a big gang.

Jimmy lay in bed when he got home. He wasn't drunk, but he had enough in him so that his thoughts were racing. Norman had whispered, 'Jimmy, I found her!' to him as he'd left with his new friend, Marie. Jimmy hoped he had, but doubted it. It was just the first time he'd scored in ages. Marco and Jen had left, gazing into one another's eyes and holding each other up. Katie practically carried Tsujita-san out the door and threw him in a taxi and then, to everyone's delight, got in with him. Maeve gave the black guy her number, as she got into another taxi. Aesop ended up with Carol and Rhonda from earlier. He was wearing his 'I'm riding two women tonight!' grin. Jimmy was disturbed to find himself recognising it.

And he thought of Sandra. She'd be in bed with Beano. Wearing pyjamas probably, Jimmy reckoned. Maybe it was a bit unfair to mess with her head like that, but Jimmy only did it to get at Beano, not her. Was she thinking of him? Jimmy didn't know. He didn't even know if he wanted her to be. He closed his eyes and tried to sleep. A bit of a disaster, as far as his finding the woman of his dreams went, but it wasn't a bad night overall. He'd nailed the solo in the Lizzy song, for starters. He indulged in a little fantasy, where Sandra called round, begging him to take her back, but he fell asleep before it was over, so he never found out if he did or not.

And the woman of his dreams wasn't at home.

Nine

Before Jimmy even opened his eyes he knew it was late. He could tell by the stiffness in his back. Any more than ten hours of sleep and the muscles just above his arse started to complain. He lifted his head from the pillow and looked at the clock as he reached for the phone. It was nearly one in the afternoon. Another Sunday goes down the toilet. He promised himself at least twice a week that he wouldn't waste the following Sunday, but this always happened.

'Hello,' he mumbled.

'Jimmy!' It was Aesop. He sounded like he was on top of the world. 'Are you still in bed, ye lazy bastard?'

'Yeah.'

'Remember Carol?'

'Who?'

'Carol. Big tits. I rode her and her mate last night.'

'Jesus, Aesop, I only just woke up. Can you tell me about it later?'

'I'm not calling about that. Carol's brother's mate plays the bass. Does a bit of session work from the sounds of it. Carol says he's just gotten divorced so he has his weekends back and wants to start gigging again.'

Jimmy was awake now.

'Do you have a number for him?'

'Carol's getting it for me now. And all the grief you give me for shagging loads of different women. Y'see what happens? It's called Networking, Jimmy.'

'Networking, yeah right. Okay then, give him a call when you get the number and then ring me. See if he's free on Wednesday. Maybe we should book a studio in town? If he's a session player he probably won't think much of the community centre.'

'Grand. You going for a pint later?'

'I s'pose so. What are you doing this afternoon?'

'I'm going to bed, Jimmy. I'm bollixed. You should've seen that bleedin' lunatic, Rhonda. She had this glass of water with ice cubes in it, right? And she kept dipping Carol's ...'

'Okay, Aesop, that's brilliant,' said Jimmy, quickly. 'Tell me later, all right?'

'Okay. Listen, I'll seeya, right?'

'Seeya.'

Jimmy hung up and fell back onto the pillow again. Well that was all right he thought, as he started twisting in the bed to relieve the stiffness in his back. Someone like that would get up to speed on the set in no time. He was thinking about having a shower when the phone rang again.

'Aesop?'

'Jimmy. It's Sandra.'

Oh bollocks.

'Hiya.' It was too early in the day for whatever this was going to be about. Then he remembered what he'd done last night. Oops. He was hoping he'd have time to practice this conversation in his head before he talked to her again. It had been a spur of the moment thing when he did it.

'Jimmy, I think we should talk.'

'About what?'

'You know about what. I heard you singing that song last night and I ... I s'pose I got a bit upset. You were never like that when we were together.'

'Sandra ...'

'Jimmy, listen to me for a minute. This hasn't been easy for me either, you know? I know what it feels like.'

Here it comes thought Jimmy, excitement rushing through him. She reckons she's made a big mistake. Oh yeah. This was going to be good. He felt ten feet tall. Yes! She wants me again. She's sorry. I'm better than Beano. Of course I fucking am! He swung around to sit up on the bed, legs jiggling off the edge with nerves. I'm better than Beano!

'I'm listening,' he said, trying to sound cool.

'Jimmy, there's people who can help you.'

'Excuse me?'

'You don't have to go through this alone, you know? Of course I want to help you too, but there are others. Professionals. They counsel people who are having a hard time accepting things like this.'

He took the phone away from his ear and frowned at the wall. Had he heard that right?

'Jesus, you're serious aren't you Sandra? You're telling me I should call the Samaritans.'

'Not just them, Jimmy. There's support groups ...'

'Are you *completely* deranged, Sandra?' Christ, this was the best one ever. 'Let me guess. You read this in a book, right? What was it? Broken Relationships for Dummies?'

'You're angry now, Jimmy, but you've got to give it time. I swear, soon the anger will go away and you can move on.'

'Sandra, listen to me a minute,' said Jimmy. He closed his eyes. This was to be delivered calmly. 'I'm not going to talk in clichés, so you might have to concentrate to understand me. I've moved on, okay? I'm not angry, I'm fucking grand. If I need therapy, I'll go on the piss with Aesop. Okay?'

'But ...' She didn't sound convinced. 'But Jimmy, I saw you on the stage. You meant it. Why can't you just admit that? If you could just face the reality of what you're feeling, you'll be able to deal with it so much better.'

'Sandra, don't talk to me about reality. You're not qualified. I'm a performer. I act. What I do on the stage is all an act. Did you see me doing *Basket Case* afterwards? I was hopping around the place because it's that type of song. You go mental for the mental songs, and you look sad for the sad songs. Do you understand? It's not real. It's fake. It's called pretending.'

'There's no need to patronise me, Jimmy. You can deny it all you want, but you're feeling hurt right now and all I'm saying is that there are people out there who can help you.'

Oh for fuck sake. Jimmy couldn't listen to any more of this.

'You're just a fucking loser, really, aren't you Sandra? You're so busy believing all that loser shite you read that you can't see your nose in front of your face. I sang that song for a laugh. Have you ever heard of irony? Clever people use it for comic effect.'

There was silence for a second.

'Jimmy, that's a terrible thing to say.'

'Sandra. I'm glad we're over, right? I genuinely am. The only person I'm sad for is you, and that's because I know for a fact that Beano is a fucking idiot. All right? Are we clear on that? I'm not suicidal and I'm not locking myself in the house every day, waiting for you to come back to me. And would you ever do yourself a favour and stop trying to be an American? Counselling me bollocks. You want me to call around there now so we can all have a group hug? Would you ever cop on, would you? What are you reading this week? Fucking Chicken Soup for the Guilty Soul?'

'Jimmy, I'm hanging up. I'm sorry I called. But you do need help.'

'You need help, Sandra. You think all the world needs to do is to listen to your shite and then everything will be grand. Well, they have a name for that. Look it up in one of your Idiot's fucking Guides to Being Full of Shit. It'll be under "L" for Living in a Fucking Dream World.'

He was talking to himself.

He hung up and walked to the bathroom. In the mirror, he was red in the face and his hands were shaking. God, she really wound him up that time. Still, if he wanted to avoid her in the future then that probably did the trick. Not even Sandra would try again after that. He splashed cold water on his face and turned on the shower, waiting for it to heat up. Good luck, Beano. You're going to fucking need it. He was about to step into the shower, when the phone rang again.

'Ah, bleedin' hell ...'

He trotted back down the landing and picked it up. He hated talking on the phone when he was in the nip, and it was freezing.

'Hello?'

'Jimmy, I called yer man. He's already started practising with a band.'

'Bollocks. Who's the band?'

'You're not going to believe it. Are you sitting down?'

'Aesop, I'm standing here with the shower running and me mickey flapping in the wind. Who's the bleedin' band?'

'Jaysis, what's up with you? Are you always this grumpy before you've had your cornflakes?'

'Sandra just called.'

'Oh. What did she want? Was it about last night? I betcha ...'

'Aesop. Tell me who the band is, will you, before my penis disappears altogether with the fucking cold?'

'It's Beano's band. He's got a singer already, and now a bass player. He's looking for a drummer.'

'Are you serious? And Beano's going to play guitar?! Has this bloke heard him yet? He's crap!'

'I know, but his uncle knows a lot of people so maybe that's how they got together. Apparently Beano's planning on making a CD, if you can believe that.'

Beano's Uncle Donal used to be a big sound engineer back in the Seventies. Jimmy had hoped to milk that but never got the chance.

'Ah shite. Okay, well it was worth a shout anyway. All right, I'll talk to you later. Jesus, Beano making a CD ...'

In the shower, Jimmy had to laugh. Between Sandra and the endless amateur dramatic productions going on in her head, and Beano with his delusions of mediocrity ... what a bloody pair. So, he's trying to put a band together, is he? Jimmy wondered who the singer was. Hardly Beano himself. Christ, he was bad enough just playing guitar. And just singing. If he tried to do them both together, he'd probably swallow his tongue with the confusion of it all. But you'd never know with Beano. He might do it anyway. Some people are blessed with an inability to respect their supposed limitations. It means that they're constantly challenging themselves, improving all the time as a result. With Beano it was different. He didn't even recognise his limitations when he reached them, so he'd blithely sail straight through, becoming more and more of an embarrassment to himself all the time. That's why the mixing desk on the stage was always sitting on Jimmy's amp. He could easily reach back and turn Beano down when he got excited and started to think he was James Brown. Beano wouldn't notice because he could still hear himself through his monitor, but everyone else would be spared.

He dried off and went downstairs to put the kettle on, turning the telly on to MTV. It was mostly shite these days but he liked to have some background music when he was alone in the house. When he was done with his Weetabix he sat in his armchair and picked up the guitar. He still had *Superchick* the song to sort out, even if he was no closer to finding Superchick the girl. The lyrics he already had in the notebook weren't the kind of thing he'd started out to write, but he thought he might as well keep going along those lines. Even if he didn't use them, they'd always come in handy later for something or other.

He put down the guitar and picked up the pen. It wasn't like he had any kind of decent tune worked out anyway. Supping on his tea every now and again, he scribbled out whatever came to mind. By two thirty, he had another verse. Same vein as the rest. Jimmy still wasn't convinced. He got up and put on his jacket. Time for food.

Dinner in Peggy Collins' house on a Sunday was at about two thirty in the afternoon and always had been. With the old Holy Hour, the pubs used to shut from two to four, so that gave his Dad time to get half eleven Mass, drop into his mates in The Fluther for a couple of pints, and be home by two fifteen. A quick read of the paper, wee wee, wash the hands and then he'd be stuck into his roast beef. Eating at any other time on a Sunday always felt weird for Jimmy.

He hadn't told his Mam he'd be in for dinner that day, but that wasn't a problem. As soon as his key turned in the door, she'd be swiping potatoes off his father's plate and the beef that had been put aside for his sandwiches at teatime, would be commandeered and smothered in gravy.

Jimmy shut the door behind him and strolled off down the road. He'd thought about wearing his leather trousers again, just to annoy his Dad, but he'd be in the pub later and they weren't really Sunday evening pants.

His notebook was left open on the floor beside his chair ...

> She loved to watch the soccer and her favourite food was
>   steak
> She could put her legs behind her head, she made me
>   chocolate cake
> Her idea of a quiet night in was pizza, beer and sex
> And she told me I'm amazing and way bigger than her ex.

'**Ah.** Here he comes. Peggy, do you want to turn the heat down, so Frosty here doesn't melt all over the carpet?'

'Howya, Da. No, don't get up.'

His father hadn't moved.

'Ah Jimmy, love, how are you?' said Peggy, flying across the kitchen floor to give him a kiss. She had her Sunday apron on and the whole house smelled of meat juices and cabbage. It always reminded him of being a kid.

'I'm grand, Ma. Look, here's a bottle of plonk for the dinner.'

'Ah Jimmy, you shouldn't be spending your money. Look, Seán, Jimmy's after bringing us a lovely bottle of wine. French. Look, Seán. You like Shiraz, don't you?'

Jimmy's Dad took the bottle and read the label over his glasses. Jimmy had forgotten to take off the price tag.

'In the name of Jaysis, Jimmy, what are you spending twenty euro on a bottle of wine for?'

'Ah Da, just drink it, will ye? Hey Ma, I hope there's enough food ...'

'Of course there is, love. Sure there's too much for the two of us anyway. I'd only be throwing it out.'

His Dad shook his head and picked up the paper again, a man who knew he'd be having a boiled egg for his tea.

'I saw Marco and Jennifer at Mass this morning,' said Peggy. 'God, they're a lovely couple, aren't they?'

'Gorgeous,' said Jimmy, picking up the Entertainment section of his Dad's paper and sitting down.

'Do you think they'll get married?' She was rearranging everyone's dinner so that it would go around and pretending to indulge in idle chat, but when his mother started into that kind of conversation there was only one way it could go. He might have broken up with Sandra but that wouldn't stop her. Her son was thirty and single and that just wasn't good enough.

'I don't know, Ma. They're only going out a few months.'

'Ah, they're not. Sure it must be nearly a year now. Marco's lovely, isn't he? Such a gentleman. And, God, Jennifer is beautiful. I think she was always after you, Jimmy.' She was laughing now, but it wasn't a joke.

'Not at all, Ma. She's Aesop's sister. We're just mates.'

There was silence from the kitchen. Jimmy looked up from the paper. It wasn't over yet. Not by a long shot.

'So, how was last night? Did you go out?'

'I went to McGuigans with the lads. It was a good laugh.'

'Did you meet anybody nice?'

At last.

'Not really. I think Norman found himself a woman, though.'

'Did he? Ah, that's great. Poor Norman.'

Jimmy smiled to himself. His Mam was brilliant.

'I'll probably see him later. I'll get all the gossip for you.'

'God, it's none of my business, Jimmy. Once he's happy, that's the main thing. And no one there you liked at all? It's a big pub, McGuigans, isn't it?'

'Ah Ma, stop. I was just out for a few pints with the lads. Sang a song with Ronnie Fitzgerald. You remember Ronnie? Used to live up in the Gardens. He's got a band now.'

'Doreen's little fella? I do of course remember him. And he has a band now too? God, did you hear that, Seán?'

'I did, yeah,' said Jimmy's Dad, lying.

'His sister married that fella from Finglas, didn't she? I think Gertie told me that. A lovely wedding. Out in Glendalough or something, wasn't it? The uncle is the curate out there.'

It went on like that all through dinner. Small talk, but with strong nuptial emphases. Jimmy's sister Liz was engaged out in Chicago to a bloke from Donegal. His cousin was doing a line with an airhostess. Young Eamon Thompson from down the road was on his honeymoon in Greece. Jimmy was used to it and his Dad had learnt years ago that once Peggy Collins got going there was no point in trying to stop her. This was Sunday dinner and her Jimmy was there. The best Seán could hope for was that there'd still be a slice of apple tart left for him when his wife was finished shovelling it into her son.

Jimmy and his Dad went into the living-room while his mother cleaned up after dinner. In the Collins household, the men did men stuff and the women did women stuff. A bit of a raw deal for Liz when she lived at home, but Jimmy could always point to the times he'd mowed the lawn or cleaned out the garage when all she had to do was peel a few spuds. Anyway, Peggy loved the idea of the two men in her life sitting down after their Sunday dinner and having a real lad's chat.

Seán sat in his armchair and picked up the Sports. Jimmy was on the couch with Entertainment.

'How's work?' said Seán.

'Grand,' said Jimmy.

They read their papers.

'So, I says to her, right, "I want to make love to your bottom," okay?' said Aesop.

The lads squealed with laughter.

'You did not!' said Norman.

'I did,' said Aesop, laughing too. 'I mean, I'd never done it, right? And you can't go pretending it was an accident, so I had to ask.'

'What did she say?' said Jimmy.

'She says "Me wha'?"' said Aesop, doing the accent. He could barely talk, he was laughing so much. 'And I said "Y'know, your hole, like. I want to make love to your hole. Do ye mind?" And she's looking at me, right? "Why?" she says to me. And I can't think up a good answer, can I? What am I s'posed to say? So I just say "Why not?" And she says to me "It's dirty." So I say ... I say, "That's why we're standing in the bath."'

The lads were howling now. Jimmy and Marco had tears streaming down their faces and Norman was clutching his pants like he needed to go to the toilet. People all over the bar were looking at them.

'And she's looking at me ...' Aesop was still laughing. 'She's looking at me, all worried like, and she's still bending over, and says, "Will it hurt?" And I says ... I says to her, "Ah no," I says, "The penis is a very resilient organ."'

They all screamed again. Beer was being slopped all over the table and Norman looked like he was in serious pain.

'Stop, stop, for God's sake,' he said, getting up. 'I'll go in me pants.' He left them there roaring and went off to the toilet.

Jimmy went up to the bar to get a cloth and some more

drinks, still chuckling away.

'What was all that about, Jimmy?' said Dave, the barman.

'Ah. Just one of Aesop's stories. He's a gas man, so he is.'

'He is all right. Had me cracking up earlier. Listen, there was a bloke in here looking for you this afternoon. About four or five. Chinky bloke. Soo ... Tootee ...'

'Zucheeto?' said Jimmy, puzzled.

'Yeah, that's it. I forgot about it 'til I saw yiz all laughing over there. He was just asking for you, that's all.'

'Right. Thanks,' said Jimmy. He picked up the drinks and brought them back to the table, fishing the cloth out of his back pocket and throwing it at Aesop. 'That mess is your fault, Aesop. Off you go. Hey, Marco. Zucheeto was in here earlier.' He thought for a second and then called up to the bar. 'Dave, was he looking for me or Marco?'

'You, Jimmy.'

'There. He was looking for me. Now, what would he be looking for me for, do ye think? And how did he know where I'd be?'

'I don't know,' said Marco, looking down.

'He had a saxophone with him,' called Dave, from the bar.

'Did he, now? Marco, what's going on?'

'Eh, sorry Jimmy. I told him that we sometimes come here on Sunday and that there is a session in the evening. I was a bit drunk. I told him that maybe he could play with you ...'

'Ah Marco, for fuck sake. It's a trad session. I haven't gotten up there in ages. When do you ever hear me playing that type of music? What did you tell him that for?'

'I was just making him feel welcome, Jimmy. It's no problem. Anyway, he's already gone, yes?' Marco looked downcast.

Jimmy sighed.

'Ah, it doesn't matter. Anyway, he's a jazz player, right?

The lads don't play that stuff either,' said Jimmy. He looked around at the small stage. There were four or five people pulling out fiddles and guitars and whistles. It wasn't a band as such, just people who'd play for the fun of it. Dave would fire a few free pints their way and everyone would have a laugh. There wasn't much call for a sax in Irish traditional music anyway, although the lads were pretty good. They'd find a use for it if there was one there.

'So, Norman,' said Aesop, when Norman arrived back. 'Tell us about this mot you were with last night. The one with the hump on her back and the glass eye. Was she human, after all?'

'Feck off, Aesop. She was lovely. Marie. Lovely girl.'

'Did you score?'

'Ah, stop. I'm not telling you all about my business.'

'Amn't I after telling you about my evening?'

'That's because you're a dirty bastard. Myself and Marie had a grand time. That's all you need to know.'

'So, are you seeing her again?' said Jimmy.

'No. No, she lives in London. Headed back there this evening. Only gets home a couple of times a year.'

Norman was trying to sound upbeat, but Jimmy knew he was devastated. There weren't many girls who clicked like that with Norman, and vice versa. Besides which, Norman had really gone out on a limb last night. He was normally far too shy to dance and chat up a girl like that. He'd really been trying. And then the cow lives in London. Jimmy felt sorry for him. Aesop didn't.

'You mean, she *told* you she lives in London. She probably lives in Coolock and was scared of her shite in case you wanted to see her again.'

Norman would usually react to stuff like that, but tonight he just gave a small, kind of sad, smile.

'No. She lives in London. I brought her to the airport.'

'Jaysis. Did you cry?'

'No. No, Aesop, I didn't cry, but I'll tell you something, you'll be crying if you don't put a gag on that big fecking mouth of yours.' Norman was grinning now. Danger. Danger.

Aesop shook theatrically to demonstrate his waning bravado, and then wisely just shrugged and took a drink. Life was short enough without bringing Norman's Grin of Death on yourself.

Jimmy wasn't really paying attention. He was wondering about Zucheeto, hoping he wasn't going to turn out to be a pain in the arse.

Ten

It was Wednesday night and the lads were at the community centre with Tsujita-san. Jimmy had tried to explain to Aesop why Tsujita-san was there, but Aesop was still pissed off with the situation. Wednesday nights were for serious practice, not pricking around.

It had all started on Monday morning when Jimmy arrived at his desk. The red light on his phone was flashing to let him know that he had a voice mail. It was a bit early in the day for people to be coming to him with their problems. When he booted up his computer, he saw a few emails. Not too unusual, but one of them was from stsujita@eirotechsolutions.ie and that meant that Zucheeto still wanted him for something. He read it:

> Jimmy-san, I will pray with you on Wednesday? Marco-san told me that your practice sessions are this day. Can you prease inform to me where to meet with you to pray? I heartily look forward to praying the great music. Best Regards, Tsujita.

Marco again! I'll fucking kill him.

What was wrong with him? The lads didn't play jazz and they didn't sit around jamming on Wednesdays. They practised some songs, worked out new stuff and tried to improve the set. Messing about for their own amusement could be a laugh but that wasn't the point of the exercise for Jimmy and Aesop in the community centre. Jimmy didn't know what to do. He didn't particularly like disappointing people – especially people who were as excited as this guy clearly was – and Marco had obviously made it his mission to integrate him into the group, but the thought of this Japanese bloke being a wart on his arse for six months was just too much.

He'd have to nip it in the bud.

He checked his voice mail, already knowing what it would be. What time did this bloke come into work, anyway?

'Jimmy-san. I send you e-mail. Wednesday, we pray. Okay. See you raytah. Oh, ziss is Tsujita by za way.'

Thanks. For a minute there I thought it was me Da. God, he was a tenacious bastard, you had to give him that.

Jimmy collared Marco later on in the corridor.

'Hey Marco. I see we have a new member in the band. Plays the sax. Japanese bloke. Do you know him? He talks about you a lot.'

'Ah. Jimmy, I was just talking and he was so excited. What could I do?'

He was giving it the big Italian shrug, but Jimmy wasn't having any of it this time.

'Marco I told you we don't need a sax player. I know you like the bloke, but now he's after inviting himself along on Wednesday night. Aesop will fucking freak if yer man starts into all that Miles Davis shite. You have to tell him he can't come. Make something up. Tell him Aesop's dead, or something.'

'But Jimmy, you told him he could go. Remember?'

'I bloody did not! When did I tell him that?'

'The first time you met him. He asked if you could play together, and you said yes.'

'Marco, I was only being polite for fuck sake. What was I s'posed to do? Tell him to fuck off? Jesus, I tell people I'll meet them for lunch all the time, but you don't see them following me around Dublin, waiting for me to take out me sandwiches, do you? It's just talk. Anyway, I had to say something. You were just after telling him that I thought he was a wanker for liking jazz.'

'Well, Tsujita-san is Japanese. Maybe Japanese believe what people tell them.'

Jimmy sighed. The smart arse fucker knew how to play

114

him. Jimmy liked to think of himself as being fair-minded and honest and here was Marco taking a small swipe at his integrity. The bollocks.

'Look. I'll talk to him, okay?' said Jimmy. 'If it was just the once, then maybe it'd be fine. But I get the feeling that this Zucheeto chap isn't the kind of bloke who'll leave it at that. He'll probably start stalking me or something. I'll have to make up a story. Where's Aesop when you need him?'

He came up with a good excuse over lunch. He'd tell Zucheeto that the band was resting up because they'd lost the bass player. They were taking some time off before they started playing again. That was reasonable, wasn't it? They couldn't gig anyway because they really didn't have a bass player, so it wasn't as if Zucheeto would see them playing if he came out with Marco. It wasn't brilliant but it would do for a month or so. He could think of something else then.

After lunch he went down to find Tsujita-san's desk. He got a big 'Harro, Jimmy-san' before he got within twenty feet of it, and saw Tsujita-san rummaging around in one of his drawers. By the time he got there, there were pages all over the place and Tsujita-san had jumped up to shake Jimmy's hand. Then he started to shove bits of paper in his face. The sheets were covered with music.

'*Anno*, this is my music, Jimmy-san. I rike Charee Pahkah berry berry match. And this is Sonny Rorrins *no* Sainto Thomas. And I rike to pray John Corutrain. You know Im-plessions? Bam bam bam.' He was playing it on an imaginary sax. 'Ah. My *ichi-ban*, besto is Chetto Baykah *no* My Fanny Barentine, *demo* I pray sax soro. Do do be doo dan dan. I pray berry well. You rike, Jimmy-san? Be bop? Jimmy-san?'

Jimmy-san hadn't got a fucking clue what he was talking about. He thought he picked up Charlie Parker and Sonny Rollins' names, but recognising a name or two didn't help much. This just wasn't his area.

'Eh, Zucheeto. Y'see, the thing is ...'

'Okay *desu*. Okay okay okay okay. Also rike Neo-bop. Phil Woods, *desho*? Airy Autumn? Stan Getsu. Ho hoh! *Desho*?' He was jigging up and down, the pages flying off his desk and spreading around the floor. People were starting to look up from their work.

Neo-bop? For fuck sake. Jimmy thought he was passionate about music but this bloke looked all set to piss his pants. He just stood there looking at him. There was no way he was going to be able to say no. Jimmy couldn't see any sharp objects on Tsujita-san's desk, but he'd heard of harry karry and didn't feel like being a witness to it at this hour on a Monday morning. He took up a pen and a post-it pad from the desk and drew a small map to the community centre. Aesop would go completely spare.

And he did.

'Jimmy, this is bollocks,' he said, when the two of them got there. Jimmy had told him on the phone that Tsujita-san would be coming along later. The lads started at seven thirty, but Jimmy told Tsujita-san to get there for eight or eight thirty. It would give them a chance to get some work done and Aesop would hopefully have chilled out a bit by then.

'I know, Aesop. Look, it's just this once, right? The bloke doesn't know anyone in Ireland and he likes playing music. C'mon Aesop, it's not the end of the world. We'll just run through a few bars with him, he'll be happy and then that's the end of it. Anyway, it's not all bad. We never played jazz before. Maybe we'll learn something. A new style of music, right?'

'Jazz isn't music, Jimmy. It's shite, that's what it is. Jesus, you even say that yourself. Remember at McGuigans that Sunday night? When you got into the row with that jazz bloke? He called you an ignoramus and you stood on his pipe.'

'Ah, I had a few pints in me. Look, Aesop, afterwards I'll tell him that we're sorry but we're too busy to jam with him again, okay? I'll ask around as well. There's lots of jazz bands in Dublin, down the south side and stuff. He'll find a gig if he wants one. This is just for tonight, all right? C'mon, maybe it'll be a laugh.'

'Me hole,' said Aesop.

They spent an hour going through their set. Jimmy even revisited *Meatloaf's Underpants* to put Aesop in a good mood, but at exactly half eight there was a knock on the door and Aesop shook his head in disgust and folded his arms.

Ten minutes later they were ready to start. Jimmy and Aesop looked at Tsujita-san. They didn't know what they were supposed to do. He was looking at them. This was their band. He didn't want to be so rude as to lead.

'Zucheeto. You start. We don't know much about jazz, okay?'

'Okay, Jimmy-san. We jast jam, okay?'

'Whatever. Off you go.'

Tsujita-san started with a fast solo run and resolved into what was very obviously jazz. Jimmy could tell by the diminished arpeggios and the way it deliberately strayed from the expected turnarounds. Aesop could tell by the way it sounded like a total bag of wank. He sighed and swung his drumsticks around to start playing. It was a bit weird. The timing seemed to be off. He tapped away on the snare with one stick for a minute or so, until he thought he had it and then, eyes closed, joined in with the other hand.

Meanwhile Jimmy couldn't figure out what chords to play. He was kneeling next to the amp, with his head practically stuck in the speaker cone, playing softly and trying to get something that would work. Nothing did. Nothing obvious, anyway.

Tsujita-san was looking at them from under his baseball cap, and slowed down. When that didn't help, he started to get embarrassed and eventually stopped, taking the reed away from his mouth and going red.

'*Gohmen*,' he said.

Right. Well that was a load of shite, thought Jimmy. They needed to find something they could all play. Aesop and himself couldn't just wing it. You needed to know your stuff to be able to do that whole Blue Note thing. Jimmy wasn't able to do it, and that pissed him off. Then he had an idea.

'Tell you what, Zucheeto. Do you like really early stuff? You know, Robert Johnson? Blind Lemon Jefferson?' These lads were early blues guitarists, but it was a time when blues and jazz still shared some fairly common ground. The jazz crowd hadn't yet taken all those drugs in the 1960s and invented Fusion. And Jimmy could do blues.

'Sure!' said Tsujita-san. 'Delta! Okay, ret's go. Brues!!'

It was much better. After thirty seconds Tsujita-san let Jimmy take over the solo and he kept up a bass line on the sax. It was actually kind of cool. Jimmy and Tsujita-san went on swapping the lead and rhythm parts, and before long even Aesop had to try not to look like he was enjoying himself. Jimmy changed key for a laugh, and Tsujita-san just smiled as he played and changed it again. For a small bloke who couldn't speak English, he was a bloody good sax player.

'Cool. What'll we do now?' said Jimmy. This wasn't so bad.

'*Anno*, you know Loly Garrahah?' said Tsujita-san.

'Rory Gallagher? Fuckin' right we know him! How do you know Rory Gallagher?' Jimmy was amazed. Rory was one of his all-time heroes.

'In Japan, Loly is berry popurar.'

The lads looked at each other.

'Are ye serious? All right then. Do you know *The Loop*?' said Jimmy. This was almost too good to be true. He only ever played this stuff when he was at home on his own.

'Yes, I know.'

They went into it, dragging it out for nearly fifteen

minutes. Jimmy kept getting faster and faster, but Tsujita-san just gave that same smile and kept with him. Eventually they were going so fast that even Aesop started to whoop and laugh out loud. After that, they played some BB King and a couple of generic blues jams. By nine twenty they were just about ready to finish up. They had to be out of there in ten minutes anyway.

'Hey Zucheeto,' said Jimmy. 'Will you play that thing again? The thing you started with.'

'Sure thing, Jimmy-san.'

He started it up again. Jimmy tried to find chords that would fit in, but it just wasn't happening for him. He stopped and looked at Tsujita-san.

'Jazz isn't easy, is it?'

'No, Jimmy-san. But you always pray root note. Don't pray root. Too flat in jazz.'

Jimmy knew his way around a fretboard, but didn't really understand what the little bloke was getting at.

'You don't play the root?'

'No. Rook. Prease?' said Tsujita-san. He had his hand out for the guitar. Jimmy shrugged and handed it to him.

'Eh, don't drop it, right? It cost me twelve hundred quid.'

Tsujita-san nodded and did a swift chord run on the guitar managing not to play any roots at all. It sounded nice and jazzy. They were chords that Jimmy wouldn't have thought of using in a fit, but they obviously worked in context. He looked at Tsujita-san's fingers and tried to put names on some of the chords he used when Tsujita-san ran through it again, slowly. There was a G6/9, some kind of F7, an F#dim and what looked like might be C7b9#11 once Jimmy did the maths, but he wouldn't have bet the farm on that. You don't go around the place betting farms on chords like C7b9#11.

'Hey Zucheeto, can I have a go on your sax?' said Aesop.

Aesop loved messing around on different instruments. He was quite good at picking things up too, unusually enough for a man who thought that music had reached its evolutionary zenith with the release of the first Slipnot album.

'No ploblem, Aesop. But, *ne*? Don't drop it, okay? Cost me four hundred thousand yen,' said Tsujita-san. 'Drop, and I kick your hole,' he added slowly. The others looked at him and he burst out laughing. 'Marco-san teach me,' he said.

Jimmy cracked up and sat behind the drums. Gas man, Marco.

They started to jam again. Aesop was just making squawking noises, but Tsujita-san and Jimmy had a nice little rhythm and blues shuffle going. Then it hit Jimmy like a brick. What the fuck was he thinking? He looked over at Tsujita-san, twiddling away on his guitar. He was bloody good at that as well. He stopped suddenly and stood up, staring at the small Japanese guy in front of him.

Tsujita-san stopped playing and took a nervous step away from Jimmy's glare.

'*Nanda?*' he said.

'Zucheeto. Can you play the bass?'

'Daburu bass?' said Tsujita-san. 'Yes. I pray in school.'

'No. Not the double bass. The electric bass. Can you play it?' Jimmy was excited.

'Sure. A rittle. Sax is my besto ...'

'Yeah, yeah. Fuck the sax for a minute. You can play bass guitar, right?

Tsujita-san nodded.

'Okay. Aesop, I ...'

They were interrupted by a knock on the door. It was Frank, the caretaker.

'Are yiz right, lads? Time's up. I want to go home,' he called.

Jimmy ran to the door and opened it.

'Frank, can you give us half an hour?'

'Are ye mad, Jimmy? The match is on the box tonight.'

'I'll give you a tenner if you let us stay 'til ten.'

'Ah Jaysis, Jimmy, I can't. You're not insured to use this place past nine thirty.'

'Twenty.'

'Twenty? How about thirty?'

'Piss off, Frank. Twenty.'

'Eh ... all right. But c'mere. Keep it down, right? I don't want Father Paddy coming around to see what all the noise is about.'

'No problem,' said Jimmy, giving him two tenners from his wallet. 'And will you get us the green bass guitar. It's hanging up in the office.'

'I'm not your bleedin' roadie, Jimmy. Get it yourself.'

'Frank, the sooner you get it, the sooner you can go home and watch the match, all right?'

'Fuck sake, Jimmy. I'm not your skivvy ...' muttered Frank, but he went off to get the guitar.

Back in the room, Jimmy plugged in the bass amp and took the sax off Aesop, putting it gently on top of its case and waving Aesop towards the drum kit. He took his guitar back off Tsujita-san and strapped it on. Frank came back with the bass and Jimmy plugged it in, tuned it to his guitar quickly and handed it to Tsujita-san. No one said a word through all this. Jimmy didn't look like someone who wanted to discuss things.

When he was happy with everyone's setup, he wiped his forehead on his sleeve and took a few deep breaths.

'Right,' he said. 'We have twenty minutes. Tsujita-san, you like U2, right?'

'Yes. I rike berry ...'

'Grand. This is easy. *Desire*. You know it? Just like Bo Diddley ...'

Jimmy started, Aesop joined in and, a bar or two later, in came Tsujita-san. He played it like a dream.

They tried a harder one. *She's Electric*. It had some little fills and Tsujita-san nailed them. They had time for one more. Jimmy decided to do a fast blues jam so that Tsujita-san could have a solo piece in it. He wanted to see what he'd come up with on his own. Jimmy was worried that if he was given space, he'd slide back into all that jazz stuff, but he didn't. It was fast, efficient and sounded great.

They stopped. Jimmy was chuffed and Aesop was twirling his sticks around, a sure sign that he knew what was up and was happy about it. They'd be gigging again soon. The only one who still seemed a bit confused about whatever was happening was Tsujita-san. He was standing there with the bass hanging almost around his knees. The strap was broken and wouldn't hold it any higher. He was tiny behind the long fretboard of the bass guitar and Jimmy did one more calculation in his head. How would Zucheeto look on the stage? Fucking brilliant, he decided.

'Zucheeto,' he said. 'We need a bass player. Do you want the gig?'

'Not sax?'

'No. Not sax. Bass. You're very good on the sax, Zucheeto, but that isn't worth a wank to me and Aesop.'

'*Nanda*?'

'Doesn't matter. Will you play, Zucheeto? Bass guitar?'

'Okay,' said Tsujita-san, smiling. 'I pray.'

'Deadly,' said Jimmy, smiling at Aesop.

Aesop stood up, grinning back. 'Now, Jimmy. Didn't I tell you this was a brilliant idea? And the pus on you all night ...'

Eleven

They were in Jimmy's place. Ireland was playing England in the Six Nations, which had been postponed again due to cows going mad or pigs getting verrucas or something farmer-related like that. None of them really knew much about rugby, but if Ireland was playing, especially against England, they'd watch it. Norman had played a few times when he was in the army, but had given it up on his commanding officer's orders. Ireland didn't exactly have huge numbers of spare soldiers as it was. The bloody last thing it needed was Norman concussing all the sporty ones.

Now that Italy was in the competition, Marco had a passing interest as well although he didn't understand the rules at all. Besides which, he had another reason for wanting to be there. The realisation of his big plan was taking place before his very eyes. Tsujita-san was sitting on the couch next to him, drinking a beer and screeching loudly whenever Ireland did something good. He was the only one who seemed to know what 'something good' actually looked like. He told the lads that rugby was 'berry popurar' in Japan, although Jimmy was a bit sceptical. Taking Tsujita-san as an example, Japanese blokes were a bit, well, *small* for rugby, weren't they?

'Bat, *ne*, Jimmy-san, you know Sumo? Sumo man, he is berry big, *ne*?' said Tsujita-san. 'And Judo?'

'Yeah. I s'pose so,' said Jimmy. That was a fair point. They couldn't all be small, could they? And some of those fat bastards in nappies were enormous. They used to show it on Channel 4, a few years ago. What was that Hawaiian bloke's name? The Dump Truck or something? He was incredible. Jimmy used to love watching him come out and squash people. He had about five arses.

'Zoocheeta, what was that for?' said Aesop, pointing at the telly where the ref had called up play.

'Offsaido,' said Tsujita-san. 'Must stay behind za ball.'

Aesop didn't even understand offside in soccer. This was way beyond him but he just nodded and took another drink, thinking that maybe the replay would make it clearer. It didn't.

The play went on.

'Knock on!' yelled Tsujita-san a couple of seconds later, but the ref didn't see it.

Marco looked at Aesop, who just shrugged. You scored when you put the ball over the opponent's line. You also got scores for kicking it over the bar. That was all grand. Other bits, though, were more confusing. Like the bit where it was okay to stamp on your opponent's bollocks if it was in the wrong place at the wrong time.

At half time Marco was in the kitchen getting more beer when Jimmy came out to put a pizza in the oven.

'Hey Marco, thanks for that. You know ... Zucheeto and all.'

'No problem, Jimmy. I told you he was a nice guy.'

'Yeah. Good bass player too. And guitar player and sax player. Are all Japanese blokes good at everything?'

'I don't know, Jimmy. But he's saved us a lot of money in work as well. He's very smart.'

Jimmy nodded. That was for bloody sure.

Tsujita-san had come around earlier to work on the set with Jimmy. Jimmy had an old bass guitar in the wardrobe. It was a cheap no-name thing and a bit knackered but it would do the trick. Anyway, Tsujita-san said he'd buy a new one. Jimmy wondered what he'd get. A man with a four hundred thousand yen saxophone could probably afford something nice. What was a yen worth anyway? Didn't matter. Four hundred thousand anything was a lot of something.

There were about thirty songs in the basic set, plus another fifteen or twenty that Jimmy liked to throw in every now and again. Every set included between five and ten originals and the rest were all covers that most people would know. Not the same stuff that everyone played though – Jimmy liked to keep it a bit more eclectic than that. He was very proud of the set. It reflected his firm belief that their job on the stage was to entertain the punters. No ten-minute guitar solos or obscure songs that only the band knew. And, at most, only one or two songs from Aesop's collection of horrible noisy shite; near the end of the night when people were good and drunk and would dance along to any old bollocks. He made sure that if they did play a few of the more obvious crowd-pleasers, they were absolutely his. His version of *With or Without You* was the best one he'd ever heard, he reckoned. Pissed on U2.

Jimmy had thought that they might get through about ten songs. If he concentrated on U2, The Clash and a few other popular tunes, Tsujita-san would already know them and it would all go much more quickly. As it turned out, they got fifteen songs done in two hours and Tsujita-san wanted to keep going but Jimmy couldn't. His fingers were getting sore. He had to swap the guitar for the bass a few times to show Tsujita-san some of the more complicated riffs, but he only needed to demonstrate them twice at most and then they were off again. Jimmy was loving it. Compared to this, showing Beano new stuff was like trying to grill an egg.

They'd finished up with one of Jimmy's own songs, *Landlady Lover*, and called it a day. Tsujita-san stuffed his notepad into a bag along with the tape that Jimmy had given him. The tape had about twenty songs on it from the set and Jimmy had been up most of the night making it.

The lads started to call around for the game just as Jimmy and Tsujita-san opened their cans of beer in the kitchen and clanked them together.

'Cheers,' said Jimmy.

'*Kampai*,' said Tsujita-san.

It was Kirin Beer. Tsujita-san had found it in an off-licence somewhere near where he was staying.

'Good Japanese beer,' he said as he handed cans out to the others, who started to make themselves comfortable around the table.

Jimmy tasted it. It was lovely. He looked at the can which was covered in Japanese writing. There was a picture of a dragon or monster or something on it. Then he looked up at Tsujita-san, who was humming the chorus to *Landlady Lover* as he went out into the hall to put his bag next to his coat.

This was going to be brilliant.

By the time the game finished they were out of Kirin, so Jimmy took a couple of six packs of Heineken from the garage and set them on the table in front of everyone. They didn't need to go into the fridge. It was one of those autumn days in Ireland where you'd be forgiven for thinking you were in Siberia. It might have snowed, but then it rarely did in Dublin. The sun had obviously given up on its annual effort to cheer everybody up and had pissed off in disgust to Spain, leaving behind a cutting wind that blew in from Russia with frightening, whipping gusts, dropping the temperature of the whole country by ten degrees and cooling Jimmy's garage stash quite nicely in the process.

'Norman. Any word from Marie?' said Jimmy.

'No, Jimmy. We talked about it. There was no point in keeping in contact, was there? She won't be back 'til Christmas and she'll be spending that with her folks in Cavan.'

'That's tough, Norman. She seemed nice,' said Jimmy.

Aesop was about to add 'if you like that sort of thing', but then looked over at Norman and thought the better of it.

'She was, Jimmy. Really nice,' said Norman. He looked sad.

'Still, we're only getting started, right?' said Jimmy, trying to sound upbeat. He didn't want Norman to lose faith.

'Ah Jimmy, I don't know,' said Norman. 'I'd prefer to just

meet someone, you know? The normal way. Not be running around trying to chat girls up and all that. I'm no good at it.'

'Jaysis, Norman,' said Aesop. 'You talk about it like it's a big chore. You're s'posed to enjoy talking to ladies. It's one of life's pleasures. Talking to them, looking at them, ridin' them. It's why we're here.'

'God, there you go again Aesop,' said Norman. 'Look, what I'm saying is that I don't know what to say. What am I s'posed to say? What do you say? You're the bullshitter. What do you do? How do you go from not being talking to a girl, to talking to her?'

'I just talk!'

'What do you say, though?'

'I say howarya, what's the story, what's your name, do you want a drink, I'm Aesop, nice pants you have on there, did you ever see me on the telly? I used to be on Ballykissangel,' said Aesop. 'Y'know? Talk.'

'But that's all bollocks! It doesn't mean anything. And you were never on Ballykissangel. What were you s'posed to be? The token Dublin knacker who robs cars?'

'Norman, they know I was never on Ballykissangel. It's just a laugh, isn't it? Once you get them laughing, you're laughing.'

Norman turned to Jimmy.

'Jimmy, tell me he's never said he was on Ballykissangel.'

'Sorry, Norman. He even had his own slot on MTV there for a while,' said Jimmy, smiling. 'Didn't you, Aesop?'

'Metal Mania. Two hours on a Friday evening. Bastards shut me down, though. Said I was too scary for the kids at bedtime.'

'But what's the point of all the lies?' said Norman. 'How is a girl s'posed to get to know you, if all you're doing is bull-shitting her the whole time?'

Aesop looked at Jimmy and shook his head. Then, to Norman, 'What the fuck are you talking about? Getting to know me. You've known me for twenty years, Norman. What do you think of me?'

'I think you're a scumbag.'

'Right. And thanks by the way. Now if a girl were to get to know me, she might come to the same conclusion, right? Now tell me this Norman, okay? What chance do I have of getting into her knickers if she thinks I'm a scumbag? No fucking chance at all, right? None. So why don't I just feed her a big line of bollocks instead? Believe me Norman, she's better off if I do. We both are.'

Norman sat there with his mouth open.

'You're some feckin' piece of work, you are, Aesop. That's all I'll say. Some feckin' piece of work. It's a wonder you're *not* on the telly. They could make documentaries about you. Nuns could show them to schoolgirls to scare them off men. Good God. And Subbuteo sitting there listening to you. A fine example of Irish manhood you're showing him. Sorry Subbuteo. Aesop isn't well.' Norman was twirling a finger around the side of his head and nodding at Aesop. 'He's mental.'

'Eh? Mentaru? *Nanda?*' said Tsujita-san.

Actually, Tsujita-san didn't have a clue what they were talking about. He was getting used to the idea that he had some new buddies, but he found them very difficult to understand, except when they spoke to him directly and slowed down a little.

'Mental,' said Norman again. 'He's a bit, y'know ...'

'Don't mind him, Tooteeto. When he was twelve he looked down and thought he'd found his first pubic hair. Until he started pissing through it,' said Aesop.

'Aesop is gay,' said Norman, pointing at Aesop.

'I could be gay, Norman, and still get more women than you,' said Aesop. 'You're an embarrassment to your sex. Do you even have a sex? Are you sure you're not a caterpillar or something?'

Tsujita-san was following this like it was a tennis match, desperately trying to keep up. Marco was beside him, nudging his arm all through it and laughing. He'd explained the whole slagging thing to him that week, but Tsujita-san hadn't understood. Here it was in action but Tsujita-san couldn't see the funny side. The big guy with the strange accent would surely hit the drummer soon, no?

'Okay lads, enough!' said Jimmy. 'I think you're freaking out our new bass player. Marco. You and Jennifer. What's the story? Are we getting anywhere?'

'Difficult, Jimmy. Very difficult. Jennifer is, how you say, independent? I cannot change her. She changes me. Here, look at my socks.'

He pulled up his trouser leg and pointed. They were red and yellow.

'Jaysis Marco,' said Jimmy. 'You're s'posed to be turning her into Superchick, and she's there turning you into Superpansy instead. C'mon, you have to be able to do better than that. Look at you. I thought Italians were s'posed to have a bit of style. They're bleedin' girl's socks.'

'They are Boss,' said Marco, looking at them. 'They were a birthday gift.'

Aesop wasn't impressed.

'Boss me arse, Marco. You know what they are? They're her telling you "I'm the fuckin' Boss around here". The state of you. It looks like you have two pairs of knickers wrapped around your feet. What did you give her? A bleedin' whip? I know my sister, pal. You need to get the boot in soon, or she'll have you by the bollocks.'

'Aesop, what are you suggesting? I should hit Jennifer?' Marco was scandalised.

'No! God, no! Jesus, don't ever do that. Ever. She'll fuckin' kill you. And then she'll fuckin' kill me for knowing you. Anyway, you don't hit girls. What kind of knacker are you? Were you dragged up?'

Marco was confused.

'I have never hit a girl, Aesop. It was you who said to kick her, no?'

'I said put the boot in. It just means you have show her that you're in charge and no amount of fuckin' homosexual socks will ever change that. But you have to do it soon. Look at you. She already has you on the turn. If you wait any longer, she'll have you buying her bras for her.'

'Yes, yes. So, what do I do?' Marco wanted to move this along. He was intrigued.

'Fucked if I know,' said Aesop.

'What?'

'I don't bleedin' know, do I? You're the one in the ankle panties, Marco. You figure it out.'

'But you said you know your sister! I thought you were going to help me, to suggest something. How do I show her that I am the boss?'

'Have you ever sat on her face and farted?'

'What?' said Marco, again.

'Used to work for me. Mind you, it drove her fucking insane. Don't tell her it was my idea, right?'

Marco turned away and looked at Jimmy.

'Anyway, she is feminist, I think. And this Superchick, she cannot be feminist, can she? She must be more, eh, relaxed no? I tried to tell her last night that in Italy, the woman, she learns how to cook. But she gave me the funny look and so I went for a walk. Jimmy, I was afraid.'

'Ah, don't worry about it Marco,' said Jimmy, laughing. 'It'll be grand. You just have to give it time. Stay away from the feminist thing, maybe. Work on the shopping. Make up some excuses why you can't go with her and stuff. You could try getting her to dump some shoes as well. But take it easy; if you move too fast you'll get into trouble. You've got the hardest job in some ways, Marco. It's easier with a new girl. You can start with a clean slate. Jennifer already knows you, so you can't suddenly turn into a big chauvinist bastard, can you? Eh ... not that that's what you're s'posed to be doing ...'

'Yeah,' said Aesop. 'New girls are best. Preferably virgins.'

Everyone looked at him.

'What are you on about, Aesop?' said Jimmy.

'Virgins, Jimmy. They're brilliant.'

'Okay, Aesop,' said Jimmy, leaning back and folding his arms. 'Tell us why virgins are brilliant. Keeping in mind that you're thirty years old and unless you're an even bigger dirt-bird than we all know you to be, you wouldn't be going out with too many virgins.'

'It's obvious, right? You're with a virgin, okay? She doesn't know what to expect. Not really. So you can get her to do all this stuff that a more experienced girl would tell you to piss off for trying. A virgin'd just think that everyone must do it, y'know? How would she know they don't? That it's actually unnatural or illegal or whatever ...'

He stopped and looked around at them.

'What?'

'Aesop,' said Jimmy. 'We're talking about meeting a girl that we like and how we'd work out if she was the one woman in the world that we'd give everything to stay with. What the fuck are you talking about?'

'Ridin' virgins,' said Aesop.

'Right. Well, can we talk about that another time? Marco was trying to get some stuff off his chest.'

'I'm done,' said Marco, who was still looking at Aesop with his mouth open.

'Okay,' said Jimmy. 'Good man Aesop. Thanks for the input there. Hey Zucheeto, what happened with you and Katie the other night? Your first Irish girl?'

Tsujita-san had been sitting there quietly, trying not to distract anyone. He didn't really want to join in these heated discussions. For one thing, he found them too hard to follow, and for another they made him uncomfortable. In Japan, people tended to be more accommodating. If you had a different point of view to someone else, you'd pretty much keep it under your hat. Irish people, on the other hand, seemed to like nothing better than a bloody big argument. It was a bit unseemly, all this shouting and insulting one another. Yet they were apparently still good friends. Strange.

'Katie berry different from Japanese girl. *Anno*, bigger, yes?' He motioned shyly towards his chest area.

'Ah, yes. Katie is well equipped,' said Aesop. Then he frowned. Something was suddenly nagging at him with regard to Katie but he couldn't quite put his finger on it.

'Will you be seeing her again, Subbuteo?' said Norman quickly, before Aesop had a chance to expand.

'I sink so. Maybe. She is nice girl.' He didn't want to say anything else. The lads were all smiling at him, like he was a little brother who'd just gotten his first snog.

'Well, that's something, isn't it?' said Jimmy to everyone. 'The night wasn't a complete loss. Two people met who like each other, and both will be around for a while in the same country.'

'They would've met anyway Jimmy,' said Aesop. 'They weren't even in on your sad little game.'

'Doesn't matter. We spread a little love around. That's what it's all about.'

'Homo.'

Jimmy ignored him. He took a drink and looked out the window. They'd have to step things up a bit.

'Anyone on for a trip out to Portmarnock this evening?' he said.

'What's out there?' said Aesop. 'Ah, hang on. You're not talking about The Knights, are you?' Discos weren't Aesop's thing.

'Why not?' said Jimmy. 'C'mon, we haven't been out there in ages.'

'That's 'cos it's brutal, Jimmy.'

'Ah, it's not that bad. Norman? You on for a bop?'

'I s'pose so, Jimmy. If everyone else is going, like.'

'Marco?'

'I can't, Jimmy. I'm staying in tonight with Jennifer. Bottle of wine and a movie, I think.'

'You think?' said Aesop.

'Jennifer said she wants to stay in.'

'Oh well, in that case ... I mean if Jennifer wants to stay in then that's the end of the discussion, isn't it? I'm amazed you're here at all. You should be around there now, rubbing her feet for her.'

'Aesop, I want to stay in too.'

'Of course you do, Marco. Sure why wouldn't you? She might let you try on her leg warmers and ...'

'Aesop,' sighed Marco, 'Fuck off please, yes?'

'Lads, shut up a minute. Aesop, are you on for it?'

'Ah all right. Nothing else on, is there?'

'Hey Toocheeto,' said Jimmy, 'Are you on for a dance? You know? Disco? Tonight?'

'Okay, Jimmy-san. Disco. I rike.'

'Brilliant. How about we meet ...'

'Hang on a minute Jimmy,' said Aesop. He turned to Tsujita-san.

'Chuteeto, why do you keep calling us whatever-san? Jimmy-san, Aesop-san, Norman-san? What's the story?'

'Is porite, Aesop-san. In Japan, is porite.'

'But we're all mates here. You don't have to be polite. I'm just Aesop, he's just Jimmy and Norman there is just Norman, but you can call him Farmer Norman. Or Smelly.'

'Okay Aesop,' said Tsujita-san. 'But, why "Chuteeto" and "Zucheeta" and "Tooteeto"? Is not my name, *ne*?'

'Well ... what's your name, then?'

'Tsujita.'

'Zoo ... Chutee ... ah, bollocks to that. What's your surname? You know, your family name?'

'Tsujita.'

'So your name is Tucheeta Tucheeta? What the fuck kind of name is that?'

'Aesop, my first name is Shigenori.'

'Shiginorry? So we've been calling you by your surname all this time?'

'Not exactory,' said Tsujita-san, with a small sigh.

'So your mates call you Shuginorry, then?'

'My friends call me Tsujita.'

'But, that's ... ah me hole. What was your first name again?'

'Shigenori.'

'Shiginorry ... Shigaynorry ... Shigi ... Shiggy ... ah, fuck it. Shiggy will do. Is that all right? Can we call you Shiggy?'

'Oh ... kay,' said Tsujita-san, slowly. He couldn't decide if he was bonding or being insulted.

'Grand. We're all set then. We're not san, and you're Shiggy. Sorry, Jimmy, what were you saying?'

Jimmy was looking at him.

'Jesus, Aesop ... I'm very sorry, Zucheeto. Don't mind fuckin' Henry Kissinger over there. We won't call you Shiggy.'

'Is okay, Jimmy. Shiggy is okay.'

'Are you sure?'

'Yes. I rike Shiggy.' He was smiling now. He'd never had a nickname before.

'Okay, then. If you're okay with it. Shiggy it is.' Jimmy looked at Aesop, shaking his head at him. 'You're some bol-locks.'

'What? I was only clearing things up, Jimmy. What were you going to say before?'

'I was going to say we meet back here at seven. Okay? Eh ... Shiggy, seven o'clock here? We go to disco together?'

They all nodded, Shiggy trying out his new name in his head. It was kind of cool. If nothing else, at least these bloody Irish people would be able to pronounce it properly.

Twelve

'Fat bastard,' said Aesop in disgust, looking at the bouncer. 'How does a bloke that size even wipe his arse? I wish he'd get a bleedin' move on.'

The lads were standing in the queue and it was bloody freezing. Shiggy was dressed for an Antarctic trek, with a big brown wool scarf tied neatly around his neck and his hands stuffed deep into his coat pockets. Aesop was smoking a cigarette between his cupped hands, his back to the wind that howled in from the sea, while Jimmy was shivering in his thin leather jacket, wondering why none of his clothes could be cool and warm at the same time. Only Norman seemed unaffected by the cold, looking around at the others in the queue. He wasn't even wearing a coat.

'Arra, come on Aesop,' he said, punching him lightly on the shoulder. 'A little bit of an oul' wind and you turn blue. Look at you, you big baby. You'd swear it was the worst day of your life.'

'I'm not like you, Norman. I didn't spend my youth running around fields in the winter, chasing cabbages or whatever. When I was growing up, we had telly.'

'Well, that's what has you like a big handbag, so. In the army ...'

'Oh Jaysis, another GI Joe story. Go on ...'

'When I was in the army, we'd camp out in this. It was nothing. I'll tell you something, you should go to the Lebanon ...'

'No thanks.'

'Try spending some time there, Aesop. At least when you're cold, you can put a coat on you. There's not much can be done when you're in forty degree heat, with a helmet and a full pack.'

'Piss off Norman,' said Aesop, unimpressed. 'If I'm going to freeze to death out here, I don't want your thick fuckin' culchie voice to be the last thing I hear, right? Jesus, what is that prick doing? It's not that hard is it? "Have you any ID?" Either you do or you don't. What's with all the questions? He's like fuckin' Michael Parkinson up there.'

The queue was moving slowly. There were over fifty people waiting to get in and only about the first ten had any kind of shelter under the awning. The lads were about twenty back from the front.

'Jaysis, they're a bit young, aren't they?' said Jimmy, looking around.

'It's a disco Jimmy,' said Aesop. 'What did you expect? We should be at home in the pub.'

'Ah, we're always in the pub. Anyway, they're not all young. Look at that bloke up there. I don't believe it. He's about fifty and the bouncer is still looking for ID off him,' said Jimmy. 'Do you have to do a special test to be a bouncer? If they detect a brain then you're out.'

'Hey Shiggy, you okay there? You're a bit quiet,' said Aesop.

'Yes. I am okay. But cold, *ne?*' Shiggy's neck seemed to have disappeared. His head was threatening to fall down into his coat.

'Yeah. I know. We should be okay in a minute, once this arsehole gets his shit together,' said Aesop. 'Hey, did you never think of being a bouncer, Norman?'

'Why's that, Aesop?'

'Well y'know, you're a big lad. You can take care of yourself. Polite. Not great at maths, y'know?'

'It's not the big lad I'd be worried about,' said Norman. 'Look at his pal.'

They all looked. The other bouncer was at least a foot shorter than his colleague and not even half his weight.

'I'd say that lad would put manners on you, if you started

annoying him,' Norman went on. 'You don't put a bloke like that on the door unless he's handy enough.'

'But can he run, Norman?' said Aesop. 'Can he run after you kick him in the goolies? That's the question. 'Cos I can be very quick off the mark when I have to be.'

They were nearly at the front now. There were just two couples ahead of them, being grilled by the fat bouncer.

'How old are you?' said Fat Bouncer to the first girl.

'Twenty-four,' said the girl, handing him some kind of student card.

The bouncer studied it.

'And what year were you born?'

'1981.'

'And how old will you be next year?'

'Eh, twenty-five.'

Shiggy was following this and looked at Jimmy, puzzled. Jimmy smiled at him and shook his head. Don't worry about it.

The bouncer moved on to one of the guys.

'How old are you?'

'I'm twenty-five.'

'Where do you live?'

'Malahide.'

'Where in Malahide?'

'Seapark.'

'How old were you last year?'

'Twenty-four.'

'What year were you born?'

'1980.'

The bouncer looked the guy up and down and then took another look at the ID in his hand. He scratched behind his ear with it and looked like he was trying to remember something important.

Shiggy was perplexed. He turned to Jimmy again.

'This man is stupid, ne?' he said, pointing to his head.

'Shush, Shiggy. It's just something they do. Forget about it.'

Eventually the smaller bouncer, obviously the brains of the operation, nodded at the fat one and the latter stepped to one side to let them in, still watching as if you couldn't be too careful. Then he turned to Jimmy.

'Have you ID?'

Jimmy handed him his driver's licence.

'Are you all together?'

'Yeah.'

'Who's this fella?' said Fat Bouncer, pointing at Shiggy with one index finger, the other being on earhole duty.

'He's a friend of mine from Tokyo.'

'Tokyo?' said Fat Bouncer.

'Is in Japan,' said Shiggy, slowly emphasising the last word and pointing back at the sea behind them. Aesop and Norman started sniggering.

'How old are you?' Fat Bouncer asked Shiggy.

'I am thirty-seven years old. Next year I am thirty-eight. Last year, I am thirty-six. See? I can count. How old are you?'

'What?' said Fat Bouncer.

'Where do you live?'

'I ... eh ... what?'

'You rook rike Sumo. Berry, berry fat,' said Shiggy, laughing and blowing out his cheeks. 'Ret me in now prease? Is cold.'

Jimmy jumped in.

'Eh, sorry about that. His English isn't very good.'

Fat Bouncer looked at them all for a minute, frowning, and then stood to one side. Brainy Bouncer had turned away and seemed to be laughing into his gloves.

'Right. Go on.' He was looking at Shiggy as he walked past, but Shiggy just grinned back and kept going. They all followed him, trying not to laugh.

'What the fuck did you say all that for?' said Jimmy once they were in. 'Jesus, I thought we were dead.'

'Stupid man is okay. But, he also not porite, *ne*? So I not porite. Anyway, now is warm. So okay, *ne*? No plobrem.'

They stood in the cloakroom queue, still giggling. It looked like hanging around with Shiggy was going to be good for a giggle. Mad bastard. Fat Bouncer could have fit him in his mouth.

In one sense Jimmy actually had high hopes. They were in a disco, there were loads of women around and there was a pretty good chance that at least some of them might be on the lookout as well. In another way, though, he knew it was a long shot. If he was just after someone for one night, or even just a snog on the dance floor, then that was easy. But he was still gripped by this idea of meeting someone, falling in love and living happily ever after. Maybe it could happen here, tonight, but it was a bit unlikely wasn't it? If it were that easy, everyone would be doing it.

Once they were settled at a high table, close to the bar and with a good view of the dance floor, the lads immediately started to look around. Shiggy, it turned out, was a bit of a revelation. Even Aesop was impressed with his lack of inhibition.

'You see that, Norman?' Aesop said. Shiggy was at the bar chatting to a girl who was about six inches taller than he was. She was laughing. 'There's a man who's only off the boat and can't string three words together without confusing himself and everyone around him, and he's up there getting stuck into some bird. You should be ashamed of yourself.'

'Piss off Aesop,' said Norman. He was looking over at Shiggy, impressed in spite of himself.

'Jaysis. Do you kiss your mother with that mouth?'

Norman looked over at him. The very mention of his mother was enough to put him on high alert in any conversation. Jimmy came in before Norman said anything.

'Lads, look at yer woman. In the black, with the colourdy thing in her head.'

Norman and Aesop looked over.

'Very nice,' said Aesop.

'Ehh ...' said Norman, following Jimmy's gesture with a scrunched-up face. He'd had to rush out the door without his contacts to catch the bus. He was okay for about ten metres but after that things got a bit blurry.

She was beautiful. Short blonde hair, with some kind of scarf thing holding it up off her forehead. She was laughing at something her mate was saying. Her mate was no pig either, Aesop noted. Jimmy couldn't take his eyes off her. She was about twenty yards away, but it was as if she was sitting right next to him. Jimmy could almost smell her perfume.

'Will we go over?' said Aesop.

'Hang on a minute,' said Jimmy. He wanted to look a bit more. It was early in the night. No hurry.

Shiggy came back from the bar.

'Hey, Karaoke tonight! We can do Karaoke!' He held a tray of drinks. With his small hands he wasn't going to be trying Marco's four-drink trick for a while yet.

'What?' said Aesop.

'Karaoke. Here. They have competition.'

Aesop looked around and saw what he was looking for on a beer mat on Shiggy's tray. One of the beer companies was sponsoring a Karaoke competition. There were a few different categories, but the one that caught his eye was first prize in the singles competition.

'Holy shit, Jimmy. Are you on? A free keg for singing a song!'

'Ah, I don't know Aesop. We'll see what happens, right? Anyway, I thought you didn't drink draft lager.' Jimmy was still glued to the mystery girl across the floor from him.

'Jimmy. Will you ever drag your eyes away from that tart and look at me for a minute? I'm all on for you scoring, right? Christ knows, you could bleedin' do with a portion. But we're talking about a free keg of beer here, okay? I don't care what colour beer it is. Get your shit together. You're the singer, so you get up there and sing. I can't do it, can I? I'm shite. Norman's too shy and Shiggy ... hey Shiggy, do you sing?'

'A rittle,' said Shiggy.

'Well that's what you said about playing the guitar, isn't it? Right, where's the yoke ... hang on ...'

He went off to ask a barman what the story was and came back with a sheet of paper. On one side was a list of about a hundred songs, and on the other was a place to fill in your details so you could enter.

'Now. Have a look at that, Shiggy. Anything you like?'

Shiggy took the page and started to look down the songs, Norman humming the tunes if Shiggy didn't recognise them by name. Aesop was reading the rules at the bottom to make sure they had all the angles covered. He didn't want Shiggy to be disqualified for being in a band, or foreign, or something stupid like that. This was too important to be fucking about. This was a free keg of beer.

Jimmy left them to it and walked closer to the table where the girl was sitting. She definitely wasn't getting any worse looking, the closer he got. He pretended that he was just standing there with his pint in his hand, looking at the dance floor, but he kept stealing the odd glance in her direction. After half a song, he had what he was looking for. She was drinking Baileys on ice. He moved back to the lads.

'No, no. That's fucking crap,' Aesop was saying to Norman.

'Piss off, Aesop. Shiggy likes it.'

'You can't get up there and sing the bleedin' Carpenters, for fuck sake. They're not going to give away free beer to someone who sang fuckin' *Close to Me* are they, you big blouse?'

'I don't see you putting your name down to sing? Let him

sing it if he wants to. He's Japanese, right? He knows what he's doing in Karaoke.'

'No way. Listen Shiggy, pick a different one. That's shite. Here, look, here's Guns and Roses.'

'Ah, not so good,' said Shiggy, sucking a big breath between his teeth and cocking his head to one side. 'Too, ah ...' He pointed at his throat.

'There. Leave him alone. Don't mind him, Shiggy. Sing whatever you want to sing,' said Norman.

'Maybe za Beetaruz?'

'Yeah, all right. The Beatles. Which one?' said Aesop.

'Ah, *I wanna hold your hand*?'

'Brilliant. Grand. Here, write that down. Do you know the words? Oh, you don't have to, right? Hey Jimmy, Shiggy here is going to do a Beatles song to win us the beer. Are you going to do one?'

'Ah, I won't bother, Aesop. I might try talking to yer woman over there.'

'Are you sure? They've other prizes as well.'

'Nah, I'm grand tonight. Anyway, I already have an mp3 player and I don't wear crap T-shirts.'

'All right, then. So, c'mere, will we both go over? To yer woman?'

'I'll tell you what, Aesop ...' Jimmy said, remembering Carol and Rhonda. 'How about I do this on me own, right? I just want to say hello and see how it goes. I need a bit of practice before I can go in there with you and start all that bollocks you come out with.'

'Yeah, all right. Whatever,' said Aesop. 'But listen, if it's going well give me a nod and I'll be over to take her mate off your hands.'

'Cool,' said Jimmy. If it was going well the last person in the world he'd be introducing her mate to would be Aesop.

Aesop turned to Shiggy who was filling out the entry form.

'Are we nearly done there, Shiggy? Eh, there's no "r" in Beatles.'

Shiggy finished filling out the form and went up to hand it to the DJ, who put it in a big box. By the time he came back the lads had another round up on the table. Their last round wasn't even finished yet. Shiggy's first pint only had a couple of mouthfuls gone out of it.

'Guys,' he said. 'Srow down, *ne*? I can't drink so fast.'

'No problem, Shiggy. We'll leave you out of the next round, okay?' said Aesop. 'We don't want you falling asleep again, do we? You're in charge of winning us free beer, so whatever you want. If you want an orange juice or something, just tell Norman here. He'll get one for you.'

'What's that?' said Norman. He was looking into one of the corners, where a few girls were sitting on some kind of sofa.

'I said you'll buy Shiggy whatever he wants. Won't you?'

'Yeah, whatever.' Norman wasn't listening. One of the girls had caught his eye and smiled. She was just out of his twenty-twenty range, so he couldn't make her out too clearly, but a smile was a smile and Norman wasn't about to pass up any potential encouragement in that department. He smiled back.

'What are you squinting at?' said Aesop, looking over his shoulder to where Norman was now grinning like big child. 'Oh Christ, which one is it? The one with the wonky teeth, the heifer with the seven chins or the beast with the wooden leg?'

'Aesop, for God sake, will you give over?' said Norman, standing up. 'I'm going over there to say hello and I don't want to hear a fecking word out of you when I come back, okay?'

'Fair enough, Dr Doolittle. Listen, find out what circus they're in and try and get a few free tickets, will ye? It's Andy's kid's birthday next week and he'd love to go.'

Norman glared at him and walked off with his drink.

Aesop turned back to Shiggy, who had his eyes closed and was singing The Beatles to himself under his breath.

'Good man, Shiggy. We're going to be drinking this beer for weeks, yeah?'

'I hope so Aesop,' said Shiggy.

'Course we will! Won't we, Jimmy?'

'Yeah,' said Jimmy. He was still distracted by the girl in black.

'Jaysis, you and Norman,' said Aesop. 'Am I the only one who's going to give Shiggy here a bit of encouragement? He's doing this for all of us, y'know? Aren't you, Shiggy? Poor bloke's going to get up and sing a song in English in front of all these people, and all you can do is sit there mooning over some bird you haven't even spoken to yet, and Norman doing his PT Barnum over in the corner. Yiz don't even deserve the beer. Shiggy, I think you and me should drink it ourselves. We're the ones putting in all the work.'

'Okay, Aesop. Ask me borrocks, Jimmy. No beer for you.'

Jimmy looked around and laughed.

'All right, all right! Which one are you doing again?'

'*I wanna hold your hand.*'

'Grand. Now, y'see, the thing with The Beatles, right, is this. The harmonies are usually in diatonic thirds. Now, what that means is that you have to ...'

He went through the whole song with Shiggy, the two of them singing with their heads nearly together over the table, explaining which harmony line to sing for best effect on the stage. By the end of his pint Jimmy thought that Shiggy would probably be grand. It was only a laugh anyway.

Thirteen

It took Jimmy nearly two hours to get moving. The first hour was just to get up some courage and was mostly spent casting furtive glances in her direction. He was on his fourth pint before he started to get that numb feeling in his head that he recognised from the old days. When he was still with Sandra it just meant that he was a bit drunk and was probably about to start getting amorous with her, but before he knew her it had always been a signal to himself that he was at his most desirable and should definitely start making a move. The problem was that there were two of them over there and he wanted to get Mystery Girl alone.

He eventually went to the bar and came back with a Baileys and a glass of ice. He didn't want them mixed because he wasn't sure how long it would take before he got an opening and he didn't want the ice melting in it and the drink turning to shite on him.

'What are you drinking now?' asked Aesop, frowning at the glass that Jimmy put down next to his pint.

'Baileys. It's for yer woman,' said Jimmy.

'I see. And c'mere, did you get a thirty foot straw for her as well, so she can drink it?'

'I'm going to bring it over to her in a minute. Shut up, will ye?'

'The old Jimmy would be over there now, handing her the drink and telling her she has lovely baps.'

'He fucking would not!'

'Well, whatever. He wouldn't be sitting here with me and John Lennon, getting a crick in his neck trying to look at her without being seen. You've been hanging around with Norman too long.'

'Yeah, yeah. Where is he, by the way?'

'He finally managed to go over to yer one. That was his fourth attempt. He's on nine faults. Cian O'Connor couldn't have gotten him past that pillar there, the last hour. It's a wonder he made it over at all.'

'Well at least he's making the effort. You've been sitting here all night. What's the story?'

'Sure Jaysis, Jimmy, I can get a woman any time. How often is someone going to give me eighty free pints? Shiggy here is a little bit nervous about the song, so I'm here for some moral support. He's never sung in English in public before and I don't want to leave him alone in case he bottles out. This is the chance of a lifetime. For him, like, y'know?'

'You're a good pal Aesop,' said Jimmy, smiling.

'Thanks, Jimmy. And me offer still stands. If you want me to get yer woman away from your bird, just look over at me. It'll only take me a minute and then you'll be away.'

'Ta,' said Jimmy. 'But I think I'm all right for the moment. Hey, look ... her mate is going out for a smoke. This could be it. Yeah ... yeah ... okay Aesop, I'm in. Talk to you later.'

Jimmy put three cubes of ice into the Baileys and scooped it up, along with his pint. He had about ten minutes to make his move. He took a deep breath and started to walk over, heart thumping. Christ, he was like a young fella at a school disco. She looked up at him when he was just at the table.

'Howya,' he said, smiling. 'I'm Jimmy.'

Shiggy had taken to writing out the words of the song. He wasn't sure he'd be able to read them off the screen on the fly so he was going to practice it this way first. He was crouched over the table, trying to squeeze the lyrics onto the back of a beer mat. Aesop was leaning over him, helping with the spelling, humming along and generally being Shiggy's best mate in the world, ever. Out of the corner of his eye he saw

Norman come back and sit on a stool, and half looked up.

'Howya, Norman. Jaysis, that was quick even by your standards. What's after him feeling all happy and stuff inside?'

'Hmm?'

'Y'know, after he's feeling happy inside.' He started humming. 'Something about hiding something ... eh, what the fuck is wrong with you?'

Norman was pale. Even in the dim light at the table, he looked like he was about to vomit. He took a drink from his pint, his hand shaking, and sat back, eyes closed.

'Are you all right?' said Aesop, looking at him properly now. Shiggy had stopped writing and was looking over too.

Norman muttered something under his breath.

'What?' said Aesop, leaning in to catch it.

Norman turned to him and opened his eyes, snarling.

'I said, she only has *one fucking LEG!*'

'Yer woman? Sure, I told you that before you went over.'

'Oh, I know you did, Aesop. Of course you did. But you're always telling me shite like that, aren't you? I thought you were just slagging me.'

'I wasn't slagging you. Not about the leg anyway. So what happened, then?'

'I asked her up to dance.'

'You fucking did not!'

'I did. Of course I feckin' did. That's what you do at a feckin' disco, isn't it? You feckin' dance!'

'Not if you only have one leg. Jesus, Norman, you've fucking outdone yourself this time. What were you thinking?'

'I didn't know! I couldn't see.'

'You couldn't see?! She's sitting next to a pair of crutches, for fuck sake! The big silvery sticks there next to the table, you stupid bastard. And anyway, everyone saw her coming in.'

'It's dark. I didn't have my contacts in, did I?'

'Jesus Norman, we're not talking about picking out the exact shade of her eyes. She's missing a limb for fuck sake!'

'Well, she wasn't exactly waving a stump around, was she?' Norman shouted. 'She's just sitting there. She has a false leg. It was there, attached to her, under the table next to her good one. How the feck was I s'posed to know?' He was nearly crying.

'What did she say?'

'She said she couldn't dance.'

'And?'

'And I said, "Arra, of course you can. Sure, haven't I got two left feet and I don't mind making a show of myself." Oh God, I didn't know, Aesop. She thought I was taking the piss. She just looked at me and then her friend told me to fuck off with myself. I thought I was just getting the elbow, you know, like normal except a bit ruder and then the girl, Anne, stood up to go to the toilet and I saw her leg. Oh, holy heart of Jesus.' He had his head in his hands.

Aesop tried not to laugh but couldn't help it.

'Norman, you are priceless. That could only happen to you. You absolute fucking muppet.'

'Aesop, feck off. I didn't know. And now she thinks I'm a real bastard. God, and the way she smiled at me when I went over first. I'm never talking to a girl again. Never. Feck Jimmy and his Superchick. I've had enough. Look at me! I'm still shaking.'

'Well, did you say anything to her when you saw her leg?'

'What was I s'posed to say? I nearly ran into the pillar I was trying to get back over here so fast. God, I'm an eejit.'

'Norman,' said Aesop. 'You know me. I'm not known for being the most considerate bloke in the world, but that was pretty bad. You need to go back there and say something. It was a simple mistake. I won't say anyone could have made it, because they couldn't, but you should go over there and say something to her.'

'I will in my hole go back over there! I'm mortified!'

'Norman ...'

'Ah Jaysis,' whimpered Norman, glancing back at the corner. 'This is all Jimmy's fault. Two disasters out of two. The last girl I talked to doesn't even live in this country and now this one thinks I'm a mean ... you see what happens? Bloody Jimmy ... I'll kill him. God ... what were the feckin' chances?'

Jimmy didn't know any of this and at that particular moment in time wouldn't have cared anyway.

'Kayleigh. God, that's a beautiful name.'

'My Dad's Scottish.'

'Were Marillion Scottish? I think Fish might have been ...'

'I'm not sure. I don't really like that type of music. Nice song though, but I used to get a terrible slagging over it when I was younger.'

'Just jealous. Having a song named after you. No one ever wrote a song called "Jimmy". Well, Tool did, but it wasn't exactly Number One, was it? And then there was *Dr Jimmy*. That was The Who. Oh, and *Jimmy Jazz* by The Clash.'

'Well, I don't think he wrote the song for me. It would've been nice though. People singing along to your song on the radio like that. So, I take it you like your music then?'

'Yeah. Actually, I'm in a band.'

'Really? What do you do?'

'I'm the singer. And guitar player.'

'No, I mean what do the band do? What kind of music?'

'Oh. Eh, y'know, Offspring, U2, Ash, Foo Fighters. That type of thing. Our own stuff as well. You should come along and see us sometime.'

'Oh, I don't know. I don't much like loud music. I'm more of a Tony Bennett girl.'

'Tony Bennett? Wow, you don't get too much of that these days. Me Mam likes him, though. Him and Burt Bacharach.'

'Oh, I love Burt too. I'd get on well with your Mam.' She gave Jimmy a strange kind of look that flustered him a bit. He took up his pint.

'So, Leslie ...' she said.

'Eh, it's Jimmy,' said Jimmy, putting the glass down again, disappointed.

'No. Behind you,' said Kayleigh, laughing. 'Leslie.'

Jimmy turned around.

'Oh, right. Sorry,' he said, standing up. Leslie had come back and was standing behind him. He'd been in her seat.

'Thanks,' said Leslie, sitting down.

'Les, this is Jimmy. Jimmy, Leslie.'

'Howya,' said Jimmy, feeling like a bit of a prat now that he was standing up on his own at the table. He didn't know what to do with his hands, so he just put them in his back pockets until he could think of a better place for them. On her bum would be lovely, for instance, out on the dance floor.

'Hi,' said Leslie, smiling quickly at Kayleigh. 'Do you two want to be left alone or anything?'

Yes, thought Jimmy.

'No,' said Kayleigh. 'Jimmy was just telling me he's in a band. They do all the rock music stuff. Les likes all that, Jimmy. That's why we're here. I never usually go for discos and that type of thing, but she drags me out somewhere every month or so to be sociable.'

'Are you singing in the Karaoke tonight so, Jimmy? We'd love to hear you,' said Leslie, smiling at him.

'Eh, not tonight, no. My mate is, though. That Japanese bloke over there at the table. He's doing The Beatles.'

The girls looked over.

'He looks nervous,' said Kayleigh.

'Yeah. His English isn't the best. But it's just a laugh though, right? Did you hear the ones they've had up there already? Brutal ...'

'Yeah. I suppose it must be hard for a real singer to have to listen to that all night,' said Leslie, looking at him.

'Ah no, that's not what I meant,' said Jimmy, quickly. Christ. Bloody Irish women. You had to watch yourself.

'Only joking, Jimmy. Why don't you sing with Kayleigh? She's a great singer. They have duets too, don't they?'

'Will you stop messing Les,' said Kayleigh, grabbing her drink quickly. 'I'm not getting up there. Sure, I don't even do all that stuff.'

Leslie picked up an entry form, from where it had fallen onto the ground, and looked at it.

'Hey, they have Frankie here! You'd do a Frank Sinatra song, wouldn't you? Look, it's the one he did with Nancy. And didn't Robbie Williams do it as well, with your one? There's a duet. Go on. You'd have a laugh!'

'Give over, Les. Anyway, Jimmy doesn't like Sinatra, do you Jimmy?'

Jimmy thought that Frank Sinatra was an old gangster with an all right voice and very suspicious associations. He couldn't act to save his life and looked like a smug prick every single time he took up a microphone. He depended totally on other people's songwriting talent, and even then tried to fuck up excellent songs by giving them a smarmy 'Frankie Touch'; his take on evocative delivery. In short, Jimmy thought he was a second-rate warbler, who conned a whole generation with his magnetic eyebrows, the wanker.

'I love Frank Sinatra,' he said.

'Really?' said Kayleigh. She didn't believe it for a minute.

'Absolutely. Sure I grew up listening to him! What's that? *Somethin' Stupid*? I used to sing that with me Mam at Christmas! C'mon, Kayleigh. It'll be a laugh. Will we? Leslie, tell her.'

'Come on, Kay. You love singing.'

'Ah no. No, it's silly.'

'Kayleigh, if you say no I'll walk away and never speak to

you again,' said Jimmy, laughing. 'And then where would you be?' He hoped to God she had a sense of humour. She sat for a minute, looking up at the stage. Then she turned to him.

'Okay, so. Right. We'll do it. Do you really know the song?'

'Course I know it!' said Jimmy. Actually, he did. When he was learning how to woo audiences, he must have watched Frank do it on video a hundred times. He fucking hated it. When Robbie Williams came out with his version, Jimmy had to stop listening to the radio for a month until the bastard thing went away.

'Oh God, I can't believe it ...' squealed Kayleigh, as Leslie filled out the form and handed it to Jimmy to give up to the DJ.

As he went up with it, another couple was doing *I Got You Babe*. They were shite. He was passing the lads on the way back and was giving Aesop a wink just as the next name was called.

'Shiggy! Can we have Shiggy up here, please?' said the DJ.

'Hey, good luck Shiggy,' said Jimmy, passing. 'You'll be grand!'

'Yeah, think of the beer Shiggy,' said Aesop. 'Just keep thinking of the beer. That's what this is all about.'

'Best of luck,' said Norman, quietly. He still looked like he was going to top himself.

'Maybe I puke now,' said Shiggy, getting to his feet. He was the same colour Norman had been earlier.

'You're grand,' said Aesop. 'Go on, up you go. We'll be here waiting for you. Ye-hay! Go on ya mad fucker!'

Shiggy made his way to the stage, and Jimmy got back to the girls.

'This should be good,' he said half to himself, standing next to the table and picking up his pint again.

The song began and immediately Shiggy started moving. He looked about as nervous as James Brown, like he'd been doing it all his life. One minute he was standing, doing the claps like a matador and stamping his feet. The next he was off across the small stage with the microphone stand, like a miniature Chuck Berry. The crowd was going nuts. It came to the middle part and he got down on one knee and started singing to a group of girls, who were dancing right in front of him. They roared. Jimmy looked around and saw Kayleigh and Leslie clapping along and laughing.

Shiggy was having trouble with some of the lyrics, but 'Prease say tsoo me' and 'I feeru happy insaido' only added to the performance. For the second middle section he stepped down from the stage and took the hand of the girl to whom he'd been chatting at the bar earlier, singing to her with heaps of sincerity considering the pandemonium going on around them. She was far taller than he was. As a spectacle, the whole thing was perfect. Back up on the stage, Shiggy wound it up with a flourish, putting the microphone back on its stand, from where he'd yanked it a moment before, and bowing his head as the last chord faded out, his arms stretched out like Christ. Jimmy found himself shaking his head in wonder. This fucking Japanese bloke was amazing.

The yelling and cheering at the end of the song went on for so long that the DJ eventually had to shout to get everyone to shut up. Shiggy stood there looking shy and vulnerable, just to make sure he had all the angles covered. He wasn't going to let Aesop down.

Kayleigh and Leslie stood up next to Jimmy to join the ovation.

'He was brilliant!' said Leslie, turning to him.

'And he's not even the singer in the band. You must be pretty good yourself, Jimmy. I don't think I can get up there after that,' said Kayleigh.

'Ah, it's not us has to worry. It's the poor bastard up there now. Look, he's going to do Elvis,' said Jimmy.

The guy on the stage looked stricken. He'd seen Shiggy's

act and was now wishing the stage had a trapdoor. His mates had to push him up there and stand around in front of him, so he couldn't get down again.

'I don't know, Jimmy. After that ...' said Kayleigh.

'No chickening out Kay,' said Leslie. 'C'mon. For the craic.'

'Hmm ...' said Kayleigh. She was looking at Jimmy, one finger in her mouth, as she tried to work out what to do. 'Okay, then. Okay. Oh God, what am I doing?!'

'Cool. Listen, I'm getting a beer. Do you want anything?' said Jimmy.

'No. I'm fine thanks,' said Kayleigh, holding up her nearly full Baileys. 'I've lots, look.'

'Leslie?' Leslie was turning out to be a good ally. She was definitely worth a bottle of Satzenbrau.

'Thanks, Jimmy.'

He headed back to the table where the lads were still clapping a very tired-looking Shiggy on the back. Even Norman was smiling.

'Brilliant stuff Shiggy,' said Jimmy, shaking his hand. 'If that doesn't win you the beer, then I don't know what will.'

'Sanks Jimmy,' said Shiggy, sweating. 'I try.'

Aesop looked at Jimmy.

'How's it going over there? You need a hand?'

'Nah. I'm grand. Sure, Jimmy Collins can handle two women, right?' he said, winking at Aesop.

'About bleedin' time,' said Aesop, smiling back.

'I'm going to the bar. You want anything?'

'Nah. I just got a round in. I had to. Norman was about to start crying and I didn't want to be here.'

'What happened?'

'Ah. I'll tell you later. Go on. Yer woman over there will be wondering what happened to you. What's her name?'

'Kayleigh.'

'Marillion?'

Jimmy nodded.

'And what's her mate's name?' said Aesop, one eyebrow shooting up.

'Sorry, Aesop. She's not your type.'

'How do you know?' Statements like that didn't make sense to Aesop. The beer was in the bag now, so normal service was about to be resumed. It was just a question of who the lucky girl was to be.

'Because I said so,' said Jimmy. 'Piss off.'

'Okay. But if you make a balls of her mate, I'm in, right?'

'Yeah, whatever ...'

Jimmy went up to the bar for the Guinness and Satzenbrau. He'd never ordered Satzenbrau before and it wasn't cheap for the poxy little bottle you got. Leslie would need to be on form before she got too many more of these this evening. As he turned away from the bar with the drinks, Elvis was about to get off the stage, and probably leave the building, after his performance. He would've been okay but Shiggy had completely thrown him. He'd been shitting himself up there and looked it, but the crowd gave him a big cheer anyway for having the balls. Two mates got up to sing a Queen song. They were plastered, both leaning into the same microphone and yelling. With competition like that, Jimmy could see many, many pints of free lager in his immediate future.

Half an hour later, he was still talking with Leslie and Kayleigh. It was actually fairly easy. He felt like he'd known them for ages, just sitting there and bullshitting away about Shiggy and the band and Leslie's undying love for Galaxy chocolate bars and Kayleigh's for Terry Pratchett books. Leslie was lovely, but there was something about Kayleigh's eyes that kept his own glued to her face. She seemed gentle. Serene, or something. As if she was cool with what was going on, whatever it was.

Not a bit like Sandra. He didn't even know Kayleigh, but he couldn't imagine her constantly trying to 'improve' herself by reading all those books or always coming up with some ridiculous, abortive project to help the less fortunate. Jimmy didn't think he was perfect or anything but he couldn't see the point in relentlessly trying to become someone you weren't. And surely it was possible, and probably more productive, to be charitable without being so neurotic and defensive about it all? Sandra could be very tiring that way. One week it was the homeless, the next it was rape victims. Later on, it would be refugees or drug addicts or women in the workplace. No focus or logic. Just endless statistics and self-righteousness all rolled up into bitterness at the world and flung at Jimmy because he happened to be sitting there and didn't look enough like he cared.

Jimmy cared. The band did charity gigs. He put a fiver into more rattled cans than most people. Maybe even a tenner at Christmas. If you want to help, then help. If you want to improve yourself, then off you go. Good luck to you. But just talking about it all the time and being angry was no bloody use to anyone as far as he could see. Jimmy was seeing his relationship with Sandra in a whole new light, and it appeared to be shining straight out of Kayleigh's bum.

'Sorry?' he said.

He'd missed that. He'd been thinking instead of listening.

'I said you look all funny,' said Kayleigh.

'Oh. Sorry. I was just thinking about something.'

'Am I boring you?'

'No. God no,' said Jimmy, smiling. 'I was wondering what key you sing in.'

'God, I don't know. Something flat probably,' she smiled back.

'Okay, you two. You're on next,' said Leslie.

There was a girl up singing a Madonna song, but the DJ had started to announce two songs in advance to warn the singers. It saved time with people being missing in action in the toilet or somewhere, when it was their turn to go up.

Jimmy looked at Kayleigh. She was knocking back the rest of her Baileys.

'You okay?'

'No. Ah, I suppose I'm grand. A bit nervous. You?'

'No problem. Hey, I'm a rockstar, remember?'

She laughed. Jimmy was just thinking that she had a beautiful laugh when Madonna finished up. As their names were called again, he realised that he actually was nervous. He wasn't surprised. He always maintained that the day he got up on a stage without being nervous would be the day he was shite. You always respect your audience.

They passed the lads on the way up to the stage.

'What are you bleedin' up to?' shouted Aesop, over the cheering.

Jimmy just winked and kept walking. He got up onto the stage first and then turned to help Kayleigh up. It was only a ten-inch step, but it looked good. They took a microphone each and Jimmy moved the stands behind them, so they wouldn't get in the way.

They stood for a second and then the guitar intro started.

They started together and Jimmy knew straight away that she was good. Nancy's part was low and a bit monotone but Kayleigh nailed it, harmonising perfectly. Before he knew it the first verse was over and he turned away from her, looking out into the audience and working the eyebrows. A couple of Frankie finger clicks got a big cheer. She took his hand then, as they started the third verse, and he looked down at her. Her dark eyes gazed back and he nearly melted. The music, the spinning lights, the six pints. Jimmy got a sudden pang inside, followed by a warm creeping sensation up his face. It was something like the feeling a guy gets when the car he's travelling in goes too fast over the crest of a hill – difficult to describe, but not entirely unlike having a feather duster gently stroke your scrotum.

The eyebrows and clicks were forgotten now, as she turned to face him and led him through a few steps of a waltz for the short instrumental break, leaning back and looking up at him, her breasts resting lightly against his middle. Her eyes were like a clear night sky, or something similarly proverbial, huge and sparkling. Then she turned away again and went back into the last verse, still holding his hand and giving it a little squeeze. He didn't even remember singing any more, but he must have because the crowd went wild again. He turned to her, stunned, and got a kiss on the cheek and a beaming smile. He was fucked. Totally. He wasn't attracted to her sexually. Well, he was – a lot – but that wasn't what he was feeling. He didn't even know what he was feeling. He was completely numb. Kayleigh had him. Dazed and confused. So this is what it felt like.

They got down from the stage together and started walking back to the table through the clapping crowd. His legs were moving, but he wasn't doing it. He wasn't making anything happen. He couldn't hear anything and he couldn't speak. Aesop stood in front of him and punched his arm.

'Not bad for a shite song Jimmy,' he said.

'Ng ...' said Jimmy.

Then they were back with Leslie, who was cheering and clapping. She kissed them both.

'Brilliant! That was great. So you can sing then, Jimmy. I thought you were just trying to impress us with a story.'

'Ng ...' said Jimmy, again. He was more his father's son than he sometimes liked to admit.

Shiggy won the singles. It was a clapometer type of affair. The loudest clapping and cheering won the prize. Everyone yelled for his or her own mates, but Shiggy's reception was thunderous with almost every girl in the place screaming for him. He got up on the stage and took his voucher for the free keg. He stood there, grinning his head off and bowing at everyone. Second and third prizes were handed out, along with some smaller prizes for best dress and stupidest dance routine and stuff. Then they moved to the duets.

'Jimmy and Kayleigh!' shouted the DJ.

The roar nearly lifted the roof. They had it.

As they made their way up to the stage, Kayleigh took his hand again, linking her fingers through his this time. Jimmy's heart did another backflip. Jesus, he'd never make it home alive at this rate. His chest was thumping, his brain wouldn't work and his belly felt like there was a troupe of little pixies in it, having a party.

On the stage, Barry, the guy from the beer company, handed him an envelope and shook their hands. Jimmy absently wondered what the prize was as he took it. This made him unique among every other guy in the place, all of whom were wondering about the two tiny mini-dresses just behind Barry and their stunning, smiling, large-tittied contents.

Back at the table Jimmy started to open the envelope. Barry hadn't said what it was. Just that it was a romantic evening. As he pulled the card out from inside, he heard a familiar voice from the stage. They'd gotten Shiggy up for an encore before they finished for the night. The cheeky bastard was going to do The Carpenters.

'Ziss is for my friend Aesop ...' he said, pointing down to him. Jimmy looked over at Aesop, who was hiding behind his hand and furiously going red. Norman was laughing beside him, both hands showing everyone who Aesop was. Nice one, Shiggy.

'So?' said Kayleigh. Leslie was next to her, grinning.

Jimmy read it.

'It's a night out for two! A date, it says here,' he said. 'Dinner in La Parisienne, then a box in the cinema and then ... oh, holy shit ...'

'What is it?' said Kayleigh.

'Eh ... a suite in The Clarence for one night. Jesus. Bono's gaff!'

Leslie screamed with laughter. Kayleigh looked at her and then back at Jimmy.

'That's a bit forward of you Jimmy,' she said. She wasn't smiling now, but she wasn't pissed off either. Not a bit.

All Jimmy's organs started playing musical chairs again.

'Eh, will you go out with me?' he said, 'For the meal anyway. And the flicks?'

Leslie excused herself to the toilet, bless her.

Kayleigh took the card and read it herself.

'Just checking. You might have added that last bit in,' she said, with a little grin. Jimmy wouldn't have even thought of doing something like that. That kind of thing was Aesop's department. But he didn't need to make anything up. It was there. A night in The Clarance.

'Tell you what, Rockstar, why don't you call me tomorrow?'

Jesus. She'd called him Rockstar.

She was punching her number into his mobile phone when Leslie came back. Kayleigh stood up.

'C'mon, Les. We should go. We'll never get a taxi otherwise. Do you want to get the coats? I'll see you at the door.'

She handed her the ticket stubs and turned back to Jimmy, as Leslie went off with a wink. She was great. Aesop would've just told Jimmy to fuck off and get his own coat for a laugh.

'I really enjoyed that. Thanks.'

Jimmy shook his head at her.

'Thanks yourself. What time tomorrow? You a late sleeper?'

'Around twelve? Should be up by then.'

'Twelve then ...' He didn't know what to do next. Shake her hand? No way. But he couldn't very well make a grab for her arse either, could he? Maybe if he just ...

She put one hand on his arm and stood up on her toes, turning her face to his. He bent down and they kissed. It was a pretty long one but not a big wet snog. It was all lips. Her

160

lips were full and soft. Jimmy closed his eyes and kissed her back. Any lingering doubt he might have had up to that point vanished. It was her. He'd found her and he was high as a kite on it.

He watched her leave with a wave and turned to go back to the lads' table. The DJ was playing the last song so the place was starting to clear out. He came up to them, feeling like a child on Christmas morning. Aesop looked up and saw him.

'You look happy,' he said.

'Like you wouldn't believe, man.'

'Yeah, I know. A free fucking keg of beer!'

'Where's Norman?'

'He went back over to yer woman in the corner as she was leaving. Said he'd see us outside. You won't believe what the fucking idiot's after doing. Oh, by the way, this is Sharon.' He gestured to the girl standing next to him. Jimmy looked and smiled to himself. How did Aesop do it? He hadn't left the table all night.

'Howya Sharon.'

'Hi Jimmy,' she said. 'And congratulations again.'

'Thanks.'

She smiled and coyly tried to pull down the hem of her tiny mini-dress.

Aesop didn't fuck about on Saturdays.

Fourteen

The lads were standing outside, trying to burrow down into their coats. Aesop's new pal, Sharon, had an enormous woolly affair on her, with a big collar up past her ears and the bottom only inches from the wet ground. Her hands were lost in its folds and only her eyes and her great mop of blonde curls were visible sticking out the top. It was, if possible, even colder than when they were queuing up to get in and given that her working clothes consisted entirely of about twenty square inches of elasticated cotton, no one was questioning her choice of outer garment. She was looking at Aesop with what might have been an air of impatience, but it was difficult to tell with all that hair. The promotion girls usually got a lift home but she couldn't bring Aesop with her that way. It was okay to use the suggestion of sex to sell beer, but actually bringing a punter home to do the business after a gig was not allowed. Or at least shouldn't be seen to be encouraged.

'Where is the eejit?' said Aesop. 'It's bleedin' polar out here.'

There was no sign of Norman. There was still a lot of people around, looking up and down the road for taxis with that mixture of fury, despair and resignation that you could only truly appreciate if you've ever tried to get a taxi in Dublin late on a Saturday night when the weather's crap.

'Look, there he is,' said Jimmy. He pointed to the car park without taking his finger out of his pocket, where Norman was walking towards them. He seemed to be happy.

'So?' said Aesop, when he got closer. 'What happened?'

'It's grand,' said Norman, smiling. 'I explained that I didn't know she only had the one leg and that I wasn't trying to take the piss. She just said it was fine. Actually, she wasn't even the one who got annoyed, she said. Apparently her friends are a bit protective. Told her about me contacts. She wears them too, so she knows how it is. Lovely girl. Anne.'

'Grand so,' said Jimmy, shivering and not really interested now that it was all sorted out. Aesop had told him the story when they were getting their coats from the cloakroom. He thought it was hilarious, but Jimmy just felt sorry for Norman. He was sure that the girl was well able to look after herself. It was Norman who'd be traumatised about it for months, the poor sap. 'Are ye right, then? We might as well start walking – get the taxis on the way back out.'

They all started walking back along the road in the direction of town, bitching about how hard it was to get a taxi.

'Bastard,' said Jimmy through gritted teeth, looking at yet another taxi rush past, its driver completely ignoring his frantic waving.

'Absolute fucking scum of the earth,' said Aesop, his voice all muffled. He seemed to be trying to get inside Sharon's coat with her.

'*Nanda?*' said Shiggy.

'Taxi men Shiggy,' explained Jimmy. 'They're the fucking pits.'

Shiggy frowned.

'They should be strung up by the goolies for what they're doing to Dublin. Understand?'

Shiggy just shook his head.

'Very bad men,' said Jimmy. Shiggy smiled and nodded.

'Ah. I see. But why?'

'Why?! I'll bleedin' tell you why, Shiggy ...' said Aesop. He went off on a rant that lasted for about five minutes, effing and blinding, his hand leaving Sharon's coat every now and then to swipe angrily in the air. 'Fuckin' taxi plates ... bleedin' blockading the place ... queuing for two poxy hours ... women having to walk home and getting attacked ... new plates didn't make a bit of difference ... bastards don't give a shite ... hope they all catch the pox ... in this day and age ... can't feel me bleedin' toes ...'

It went on and on. At the end of it, he stared at Shiggy and said 'Now do you understand?'

Shiggy looked at him.

'No,' he said. 'Say again, prease.'

They all laughed.

'I sink I understand,' said Shiggy, smiling. 'But, *ne*, different in Japan.'

'How is it different, Shiggy?' said Jimmy.

'Takushi man has job, *ne*? So, takushi man just do his job. People get in takushi, takushi man drive people home. Easy. In Tokyo, takushi like bus, like train. Not money. Money is not ah, pry ... plyor ...'

'Priority?'

'Yes, plyority. Train stop at night, so people need takushi. Most important sing is serbiss, *ne*? For people.'

'Bloody right,' said Aesop. 'Well, we barely have a bleedin' taxi service at all. It's not my fault they paid eighty grand for a taxi plate, is it? So why am I the one walking down the road in winter with me nipples stinging the fuck out of me? Look, there goes another one the fucking dirty ...'

The taxi stopped.

'Howyiz, lads. Where yiz off to?'

'Eh, mostly around Collins Avenue. Will you take five?' said Jimmy.

'Ah lads, can't take five. They'd fuckin' have me, y'know?'

'Please. It's bloody freezing out here ...'

He looked at them for a few seconds, especially Sharon, and then checked his watch. Sharon had the kind of face that men want to see smile for them and taxi men, despite Aesop's observations to the contrary, were only human. Luckily he could only see her face. If he'd been able to see what the lads knew was under the coat, he wouldn't have stopped for them so much as crash into the nearest lamppost.

'Ah, fuck it. Get in. Keep that little fella's head down and we'll be all right. It's me last run in tonight, in annyway.'

'Good man,' said Aesop, getting in after Sharon. 'Thanks very much.' He was all polite now. Aesop was like everyone else. No matter how strong your feelings were, when you were sitting in a taxi man's car at two in the morning you kept them to yourself. Getting thrown out and having to find another one was far too horrible to contemplate. The fact that this bloke would take five at all was practically miraculous. The scene was probably being repeated all over the city. Passengers nodding politely and agreeing with everything the taxi man says, the latter blissfully unaware of what the former really thinks of him – that he is essentially an utter, out and out, taxi-driving bastard.

'I thought we'd have to walk home,' Aesop went on.

'Jaysis, that'd be a long fuckin' walk,' said the taxi man, adjusting his mirror so that Sharon's face was in it. She was smiling beautifully now. The taxi man thought it was because he'd stopped for them and she was warming up at last, but in fact it was because Aesop's left hand was squeezing her big right tit under the coat. The taxi man didn't know this of course, and so the lampposts of Dublin were safe enough for another few miles yet.

Norman was in the front, leaving Jimmy and Shiggy to squeeze into the back. It was cramped and smelled of cigarettes, but it was warm and it was bringing them home. The taxi man was one of the chatty types but, amazingly for a Dublin taxi man, he didn't once mention the scumbag blacks that hung around the hoors on Fitzwilliam Square, or the refugee knackers that were sponging off the country, or rich students puking in his car, or smelly culchies ripping off the social welfare system or any of the other myriad of things that his colleagues were invariably given to whinge about.

He didn't even talk about driving a taxi, which was a first for the lads. He was a moany bastard, but at least he wasn't a moany fascist bastard.

'Cold out there.'

'Freezing.'

'Me missus has a terrdilble cold, y'know?'

'Yeah?'

'Shockin'. Doctor thinks it's the bleedin' flu.'

'That's awful.'

'Ye see the rugby? Bleedin' brutal, weren't we?'

'Terrible.'

'Sure we haven't the jaysis numbers for rugby. Who plays it, only a few a dem schools over the south side?'

'I know.'

'Do yiz follow the oul' racing, do yiz?'

'Norman there does.'

'Put a fiver down on Start of Gold, Norman. Galway. Saturday.'

'Yeah?'

'Ah, deffny. The missus' Da knows the trainer.'

'Thanks.'

'Where're you from? Hey, little fella. Where're you from?'

'Japan.'

'Jaysis, wha'? Me nephew went out to Singapore a few years ago, teaching. Very expensive, so it was. Tenner for a pint. Sure, how are you s'posed to go out for a night paying that sort of money? Madness, so it is. Fuck that. I'd be on the bleedin' wahter, d'yiz know what I mean? Sure that's all beer is in annyway, wahter and hops, isn't it? A tenner me bollix. I wouldn't pay a tenner for a pint. I'd rather starve. Will ye stop? And c'mere, I says to him, says I, is it even a nice pint? Ah, it's all right, says he. Only all right, I says! Sure Jaysis, I says, for a tenner ye'd want to be able to bring it home to your Mammy. A tenner, wha'?'

'I know.'

'And, c'mere, do youse eat raw fish, do yiz?'

'Ah, yes, sometimes I ...'

'Jaysis, you're all mad out there. And warribou the sam-nella? Do yiz not be getting terrdilble bleedin' sick from eatin' stuff dar isn't cooked proper. My missus had a dose a sumtin once off a battered cod. Jaysis, it was woeful. Couldn't leave the house for a week for fear she'd be caught away from the jacks. Would you look at that gobshite, all over the bleedin' road. The coppers'll have him. Wait'n y'see. There was a terrdilble accident in Fairview tonight, so there was.'

'Was there?'

'Shockin'. A bus took the side of a car. No one in the car, thank God, but I'll tell yiz, there'll be two hundred people down the Four Courts on Monday morning sayin' they were on the jaysis bus. Ye had to go through Ballybough to get into town. Down Parnell Square way, y'know? Have ye seen Croker since? Jaysis, that's some fuckin' building job, wha'? And they say they've no money? They've bleedin' money all right. Won't let soccer near the place, but. The foreign game, d'ye see? Sure what the fuck is American Football and they do have that in there. Ah yeah, they have money all right. C'mere, these two hunters are out shooting pheasants, y'see, when one of them falls on the ground and starts twitching. Then he stops moving and just lies there with his eyes closed, right? So his mate takes out his mobile phone and dials 999, right? So the bloke answers and yer man says "Me mate is dead! What do I do? What do I do?" And the operator says "Calm down, calm down. Now first, let's just make sure he's actually dead, right?" The next thing the operator hears this massive gunshot and yer man comes back on the phone. "Right. Now what?" Ha ha ha. Jaysis, that's a good one, isn't it? "Now what?" Me brother told me that in the pub yesterday. Broke me bollix laughin'. He does work over in Baldoyle. Gets some deadly bleedin' jokes, so he does. Do yiz know the Racecourse out there? C'mere 'til I tell yiz. Do yiz know how they got planning permission for that ...?'

It went on like that most of the way home. Neurons firing randomly and triggering the mouth to say things. They took turns with small encouraging grunts – ah stop ... yeah ... no ... Jaysis ... me hole ... sure what do they bleedin' know – but it was mostly monologue. Shiggy was fascinated by the man's swearing, which he thought put even Aesop in the shade. Aesop and Sharon had their own fascinations to deal with, and Norman was just sitting up front, staring out the window and looking tired. Jimmy was glad the driver kept it up. It meant that he didn't have to talk to the others and that meant he could lose himself again, thinking of Kayleigh. Anyway, the way this bloke was going on, none of them probably needed to be there. He sounded like he waffled on like that even when he was on his own. A thirty-minute walk in the cold could put a damper on the best of evenings, but now that they were nearly home, Jimmy was starting to recapture the mood he'd been in earlier. Grand girl. Amazing. Great personality. Beautiful. Friend was dead-on. God, this could be it Jimmy, me oul' flower, this could be it.

Twelve o'clock tomorrow afternoon. He'd see then.

Jimmy had left the heat on in his bedroom when he went to bed, so when he woke up at about ten on Sunday morning, the quilt had been kicked off during the night and he found himself lying naked on the mattress. He quickly grabbed it from the floor and covered himself. You never knew when a fireman would burst into the room or something. His mouth tasted of sour milk and he had the start of a bruise on his arse where Aesop had accidentally kicked him when he and Sharon were getting out of the taxi. Sharon. Taxi. Disco ...

Kayleigh.

He smiled as it all came back to him. God, that was a good night. Sometimes you could go to bed at night feeling great, and then the next morning, with the sun shining – or at least, if you lived in Ireland, up in the sky somewhere – the whole thing seemed different. He remembered idly wondering how he'd feel when he was going to bed, if he'd still think she was brilliant and if he'd still have the buzz in his belly when he woke up. Now that he was awake and grinning like a fool to himself in the bed, he knew that it wasn't just the drink or the strobe lights or the Saturday night that did it. She did it. He felt good. Strangely nervous and a bit queasy, but very, very happy.

He reached out and grabbed the remote for the stereo. Jimmy wanted to be able to have music in every room of the house, but until he could afford to wire the whole place to a five hundred CD changer downstairs, he had to make do with a stereo in the living-room and one up here. This one had three CDs in it and Jimmy mentally flicked through them, to see what he was in the mood for. Ten seconds later, the Barenaked Ladies were lending their manic musings to his Sunday morning reverie. Happy music for a happy Jimmy.

He was lying there, still smiling away to himself, half an hour later when the phone rang. He turned the music down with one hand, grabbing the receiver with the other.

''Morning, Jimmy.'

'Howya Aesop. What's the story?'

'Well, Jimmy, do you remember a girl called Sharon?'

'I do, yeah,' said Jimmy, sitting up in the bed and laughing. If he had to hear about it at all, Jimmy normally preferred to have had his Weetabix first, but today he felt about sixteen years old and was on for getting all the gruesome details.

'Jaysis, Jimmy. Un-fucking-believable. That's all I can say. If you thought she was stacked in that dress, you should have seen her in the shower.'

'But what about your Da? And Jennifer.'

'Jennifer stayed over in Marco's, the slapper, and me Da

is playing golf this weekend in Cavan. Had the gaff all to meself. It was probably me best performance ever, Jimmy. You could've hung a wet duffel coat off me. I even let her stay for breakfast I was that proud of meself. Made her toast and everything. And d'ye know what she says to me when she was leaving?'

'That your mate Jimmy is a ride?'

'No. She said she's a few friends that'd love to meet me. Can you believe that? Jimmy, I know I was sceptical before, but I think I've found this bird you were looking for. Sharon. See? Sharon and Superchick. They even have the same initial. Jaysis, I'm in love.'

'So then, this mot that you think you love wants you to meet her mates so you can shag them all?'

'Yep. I presume that's what she meant anyway.'

'Aesop, that's not really what I had in mind when I was laying down criteria for Superchick, y'know?'

'Ah Jimmy, don't be bursting me bubble now. You have your criteria and I have mine. I'm meeting her this evening in town for a pint.'

'You're meeting her?! Jaysis, Aesop, maybe it is love!'

'Isn't that what I'm telling you? Look, me Da isn't back 'til tomorrow morning and I can always get Marco to bring Jennifer out. I want another portion of that, Jimmy. I think me and Sharon could be a big thing. I've never felt this way about a girl before. I might even write a song abou ...'

'Ah, for fuck sake!'

'No serious, like.'

'What are you going to call it? I *Love Your Sweet Sweet Smile and The Way You Share Me With Your Mates*?'

'Maybe, Jimmy. That's a good one. Unless you've already got something going with that title, do you?'

'No, you're grand. I'm still working on *Me Mate's a Knacker and His Mot Has Big Tits*.'

'Ah, that's nice. A song for Aesop. Listen Jimmy, seriously, do you need me for practice this evening? We said we'd get together with Shiggy in your gaff and go over some stuff tonight.'

'Nah, it doesn't matter. Anyway, I might be hooking up with Kayleigh from last night.'

'Oh yeah. So what d'ye think?'

'Nice. Very nice, Aesop. I'm calling her this afternoon.'

'Nice? So, does that mean she's Superchick, or that she'll do for practice?'

'What do you think?'

'Knowing you, Jimmy, she's round your Ma's now learning how to crochet. Well anyway, look, I'll give you a shout later, right? It's just me and Sharon tonight, but if I play me cards right, I might be able to get her to call one of her pals. Ye never know.'

'Yeah, ye never know Aesop. Right, I'm getting up now. I'll seeya later, right?'

'Yeah. Seeya.'

Jimmy hung up, got out of bed and went into the shower. Downstairs would be cold, so he stayed under the hot dribble for twenty minutes, thinking dreamy thoughts about Kayleigh, exasperating ones about Aesop, and some fairly dirty ones about Sharon. He closed his eyes and tried to imagine Kayleigh in the shower with him, but she kept turning into Sharon in his mind. Bloody Aesop, hijacking his morning ablutions with an image like that.

He ran down to the newsagent for the paper once he was dressed. It was mobbed. Half ten Mass was just finished and all the Daddies were in there getting the *Sunday World*, the Mammies getting a half pint of cream for the dessert and the kids running around, screeching for a Curly Wurly or a bag of crisps. Everyone's carefully arranged clothes and hair were already beginning to fall apart, but no one seemed to mind. Mass was over for another week.

Jimmy waited patiently in the queue, smiling at the little

ones and their mothers. It was amazing how mothers knew what their kids were up to, no matter where they were.

'Conor, leave your sister alone. Fiona, give him back his SpongeBob.'

Conor and Fiona's Mam was talking to another woman, her kids about ten feet behind her over at the magazines. She hadn't even looked around. Dad was scowling at the back page of the paper, oblivious to the kids' dispute but still looking very uncomfortable in his dark grey suit and yellow tie, clearly wishing his wife would gather up the brats and stop her yapping, so he could get them home and piss off for a pint before his dinner. Jimmy remembered the scene well from his own youth, except with him and Liz it was always about his Steve Austin figure. Liz wanted Steve and Cindy to get together, and could never seem to understand that Steve had more important things to do – things involving exploding Lego houses and plastic German soldiers and slow-motion sprints across the kitchen floor. When the Jamie Somers doll came out, it nearly caused a riot in the house. Steve didn't want some girl helping him defeat evil, and anyway everyone knew that bionic ears were shite compared to a bionic eye. Eventually, Liz pulled Steve's head off and flushed it down the toilet and Jimmy fed Jamie to Rusty next door. It was days before they spoke to each other again.

Back in the house, Jimmy flicked through the paper and some of its many supplements but he wasn't really taking anything in. He kept looking at the clock in the kitchen. Eleven thirty, eleven forty, eleven forty-five. What time should he call? He'd said twelve, but did that mean twelve on the dot? Nah, he'd look too anal. Five past twelve? Well, what if her clock was five minutes slow? It would say twelve exactly, and he'd still look anal. Same for five to twelve if hers was fast. Twelve fifteen? She might think he wasn't going to call and go out or something. And if he called early, he'd sound too keen. That could put some women off. It was ten to twelve now. God, what would he say? He decided to practice in his head ...

'Hi, Kayleigh? It's Jimmy.'

'Hi Jimmy. How are you?'

'I'm great, Kayleigh. You?'

'Yeah, great. I didn't drink too much, so you know ... ?'

'Yeah. So, eh ...'

Then what? Eh ...

'Eh ... you want to go out for lunch this afternoon?'

'I'd love to. What time?'

'I'll pick you up at ...'

No. Bollocks. That wouldn't work. His car was manky. He'd have to clean it out before he let her near it.

'I could meet you in Howth, maybe? There's a nice sea-food place out there.'

'Great! I love seafood. What time?'

'How about three? Give you time to get over your Weet-abix.'

'Sounds perfect. Which place?'

'It's called ...'

What was it bloody called? He ran to get the Dublin tourist guide that Marco had left lying about the place.

'Shandlers. You know it? Just opposite the Club.'

'Oh, right. I think I know it, yes. Blue décor in the front?'

'That's it. So, seeya there at three?'

'Perfect. I'm looking forward to it, Jimmy. I had a good time last night.'

'Yeah, me too. Seeya, then.'

'Seeya, Rockstar.'

Brilliant. That would be completely fucking brilliant. Rockstar. God. He didn't want to get ahead of himself or anything, but imagine her calling him that in the sack? It was five to twelve now. Oh shite, what would he wear to the restaurant? Everything was in heaps on his bedroom floor. Since Sandra left he hadn't gotten around to getting a proper laundry routine going. He got up and ran around the house, picking things up, sniffing them and throwing them down again. Eventually he settled on a pair of jeans and a denim shirt. Nothing too mad. And his leather jacket would do fine. He'd wear a T-shirt under the shirt. It could get pretty windy out in Howth.

Five past twelve. Right. That'll bloody do. He got his coat from where it hung on the banisters and brought it into the kitchen, reaching into the pocket to pull out his mobile phone. His hand came out empty, and he stared at it for a second before realising what that meant.

'Oh bollocks ...' he whimpered.

Fifteen

For a second or two every sound in the house and on the street outside was gradually squeezed out of Jimmy's head by the rising sense of panic that started in his chest, moved up his neck and settled into the back of his skull with a muffled thump that made the tops of his ears go all tingly. He quickly searched all the pockets in his coat three times each. Then he checked them again for rips and turned the coat over to pat the lining, in case the phone had somehow managed to slip between the stitches. Nothing. He stood up and spread the coat open on the kitchen floor, getting down on his hands and knees and running his palms over its entire area, head cocked to one side and face scrunched up trying to detect a bump. Only buttons. He sat back up and took the coat onto his lap again, searching the pockets once more to make absolutely sure. Eventually he threw the coat over a chair and stood up, looking into the back garden with his arms folded.

The phone was gone. And that grass needed cutting.

Jimmy spent the next thirty minutes running around the house, concentrating first on every room he'd been in between getting home the previous night and sitting down to call Kayleigh, and then looking in the places he knew the phone couldn't possibly be. He checked everywhere – under clothes, on his bed, under his bed, around and down the side of the sofa, under the newspaper, on and in the fridge. He even took a peek in the cereal box, hoping that maybe he'd been so preoccupied with his daydreaming, he'd somehow contrived to drop the bloody thing in there. He knew he was wasting his time when he found himself lying on the floor, shining a torch under the oven.

He wasn't panicked any more. Just monumentally pissed off. He'd never lost a mobile phone and he'd had one for about six years. When Sandra had gone through three in a six-month period once, he'd been the first one to tell her that she was an airhead. He distinctly remembered dancing around her in this very kitchen singing 'Sandra is an airhead, Sandra is an airhead', and her telling him to feck off. He found a pack of Aesop's cigarettes and sat down with one to think. He only ever smoked the things when he was plastered, but he was trying to clear his head and Aesop swore by them for calming himself down. Like Aesop needed calming down. Okay. First things first. He rang his mobile number. Should have bloody done it half an hour ago. It rang but no one picked up. His voicemail kicked in after five rings, and he left a message to whoever found it to call his home number. Then he remembered that he'd password protected the message box. Brilliant.

He rang again, twice, running around the house listening for the tune to *The Lion Sleeps Tonight,* that he'd put on it to annoy Aesop. Wherever it was, it wasn't in the house. Then he jogged down to the newsagent to see if he'd left it there, but he knew he hadn't.

'Did anyone hand in a mobile phone this morning?' he panted to the fourteen-year-old girl behind the counter.

'Eh ...' she said, looking at him.

'A mobile phone. I lost mine, and I was here this morning. I'm wondering did anyone find it and hand it in.'

'I don't know,' she said. 'I wasn't here.'

'Well, if someone did hand it in, where would you put it? Next to the cash register or something?'

She looked next to the cash register.

'There's no phone there.'

Jimmy wondered if she was taking the piss. There had been about four shop assistants there earlier, but that was for the post-Mass rush. Now Daddies were in pubs, Mammies were in kitchens and kiddies were out playing. This dopey cow was on her own in the shop.

'Okay,' said Jimmy, reaching into his pocket and taking out his wallet. 'I found this outside on the path. Do you want to take it and put it somewhere in case its owner comes back?' He handed the wallet to her.

She took it in her hand and looked at it for a second before looking back at Jimmy.

'Go on. Put it where you put things that are lost,' said Jimmy, making shoo-shoo motions with his hands. He was starting to lose it.

The girl moved slowly to her right and put the wallet next to the cash register, casting a hopeful look back in Jimmy's direction.

'Oh for fuck sake. Here, give it to me. It doesn't matter. Just give it to me. It's my wallet.'

'You said you found it.'

'Look, just give it to me, okay? It's my wallet. My work ID is in it, with my picture. Can I have it please?'

She didn't know what to do.

'Listen to me. Take the wallet and give it to me. Please, for fuck sake, just give me my wallet, will you?'

The girl looked like she was going to start crying but she threw the wallet onto the counter again and moved back, watching him.

'Thanks. Sorry for bothering you,' said Jimmy. He felt a bit bad now, but then he was in uncharted waters. He'd never been in a situation before where the most important thing in the world was a phone number he couldn't find. And he was supposed to be the clever one in the family.

He ran home again and called Aesop.

'Aesop.'

'Jimmy!'

'Aesop. Do you have my phone? I lost it last night.'

'No. I didn't see it. Are you sure you had it with you?

Why would you bring it to a disco?'

'I had it, Aesop. Kayleigh's number is in it.'

'Oh-oh.'

'Yeah. I must have lost it in the taxi. We were all squash-ed in, remember? You didn't see it? Sharon didn't see it? Re-member you gave me a boot in the arse when you were getting out?'

'No. Sorry, Jimmy. Did you check down the side of the couch? I'm always losing stuff there. One time me Da threw out a twenty spot he found down there. He thought it was ...'

'I checked, Aesop. It's not in the house.'

'Okay. Well, did you try Norman and Shiggy?'

'No, I'll do that now. Seeya.'

Click. Dring. Beep beep beep. Click.

'Shiggy?'

'Jimmy-san. Ah, sorry, Jimmy. Harro.'

'Yeah. Listen, Shiggy, did you see my phone? My mobile phone? I can't find it. I think I lost it last night.'

'Ah, *wakarimashita*. Sorry, Jimmy. I not have. *Gohmen*.'

'Are you sure? Did you see it at all last night?'

'Ah, maybe. You had in disco, right?'

'Yeah, but I can't find it.'

'Ah, maybe, Jimmy call phone and rissen, *ne*?'

'I tried that Shiggy,' said Jimmy. Christ. Everyone was full of bloody useless suggestions this afternoon.

'Sorry ...'

'Doesn't matter. Okay, I'll talk to you later, right?'

'Okay, Jimmy. Bye bye.'

Click. Dring. Beep beep beep. Click.

'Norman?'

'Robert is having his dinner,' said a stern voice.

'Ah, hello Mrs Kelly. This is Jimmy. How are you? Lovely day, isn't it? Very sorry to interrupt your dinner. Do you think I could have a quick word with himself? Won't take a minute,' said Jimmy. He'd been moving fast, pacing the kitchen with the phone under his chin, but hearing her voice had made him stop and sit down. You didn't hurry Norman's Mam. She could freeze the piss in your belly just by looking at you sideways and you don't want to be rude to a woman like that.

'He's having his dinner, Jimmy. Can you call back later?'

'Oh, sorry. Of course I can, Mrs Kelly. I didn't realise the time.'

'His dinner will get cold on him.'

'Yeah. Sorry about that. I'll ring back later.'

'Mine's getting cold now.'

'Eh, right. Goodbye, so. I'll talk to him again.'

'It's no good to you cold.'

Well go back and eat it then, you mad fucking cow.

'Okay, Mrs Kelly. Bye- ...'

She'd hung up. Jesus, she was a spooky oul' bastard. When they were young, a ball going over her wall was doomed. She even took in Norman's ball once and wouldn't give it back. You never knew when she was looking out the window. Sometimes she'd be out the door before the ball bounced twice, but other times she'd wait until you crept into the garden and then the door would fly open and she'd come careering down the driveway, yelling about her roses and letting fly to the ear with her backhand. She had the reflexes of a cat, the temperament of a Rottweiler, the body of a sperm whale and tits the size of your head. The kids used to call her The Thing.

Jimmy tried to think. There was no point in calling the disco. There'd be no one there at this hour on a Sunday. He checked his watch. It was going on one. What was Kayleigh doing? Sitting there watching the phone? He'd spent most of the night talking to her and hadn't even asked her what her surname was, so the phone book was no good. All he knew was that she was Kayleigh and she was from Clontarf. He could tell you all about her musical tastes, what she liked to read, her favourite movies, how herself and Leslie went to Tenerife on holliers that year. He didn't know Leslie's surname either. Think, Jimmy. He checked the phone book anyway, as if she'd have an entry under 'Kayleigh', then started opening random pages and looking for Clontarf numbers. This was going nowhere.

Hang on. Norman! Norman had been last out of the taxi, which meant he paid! And he was always keeping receipts. Aesop said that it was the tight culchie bastard in him. Okay, okay. Maybe it would be fine. The receipt would have a phone number for the taxi company on it, wouldn't it? There was a number on the car roof too. Which one was it? Something easy to remember. 888-9999, or something. Norman might remember, even if he didn't have the receipt.

All he had to do was wait. It was after one now anyway. Kayleigh wouldn't exactly be sitting at home with one hand on the receiver, would she? He might have been if it had been him, but a girl would never be that sad. She'd be gone out or something, so there was no hurry any more. He tried ringing his mobile again, but only once. Wherever it was, he didn't want the battery running out or he might be in trouble. The taxi man had said it was his last run last night, so he was probably still in bed or having his dinner. The phone would be in the car, that's why no one was picking it up. If he'd gone straight home, then no one else would have been in the taxi to rob it. So. Just wait a bit for Norman to call. Or give it another hour or so and call him. He wouldn't risk calling sooner than that. He'd known Mrs Kelly for the best part of twenty years, but she still scared the shite out of him.

'Jimmy?'

'Oh, thank Jaysis. Howya Norman.' It was twenty minutes later.

'What's up? You sound worried.'

'I lost me phone last night. I think it fell out in the taxi.

Did you get a receipt?'

Please, please, please.

'Eh, yeah. I have it here somewhere … hang on a minute … yeah, it's here. I put it in me wallet.'

'Oh God, that's great. Is there a number on it?'

'Yeah, it's …'

'Hang on, I'm getting a pen … right, go on.'

Jimmy took down the number and told Norman he'd call him later.

'But c'mere, it's not that big a deal, is it? Will work not give you another one?' said Norman.

'They will, yeah, but Kayleigh put her number into it last night and I was s'posed to call her this afternoon.'

'Ah, right. Well, I hope you find it. She looked nice.'

'Thanks. Seeya.'

Click. Dring. Beep beep beep. Click.

'North Dublin Limousine Service.'

'Hello. Eh, I was …'

'Please press one to pre-book a taxi …'

'Ah, Jaysis …' moaned Jimmy. He hated these menu things. And what did a bloody taxi company in Dublin need one for?

' … or press two to speak to a customer service representative.'

Two choices, the pricks. Whichever button he pressed, Jimmy was sure he'd be talking to the same person. He pressed two.

'North Dublin Limousine Service.'

'Hello. My name is Jimmy Coll …'

'All our operators are busy at the moment, but if you wait …'

'I don't fucking believe this,' said Jimmy, amazed.

He waited for a while, listening to a horrible rendition of *The Wind Beneath My Wings* and being assured of his valued customer status every thirty seconds. After about five minutes his patience ran out and he hung up, cursing. They must have someone in there on a Sunday, right? He tried again ten minutes later but got no further that time either. Then he tried pressing one to pre-book a taxi. Nothing. He tried pressing two again. He was fuming now. One again.

'North Dublin Limousine Service.'

'Ha! Limousine Service my bollocks. The state of the shit heap I was in last night. And why don't yiz have real people answering your bleedin' phones?'

'I'm sorry?'

'Oh. Eh ... nothing. Hello. I got one of your taxis last night and I lost my phone. I think it fell out of my pocket in the car.'

'I'm sorry sir, this number is for booking a taxi. I'll need to transfer you to our customer service desk ...'

'But ...'

'Please hold on, sir ...'

'No don't! Wait a minute! There's no one ...'

The phone went silent for a second and then he was back to square one, being asked in song did he ever know that he was some tart's hero.

Jimmy slammed the phone down and stood up, running his hands through his hair. He couldn't take it any more. He grabbed his coat off the back of the chair and started to rifle through it again. Then he had an idea. He looked out the window to make sure that the weather was still okay, and then he slipped the coat on and left the house. He was going for a walk. Down around Clontarf way. You never know.

'No sign, then?' said Norman, later that evening.

Jimmy shook his head.

'Well, I s'pose it was a bit of a long shot, walking around Clontarf like that. It's big enough.'

'Yeah.'

'Nice though.'

'What?'

'Clontarf. Some nice houses there. Big gardens and all, y'know?'

'Yeah. It's lovely,' Jimmy said. He hadn't even noticed the nice houses and big gardens, except that there were bloody loads of them. He stood up to put the kettle on again, wincing as he put pressure on his sore feet.

'So you've no clue what her last name is?'

'No. She didn't say. We were talking about other stuff, y'know? Music and telly and all. I didn't even think to ask her. Thought I'd find out soon enough. And we only used first names for the Karaoke competition.'

'Right, yeah. Ye were very good, by the way.'

'Thanks. For all the bleedin' difference it makes now.'

'What did the taxi man say?'

'He said he always checks the car before he finishes. There was nothing there. But he was after picking up someone else around here when he left you off, and drove him out to Finglas. He lives in Glasnevin or something himself, so it wasn't out of his way.'

'So, that's the fecker that robbed it? The Finglas bloke?'

'Probably. I don't give a shite about the phone. He can have it. I just wanted that number out of it. I rang a few times but no one was answering it. Bastards'll probably just get a new card and change the number tomorrow and that'll be the end of it. It's definitely not out in Portmarnock. I rang before you came over. Nothing handed up. Fuck.'

'Arra, come on Jimmy. It's not the end of the world, is it? Sure, you might bump into her again.'

'Ah, I won't Norman. How would I? She doesn't go out much, she was saying. And anyway, I was s'posed to ring her this morning. She probably thinks I'm just another bastard by now. She wouldn't even take my number last night – like it would make her some kind of a slapper if she called me instead of me calling her, y'know?'

'But it's not your fault.'

'Yeah, but she doesn't know that, does she? "Ah right, the old lost-me-phone story." Me arse. Even if I bumped into her, she'd think I was full of it.'

'You could take out an ad ...'

'Ah, come on Norman. Where would I put it? In the personal section of the *Herald*? "Hi Kayleigh. Listen, I'm after losing your number like a dopey fucker. Please call me at home, love, Jimmy." She wouldn't read those yokes anyway.'

'You never know, Jimmy. She might,' said Norman.

'I don't think so, Norman. If she was a fucking loser, we wouldn't be having this conversation, would we? But I was thinking, I'll call up the restaurant where we were supposed to go out. Maybe she'll call as well just to see if I made an enquiry or something. Probably won't though. The point is, she doesn't know about the phone, so she just thinks I didn't want to call her. She's not going to go out of her way to find me then, is she?'

'Worth a try, though.'

'Yeah.'

'No way she'd come and see the band?'

'I wouldn't say so. For starters, she doesn't like the music. And anyway, even if she did she's not going to come and watch us when she thinks I stood her up, is she? Same reason she won't ring the restaurant.'

They said nothing for a while and then Norman stood up.

'Sorry, Jimmy, I have to go. I told Mam I was just coming down for an hour, so she'll be wondering where I am.'

'Yeah, grand. Thanks for coming over. I wasn't much of a laugh tonight though, was I?'

'Ah, it's just shite luck. And sure, you never know, right? Was she that nice though? I mean she looked grand and all but the pus on you, you'd swear she was Meg Ryan.'

'I'll tell you something Norman, Meg Ryan is a hound next to her.'

184

'God. Yeah? There's shite luck now for you. You'd never find her with all your computers in work or something?'

Jimmy laughed.

'Nah. It doesn't really work like that, Norman.'

'What does she do?'

'She's a teacher. Kids. And no, I don't know where she teaches. It could be anywhere.'

'Well, I don't know. Short of going on the telly or something, I don't see how you can find her unless it's by accident. Listen, I'd better go.'

'Yeah, okay. Tell your Mam I said hello.'

'Will do. She was asking for you.'

'Was she?' Jimmy was surprised.

'Ah yeah. She always liked you, Jimmy.'

Liked me? Fucking hell, thought Jimmy. What was she like when she thought you were a prick?

'Eh, good. Right then. Seeya during the week, Norman.'

'Good luck, Jimmy. Sure, you never know ...'

'Yeah.'

Jimmy let him out and got back to his seat in the living-room, feeling depressed. Sunday evenings were a bastard at the best of times. Work in the morning, the clock gone back so it'd be even colder and darker than normal, and of course he'd have to explain to Eileen in work that he'd lost his phone and could he have another one. She'd look at him like he was a spa, and her without two brain cells to rub together.

He picked up his guitar for a minute but he didn't even have the heart to play tonight. He put it down again and turned on the telly. MTV were doing a Beyoncé special. God, had that slapper not gotten her fifteen minutes yet? Some crap comedy repeats that weren't even funny the first time around were on Sky. He settled on an English talent show. Some eejit thought he could do a good impression of Val Doonican, and that seemed to be the extent of his gift.

Christ, they let anyone on the telly these days. He smiled at what Norman had said. He'd have to go on the telly to find her. He turned down the eejit's crap Irish accent and closed his eyes, thinking of her and wondering what she was doing. God, he'd been close. Of all the times to lose a phone. He really thought she could be it. Kayleigh. Like the song. She'd even said she liked the song, and Marillion weren't exactly her cup of tea.

He opened his eyes and sat up suddenly.

Maybe there was one thing he could do. In fact he was doing it anyway, right? For the first time since he'd poked his hand into his jacket earlier, he didn't feel terrible. Of course! Well, it wouldn't be easy, but ...

He picked up his guitar again. As Norman said, you never know ...

Sixteen

They decided to go for a pint after rehearsal on Wednesday. They didn't always do that but Jimmy thought that it would be good for the new line-up to bond as a band, as well as just being mates who hung around together when they weren't playing. Marco and Norman weren't there so it meant that the three of them could talk about music and gigs and stuff without boring the others. That was the plan anyway.

'She has me worn out,' said Aesop, grinning.

Jimmy and Aesop were on pint number four, with Shiggy trailing on two. It was hard to keep to any sort of agenda after the third one, so Jimmy stopped trying. All they'd agreed was that they'd play a fairly easy set in McGuigans on Saturday, to give Shiggy a chance to get used to it. A few gigs down the road, they'd see about giving Shiggy some vocal parts and maybe even let him swap the bass for the guitar on a few songs. It would make it interesting for the band but Jimmy was wary of too much messing about on the stage. If you've got the punters' attention, it wasn't a good idea to let it go again by pricking about up there.

'Sharon?' said Jimmy.

'Yeah. She's a bleedin' looper. All night, she wants it. I had to start going to her place, with Da back from the golf. He might be a bit inattentive, but he's not deaf, y'know? Sharon's a bit of a screamer, God Bless her. Backwards, frontwards, sideways ... I'm wrecked, so I am.'

'But are you happy?' said Jimmy, looking at him over his pint glass.

'Oh yeah,' said Aesop. 'I haven't been this happy since Hector Grey's burned down. Remember that?'

'Yeah. I think I still have that pencil case you sold me.

So, Sharon is the one, is she? I have to tell you Aesop, I didn't think you'd be the one to get a bird out of all my brilliant scheming.'

'Ah now, hang on a minute. I never said I got a bird out of it. We're just ridin', like, y'know?'

Jimmy smiled. Same old Aesop. A dead Mam and a fear of getting close to women. Freud or someone would probably have loved that.

'Whatever,' said Jimmy. 'So Shiggy, have you talked to Katie since?'

'Ah, no Jimmy. I don't sink so,' said Shiggy. 'Katie was, ah, serious? I don't rike serious.'

'You're a wise man Shiggy,' said Aesop. 'I don't know about Katie, but you just keep thinking like that and you'll be grand.'

'Anyway, I hab girlfriend. In Japan.'

'What?' said Aesop and Jimmy, together.

'Why didn't you say that before?' said Jimmy, bemused.

'Not so important. She is in Japan. I am here. No ploblem. I go back, we get married, maybe.'

'But you said you didn't like being serious?' said Aesop. 'Jaysis, you can't get much more serious than that, Shiggy. That's funeral serious. It's the fucking end man, what are you thinking?'

Shiggy just smiled.

'Ah, in Japan, is ... different,' he said, a bit too slowly even for him.

'How is it different?' said Aesop. This was getting interesting.

Shiggy just smiled again and took another drink.

'Oh, Aesop,' he said. 'By za way. Katie say you shag her.'

'I fucking will not shag her!' said Aesop. 'Jaysis, and the lad hanging off me with the ridin' ...'

'No no no,' said Shiggy. 'You shag her before. Rast year, I sink?'

Jimmy looked at Aesop. This was a new one.

'Aesop? I thought you didn't shite where you eat? Katie is good mates with your sister. What have you been up to?'

Aesop was frowning, looking off into the distance.

'Ah, I don't think so ... did I? Nah. Sure, I'd remember that.'

'She say you shag her,' said Shiggy. He was adamant.

'Well, I s'pose it's possible. Where?' said Aesop.

Shiggy looked confused. He pointed between his legs.

'No. Fucking hell, I mean where was it? In her house? In the back of ... ah, hang on a minute. Wait, wait ... something's ringing a bell now. Did she say it was in Jimmy's?'

'What?' said Jimmy. 'In my gaff? Ye dirty ...'

'Yeah, remember your birthday party that time? You only invited a few people, so there wasn't much in the way of choice, y'know? No offence, Shiggy. So I think I might have given her one out the back garden. Must have been her. Yeah ... yeah, I think so 'cos we went back to her place afterwards. Ah Jaysis, I remember now. The things ye do, hah? So c'mere Shiggy, did she say I was any good?'

Shiggy shrugged.

'I don't know. But I don't sink she rike you now.'

'Ah, right. Well that would explain the fucking head on her then. That's one mystery solved. Must've broke the poor girl's heart. Ah well. Nice tits, but, yeah?'

Shiggy nodded, frowning.

'But, *ne*, too ... ah ... bouncy?'

Aesop laughed.

'Ah, yeah. Go on, ye dirty bastard! You'll get used to that, Shiggy. Irish girls like their spuds.'

'Will you fucking leave him alone, will you?' said Jimmy. 'Christ, you're bad enough on your own without having Shiggy as a disciple. He's got his mot at home, so don't you go corrupting him any more than you have already.'

Shiggy didn't understand what corrupting meant, but he

wasn't too worried. He was kind of getting the knack of these conversations and had almost stopped worrying about accidentally insulting someone. After all, he'd just been called a dirty bastard and *he* wasn't insulted. It seemed to Shiggy that in this country, you really had to go out of your way to cause offence. If your best buddy could be a wanker, a bollocks, a fucker and even a geebag – whatever that was – what exactly did you call someone you didn't like? The mind boggled. There must be some seriously bad words out there.

'So, what about your mot, Jimmy?' said Aesop.

'Ah, what about her ...'

'No sign?'

'No. It's a real fucking bummer. Can't believe it. Jaysis, I don't even want to talk about it.'

'Eh, so c'mere, with no mot ...'

'Yeah?'

'Well, I was just thinking ... with no mot, you won't be needing that prize you won, will you?'

'Piss off, Aesop!'

'Come on, ye stingy fuck! You won't be using it, will ye? Me and Sharon could go out for dinner and use the hotel room.'

'No bleedin' way, Aesop. You've already got your beady eyes on Shiggy's keg. Jaysis, you want to clean up from Saturday? You didn't even sing!'

'Go on, ye bollocks. Just 'cos I met someone nice. You were the one going on about spreading a little love around, remember?'

'You and Sharon? Are you winding me up? All you do is go at each other like a pair of mad rabbits.'

'That's a kind of love, isn't it?' Aesop said. 'Anyway, a nice meal, clean sheets ... ye never know, it might add a whole new dimension to it. Advance things along, y'know?'

Jimmy looked at him and shook his head.

'What a complete load of me bollocks. I'll tell you what,

Aesop. If I don't find Kayleigh in three months, and if you're still seeing Sharon, then you can have it. Okay? Christmas.'

'Ah Jaysis, Jimmy ...'

'Three months, Aesop. If she's your Superchick, then we'll find out and you're welcome to the prize. It's only three months. You're telling me you found Superchick and I'm telling you that if you did, then you'll still be with her at Christmas. I'll even throw in the taxi fare out of me own pocket so you don't have to give her a crossbar into town.'

'You have no faith in me, do you Jimmy?' Aesop was trying to act hurt. It worked on nearly everyone but Jimmy knew him too well.

'Of course I don't! I know what's going to happen, Aesop. She'll turn around one day and tell you that she'd like you to meet her folks. Ten seconds later you'll be halfway down the road hiding in a bush, rocking back and forth and sucking your thumb.'

'No I won't! Right. We'll fuckin' see. And c'mere, if I'm not with her at Christmas, then you keep the prize and I'll buy you the Zeppelin Remasters collection. Right?'

'You're mad, Aesop. Okay. Zeppelin versus the prize. Shiggy, you heard that, right?'

Shiggy heard, but hadn't a clue. He nodded anyway.

The other two sat back, Jimmy smiling confidently and Aesop wondering if he'd been a bit rash. Three months? That was about twelve weekends. He adjusted his crotch absently. It was a bit achy down there.

'Anyway, how are you going to find Kayleigh?' he said.

'I have a cool plan.'

'What plan?'

'The song.'

'What?'

'*Superchick*. It's a song, right? That's how this whole thing started. I'm going to write it. Properly, this time. Me last attempt was shite. I'm writing Superchick and then I'm going to get it on the radio and she'll hear it and know I lost the phone.'

'Are you serious? That's your cool plan, is it?'

'Yeah. Why not?'

'Jimmy, we've been in a band for years. What's the closest we ever came to getting a song on the radio?'

'Doesn't matter, Aesop. It's all about focus. I'm going for the Christmas Number One with this one.'

Aesop laughed.

'Yeah, right. We'll be on *Top of the Pops* so, will we? Dressed up as Santy, next to Slade?'

'Yep,' said Jimmy. There. He'd said it now. He'd hoped that putting the idea out there would give him confidence, but it hadn't really.

Aesop laughed again and headed to the toilet, singing.

'Jingle bells, jingle bells, I lost me bleedin' phone ...'

Jimmy gave him the finger and turned to Shiggy.

'What do you think, Shiggy. Ever record your own stuff?'

'Sree times, Jimmy. Difficult. And berry expensive.'

'Yeah, well, we'll see about that. I might be able to call in an old favour if I have to.'

He sat back again, drinking and thinking. It was a good idea. All he needed was to write a brilliant song and to be a lucky bastard. How hard could that be?

Aesop came back, still singing.

'Her number's gone, this nice young one, and now I'm on me own, Oh! jingle bells, jingle bells ...'

'Piss off, Aesop.'

'I think it's a great idea, Jimmy. And if we're playing Slane next summer, I want to abseil in from a helicopter, right? Would U2 be free to support us, do you think?'

'I'll ask The Edge when I see him at bingo later.'

'Ah, listen Jimmy. Are you serious? You've been moaning about finding this Superchick bird for weeks and the best idea you can come up with is to get yourself on the radio, singing her some homo fuckin' love song? Jimmy, get real. You need a better plan.'

'Like what?'

'I don't know. You must know people from Clontarf. Ask them do they know her. Look, she's not called Mary, is she? Can't be too many Kayleighs around. I'm not great at remembering girls' names, but I'd remember that one.'

'Aesop, you can't even remember spending the night with Katie, and you've known her for about fifteen years.'

'Yeah, well. It was a birthday party. There was a lot of jelly vodka shots in your fridge that night. Anyway, we're not talking about me. What's the chances of your song being Number One?'

'It doesn't have to be Number One, Aesop. Jesus. Once people hear it, that's a start.'

'But who's going to hear it?'

'We're in a band, Aesop, remember?'

'Ah, wait a bleedin' minute, Jimmy. You're not going to start asking the punters to help you find her, are you? Ah Jaysis, come on Jimmy. I'd be mortified! It's a rock band, not Sergeant Pepper's bleedin' Lonely Hearts Club Band.'

'Relax, will ye? I'll write the song, we'll play the song. Same as always. We'll record it and I'll try and get it on the radio. See what happens.'

'Does she even like you?'

'What?'

'Kayleigh. Does she even like you? Was it even her real number? Or her real name? You don't even know the girl, Jimmy. Maybe she's not interested.'

'Of course she's fucking interested! Why wouldn't she be? I sang a Frank Sinatra song for her, the prick. She was holding me hand and gazing into me eyes like I was ice cream. Big kiss at the end. Of course she likes me. Used to anyway. I didn't call her, so she might be a bit miffed now, but I'll sort that out. Her mates used to slag her when *Kayleigh* came out, but they'll be jealous as fuck by the time I'm finished with *Superchick*.'

'Ah Jimmy, you can't call it *Superchick* now.'

'Why not?'

'*Superchick*. Jimmy, it sounds like a bleedin' cartoon character. A cuddly little yellow bird in red underpants with a cape and X-ray vision. Call it something else. Call it ... well, you can't call it *Kayleigh* after Marillion, but call it something else. A girl that age wants a proper song.'

Jimmy smiled at him.

'So, you're coming round to the idea, then?'

Aesop sighed.

'I never said don't write the song, Jimmy. I just said don't get your hopes up about it being in the charts. And especially not a Christmas Number One, okay? Anyway, Wham are always Number One at Christmas, the bastards.'

'I sink it work.'

'What's that, Shiggy?' said Jimmy.

'Good idea. Write song. Good idea.'

'Thanks, Shiggy. Now do you hear that, Aesop? Shiggy reckons it's a good idea.'

'Shiggy's a spacer, Jimmy. He thinks jazz is a good idea.'

'And you think you and Sharon are a good idea. So we're all mad. Grand. Rock bands are s'posed to be a bit eccentric. What's the worst thing that could happen? We have a new song and I can finally stop trying to find words that rhyme with chick that aren't another word for penis. Jaysis, that's reason enough to do it; it has me fucking tormented. Fame and fortune will just be a bonus. Now. Up you go. It's your round.'

'It's Shiggy's round!'

'Aesop, Shiggy is currently in possession of a voucher for eighty pints of lager, most of which you'll probably end up drinking. Now get up there and buy him a pint. And me.'

'See that, Shiggy?' said Aesop, standing up. 'Singers.

They're all the bleedin' same. Never happy unless they're bossing people around the place.'

He started counting the change out of his pocket like he was broke.

'And c'mere,' said Jimmy. 'While you're up there, ask Dave will he ever turn that bleedin' CD off and play something else? It's doing my head in.' He drained his pint and looked at Shiggy.

'Babylon me bollocks ...'

Seventeen

Jimmy was trying really hard. It didn't help that he was just beginning to realise that most of the songs he wrote before were bollocks. Funny lyrics and a catchy tune, but not songs that you could look back on when you're sixty and say to your grandson, 'See that, young Billy? See how cool Grandad used to be?' It always came back to that for him. Art. Not in the sense that it had to be highbrow and arcane, but just ... ethereal or something. Timeless. Okay, so a funny pop song was a type of art, but he'd already tried that for *Superchick* and the result was just like everything else he'd ever written. He wanted this one to be different. Not just a three-minute giggle for people who were pissed off at work and wanted to unwind. He wanted people to hear this one and find themselves yearning to make love to the one they cared about most. Assuming it wasn't the cat or something weird like that.

He picked up the final result of his last effort. It wasn't that bad. He didn't really have a tune, or even a chorus, but that wasn't the point. The point was that Aesop had been right all along. It was juvenile. It had its place, but its place wasn't in Jimmy's current project:

I
I've loved a lot of women in my time on this blue ball
Some cute some smart some sexy, didn't matter loved them all
Dancer, lover, drinker, never knew which one to pick
'Til I found them all in one girl and I called her Superchick

II
That chick was unbelievable, I swear she'd read my mind
She knew exactly what I'd want, never bitched and never
    whined
She never dragged me shopping and I never met her folks
But she always looked amazing and she laughed at all my jokes

III

She loved to watch the football and her favourite food was
    steak
She could put her legs behind her head, she made me choco-
    late cake
Her idea of a quiet night in was pizza, beer and sex
She told me I'm amazing, and so much bigger than her ex

IV

She never wore a stitch in bed and she loved to wash my car
And when I got too drunk to drive, she'd collect me from the
    bar
She paid all her own phone bills and the fridge was never bare
Her favourite show was Star Trek and she hated Richard Gere

V

So what am I s'posed to do now that our love is on the rocks
How can I go back to normal chicks and dirty socks
I've thrown it all away because I listened to my dick
And she caught me with her sister – now I've lost my Super-
    chick

No. That wouldn't do at all, at all. If that ever went out on
the radio with a dedication to Kayleigh, he could pretty
much kiss her lovely arse goodbye. She was a Tony Bennett
girl, right? There had to be a middle ground between rock
and elevator music. Look at Tom Jones these last few years.
Young bands were queuing up to try and get the hairy Welsh
bollocks singing on their albums. He'd even heard Joe Dolan
doing a Lenny Kravitz song on the radio the other day. Yeah,
but what has that got to do with anything? Focus, Jimmy!

What about the title? Superchick. Jimmy wasn't sure any
more. *Superchick* wasn't really the name of a song you'd make
love by, was it? You might ride someone while it was on, but
probably only by coincidence. And anyway, what *was* making love as opposed to anything else? Jimmy thought about
it. He was pretty sure he'd done both – made love and ride.
What was the difference? He knew when he was doing one

as opposed to the other ... hmm. Making love. One. There had to be soft light. Two. You had to have brushed your teeth fairly recently. Three. Both of you had to be trying not to make fart noises from anywhere. Those were the three main ingredients. He couldn't remember ever having made love without at least two of them being in the picture. If they weren't, then it was just riding. Of course, the fact that at least two of them were in the picture meant you probably also gave a shit about the person you were with, so that took care of that side of things.

So anyway, could a song called *Superchick* set the mood? Eh, no. Probably not. Right. So he'd have to change the title. No point in doing that until he knew a bit more about the song. He'd get back to that later. Christ he was getting nowhere, he thought, looking dejectedly at the blank page in front of him and the clock over the mantelpiece. He stood up and went to the toilet, splashing water on his face and looking in the mirror. He'd been at it for a solid hour and all he had to show for it were two red, fist-shaped marks on his cheeks.

Back at his notepad he decided that he wouldn't get up again until he had a verse done. No coffee, no wee-wee, no messing about on the guitar. Okay, now where were we?

Making love. Yes. No. Hang on a minute. Since when was that the point of the song? He'd never even made love to Kayleigh. Imagining it at a time like this would only be a distraction. He was writing the song for a girl he barely knew. He'd need to go easy on the whole lovemaking side of things. Some women could be funny like that. She'd said something about the Marillion song being nice, but it wasn't for *her*. Well this one would be. And Tony Bennett, Bobby Darin, Sinatra and all the rest of them could get stuffed. This was Jimmy's song and he'd do it his way. *My Way.* Sinatra again. Ah will you stop getting distracted, you arsehole?

He closed his eyes and tried to remember what he'd felt

when he saw her first. Well, the first thing he'd felt was lust. No point in denying that. He'd wanted nothing more than to walk over and give her one right there and then, yelling 'Who's yer Daddy?' and 'Go on ye good thing!' at the top of his voice, one hand twirling overhead and the other one smacking the arse off her. Hmm ... yeah ... wasn't really the tone he was after though, was it? So, what about later on? When he went over and spoke to her. God, he just felt blown away by her. *You blow me, just blow me away ...*' You blow me?! Oh, I'd say she'd love that, yeah. Oh Jimmy, no one's ever said that to me before. C'mon, Jimmy! What blew you away, you useless bastard? Her eyes. Yeah. And smile. Seeing her smile made him want to own her. To be able to take her out when he was feeling down and look at her. No, you couldn't say that either. Sounded like he has her locked under the stairs or something. Women could be funny about that stuff as well.

But it *was* her smile. It made her face shine. Was there any way to say that without sounding like Chris De Burgh? He scribbled a few words down – smile, shining face, bright eyes – and sat back again to think. So she was pretty, but it had to be more than that. Jimmy knew lots of pretty girls, but none of them made him feel faintly nauseous when he spoke to them the way she did. She had some kind of aura around her. It grabbed you like a tractor beam and held your attention, even when she wasn't looking at you. It was her presence. Like she wasn't there in the same way everyone else was there. She was like a princess or an angel or something. Kind of otherworldly. He wrote down some more snippets and looked over them. He grimaced, cursing himself. Otherworldly, tractor beam, princess ... Jesus, throw in a Wookie and you had *Star Wars*.

He closed his eyes tightly again.

When she talked to him he felt special. At one stage, when some bloke had walked past the table and she glanced up, he'd gotten a pang of jealousy, like the guy was an interloping bastard coming to spoil everything. The bloke hadn't even stopped or looked down, but Jimmy knew his type all right as the smug prick glided past. So she made him feel special. And a bit psychotic. Oh, perfect. What rhymes with psychotic? Neurotic? This is brilliant stuff, Jimmy. You should put this in for the Eurovision, you muppet.

There was half an hour of going around in circles, wondering why every single heartfelt lyric he came upon sounded old and clichéd, before Jimmy finally caught on to the reason why she made him feel the way he did when he thought of her. It wasn't because she was beautiful, although she was. It wasn't because she was a cool person to talk to, although she was that too. It was more subtle than that. It was because when they talked, and even when they were singing together, he got the impression that there was nowhere on the planet that she'd rather be than right there with him. He didn't think he'd ever commanded that kind of attention before. Not on the stage. Not at work.

Even Sandra – and Jimmy and Sandra had been close – could be sitting astride him; eyes closed, head back and loving it, but Jimmy knew in his heart and soul that it was no coincidence that, in all their time together, they had never once made love at the same time that Coronation Street was on the telly.

He didn't get that with Kayleigh. He had her full attention. Completely and utterly. That's what had overwhelmed him. Jimmy stood up and shook his head. Jesus. What did that mean? That he loved being the centre of attention? Sure, he knew that already! No, he knew what it meant. It meant she felt the same way as he did. He had been rapt. So had she. Whatever she'd been looking for, she'd found it. So had he. Love at first sight. For both of them. Oh fucking hell, was it that? And then he goes and loses his phone?

He picked up the pen again. Ten minutes later he threw

it at the wall. He picked it up and sat down. He was in his underpants now, the heating on full and the house roasting, but he didn't want to move until he had a start. He was sweating and uncomfortable, the pen slipping in his hand and his arm sliding off his bare leg. The fabric of the arm-chair was making his back itchy. He looked at the clock. Going on two in the morning. He'd be completely crap in work. Just write something, Jimmy. Anything at all. Just get started for fuck sake!

He tried, but scribbled it out again. A thousand love songs were whipping through his mind but they all sounded the same – *I love you, it's true, hold me in your arms, you make me feel so good, the day I met you, I need you, please say you will, the fire in your eyes, the love I feel, I need your love, I love your smile* ...

Faster and faster ...

You're my love, take my hand, hand in hand, hold my hand, share my life, be my wife, only you, tell me please, love of my life, big love, happy in love, the greatest love, my only love, love me love, I can't live, I love my love ...

'Ah, fuck this!' Jimmy yelled at himself and stood up again. He went out and turned off the heat. This was stupid. He ran upstairs to the bathroom and took off his jocks, throwing them on the floor and hopping into the shower. Full blast on cold. Ten minutes of that would bloody-well wake him up. Two seconds later he screamed and jumped out again, landing on his underpants, slipping and putting his hand down the toilet to stop himself from cracking his skull open on the sink. He sat there for a minute, shivering, wet and naked on the floor, and then pulled his hand out of the bowl, looking at it like he'd never seen it before. Then he started to laugh. Okay. So, you reckon you're in control of the situation yet, Jimmy?

He stood up, washed his hands. He needed to stay calm. He'd been going about it all wrong, he decided. You didn't have to write verse by verse. If he was going to write a special song, he couldn't expect a normal approach to work, could he? So, he needed a new approach. Something he'd never done before. He looked around his living-room; hoping for something to catch his eye, kick it off. The place was a complete mess. There wasn't much inspiration for the Love Song of the Century in an empty pizza box, four coffee mugs and a small pile of beer cans, was there? He decided to do a quick tidy-up. It was late and he was tired but some type of activity might do the trick. He collected an armful of crap from around the room, bringing it out into the kitchen and dumping it on the table. He stood there for a minute, looking at it. Nothing.

The cans collapsed and fell clanging to the floor. He bent to pick them up and then it all happened very suddenly.

One of them was a can from Shiggy's Japanese beer, covered with the funny writing and the picture of the dragon-thing. He stood up, looking at the can in amazement. The problem he was having with the song was that he couldn't come up with a single, solitary lyric that wasn't immediately recognisable from some other bastard's song. Everyone had heard it all before ... in English!

Who said the song had to be in English? He ran back into the living-room with the can and sat down, placing it on the coffee table in front of him. There was only one choice. Obviously, he couldn't write it in Japanese, could he? This was his song. He didn't want to have Shiggy write it for him, or even translate. And how would he get a Japanese song on the radio? French was out too. He hadn't spoken a work of it since the Leaving Certificate, and he was crap even then. And Irish radio wouldn't play a song in French either. Which left ...

Why not? He'd spent five summers in the *Gaeltacht* – an Irish-speaking region in the west – speaking it all day, every day. Okay, he was only a kid then but he was sure he was still pretty good at it. Honours in the Leaving. There weren't too many songs on the radio in Irish, but there were some, right? Sure Clannad even got onto *Top of the Pops* in England with *Harry's Game* and even he didn't know what the hell that was supposed to be about. Hot House Flowers did it. Sinead O'Connor did it. Enya. Kila. The Corrs probably did it, although he couldn't think of a song offhand. He was excited now. He could say whatever he wanted in Irish and not have it sound like a zillion other songs. Would Kayleigh remember it from school? She'd need to be able to understand it. He didn't know. He'd have to make the Irish fairly easy just in case. Well, that wasn't a problem. He wasn't exactly bloody Seán Bán Breathnach, was he?

There was another advantage too. The song would probably end up being a bit sad, and there wasn't a language in the world could hold a match to Irish if you were a miserable bastard trying to express yourself. All you needed to do was go through the Irish education system to see that. They were beautifully written, but Jimmy must have studied about fifty poems in Irish and he couldn't remember a single fucking happy poet among the lot of them. The closest they ever came was if they were writing the poem when they were old, and then they were only happy because they'd be dead soon. The rest of them were fighting the British and getting hung, weeping after some bird that didn't love them because they had no land, having their marriages arranged, getting excommunicated or transported to Van Dieman's Land for robbing grain, digging up ruined spuds, being cold, hungry, afraid of the priest and generally having a shite time of it and it pissing rain.

Plus, you could never be in control of your emotions in Irish. It was always passive. You could never just *be* angry or sad – there had to be anger or sadness *on* you. Like you were minding your own jovial business when all of a sudden this sensation came out of nowhere and put a bummer on you. It could be incredibly expressive when translated directly into English. Irish guys had been using that for ages. It only worked, though, on foreign girls. Try telling an Irish girl that gazing into her eyes brings a terrible feeling of helplessness to your heart, and you're probably setting yourself up for a nasty fall. But foreign women loved it. It may take a bit longer to get your message across in the disco in Crete, and you trying to throw a length into the little English tart with the sunburnt tits, but the thinking is that she'll always appreciate the extra little bit of glamour, and there could be a blowjob in it for yourself.

Four hours later he was done. The sun was half-heartedly trying to poke through thick grey clouds and Jimmy lay back on the armchair, shattered, his notebook still gripped tightly.

Caillte

Fíon a dhéanu sí d'uisce
An falla a dhéanu mé, briste
Tugtha di

Ag luí dom san oiche gan sos,
Á smaoineamh, le fuarallais ar bos
Á lorg, fós

Go gcloise sí, gcuimhní sí, tá súil a'am
Go dtuige sí nach rogaire mé, tá dúil a'am
Caillte atáim.

Amharc uirthi, a maolódh mo chroí ... caillte
An leannán ba cheart a bheith a'am, ach níl neart ... caillte
An seáns canadh uair eile, casadh uair eile,
Le chéile
Le Kayleigh
Caillte

Next to it was the translation. God, it even worked in English he thought, as his eyes closed. The last thing he remembered doing was calling the office to say he was sick and then he conked out and dreamt of himself and Kayleigh being fourteen years old, dancing the Walls of Limerick in a field, and it pissing rain ...

Lost

She made wine from water
The wall I made is broken
I need her

I lie at night without rest
Thinking of her, a cold sweat on my hands
Still looking for her

That she might hear, might remember, I hope
That she understands I'm for real, I hope;
I'm lost

A glimpse of her, to ease my heart ... lost
The girl that should be mine, what can I do ... lost
The chance to sing again, dance again
Together
With Kayleigh
Lost

Eighteen

Early on Saturday afternoon, Jimmy picked up the phone and dialled. It wasn't a number he thought he'd ever find himself punching into a phone again, but sometimes you just had to do things even when you didn't want to. He'd spent a whole week in the Isle of Man with his folks when he was fifteen and that hadn't killed him. He just needed to keep his head. He took a deep breath.

'Hello?'

'Sandra?'

'Jimmy?!'

'Yeah.'

'Ah, Jimmy why are you calling? There's nothing to talk about, okay? We've gone over it all already. You have to just try and move on.'

'Sandra ...'

'No Jimmy, I won't do this. Please, you're only making it more difficult than it has to be. Please, Jimmy.'

'Eh, Sandra ...'

'We had our time together, Jimmy. It was great, but it's over. I mean, of course I'd like us to be friends but you made it very clear the last time that you're not interested in that. I mean, why do you want to talk to me now? Can you not see ...'

'Actually Sandra, I wanted to talk to Beano.'

'Oh.'

'Is he there?'

'Em ... yes, he's upstairs. But Jimmy, you're not going to start any trouble, are you? Don't even go there. Because I can tell you, if you're just trying to ...'

'I just want to talk to him, Sandra. It's not about you and me.'

There was a slight pause.

'Well ... okay. Hang on.'

Jimmy waited while she went to get him. He was standing in the kitchen, one hand clenched into a fist. He hated that one, 'Don't even go there'. Nearly every girl he knew was using it now, like it made them feel empowered or something. Real women's libbers – the ones with moustaches – were probably going mad.

Sandra was really starting to bug him now but he couldn't afford to lose the rag with her. His jaw started to hurt and he realised that he'd been grinding his teeth to keep from yelling at her to just shut the fuck up and get Beano on the phone. Did she really think he was that sad? That he'd be calling her up to try and get her back? Bollocks to that. He wouldn't take her back now if she came with a year's supply of Jaffa cakes.

'Yeah?'

'Beano, it's Jimmy.'

'I know.'

'You want to do me a favour?' Jimmy had decided to take the direct approach. There was no point in pretending that nothing had happened and that they were all best mates.

'Do you a favour? Jimmy, every time I see you all you do is tell me to fuck off. Why should I do you a favour? The last thing ...'

'Will you shut the fuck up Beano and listen a minute, will ye?'

'What? You called me, you cheeky bollocks. You can't talk to me like that. Who the fuck do you think you are? Me and Sandra are together now, Jimmy. We're getting on grand. You calling up and fucking giving me abuse about it just makes you look like a stupid bastard and ...'

'Blah blah fucking blah Beano. I don't give a shite about you and Sandra, okay?'

'Well what do you want, then?'

'I hear you've put a band together and you're making a CD.'

That seemed to throw Beano a little.

'Yeah ... so what?' He was on the defensive now, sounding guarded.

'So I presume that your uncle is helping you out.'

'He might be.'

'He is, Beano. How else could you afford to record a CD? You can't even afford to buy a CD.'

'Are you going to tell me what you want, Jimmy?'

'When you're in the recording studio, I want to record a song of me own with the band. My band.'

'You what?! Why should I let you do that? We only have the place for a weekend. I don't believe this! Anyway, you've been such a prick about everything for the last ...'

'I've been a prick? Who's the one who started riding my girlfriend? And you call me a cheeky bollocks?'

'I thought you said you didn't care about that.'

'I don't care about it now, Beano, but I fucking cared about it when I found out about it. I cared about it when every cunt in Dublin was talking about me behind me back. And I cared about it when I had to tell me Ma that her darling Sandra wouldn't be coming around on Wednesday to help her make the curtains. You fucking owe me.'

'I don't owe you fuck all. I don't believe you're even asking me. You're the one with the big job. Why don't you get your own studio?'

'Because, Einstein, if your uncle has set this up and he's been in the music business for years, he's not going to go to all this trouble to help you out only to let you in there on your own, is he? Do you know how to set up all the instruments? No. Do you know how to work professional mixing and recording gear? No. Do you know the first thing about making an album? Do you fuck. Unless being a dopey, dopey bastard runs in the family, your uncle will have an engineer there who knows what he's doing. And someone to produce it. Am I right?'

'Do y'know something Jimmy ...?'

'Am I right, Beano? It's not a brain teaser.'

Jimmy heard Beano sigh.

'Me uncle's producing it. Someone he knows will be helping out with the sound and all. But I still don't know what any of that has to do with you.'

'I told you. I want to record a song and I want to do it properly. I can get a studio but where am I going to get a decent engineer and producer?'

'I don't give a shite where you get them Jimmy, but you're not using mine. The only thing I owe you is a pain in the arse.'

Jimmy started pacing the kitchen. He was hoping it wouldn't come to this, that he'd be able to pull a guilt trip on Beano. Apparently not. Time to put an ace on the table.

'What if I helped you on the CD?'

'Help me? Help me what? I don't need your help. This is my band, Jimmy. The last thing I want is Jimmy Collins waltzing in like he owns the place and telling everyone what to do. Ah, now I see. That's what this is all about, isn't it? You want to be able to say you made the CD. It was all your ideas and your work. You're bullin' that I'm doing this before you are. No chance, Jimmy. Nice try, but fuck off.'

'Beano, cop on. I've been playing music for years. Why the fuck would I want to record a CD of someone else's work? Especially yours.'

'Well then tell me, Jimmy the big bleedin' star, what can you do that I can't do?'

'Well, for one thing, Beano, I can play the guitar. How's that for starters?'

'I can play the guitar, Jimmy. Maybe I'm not as good as you yet, but I will be. And anyway, you don't have to be a brilliant guitarist. Once you can play what you need to be

209

able to play. I won't be putting big solos in everything because I'm not a fucking egomaniac like some people.'

'Whatever, Beano. What I'm telling you is that I'd be willing to play the guitar on your CD. I'll come in and play whatever you want. Rhythm, solos, whatever. You say what you want, and I'll do it. I'll play stuff, show you how to play it for afterwards, and I won't even tell anyone it was me playing. Your CD won't sound like it has some ten-year-old with a toy banjo banging away on it, and you'll be able to learn all the bits so you can play them live once it's done. The whole weekend, Beano. When I'm not recording for you or doing my own song, I'll be teaching you and I'll sit there and say fuck all unless I'm asked. No one will ever know I was playing on the CD if you can learn the parts and play them in gigs. No mention of me on the sleeve or anything. Now, what do you think?'

'Eh ...' Beano was trying to think fast. It wasn't his strong point.

'I'll tell you what, Beano. Have a think about it and call me back in half an hour, right? I'm at home.'

'Okay.' Beano hung up. Jimmy finally stopped pacing and went over to the sink to turn on the kettle. Beano would go for it. He probably thought Jimmy was trying to pull some kind of fast one, but the temptation would be too great. Even he couldn't be insane enough to think he was a good enough musician to make an actual album. In fact, he'd probably been shitting himself about the whole thing, worried that his uncle would find out just how crap he was. This would be his way out. He was deluding himself if he thought Jimmy could really teach him a whole CD worth of guitar parts in a weekend, but that wasn't Jimmy's problem.

It didn't even take half an hour. Ten minutes later the phone rang.

'Jimmy?'

'Yeah.'

'What's to stop you going ahead and telling everyone you played on the CD?'

'Me. I told you I wouldn't do that.'

'Yeah, but what's stopping you doing it anyway?'

'Beano, I might think you're a wanker but I've never lied to you, have I? Believe me, I won't want anyone knowing I played on the stupid fucking thing any more than you will. I've got me reputation to think of, y'know?'

'Jesus, for someone who's trying to get a favour you've a strange way of going about it.'

'It's not a favour any more, Beano. If I'm playing on the record, then it's a simple business arrangement. You get me; I get the studio for a couple of hours. How many songs are you doing anyway?'

'Four.'

'Four? Ah, right. So it's a double album, then?'

'It's an EP, smart arse. I've only been writing for a few months and I've four songs that I think are good enough. You could have heard three of them when I was playing with you but you don't exactly welcome other people's artistic input with open arms, do you?'

'I never knew you were writing songs, Beano. All you had to do was play them for me. I was never a bastard about things like that. We played a few of Aesop's songs didn't we?'

'Yeah. Your best mate Aesop. Anyway, bollocks. Even if you liked them, which you wouldn't have, you'd just have made them sound like your own songs. They're mine.'

'Beano, there's no point in having a row about that now, is there? I'm sorry you felt that way about your songs but I didn't know, and anyway I didn't think you were the kind of bloke that wrote music, okay? I'm still having fucking difficulty with it, to be honest. It's not like I ever mistook you for a talented bastard, is it? Who's your singer?'

'Sandra.'

'Sandra?! Ah, for Christ ...'

211

'See what I mean? When did you ever give her a chance to sing? Too busy being fuckin' Mick Jagger, so you were. No one else was allowed to have a bit of the spotlight.'

That was stupid. Sandra never wanted to sing. He'd asked her a few times and she always said no. It wasn't that she had a crap voice, because she hadn't. She was no Bette Midler but she was all right. The problem was that she was too shy for it. He'd even asked her up when they were in the middle of a gig once, hoping that putting her on the spot would do it, but she just ran into the toilet. Jimmy would have loved her to get up there but he couldn't keep an audience hanging on in the middle of a gig while he tried to coax her into it. Ah go on, go on, go on, go on, go on, and the punters all pissing off to the bar. He'd never asked her after that and she never seemed to mind. So, what did this mean? That he should have been more patient? Ah Christ, this wasn't the time ...

'Okay Beano, Sandra's the singer. Good for her. I'm glad, right? So are we set, then? I play the guitar for you and we get the studio for a few hours?'

'Yeah. Except on one condition.'

'What?'

'You've a gig tonight, right?'

'Yeah ...'

'Right. During your break, my band gets up and plays the four songs. We've been practising them, but I want to play them for an audience.'

'No fucking way, Beano. Are you mad? Between sets? The audience will all go home!'

'They won't go home, Jimmy. Ye never know, they might even like us more than they like you.'

'What are the chances of that, you amazingly stupid bastard?'

'That's the deal, Jimmy. Take it or leave it.'

Jimmy thought about it for a minute. He wasn't concerned that Beano's band would blow them off the stage, but he was worried that they'd be crap and that was the last thing he wanted. It would reflect badly on him and it would be embarrassing for everyone. If Beano got laughed out of it, then he might chicken out of doing the recording too.

'Beano ...'

'I'm serious, Jimmy. That's the way it is.'

Jimmy took the phone away from his ear and looked blankly at the wall for a minute. He really didn't want this. On the other hand, he really wanted an experienced engineer and producer. He didn't know how to work a studio any more than Beano did and radio stations don't play songs that were put down in someone's garage with a tape recorder. And he thought of Kayleigh. There was no point in backing out now.

'Okay,' he said.

'Grand. We start recording this day week. Six in the morning. Are you free?'

'At six on a Saturday morning? No I'm washing me hair ye spa. Of course I'm bleedin' free.'

'Good. So, what time tonight?'

'We'll break between ten and half ten. That's as long as you've got, Beano. No fucking around. At half ten, you're off. If you want to do a sound check, then be there before six. Call John and tell him I said it's okay. At seven we're setting up and I don't want your shit all over the stage, right?'

'No problem, Jimmy. We'll be gone before you even get there.'

'Good. I'll introduce you at ten when we're done. If you're not there, then tough shit.'

'Why wouldn't we be there?'

'I don't know. I'm hoping you'll get lost or something. What's the name of your band?'

'Lavender's Teardrop.'

'Right. Ten o'clock, Beano.'

'Grand. Seeya so, Jimmy mate.'

'Fuck off, Beano.'

Jimmy hung up and shook his head.

Lavender's Teardrop. The arse hole.

Jimmy went to the pub a bit earlier than usual. He wanted to see Beano's band doing their sound check so he'd know what to expect later on. If they were really terrible he'd have time to think of something to do about it, although he was committed now and couldn't really tell Beano he wasn't going to be able to play. He also wanted to get a look at this bass player that might have been in the band instead of Shiggy and, of course, seeing how Sandra got on would be interesting. When he got there they were nearly finished. He stood at the bar, gave John a nod and waited for his pint. There was no one else in the place and he stayed well back where they wouldn't notice him.

It wasn't as bad as he'd imagined it would be. They were using a drum machine, so Beano was obviously still looking for someone there. The bass player was clearly talented but he looked like he was trying too hard to impress everyone. There was a lot of flashy slapping and popping going on where a simple rhythm would have suited Beano's mediocre guitar parts, and the lyrics, much better. Beano himself was bent over slightly, scowling pointedly at his left hand like he thought he could intimidate his fingers into playing the right notes. He wasn't trying to do anything spectacular, but he was concentrating so hard on not making any mistakes that he looked constipated. Sandra's singing sounded pretty good but she was stiff as a board, hands down by her side and her face a pale green even from ten metres away.

Jimmy saw immediately that there were two main problems. For one thing, the song itself seemed to be about loving all the little animals in the world. That would go down like a fart in a Ford Fiesta in McGuigans on a Saturday night.

Jimmy could only suppose that Sandra had had something to do with the lyrics. The other problem was the way they looked. Scared shitless or, in the case of the bass player, bored. When the only member of your band that seems to be having a bit of a laugh is the drum machine, then you've got a problem.

But they weren't completely shite. It came naturally to Jimmy after all these years, but he knew that being comfortable on the stage took some time. A band like Lavender's Teardrop – Jesus, what a fucking name – would be fine for a Monday or a Tuesday night in a pub, but this was Saturday night in McGuigans. By ten o'clock, the punters would all be well on the way and they might start taking the piss. Jimmy was a bit nervous about that. Beano could bottle out of the whole thing and, despite everything, he didn't particularly want to see Sandra cry in front of everyone at his gig.

When they finished the song Jimmy took a deep breath and walked up towards the stage, clapping and smiling.

'Good stuff, lads. I think you might have something there.'

'Oh God. Jimmy!' said Sandra, hands to her mouth. 'I'm scarlet!'

'Howya, Sandra. Beano,' he said. Then he turned to the bass player. 'I'm Jimmy Collins. Howzit goin'?'

'Mick Fegan. Howya.'

'What did you think, Jimmy?' said Beano.

Jimmy wasn't about to tell him what he really thought, and he didn't really want to tell him to fuck off this time either. Beano looked like a little child who had just come off a football pitch and wanted his Daddy's approval. Jimmy took another breath.

'A lot better than I was expecting, to be honest. You sounded really good. Fair play to yiz,' he said. He knew that anything better than that would sound like bollocks.

'Thanks. I'm not sure about the timing, but I think we're getting there. I'm a bit nervous though,' said Beano.

'Sure, I'm always nervous,' said Jimmy. 'Don't mind that. It means you'll do your best. The crowd in here later will be up for a good time. They'll love it. You'll be grand.'

He turned to Sandra.

'Sandra, you sounded brilliant. Well done.'

'Ah, give over. God, I was shaking and there's no one even here. What will I be like later on? This all sounded like a great idea a few weeks ago. I'm not even sure I can do it now.'

'Listen, Sandra. You've got a great voice. You're bound to be a bit shaky with a crowd of people watching you, but there's nothing you can do about that. Look, see that light up there? And that one? And the one over the bar? They'll all be on when you're playing tonight and they'll be shining right in your face. You won't even be able to see most of the people in here, just the ones at the front. It'll be grand.'

'Easy for you to say, Jimmy.'

'Ah stop. I'm always shitting myself before I go on. Once you get going you'll be flying and when it's over you'll be buzzing all night. Have a couple of drinks beforehand. Calm you down.' Jimmy smiled. He wasn't just being nice. He actually felt a bit sorry for them. He'd been where they were at one time, and in a weird way he knew that all the shit that had gone on between them would have no place here to-night. Tonight was about the gig. They were too worked up to concentrate on that and still be defensive and guilty in front of Jimmy and that suited Jimmy just fine. This was a big gig for him too. He didn't want to be distracted.

'Thanks, Jimmy. And thanks for letting us do this. Beano told me about the arrangement.'

Jimmy shrugged.

'Something for everyone, Sandra.'

'Well, thanks anyway. Maybe we can all get on with each other afterwards? I hope so ...'

She didn't look much better after his efforts to reassure

her, but at least she was smiling now, Jimmy saw. That was important. Even if she was completely crap later on, she was still a gorgeous-looking bird and a smile would go a long way towards keeping any bastards in the audience from giving her grief. Tucking in that shirt so that her diddies stuck out wouldn't hurt either, but he wasn't going to be the one to suggest it.

'Sure we'll see, right?'

'Hmm. Well, we're off for to get some dinner now. Not that I'll be able to eat anything. Seeya later, Jimmy.'

'Seeya,' said Jimmy. He nodded at the others and went back to the bar to drink his pint while they cleared their gear off the stage. Aesop and Shiggy would be here in another fifteen minutes.

'Is that your Sandra?' said John, stacking glasses on a shelf.

'Not any more John,' said Jimmy.

'Oh. Right. Sorry about that.'

'Nah. Didn't work out. She obviously thought her musical career would go further if she started going out with Beano.'

'Well it might Jimmy, but I seriously fucking doubt it. They're a bit shite, aren't they? What was that she was singing, something about a cat and a dog and a little hedgehog? From *Bosco*, is it? I think I heard my little one singing along to something like that on the telly.'

Jimmy smiled.

'Ah, they're only starting out, sure.'

'Yeah, well good luck to them. You're being very nice, though. Letting them play during your break. With Sandra and Beano and all, y'know?'

'Bygones John,' said Jimmy, sipping his pint.

'Bygones me hole,' said John, walking away down the bar to get more glasses out of the dishwasher. 'I know what I'd have fucking told Beano ...' he was mumbling, as he went out of earshot.

Jimmy smiled. Tongues would be wagging again tonight.

'Where's Shiggy?' asked Aesop.

'He's in the jacks,' said Jimmy. 'You look like shite.'

Aesop was pale and looked like he had a cold.

'I'm a bit run down.'

'Do you have Vitamin C? Me Mam always gave us that. It's cool.'

'It's not vitamins I need, Jimmy; it's a pint of coffee and a fresh mickey,' said Aesop, plonking himself onto a bar stool with a grimace.

'Oh right,' said Jimmy, smiling. 'Going well with Sharon, then?'

'Brilliant,' said Aesop, with his eyes closed. 'I'm in love. And y'know something? They're right. Love hurts.' He stood up to stretch with one hand on his back like an old gardener, and sat back down again.

'Jesus, look at you. Why don't you just tell her you're tired or have to get up early or something?'

'Jaysis, I can't do that, Jimmy. She might tell people. I have a reputation with the ladies, y'know?'

'Yeah, I know all about your reputation with the ladies, Aesop, but I think you might be overestimating how much it endears you to them.'

'No way. Me and Sharon are going all the way. You're just trying to get out of giving me that prize you won.'

'Believe me Aesop, I'm not. But do you think it's worth it? You can't keep this up for three months. Look at you! She'll have you destroyed.'

'It's not her that's the problem. Since Wednesday she's had two mates around. That's four of us going at it, in one queen-sized bed. I've only ever dreamt about it. Who was it said that? The writer bloke? Y'know, about not wishing for something too hard or you might get it and then you'd be completely fucking fucked.'

'You'd be completely fucking fucked? Yeah, that sounds like something George Bernard Shaw might say. I'll tell you something Aesop, it all sounds a bit weird to me. Normal women don't go around hopping into bed with a gaggle of their mates and some bloke. You'd want to watch yourself.'

'I know, I know. I might say something tomorrow.'

'Is she not coming tonight?'

'Jaysis, no. They have a gig in Athlone, thank fuck. She'll be back up tomorrow morning. Jimmy, can I sleep in your gaff tonight? She knows where I live and if I'm not in her place when she gets back, she'll be around to my place first thing for me to sneak her past me Da. I need a decent night's kip. Please?'

'Yeah, whatever. You're a terrible gobshite though Aesop, y'know that?'

'Don't, Jimmy. I'm feeling fragile. I'll be grand in a bit if no one talks to me.' He paused. 'Eh, what's Shiggy doing?' Shiggy had just come out of the toilet and was standing under a stage light, holding a small mirror up to his face.

'I don't ...' said Jimmy, looking over. 'Hey Shiggy, what are you doing?'

'Hi. Hey, hi Aesop! *Anno*, pruck eyebrow,' said Shiggy, holding up the mirror and a tweezers for them.

'Did he say he's plucking his eyebrows?' said Aesop, who had his eyes closed again.

'I think so,' said Jimmy.

'For what?'

'I don't know. Should I ask him?'

'Well, I think someone should ask him. If he's a fag then I want to know before the band goes on the road and we're sharing hotel rooms.'

'Shiggy, why are you plucking your eyebrows?' called Jimmy.

Shiggy walked over.

'See?' he said, facing into the light and holding his head up to them.

'See what?'

'Straight ryne.' He turned his face so that the other eyebrow was illuminated. 'Straight ryne,' he said again. 'See? Good, *ne*?'

'Eh, yeah. That's lovely,' said Jimmy, nodding slowly. 'Very straight line.'

'Sanks,' said Shiggy, smiling and walking back to the stage. He put the mirror away and starting unpacking his new bass.

'Well that was a bit weird,' said Aesop, looking after him.

'Hmm ...' said Jimmy. He was running a finger along his own eyebrows, thinking.

'So, would you say he's a fag?' said Aesop.

'Hmm? Oh God. What is it with you and gay people, Aesop?' said Jimmy. 'It's not as if they're always following you around the place, is it, waving and winking and blowing fucking kisses at you. Can you not just leave them alone? Maybe Shiggy just has a thing about eyebrows.'

'Yeah. That must be it. Why would he want straight eyebrows, but?'

'I don't know, do I?' said Jimmy.

'Hmm ... maybe I'll ask Jennifer later. Do you think he shaves his legs as well?'

'Oh, fuck off Aesop,' said Jimmy, starting towards the stage to set up. 'Maybe it's a Japanese thing. He can shave his arse and wear a peephole bra, for all I care. Once he plays that bass, I don't give a shite what else he's into.'

'Yeah. Still, but. It's not normal ...' said Aesop.

'You're bloody one to talk Aesop,' said Jimmy, turning back. 'What have you been up to all week, you fucking strange bastard? Now get your shit together. There'll be a lot of women in here tonight and they'll be wanting you to be on form for them.'

'Fuck them,' said Aesop to himself, wincing.

He sat there on his own for a minute, and then slowly stood up. There wasn't a bit of him that wasn't sore from those three mad tarts and now he had to play the drums for two and a half hours, while fending off a pub full of women.

He moved slowly towards the stage, idly wondering if this George Bernard Shaw bloke ever had these kinds of problems and deciding that he probably did.

Nineteen

Marco and Jennifer arrived holding hands, grinning and gazing at each other.

'Howyiz lads,' said Jimmy.

'Hi Jimmy,' said Marco. 'All set for tonight?'

'Ah yeah. I've even organised a surprise act for the break. Should be good,' said Jimmy. Or interesting anyway, he was thinking.

'Hiya Jimmy,' said Jennifer. She was blushing. Were they after doing it around the back lane before they came in?

'Jen. You look great.'

'Thanks,' she said, smiling and pulling Marco closer. He giggled back and hugged her.

Ah fuck this, thought Jimmy. If that's the mood this pair is going to be in all night then I'm keeping the hell away from them.

'Listen,' he said, 'I need to get ready. We're on in a few minutes. I'll talk to yiz later, all right?'

He walked over to where Shiggy and Aesop were looking at the set list next to the stage. The place was nearly full now and it was getting noisy. Jimmy was nervous. For one thing, his arrangement with Beano was starting to feel like a bad idea. That stupid fucking band wasn't nearly ready. And it was Shiggy's first gig, so anything could happen. As well as that, this was his first 'public appearance' since he'd met Kayleigh. There was always the chance – a tiny, tiny chance – that she'd turn up. She knew the name of the band. She knew how to read the entertainment section of the paper. If she wasn't too pissed off at Jimmy for standing her up, then she might come along to give him another chance. Jimmy had the jitters.

'All ready, lads?' he said, rubbing his hands together.

'Excuse me?' said Shiggy, still frowning at Aesop's terrible handwriting.

'I said, are you ready? You know – bass tuned up, mike levels set, eyebrows nice and straight?'

'Oh, yes. Sure. No ploblem.'

'Aesop?'

'I think so, Jimmy. I just need to stretch me back out a bit. Shiggy's been showing me some stuff. Eh, Chee Chai or something.'

'*Tai Chi*,' said Shiggy, without looking up.

'Yeah, that's it. Look Jimmy, this is The Cobra. He moves quickly and gracefully, in harmony with his prey, doesn't he Shiggy?' He stood on one leg and reached over his head with both hands, linking his fingers together. Then he leaned his head back. This threw him off balance and he fell sideways into a mike stand on the stage, taking it with him to the floor and ending up with his feet tangled in the lead and his head poking into the bass drum, moaning.

'Me fuckin' leg ...'

'Yeah, that was beautiful Aesop,' said Jimmy, helping him up. 'He sneaks up on his prey, does he, this fucking cobra? Christ. He wouldn't want to be fucking hungry, would he? Stop messing, ye spa. You're bad enough without a broken neck as well. Shiggy, could you not show him an easier one? The Sheep or something.'

'No sheep, Jimmy.'

'Well, something then. Jesus. Come on. We'd better get a move on before he tries the Kangaroo and fucking wrecks the gaff.'

Jimmy gave John at the bar a nod and the three of them stepped onto the stage. This was it. Shiggy the bass player. There was no doubt that he could play the thing but this was a real gig. This was where they'd all know if it was going to work out or not. Trial by fire.

When they were ready to go Jimmy looked at John again, the house system died down and all the stage lights came up. There was a big cheer and Jimmy smiled out into the crowd. He could make out Marco and Jennifer and Norman at their table, clapping and waving. He tried squinting towards the back of the room to see if ... maybe ... but he couldn't see back that far.

Right. Here goes.

Halfway through the first song, he decided that he could stop glancing across at Shiggy and chill out. The guy was going a great job, adding some neat fills they'd never practised but nothing that got in the way. He was moving well too; hopping up and down, arching his back, kicking out or just standing there with his legs wide open, like Phil Lynott except with legs about two feet shorter. The audience was loving it too. They already had a few boppers up and everyone seemed to settle in for a great night out on the piss. Only Aesop wasn't himself. Jimmy looked around at him quickly at one point and found him playing with his eyes closed and wincing. Good, thought Jimmy. That'll teach you, you trollop.

The set went really well but, by nine forty-five, Jimmy found that he was still nervous and it was getting worse. This never happened. Usually he was grand as soon as they started. There was still no sign of Kayleigh but he looked across during a solo and saw Lavender's Teardrop standing by Shiggy's side of the stage with their instruments, and his heart suddenly flipped. Christ, what was he thinking, letting them up here? They were brutal! He checked the crowd. Some people would know them but a lot of punters wouldn't and might not appreciate having to sit through Amateur Half Hour for their fiver. He messed up the end of the solo, getting a quick glance from Shiggy, and tried to put it out of his mind. This wasn't his problem. Beano wanted this! No one could blame him, could they?

They had one song left before the break and before it started he called over to Beano.

'You ready? This is our last one.'

Beano nodded and gave a thumbs up, but Jimmy could see he was just about ready to shit his pants. Sandra looked beautiful, done up to the nines, but her eyes were wide open in fright at the cheering and clapping that Jimmy was getting and no amount of make-up could hide the fact that she was going to vomit at any minute. Even Mick looked uncomfortable. He hadn't gigged in ages and this was a big crowd. Oh fuck, thought Jimmy. This is going to be bad. He chose one of his own songs, *Alibi*, for the last song of the set, calling the change to Shiggy and Aesop. The last thing he was going to do was play The Darkness or Metallica and then hand everything over to Sandra, so that she could sing some fucking crap hippy song.

'Thanks very much,' he said into the mike, when they were done. 'And now folks, we're going to take a little break. But while we're gone, there's a little surprise waiting in the wings. A new band on the scene, giving their first live performance tonight. Ladies and gentlemen, will you please give a big welcome to Lavender's Teardrop!' He took off his guitar and clapped into the mike and the crowd, to their credit, started whistling and stomping. He saw a few people immediately turn to their friends and start talking and pointing. The word was obviously out. This would be bigger than his *Still in Love With You* piss-take a while back.

He walked off the stage, passing Beano on the way.

'Good luck, Beano.'

'Thanks, Jimmy.' The poor bastard was planking it.

'You'll be great, Sandra. Break a leg,' he said to her, as she stood waiting for him to pass.

She didn't move when he got out of the way.

'Sandra?'

'Jimmy, I can't.' Her hands were on her face, pulling her

skin down from under her eyes.

'Sandra, of course you can. It'll be grand. Really.'

'I'm going to be sick.'

Oh fuck.

'Sandra, listen to me ...' He looked around. Beano was plugging the drum machine into the PA and Mick was looking for a pick. 'Sandra, you've got a great voice and the songs are good. I wouldn't say that if it wasn't true, would I? You know me and my music. Would I let you up there if I thought you weren't ready for it? C'mon. Get up there and do it. This crowd will love you. I swear. They will.'

'Really, Jimmy?'

'Really.'

'Okay. Okay.' She started taking deep breaths. 'I can do this.'

'Course you can.'

'Right. Thanks, Jimmy. Okay.'

'Yeah. Oh look, there's something on your shirt there. At the back. A stain or something.'

'Oh no! Shit! Where?'

'It's fine, Sandra. Look, just tuck it into your jeans. No one will see it.'

'Oh yeah. Okay. Thanks, Jimmy.'

She tucked the shirt in good and tight.

She gave him a final pitiful look and he winked at her, smiling. Then she got up onto the stage and Jimmy let out a big breath. Christ, never mind Sandra, he was fit to throw up himself. He watched her walk into the main spotlight to huge applause; the girls in the audience overdoing it to show that they weren't a bit jealous of her good looks, the lads showing their genuine appreciation for a spectacular pair of breasts well presented. There. Jimmy had done all he could.

The crowd hushed up and Sandra stepped up to the mike. Jimmy stood against a pillar next to Aesop, who was chewing on a plastic cigarette and watching the stage, be-

226

mused. Shiggy was gone to the Gents.

'Eh ... hello everyone,' she said quietly, looking out from under her hair.

Silence.

Jimmy started to sweat.

'Come on, Sandra. Look up. Speak up. Smile. Stick your tits out. For fuck sake ...' he was blabbing away to himself, one finger in the corner of his mouth.

Aesop was looking at him.

'What's up with you?'

'Shut up a minute Aesop,' said Jimmy. He didn't take his eyes off the stage. 'Jesus, Beano, fucking play something, will you?'

'Eh ... this is called *Sometime*,' said Sandra.

She looked around hopefully and finally Beano woke up and pressed something on the drum machine. Then he started to play a simple rhythm for a few seconds, with the bass coming in slowly, and they were off. Suddenly Beano stopped playing, said 'sorry' into his mike and turned the drums off again.

'Eh, that's the wrong beat,' he said.

Jimmy heard a quiet giggle from out front and closed his eyes. His shirt was soaked.

'That's what he gets for having a drum machine,' whispered Aesop.

They got it going again, with the proper beat this time, and Sandra started to sing. She did okay. Her voice was a little shaky, but after a few lines she seemed to gain some confidence and the extra reverb Jimmy had put on her mike before he got off the stage masked most of the worst wobbly bits. Three minutes later the song was over and the crowd gave a big cheer. It had been fairly shite but they knew it was the band's first time out and at least it hadn't been so bad that everyone had pissed off to the toilet or the bar. Jimmy whistled and clapped, catching Norman's eye down at the table and gesturing for him to do the same. Norman nudged Marco and after a few seconds there was quite a respectable round of applause going on.

Jimmy checked his watch. Five past ten. Okay, three more.

The second song didn't go so well. Mick forgot what he was supposed to do and decided that the best way out of the conundrum was to start playing very loud and fast. That completely threw Sandra, who forgot the words of the second verse and started singing the chorus instead. Then Beano got distracted and couldn't remember where he was either. They finally got it back in time for the last verse and chorus but by then the crowd was starting to shift uneasily in their seats and a low hum of conversation had started up.

'Oh bollocks,' moaned Jimmy. He scraped a beer mat along his forehead and flicked a big dollop of sweat from it onto the floor.

'This is going well,' said Aesop, moving his hips and shoulders in a small dance. He was grinning now for the first time all day.

'Jesus, Aesop. It's terrible.'

There was some more applause but, to Jimmy's trained ear, everyone had had enough of Lavender's Teardrop for tonight. They wanted to dance.

Sandra spoke up again.

'Eh, thanks very much. Eh ...' she said, looking around at Beano. You'd have to be stupid not to see that it was time to stop, and she wasn't that. She said something to Beano but he just shook his head and nodded to her mike. She turned back around to it, looking mortified.

'This one is called *Red Rage*,' she said.

'Oh shit, no,' whimpered Jimmy. 'Just stop. Beano, enough is enough. Get off the fucking stage before they start throwing peanuts at you. Please. You arsehole ...'

'*Red Rage*? Hey, maybe it's a rocker?' said Aesop.

It wasn't. It was the kind of song that Tracy Chapman

would have written if she'd had no talent.

Some punters were starting to make their way to the bar.

'He shouldn't be doing all originals,' Aesop observed.

'I know,' said Jimmy.

'Not in here. Not on a Saturday night.'

'I know.'

'Four songs, was it Jimmy? Ah, they won't want to hear four songs like that.'

'I fucking know, Aesop! Will you shut bleedin' up and let me listen?'

They got to the end of the song, and were met with polite applause from about twenty percent of the audience and some fairly manic clapping and cheering from Jimmy.

'Now, Beano. Please. In the name of God, will you stop now before it gets any worse. Please. You'll get a big cheer. You will. They'll let you away with it. Just don't ...'

'Eh, this is our last song,' said Sandra.

Fuck.

'It's called *Mother Nature*.'

'Oh Jesus. Oh no. Not the fucking Bosco song ...'

They started playing but hadn't gotten three bars in when the drum machine seemed to go all funny and miss beats. Mick, Beano and Sandra all looked around at it, a small silver box about the size of a book, sitting on a speaker. There was some static and then the thing stopped completely. Beano and Mick stopped playing.

'Keep going, you bloody fool!' Jimmy half roared and half whispered, but Beano just stood there looking confused.

Jimmy moved to the side of the stage and caught his eye.

'Get off. You're done. Get off! It's broken.'

'It's not broken, Jimmy. I just need a battery. Do you have a nine-volt ... ?'

'A battery?! You're fucking using batteries for a gig?! Beano you useless prick, you don't use batteries for a live ... you ... how the fu ... Jesus, Beano, just get off, will you?' He turned back to Aesop. 'He has it on batteries, the dickhead,' he said, blinking.

'Yeah,' said Aesop, studying the end of his plastic smoke and nodding, 'That sounds about right. Ask him what he got in his Leaving.'

'This is the last song Jimmy,' said Beano. 'Do you have a battery?'

Sandra was standing in the middle of the stage, looking scared.

'Get them off ye, love!' someone yelled from the back.

'Jimmy?' she stammered.

Jimmy looked at her. The bottom lip was starting to go. Oh for fuck …

He turned back to Aesop.

'Get up there, you.'

'What?' said Aesop, taking the fag out of his mouth.

'Get up there. Play the drums.'

'I will in my fuck!'

'You will. I swear, you'll get up there and play.'

'I don't even know the song, Jimmy. And they're shite. How am I s'posed to play along …'

'Aesop. Get up. Go on. Move. Get the fuck up there.' He was pushing Aesop in the back now, moving him towards the stage. They were almost in darkness, but a few people saw what was going on and started to laugh.

'Piss off, Jimmy. I didn't tell the gobshite he could play, did I? You play the drums if you want to.'

'Aesop. Please, get the fuck up there, will you, before the crowd goes home? I swear to Christ if you don't go up there right now, you're never getting any of my Ma's buns ever again. I'm telling you. I'll throw them in the bin before I let you have them. I fucking will. And I'll tell Katie you said she was a slag.'

Aesop was laughing, trying to push his way back to the pillar.

'Yeah, right. Katie hates me anyway. And I can call around to your Mam and she'll give me buns herself.'

'She won't. I'll tell her you hate them.'

'Your Mam loves me. Okay, hang on, hang on. Listen, I've an idea.'

'What?' said Jimmy. He stopped pushing and looked around. Beano, showman extraordinaire that he was, was just standing there looking at the crowd. Sandra was trying to get out of the spotlight and Mick had his back to everyone, pretending to do something to his amp. Even the punters were embarrassed, most of them turned away from the stage. Jimmy turned back to Aesop.

'Meatloaf and his amazing underwear,' said Aesop.

'What?!!'

'I'll play for Beano if we can do *Meatloaf's Underpants* in the second set.'

'Are you serious? In here? Tonight?'

'Yeah. Why not? You even said it was a good song.'

'Jesus, Aesop, *Chitty Chitty Bang Bang* is a good song, but this lot don't want to hear it! You can't ... that's not fair ... ye ... oh fuck it. Okay. Go on. You'd better fucking make them look good, but.'

'No problem, Jimmy. Won't I be up there with them?'

He jumped up onto the stage and Jimmy started to whistle again. Come on, Aesop.

The punters started to cheer when they saw Aesop.

He sauntered straight up to Sandra's mike and stood in front of it, his arms out wide, grinning.

'Eh, sorry about that folks. Luckily my battery never goes flat.' He winked. 'At least, that's what she said last night ...'

There was another big cheer and Aesop waved and sat behind his drum kit. Beano smiled in relief and started playing again. Sandra looked like she could kiss Aesop as she took the microphone in her hand. All of a sudden everyone was having a good time. Even the punters.

Jimmy looked on, drained but happy. The knacker. One dirty-bastard line from Aesop and the show goes on. He watched him twirling his sticks and winking over at him. For a man with the sorest lad in the world not one hour ago, he seemed to be recovering nicely now. Jimmy should have bribed him into doing this from the start. He leaned back against the pillar and finally felt the tension running out of him as *Mother Nature* got the second biggest cheer of the night.

Only *Meatloaf's Underpants*, later on, was a bigger hit.

Twenty

'So,' said Jimmy. 'What do yiz think?' He put down his guitar and looked at them.

'Fecking brilliant,' said Norman.

'Yeah. Good, Jimmy. Very good,' said Aesop.

'Eh, what does it mean?' said Marco, who hadn't been blessed with an Irish education.

'Ah, it's just about a girl, y'know? It's called *Caillte*. Means "Lost". Lost girl, lost phone, y'know? But what about the melody?'

'Very good, Jimmy. But sad?' said Marco.

'Yeah. Sad will do,' said Jimmy, looking at the guitar lying against his leg. 'I'm going to a lot of trouble and I'll be really bloody sad if nothing comes of it. What do you think, Aesop? For the drums, like?'

'Ah, Jimmy. A slow little yoke like that? No problem. I'll just tap away. Once it's recorded the way you want it, we can stop pricking around and do a proper version live.'

'That is the proper version, Aesop. I didn't write it so you could give it the Ozzy Osbourne treatment.'

'Fair enough. It's not like we have to play it live, like y'know?'

Jimmy looked at him.

'We'll be playing it live. Aesop, why does every song you like have to be about Satan or killing politicians or catching the pox? Can you not just listen to a nice gentle tune and relax. Even Metallica had a few ballads.'

'Ah, *The Black Album*. That's where the rot set in. Black is right – it was a black day for metal, so it was. Look Jimmy, I've no problem with pop music. Once I don't have to listen to it.'

'Well, whatever. This is a ballad, it's in Irish, and there won't be a metal version of it, okay? And we'll be playing it at gigs.'

'Puff,' said Aesop, picking up his beer from Jimmy's coffee table. 'Where's Shiggy?'

'I think he's off with that African bird he met last Saturday,' said Jimmy.

'Really?' said Norman. 'God, he gets around doesn't he?'

'Why's that, Norman?' said Aesop. "'Cos he's scored twice in the two months he's been here? That's about average for a healthy male in some parts of the country, y'know?'

'Ah lads don't bleedin' start, the pair of you,' said Jimmy. 'Aesop, Shiggy will be around tomorrow night to go over the bass parts. Can you come over? Just to get an idea of how it'll sound with the bass and proper guitars. I don't know how much time we'll have on Sunday, and I don't want to waste any of it.'

'Eh, Jimmy, Sharon's after catching up with me and she's not working tomorrow night. I've had a couple of days off, so she'll be expecting a bit of a session, y'know?' He was trying to look happy about it but there was a pasty shine to him that you couldn't miss.

'And this floozy is your Superchick, is she Aesop?' asked Norman.

'She is Norman. God bless her.'

'And all who sail in her,' said Norman.

'Ah. A bit jealous, are we?' said Aesop.

'Oh, I am yeah. I wish I had bags under my eyes and that I was so sore from the waist down that I couldn't even walk without looking like a sick oul' granny. If only I'd played my cards right, it might be me who's shagging the Queen of Tarts and all her mates, catching God knows what off them and making a fool of myself.'

'It'd be some hand of cards you'd want to have been holding there, Norman, for you to be riding Sharon and all

234

her mates. A fucking trick deck is what you'd need.'

'So, you're not coming over, then?' said Jimmy quickly.

'Nah. Listen Jimmy, if the song is like you just played it, we'll be grand. If you make any big changes, tape it and give it to me on Saturday.'

'Okay. We're starting at ... Marco, what the fuck are you grinning at?'

They all turned to him. He looked liked he'd just been woken from a pleasant dream. Jimmy pointed his bottle at him.

'You've been walking around in daze all week. What's up with you?'

Marco went red.

'Ah. Nothing, Jimmy. Just ... no, nothing.'

'Come on. What's the story?'

'Really, Jimmy. It's nothing. Well, just, you know, you have found your Superchick, Aesop has his. And I think I also have found mine.'

'Jennifer?'

'Of course, Jennifer. In the last few weeks ... ah Jimmy, it is very good. I am very happy with her.'

'You can probably get pills for that Marco,' said Aesop, with a burp.

'No, Aesop. No pills. You see, since we started talking about Superchick and I was ... eh ... nervous. I think I am afraid that I see it is not her. But now when I am looking at her, when I am with her ... yes ... it is her. I am very lucky. She is Superchick.'

Jimmy leaned forward and cracked his bottle off Marco's.

'Well, that's great news! I'm delighted for yiz. Good stuff.'

Norman raised his bottle as well.

'Fair play to you, Marco. The first one to find the woman of his dreams. And he had her all along and everything.'

'How is he the first?' said Aesop.

'What?' said Norman.

'How is he the first? I mean, she's my sister and I think he's off his trolley, but he didn't even realise it was her until a few days ago. I've been with Sharon for weeks. Why amn't I first?'

'Because Aesop,' said Norman, turning to him, 'Marco's girl is someone he might love and want to marry and have children and live happily ever after with. Yours is a dirty great slag you'd be afraid to let into the kitchen for fear she'd touch something.'

Jimmy and Marco burst out laughing.

'What are yiz laughing at?' said Aesop, looking around. 'That's not funny. That's a bleedin' insult, so it is.'

'Well, he has a point Aesop,' said Jimmy, still laughing.

'He does in his hole have a point! Sharon's a lovely girl. She has a healthy appetite maybe, but so do I, right? We suit each other. What's to stop me marrying Sharon and having babies and all that?'

'Will you listen to yourself, Aesop?' said Norman, with a roar. 'God, who'd marry someone like that? Does she even bother to put jocks on when she gets up in the morning, or has she decided there's no point?'

'Shut up, Norman. That's not fair. You don't even know the girl. Jaysis, I'd have expected better from you, ye poxy little virgin. Since when did you start being a nasty bastard.'

'Relax, Aesop. I'm just slagging you. I'm sure she's grand,' said Norman, giggling.

'Yeah, well keep your opinions to yourself.'

Jimmy looked on in astonishment. He'd known Aesop all his life and he'd never seen him getting defensive like this before. And letting Norman take the piss out of him like that? It was like he was a different person. What was going on? Did he really love this bird? It was unthinkable but Jimmy couldn't think of anything else that would explain it. Was it going to cost him his prize at Christmas? Jimmy didn't care. The idea of Aesop with a steady girlfriend would be well worth it. Christ, he'd throw in a new drum kit if he thought there was any chance of Aesop finally growing up. But Sharon? Nah. He just couldn't see it. Even if he was into it, she just didn't seem like the steady girlfriend type. This was going to get very interesting, he decided. Aesop finally falling for a bird and her not having any of it. Who'd have thought?

He realised that they were all staring at Aesop and probably thinking the same thing.

'What are yiz all looking at?' Aesop shouted, looking around. 'Fuckin' leave me alone, yiz bastards. Just deal the jaysis cards Jimmy, will ye?' He folded his arms and looked into the fireplace.

Very, very interesting.

They only played poker for a couple of hours before it broke up. Aesop could barely keep his eyes open, Jimmy kept humming his song to himself and Marco's inane grinning was putting everyone off. Norman was up about fifty euro without even trying and proposed that they call it a night before he started embarrassing them. No one objected.

When Marco and Aesop left, Norman hung back and started to tidy up the beer cans while Jimmy put the kettle on. They settled back with cups of tea and a plateful of bloody awful buns that Marco had brought, courtesy of Jennifer. Neither Norman nor Jimmy knew too much about the mechanics of bun making, but it was clear that Jen was struggling with the basic principles herself. They were all about five inches wide and half an inch high and seemed to absorb any little bit of moisture that they could find in your mouth. They also expanded when you chewed on them to fill all the available space, and the cumulative effect was not unlike that of having a huge mouthful of stale Liga. Except for the taste, which had more onion to it than the lads, over the years had come to expect from their confectionery. They managed one each and then sat back talking, trying to avoid looking at the plate.

'Marco seems happy,' said Jimmy.

'Yeah. Ah, sure Jennifer's a great girl. Lovely. I'm glad for them. It's nice to see your mates happy like that,' said Norman, trying vainly to get his tongue under a particularly stubborn piece of bun on one of his molars.

Jimmy nodded and grunted back. He had a mouth full of hot tea, swishing it around to try and melt the goo stuck to his own teeth. He finally gave up and swallowed. He'd go at it with the toothbrush if it was still there later.

'If they do get married, I hope these buns were an accident,' he said. ''Cos if this is the best she can do, he'll be spending the next fifty years pulling fillings out of the back of his throat. Jaysis, has your Ma ever made buns like this?'

'Ah no, Jimmy. My Mam's buns are always lovely and fluffy.'

'Mine too.'

'I think she forgot something.'

'Yeah. Flour, maybe.'

'Does your Mam make scones?'

'Course she does. With raisins sometimes.'

'Lovely.'

'Yours?'

'Oh yeah. They're brilliant with jam.'

'Ah, blackberry.'

'Stop.'

They took a sup of tea and sat there silently for a minute or so, smiling to themselves as they relived some of their greatest ever bun moments.

'Will they get married, do you think?' said Norman.

'That pair? Yeah. I'd say so. They'd be mad not to anyway,' said Jimmy.

'Aesop thinks Marco is mad already.'

'That's just Aesop,' said Jimmy, putting down his cup. 'It's all an act with him. He's mad about Jennifer, really. When his Ma died she was only a kid, but she still worked her bollocks off in the house. Looking after the whole lot of them; cooking, cleaning ...'

'Making buns.'

'Making buns, yeah,' Jimmy laughed. 'Jaysis, maybe he does hate her! Nah, but. Jen deserves a nice bloke. Marco will look after her.'

'Could have been you Jimmy,' said Norman, looking at him.

'What? You reckon Marco fancied me?' Then he laughed. 'Nah. Me and Jen are just mates Norman.'

'Well maybe you think that, but Jennifer was always mad about you.'

'She was not. I never acted the bollocks with Jen.'

'Ah, you didn't have to, Jimmy. You were always around and you could tell just by looking at her.'

Jimmy couldn't think of anything to say. The truth was that he knew Jennifer liked him. The bigger truth was that he liked her too. The thought had crossed his mind when they were teenagers that maybe he should try something. A snog, maybe. But he never did and he was thankful for it now. He was sure it would have been a great snog and all but it probably would have changed things. He could look at Jennifer now and see someone who was as perfect as he could imagine any woman being, except for the buns, but she was one of his best friends. She'd always be there for him. People say you can't really be friends with a girl in the same way you can be with a guy, because ultimately there's always the fact that the girl has breasts and sooner or later you'll want to play with them. Jimmy wouldn't argue the point. It wasn't the same type of friendship that he had with Aesop or Norman anyway. What he had with Jen he had with no one else. Jen was Superchick, there was no doubt about that at all. But she was someone else's. That suited Jimmy. It meant he and Jen would never break up.

'Jimmy?' said Norman.

'Yeah?' said Jimmy, looking up.

'Jennifer?'

'We're mates, Norman. Good mates. A bit like having a girlfriend and a sister, all rolled into one.'

'Okay, okay. Fair enough. And Kayleigh?'

Jimmy laughed.

'That's the fucking thing, isn't it? I can't even remember most of that night. Sometimes I can't even remember what she looks like. Like it never happened at all.'

'Well, it happened Jimmy. I can't remember what she looked like either, but I know what you looked like. A big happy fool, so you were.'

'Yeah. I remember that,' said Jimmy smiling. 'I don't know, Norman ... maybe it was all just timing. I broke up with Sandra, decided to go looking for this cracking bird ... I didn't exactly turn over every stone in Dublin, did I? It was only a few weeks. Maybe she was just this nice mot and it was my mind that built her up into some kind of angel, because that's what I was looking for. This song and everything ... I'm still going to do it, but Aesop's right. There's no point in getting me hopes up. For one thing, there's fuck all chance really of it getting on the radio, is there? And anyway, maybe I would've fallen for any nice bird I met that night, the way I was feeling.'

Norman looked at him for a minute.

'Jimmy,' he said. 'I've known you a long time. You and that girl clicked. It wasn't just that you liked the look of each other or that you had the few beers in you. You didn't look like that when you started going out with Sandra, and the one before that ... eh, Mairéad? Well, it's not like that either. You got down off that stage with her after singing and you looked like you were after having your bollocks kicked. In a nice way, like.'

Jimmy smiled and Norman went on.

'Look, just do yourself a favour, will you? You had that feckin' eejit Beano up on the stage and you helped him out when he was dying up there. You're going into the studio at the weekend to do your song and Sandra's going to be there and everything. You're halfway there, Jimmy, so don't just go through the motions. Make that song the best thing you've ever done. If she never hears it, then there's feck all you can do about it. But at least you did it properly, right? And anyway, don't mind what Aesop says.'

'Yeah. I know,' said Jimmy, picking up another bun and then, remembering, putting it back down. 'You're right. I was just feeling a bit sorry for meself. It's been a mad couple of months, hasn't it? So what about you, Norman?'

'What about me?'

'Superchick?'

'Ah, feck all that Jimmy. I gave it a go, but it wasn't me. Trying to chat up girls and going to discos and dancing around the place like a feckin' loo-lah. Nah. You play to your strengths and mine isn't being a charmer, believe it or not. I'm no Joe Dolan and I don't care what anybody says! Me Mam is the same. God, to hear her tell it, I'm like Marlon Brando before he turned into a sofa. I'm not in any hurry, Jimmy. My Superchick probably doesn't go to discos anyway. I'll be grand.'

'Course you will, Norman.'

'God,' said Norman, 'We're like a couple of feckin' women, aren't we? Sitting up talking about this stuff, with our cups of tea. All we need now is slippers with rabbits on them.'

Jimmy laughed and nodded.

'Yeah. I'd put on me Suzanne Vega album, but Sandra took it.'

'Do you miss her, Jimmy?'

'Yeah,' said Jimmy. 'Not like I want her back, like. But you get used to it, y'know? Maybe that's the problem.'

'Yeah, maybe. But getting used to it doesn't mean it's not still great, does it?'

'No. It just means ... look at Aesop. Didn't think he could ever have enough gee, and now he's hiding from his mot in my gaff 'cos he's worn out riding her! He was a bit weird earlier on. Do you think he's really into this bird?'

'Not at all, Jimmy. I'll tell you what's wrong with Aesop. He's finding out that there's more to life than where he puts his lad and how often, and it's scaring the shite out of him 'cos he doesn't know what to do about it. His brothers copped on years ago but Aesop thinks he has to keep the whole thing going, like he's on a mission from Satan or something. The truth is, he's not able for it any more and he knows it. Not only that, seeing Marco and Jennifer so happy and the effort you're putting into finding Kayleigh ... he's just jealous.'

'I'll give you my house and a year's salary if you could get him to admit that,' said Jimmy, sitting up straight and smiling.

'No way, Jimmy. He might be catching himself on but he's a bit of a ways from admitting it. Sure, he's even trying to convince himself that she's a real girlfriend! You can see he's heading in the right direction, but the poor eejit is only codding himself. His brain knows that something is wrong but his little fella is still calling the shots. He'll be grand once he gets that sorted out.'

Jimmy laughed again.

'Very perceptive, Norman. Actually, I think you might be right. If it was another girl who was mad for it like Sharon is he'd probably try and marry her as a point of principle, but I don't think she's interested. She's having a laugh now, but when she gets bored with him she'll just move on. Jaysis, Aesop won't like that, will he? The last of the Great Irish Lovers gets the heave-ho. Can you imagine it?'

'Imagine it?' said Norman, laughing. 'I've been looking

forward to it for the last fifteen years! By Christ, I'll be having a laugh with him that day ...'

Twenty-one

Jimmy got to the studio with ten minutes to spare. It was in the new trendy part of the city. Well the trendiness was new anyway. The area itself was a small maze of narrow cobbled streets and old buildings. He rapped on the door and a huge bloke of about fifty let him in. The guy had shoulder-length greying hair, thick black glasses and a vague smell of cheese about him. This was what Jimmy always imagined Mr Maguire, his old geography teacher, would look like on weekends. Except for the cowboy boots.

'Are you Beano?' said the guy, leading Jimmy up a staircase.

'No. I'm Jimmy. I'm playing guitar,' said Jimmy.

'Right. Well, you're the first one here. I told Donal that everyone would have to be here by six on the dot. They bleedin' better be. I'm Sparky by the way. Electrocuted, so I was.'

He stopped walking and turned around to look at Jimmy.

'Do you know what it's like to have a million volts shooting through your goolies?'

'Eh, no ...' said Jimmy.

'Lucky bastard,' said Sparky, and walked on.

'Are you the sound engineer?' said Jimmy.

'Yeah. You might say that. But for the duration of this weekend, I'm not just the sound engineer. I'm the fucking boss, okay? You do what I tell you. Donal is the boss as well. Yiz only have the place because it's not finished yet and we wanted to test the gear. Donal said he had a band that would do it, but that they're virgins. That's you. A virgin. Don't go thinking you're the fucking Edge around here, 'cos you're not. And even if you were, I still wouldn't give a shite. I'll

244

record whatever you want to do, but I have things I want to check so do what yiz are told as well. Don't bother me and don't ask me too many questions, 'cos I do get terrible fucking headaches when I'm irritated, which is all the time. Ask anyone. I'm a real bastard. Right? Annoy me and I'll bleedin' batter yiz all, I swear.'

'No problem,' said Jimmy. 'You're the boss.' Jesus.

'Good. What's the axe?' said Sparky, nodding at Jimmy's case.

'It's a Strat. Clapton signature model.'

'Fuck sake. Poor bastards have it tough these days, don't yiz? And I suppose that's a bleedin' Rolex you have on you as well, is it?'

Actually it was a Tag, but Jimmy didn't say anything. It was too early in the weekend to risk annoying Sparky. He'd leave that to Beano when he got here. Beano could be immensely annoying. If this bloke was irritable by nature, he'd be having fucking conniptions by lunchtime, if Jimmy knew Beano.

Jimmy walked into a room about the size of his bedroom at home, except that this one looked a lot cooler. There were knobs, buttons, lights and sliders everywhere. A huge desk stood up against a window, through which Jimmy could see what would be his home for most of the next two days. Right now it was practically empty except for some mike stands and the bones of a drum kit.

'This is the Trident,' said Sparky, sitting at the huge mixing desk. 'I'd tell you exactly what everything does and how it all works, except that there's no point because if I catch you touching it I'll punch the bleedin' bollocks off you. This board is very old and very expensive and the only thing that'll make you sound halfway fucking decent, so don't go near it. Right?'

'Okay,' said Jimmy, taking a step back. 'It looks complicated. I've a Yamaha desk for gigs but there's only eight channels on it. I don't even use them all.'

'Oh yeah,' said Sparky. 'Thanks for reminding me. I need to tell you that gigging is nothing like recording. Nothing at all, right? Don't presume you know the first fucking thing about what we're going to be doing in here, 'cos you don't. Everything you might think you know isn't worth a shite.'

'Fair enough,' said Jimmy. 'I'm just here to play the guitar, Sparky. It's not even my band. If I can learn a few things then that's grand, but this is just a favour to Beano, kind of.'

'Yeah. Well Beano's a lucky bastard. In about two weeks, this place will be finished and a full weekend like he's getting will cost about seven grand. Jimmy is it?'

'Yeah.'

'Well, Jimmy, it's six o'clock and your mates aren't here. That makes me very fucking sad, so it does.'

'Sorry ...'

'What amps do you want?'

'What do you have?'

For the first time, Sparky smiled.

'C'mere,' he said, leading Jimmy through a door into the main recording area.

He opened another door that Jimmy hadn't even noticed and stood back.

'Fucking hell!' said Jimmy, his mouth dropping open.

It was like a Santy's Workshop for musicians.

Ten minutes later Jimmy was plugged into a 1960s vintage Vox AC30 with top boost. This was the amp he'd wanted for years but he'd only ever played it in shops, it was usually in shite nick, and anyway he only ever got about five minutes on it before some bastard shop assistant realised that he wasn't going to buy it and started annoying him. It was in mint condition and he turned it right up, the huge grin on his face threatening to dislodge his eyeballs. Sparky smiled back through the window of the control room. Jimmy had been wondering how to get the cranky old bastard to like him but it turned out that all he had to do was love his gear. Like that was a problem! Jimmy went through two more vintage amps and a brand new Mesa Boogie. He looked at the clock on the wall. It was now six thirty. He didn't know which amp he'd use for Beano's music, so he left them all set up and plugged back into the Vox to get loosened up. By now Sparky was starting to curse loudly at the clock and he wanted to stay out of his way. Tardiness seemed to be just one of the many residents in his menagerie of pet hates.

It was quarter to seven when a breathless Beano finally showed up with Sandra. Jimmy couldn't hear anything from the main recording room, but he nodded to Sandra in the control room through the window and watched Sparky's lips as they rapidly hurled abuse in Beano's direction. When Sparky was finally done, he opened the door to the recording room where Jimmy was practising and shooed Beano and Sandra through.

'If you're late tomorrow, you can fuck off,' he said, and slammed the door again.

'Beano. Sandra,' said Jimmy.

'Hiya Jimmy,' said Beano.

'Hi Jimmy,' said Sandra, looking back nervously through the window at Sparky.

'Good gig the other night,' said Beano, putting down his bag.

'Yeah,' said Jimmy. And which fucking gig were you at Beano, ye spa?

Sparky's voice came over the intercom.

'Are yiz finished? Get a bleedin' move on. We're after wasting enough time. Jimmy, show that late fucker where the gear is. You need to set up the mikes and get a bass amp. The drummer will be in at ten. We'll be doing levels 'til then.'

'Oh, it's all right Sparky. I have me own mike,' said Beano.

Jimmy closed his eyes and shook his head. Sparky looked up.

'Do ye? And what fucking mike do you have, so?'

'It's a Shure SM58,' said Beano, proudly.

'And you're going to sing into that in my studio, are you? Jimmy, will you explain to this gobshite what I'll do to him if he ever second guesses me again?'

'He'll fucking kill you Beano.'

'That's right. Now. You. Go into that storeroom and get out a Neumann U87 and put it on a mike stand and then plug it in where I tell you, before I go out there and kick the gee off you, right? A fuckin' 58 in my studio ... you're not in the bleedin' Baggot Inn now, ye hear me?'

'Neumann?' whispered Beano to Jimmy, on their way to the storeroom. 'Whoever heard of Neumann?'

'You never heard of Shure before I told you, Beano. Listen, this bloke is a grumpy bastard. Don't ask him stupid questions. Just do what he says, right? I get the feeling he doesn't like musicians.'

'Well my uncle owns this place. He better start having a bit of manners,' said Beano.

'Yeah, well I don't know who owns what, right? It's none of my business. But that bloke out there is the one who'll be making your CD for you. I wouldn't piss him off if I were you or you'll end up sounding like fucking Leo Sayer.'

'Yeah? Really?' said Beano, smiling. 'Leo Sayer?'

Jimmy looked at him.

'That's a bad thing, Beano. For fuck sake. Look, there's the mike. Just grab it, will you, and let's go. Jesus ...'

Jimmy grabbed a big bass amp and moved it out the door behind Beano.

'Where's Mick?' he said.

'Eh, yeah. Mick. I had to let him go.'

'What?!' said Jimmy.

'Yeah. Ah, we had a few disagreements about the direction, y'know? He was all into this hard rock stuff and we're more into folk fusion.'

'Folk fusion?' said Jimmy. God. The beast had a name.

'Yeah. Anyway, it didn't work out. I'm playing the bass. Or you could play it Jimmy, if ...'

'No fucking way, Beano. That wasn't part of the agreement. That's just you being a lazy bastard. Play it yourself. Folk fusion isn't too demanding in the bass department from what I've heard. Beano, you didn't let him go, did you? He told you to fuck off, didn't he?'

'Eh, kind of ...' said Beano, looking away.

Jimmy sighed. The only one in the band with any real talent or experience, and he shags off after one gig. A typical Beano effort.

'Listen Jimmy, my uncle will be coming in at some stage, y'know? He's been hearing about me being a musician for years, but he's never heard me play or anything. That Sparky bloke out there is bad enough yelling at me and all, but could you do us a favour and not treat me like a fuckin' eejit in front of Donal?'

'Beano, I said I'd shut up and do what I'm told, right? That's what I'll do. This is your show. Are you ready for it?'

'Ah yeah,' said Beano, smiling. 'Course I am. It's going to be great! Oh listen, I'm after leaving me bass at home. Hang on, I'll just get one from in there.'

Jimmy watched him go back into the storeroom. How could a man who was about to record a CD for the very first time, be so stupid as to forget the only instrument he had to play on that CD. Jimmy had a feeling that Beano's delusions of mediocrity were about to be tested. Maybe Sparky's bark was worse than his bite, but Jimmy reckoned he was going to find out one way or the other.

It was a long morning and after a half-hour break for lunch they eventually started setting up for the first song. The drummer, a guy called Rob about their own age, had come in and started to tune his drums. For some reason, getting the drum sounds right was easily the most difficult part of the whole operation, Jimmy noticed. It wasn't like that with Aesop. Either Aesop had a brilliant ear and could tune his drums in seconds, or else he didn't tune them at all. Jimmy suspected the latter. Aesop's drums were in tune when he could hit them very hard without breaking them.

Rob had started by asking Beano what kind of sound he wanted and looked curiously at Jimmy, and through the window at Sparky, when he got the answer.

'And what the fuck is folk fusion when it's at home?' he said.

Jimmy bit his lip and said nothing.

'Y'know ...' said Beano. 'A kind of trad-folk vibe with a bit of ska.'

'Yeah right,' said Rob. 'Like Foster and Allen meets Bad Manners?'

'Yeah. Exactly,' said Beano.

Rob shook his head. At least now he knew what he was up against.

'Look, here are the four songs,' said Beano, handing Rob a Walkman. 'This is them unplugged, but it'll give you the idea.'

Rob took the Walkman and listened non-stop for about ten minutes. He finally took the headphones off and handed them back to Beano, who was trying to tune his bass.

'Okay. Grand. Actually, it's more Puff the Magic Dragon meets Play School, isn't it? Whatever ... let's get on with it. I've a gig this evening.'

'Tell you what,' said Beano. 'I don't know too much about drum sounds. Why don't you play whatever you think fits.'

'Good idea,' said Rob. He started wondering where he could borrow a bodhrán on a Saturday afternoon.

By three, they were finally set up. Jimmy found himself in the guitar booth – a room with a stool and five microphones. A guy called Tommy had come in to help Sparky and it was he who had placed the mikes. He didn't say much, but seemed to understand the bewildering language that Sparky spoke when he was talking about his equipment.

'Tommy, we need the PZMs, use the 57s, in pairs, ambient one foot behind the wave,' he'd say, and Tommy would hop to it.

Jimmy was impressed. Tommy looked about seventeen.

Now he sat there, afraid of his life to move. Sparky had told him where to sit and where to face his guitar. He was playing an acoustic now and since the sound could apparently go from sounding beautiful to sounding like a plastic cup with an elastic band strung across it if he so much as scratched his bum – to Sparky's ears anyway – he was concentrating on not budging. He heard Rob count them in through his headphones and off they went. He didn't have a whole lot to do. He was recording a scratch track, he'd been told. It would go onto tape, but he was only playing so that Rob and Beano would hear the melody while they put down the real bass and drum parts. Jimmy would record the actual guitar parts later, when the rhythm section was done. Sandra was in the vocal booth, doing a vocal scratch. She'd be last to record her real part, singing over the finished product of the rest of the band. It was all very exciting. Jimmy had loved music and playing since he was a nipper, but this was a whole different side of that world and one he was quickly coming to realise he knew absolutely nothing about.

They finished the song and Jimmy waited, looking through the window at Rob and Beano, and through another window at Sparky. Everyone had headphones on. It was like being in a rock video. He was grinning his head off, thinking it hadn't gone too badly, when Sparky eventually looked up from the desk.

There was a click over the headphones.

'That was pure shite,' he said. 'Beano, are you playing the same song as everyone else? 'Cos I'm listening to it in here and it doesn't sound like it. We'll do it again, right? And

Beano, if you could play the right notes, that'd be a great help. If you can play them in the right order, I might even not kick the jaysis out of you for wasting me time.'

Click.

Jimmy looked at Beano going red in the other room. Beano was nervous as hell and that was the problem. Even Jimmy wasn't feeling his usual cocky self. Sparky was right; this wasn't a bit like playing a gig. In a gig, if you make a balls of something it's gone as soon as you do it. The band plays on and the crowd doesn't even usually notice. But in here it was all recorded. The slightest little mistake and you had to either do it again or live with the fact that it'll be forever on tape. They did it again.

Click.

'Very good,' said Sparky. 'Oh, except you, Beano. You were brutal.'

Click.

'How was I brutal?' said Beano. He was getting pissed off.

Click.

'There's four verses in the song, right?' said Sparky. 'Well you played them all differently. And for two of the choruses, you were late coming in. And your A string is out of tune by at least half a semi-tone. And you stopped about two seconds before Rob and Sandra at the end. Any other questions?'

Click.

Beano frowned and muttered to himself.

'Yeah. How did you ever become such a fucking prick?'

Click.

'Hey, Beano?' said Sparky, 'See that microphone three inches away from your mouth? If you don't want to be heard, then you should turn away from it, you stupid bastard. And if you ever call me a prick again, I'll reef your head off and punch the fuck out of it.'

Click.

It was six by the time Sparky had a rhythm section he

was happy with. Beano had gotten more and more abuse, but was finally able to concentrate to the point where he played better than Jimmy had ever known him to. They all sat in the main room when it was finished and listened to the end result. It was pretty amazing. Even with the guitar and vocals only being scratch tracks, it still sounded like a real song. A bit of a crappy real song, but a real song nonetheless. Even Sparky was happy, although Jimmy suspected that that was because his equipment had worked well more than anything else.

Beano and Sandra disappeared for an hour for dinner. Sparky said that Jimmy could go with them while he started to work on the mix, but Jimmy declined.

'Sparky, I might never get a chance to be in a studio like this again in me life. If it's all right with you, could I stay and watch? I swear I won't get in the way.'

'All right then. But I'm warning you – if you start annoying me, out you go, right?'

In that hour, Jimmy learnt more about a recording studio than any amount of techie magazine reading would have taught him. The difference between in-line and split consoles, track bouncing, channel grouping, enhancers, gates, pick-up patterns, EQ, spillage and just about any piece of equipment that had ever appeared on any record of note in the last forty years. Sparky was a walking, talking, cursing encyclopaedia on the subject and his passion for his job made Jimmy jealous. Imagine getting up in the morning and being that happy to go to work? Sparky's hero was George Martin, who he called 'Sir George' in soft, reverent tones that Jimmy found strange coming from the same mouth that vehemently swore most modern producers were only a shower of fucking geebags.

He'd worked with just about everybody in Irish music over the years. Listening to all his stories made Jimmy feel weird. All these bands and musicians. Talking to someone who'd actually met them made them seem more real. They weren't just the music that came off a piece of vinyl or a CD. They weren't just big stars on the telly. They were real people, and they did the same thing as Jimmy, except for the fact that they were mostly rich or famous or both. Jimmy didn't know whether to be excited or depressed.

He knew now that there was never any danger of his annoying Sparky either. The crustiness wore off after only five minutes and then he was speaking quickly and animatedly, even letting Jimmy play with some of the sliders on the board to see how the different takes sounded and exactly how and where Beano had made mistakes. To his embarrassment, few of Jimmy's own efforts were flawless. It was amazing how different it all sounded back here. Jimmy faded out the bass, vocals and drums and just listened to his own guitar part, Sparky smiling over his shoulder.

'Listen! There! I fucked that up,' he said.

'Yeah,' said Sparky. 'You did. You'd be amazed at how many musicians try and convince me that they meant to do that. Young fellas and everything. I've been doing this since the Seventies and they think I don't know when they make a mistake. But you'll do all right, Jimmy. You're a neat player and you listen when people are explaining things to you. You'll be grand.'

'Did Beano tell you that my band are coming in to record a song tomorrow?'

'Yeah. Donal mentioned it. What's the song?'

'Ah, it's just a song I wrote for this girl. I'm hoping to be able to get it played on the radio, y'know?'

'Bit early for Valentine's Day, isn't it?'

Jimmy laughed.

'Yeah. More of a Christmas present really.'

'Well, anyway, no problem. If your band is any better than this nonsense we're doing today, then I'm sure you'll do all right with it. I might even let you use Gunther.'

'Gunther?'

'Ah, you'll find out tomorrow if you're a good boy. Gunther can be a great inspiration sometimes. But what the fuck do I know? I'm an engineer, not an artist, right?'

'Well, I'm new at all this,' said Jimmy, looking around at all the gear, 'but I'd fucking-well say that this is art as well.'

He got up and made his way back to his guitar booth to get ready for the next session. When he got there he looked back through the window at Sparky, who was still blushing and smiling as he looked around at his beloved Trident board with pride. He was now a friend for life.

They didn't leave the studio until after ten that night, and they'd only really done one and a half songs.

'Beano,' said Jimmy, as they went down the stairs together, 'I told the lads that we'd be on from twelve 'til four tomorrow, right?'

'Depends, Jimmy,' said Beano. 'We mightn't have time to do your song the way things are going.'

'Is that right, Beano? Well, c'mere 'til I tell you something, right? We're going to be in here for four hours tomorrow and you're not. If you're here, I'll kick you down these stairs myself. And if you think we're not playing so that you can finish this masterpiece of yours, you can kiss my hairy fucking bean bag ...'

'Jimmy ...' said Sandra.

'Sorry, Sandra. I'm not a violent person, but if Beano acts the bollocks with me on this, I swear I'll kick his teeth down his ...'

'Relax Jimmy, relax. I'm only messing. Four hours is grand. No problem, right?' said Beano. 'Hey, do you want to share a taxi?'

'No thanks,' said Jimmy. 'I'm going for a pint. Seeya tomorrow. And, Beano, six in the morning, right? If you're late again, Sparky'll reef the pubes off you.'

'Ah, don't mind Sparky,' said Beano, walking off. 'He's all mouth.'

Twenty-two

At twenty past six the following morning, Sparky was sitting on Beano's chest in front of the drum kit and slapping him on the forehead with a piece of toast.

'I fucking told you not to be late, didn't I?' yelled Sparky. 'What's the bleedin' matter with you? Do you not understand that I get very, very annoyed when people are late? Did I not give you that impression yesterday? I thought I did. I distinctly remember telling you I'd kill you if you were late. Remember that? "I'll fucking kill you if you're late," I said, so it wasn't like I was only dropping hints. I was very clear, so I was. Wasn't I?'

'Yeah. Yeah you were,' whimpered Beano, crumbs all over his face. 'I'm sorry, Sparky. I forgot the buses start later on Sundays.'

'The bleedin' buses?! You're blaming the buses now? And I suppose your Mammy slept it out as well and didn't wake you, did she? And you forgot your homework, did ye? Do the twelve times tables.'

'What?' said Beano.

'You want to be treated like a schoolchild? Well then do the twelve times tables. Multiplication. Fucking do it!' Sparky yelled, jamming the toast up Beano's nose.

'Eh, twelve times one is twelve ...'

'Fucking sing it!' roared Sparky. 'We sang it when I was fucking seven years old!'

Sparky jumped up and grabbed the mike, shoving it under Beano's mouth and sitting on him again before he had a chance to get up.

'In here,' he said. 'I want everyone to hear it.'

Beano started again, singing this time.

'Twelve times one is twelve. Twelve times two is twenty-four. Twelve times three is ...'

Jimmy watched, mesmerised, from the guitar booth. Sandra had locked herself into the vocal booth as soon as Sparky started to chase Beano around the room. Beano was far faster and only got caught because Rob tripped him up as he ran past the drum kit. Now Sandra was looking through the window at her darling Beano lying on the ground with Sparky hitting him and making him sing the multiplication tables. That kind of spectacle is bound to affect a relationship, reflected Jimmy.

Suddenly there was no more singing over the headphones and Jimmy looked back out into the main room.

'Eleven?' snarled Sparky.

'Eh ... ehh ...' said Beano. 'We ... we only did up to ten, Sparky.'

'Fucking eleven!' screamed Sparky. There was spit flying now. He stuffed a corner of the toast into Beano's ear but that only seemed to shut his brain down completely.

Silence.

The tension was killing Jimmy.

'A hundred and thirty-two,' he said, quietly, into his mike.

'Ah, don't fucking tell him, Jimmy!' shouted Sparky, looking around with wide, mad eyes.

'A hundred and thirty-two,' sang Beano. 'Twelve times twelve is ... eh ... eh ... a hundred and ... forty ... forty-four.'

He stopped.

'Good,' said Sparky, getting off him. 'Now. If you fuck up again, you're out on your ear.'

With that, Sparky got up and walked back into the control room, putting on his headphones like nothing had happened.

'We're going to start with *Red Rage*. I want it finished in an hour,' he said, eyes on his board and hands moving quickly over a myriad of sliders.

Beano slowly got to his feet and brushed the crumbs out of his hair. He made a gallant effort to pick up his bass and smile nonchalantly at Sandra through the window, but the blob of marmalade on the end of his nose marred the effect. He was trying to look like a guy who'd just enjoyed a manly wrestle with another guy for a laugh, but in fact he looked like a man who'd just been sat on and slapped around with a slice of toast. Anyone else would have been mortified, but Jimmy knew Beano. The man was incapable of shame. By this time tomorrow, the whole story would be changed. Not just in the telling, but in Beano's actual mind as well. He had a great capacity for self-deception.

It was just after eleven when they finished *Can't Think*, leaving just *Mother Nature* for later. They were moving much faster now. Beano wouldn't have noticed, but Sparky was being far less critical than he had been yesterday. Even Jimmy could now hear mistakes that Sparky ignored. He had obviously had enough of Beano and his folk fusion.

'What's it supposed to be fused with?' he'd said earlier. 'Shit?'

All four songs used the exact same gear, so whatever testing could be done with that kind of music was done as far as he was concerned. Sparky was just going through the motions now, getting the songs down well enough that he couldn't personally be held responsible for how bland they were. Jimmy overheard him saying to Rob during a five minute smoke break that he'd just have to jazz the whole thing up in the mix before he'd be able to put his name to it. He didn't know what that meant, but he got the feeling that Sparky was looking forward to recording Jimmy's own song. A whole new setup for him to play around with. That was fine with Jimmy. He wanted Sparky at his best.

Rob, Sandra and Beano were dismissed by Sparky at a quarter to twelve with orders to be back at half three.

'And Beano?' he said. 'The next time it won't be toast,

right? I'll have Rob use your bollocks for a bass drum, d'ye hear me?'

Beano laughed.

'No problem Sparky,' he said, looking at Sandra and winking.

Sparky shook his head as they left with Rob, leaving Jimmy and himself alone in the control room.

'He's a bit strange, isn't he?' he said.

'Beano? Ah. Just a bit of an airhead, that's all.'

'A bit? Donal's a good mate of mine. You know we're partners in this place? There's ten of us put the cash up. I've known Donal for years. He mentioned this amazingly talented nephew of his a few times, but Jaysis ... that Beano is some tulip all right. I'm surprised at Donal, thinking he was any good. I know it's family and all, but Donal's been at this game too long for that shite.'

'Eh, to be honest, I don't think Donal's actually heard Beano yet. Probably just heard about him from his Mam or something.'

'Yeah? Thank God. I'd hate to think Donal was losing it. If he thinks Beano has talent, Christ knows what other shite he'd be bringing in here. Cost a bloody fortune to set all this up, so it did. We need to get a good name fast, before them bastards at the bank come in and tell us to close up shop and piss off. We're not going to get the word out if Donal keeps bringing in fucking crap Cat Stevens bands. Thirty years ago, maybe, but ... oh that reminds me. Time for you to meet Gunther.'

He walked out of the control room and came back carrying a large wooden box. Jimmy eyed the box nervously.

'Jesus, Sparky. Gunther's not a fucking gerbil or something, is he?' he said.

'No. This is Gunther.' He opened the box and took out a microphone. 'Do you know what Gunther is?'

Jimmy shook his head.

'He's a Telefunken tube mike, Jimmy. I don't usually let anyone use him, 'cos he's a temperamental bastard like meself and he needs to be looked after. They usually have their own roadie these days, if you can find them at all. I got him in London about twenty-odd years ago. It was a present. From John Lennon, Jimmy. He used Gunther on *Imagine*.'

'Fuck,' whispered Jimmy. 'Are you serious?' He held it in his hands and stared. This was unbelievable.

'As true as God, Jimmy. He's worth a bleedin' fortune. I'm only letting you use him 'cos I like your attitude.'

They both sat, just looking at Gunther. John Lennon. Fuck.

A bell rang from downstairs, breaking the spell. It was Shiggy and Aesop.

Jimmy made the introductions, smiling as the two lads stared around the studio in amazement.

'Fucking hell Jimmy,' said Aesop. 'This is the *bollocks*! Howya Sparky. I'm Aesop and I'll be your drummer this afternoon. Howzit goin'? Jaysis, this is some place you've got here. Do you need to go to college to work all them buttons? Look at the size of that desk! Jesus. This is going to be bleedin' deadly. C'mere, where's the jacks?'

Sparky pointed off to one side where there was a small kitchen and toilet and watched Aesop walk off.

'That's your drummer?' he said.

'Yeah,' said Jimmy laughing. 'He's a bit of a looper, but don't mind him. He's a great drummer.'

'Preased to meet you,' said Shiggy. 'I am Shiggy.'

'Howya,' said Sparky. 'You're the bass player?'

'Yes. I pray bass.'

Shiggy took out his guitar and showed him.

'Nice,' said Sparky, whistling. 'These are new, right? Streamer JazzMan. What amp do you want?'

'Ah, *anno*, Trace Erriot?'

'No problem, Shiggy. No problem. Help yourself in there.'

Aesop came back.

'Okay, where do I sit? Tell you what. I'll sit here, right?' He sat at the drum kit. 'Brilliant. Jaysis, I'll tell you Sparky, this is some nice gear. You should see the shite I have at home.'

He sat down and started warming up.

Sparky watched for a minute and then, satisfied that Aesop was a real musician and not just a space cadet, he went back into his control room and told everyone to put on their headphones.

'We'd better get started on the drum sound Aesop,' he said. 'That'll take the longest and we only have a few hours.'

'Jimmy said there was a session drummer in here today and yesterday,' said Aesop. 'Did he set the drums up?'

'Yeah,' said Sparky.

'Well then that's good enough for me. What the fuck do I know about a recording studio, Sparky? If they sound all right to you, then I'm happy. I don't like it when things get complicated. You just tell me if it's crap and we'll go from there.'

Jimmy saw Sparky smile down at his console. Good man, Aesop. Jimmy hadn't even told him to say that.

Jimmy waited until everyone was back and ready to go, and then he sat in the middle of the main room with an acoustic guitar and his notes, explaining to everyone how he wanted things to work. After half an hour, Donal finally arrived and sat down with them.

'So, you're Jimmy, then?' he said. 'Sorry I wasn't here yesterday; I had a load of stuff on. I've heard a lot about you.'

'Yeah. I've known Beano for a good while.'

'Ah, not just from Beano. The Grove has a good name about town. For a cover band, like. About time you did something like this.'

'Well, it's not like the opportunity comes up every week-end, y'know? We've got a good few songs, but I haven't really thought about recording them properly. Anyway, how could we afford this place?'

'Ah, you don't have to do it here, Jimmy. There's lots of ways to get a start. You think U2 started out in a place like this? Anyway, come on. We're on a tight schedule here and I want to see what you're made of. And I need to listen to Beano's tapes and see if his Mammy's blinded by love for the little dote. Or deafened anyway. She has the ear bent off me about him. Is he behaving himself, Sparky?'

'Ah yeah,' said Sparky. 'I had to slap him around a bit for being late, like, but you know me, right?'

'Yeah, I do all right,' laughed Donal. He looked around at the others. 'Funniest thing I ever saw in my life. Sparky with Phil Lynott in a headlock, the two of them rolling around on the floor, fighting over bag of crisps.'

'They were my crisps Donal,' said Sparky.

'Yeah, well no one got them in the end, did they?' He turned to the lads again. 'Philo emptied them all over Sparky's head and about six of us had to separate them. The state of the place after them. Sparky was picking crumbs out of his beard for weeks.'

Aesop and Jimmy were enthralled. How could you tell a story like that and not make it last for half the afternoon? And how was it possible that Beano could be related to someone so cool?

'Anyway, no time for d'ye-remembers. We right?' said Donal.

Jimmy felt his guts tighten. This was it.

They all got into position, Jimmy in the guitar booth again to record a scratch for Shiggy and Aesop to put down the rhythm tracks to. He was singing this time as well, and tried to fight down his nerves as he adjusted the mike in front of his face and strummed the guitar to make sure everything was on and ready to go.

'Okay,' said Sparky. 'Here we go. Aesop, do the honours

will ye? In your own time.'

Aesop counted them in and Jimmy closed his eyes. Kayleigh, you cow, I hope you're listening. Funnily enough, it was the first time he'd thought of her all weekend. With everything else that was going on, he just hadn't had the time. Now he forced himself to conjure up her face. This was all a great experience, but there was a job to do now. He struck the opening chord and sang to the smiling face that was now floating about on the inside of his eyelids.

By three Jimmy was absolutely exhausted. Completely. He'd never felt so drained. The rhythm parts turned out to be the easy bit, but when it came to the guitars and vocals Jimmy found himself concentrating so hard that the adrenaline and tension built up into a throbbing pain that seemed to be all over his head at once. Donal had stopped listening to Beano's tapes and was now looking straight at Jimmy with a deep frown. Jimmy was aware of the others around; Sparky moving sliders, Donal standing there pursing his lips, Shiggy and Aesop sitting in the main room, watching everything, but they were all only barely there. He had never been this focused on anything in his life.

They ended up with eight different guitar parts and half a dozen vocal tracks. Of course it wasn't all going to end up in the song, but Jimmy had a lot of ideas and he wanted them all to be available for Sparky and Donal, when it came to mixing everything down. He just hoped that they'd do a good job on it. He wouldn't be there while that was going on and he had to trust them. If they hated the song they probably wouldn't bother too much and just use the whole thing as a mixing exercise on their new equipment.

At the end of the final vocal take, a harmony line, he stopped and opened his eyes.

'I think we got it Jimmy,' said Sparky. 'I think that's it.'

There was silence for about five seconds, and then

Shiggy and Aesop burst into applause. Jimmy came out of the vocal booth and sat down, feeling like his legs would have given out on him if he hadn't. He looked through the control window and saw Sparky and Donal looking at him. They were both grinning their heads off and Donal gave Jimmy two big thumbs up. He leaned over to Sparky's mike and cleared his throat.

'Nice one Jimmy,' was all he said, but Jimmy knew by his face. He'd nailed it.

Shiggy and Aesop came over to him, clapping him on the back and telling him he was brilliant.

'Thanks lads.'

'Nah,' said Aesop. 'You were deadly. I mean it. Christmas Number One. No fucking problem.'

'I meant thanks for doing it. I couldn't have done it on my own. Really, yiz did a great job. Fuckin' hell, I'm wrecked ...'

He hung his head down, massaging the back of his neck while Donal and Sparky made their way out to them.

'That's a good song Jimmy,' said Sparky. 'Fair play to you. All them tracks – Jaysis, we've a week's work trying to put that together, don't we Donal?' He went back into the control room.

'Yeah. Listen Jimmy, you did a good job there. Sparky tells me you never recorded before. Well, you have a knack for it. Most of the time everyone just wants to get it done and piss off to the pub. You knew what you wanted and I think you got it. God, Sparky even let you use Gunther so I know he's impressed. Are you happy?'

Jimmy could only nod. He'd never felt like this before. If there was such a thing as a truly natural high, then he was right off his tits on it at the moment.

'Lads,' said Sparky over the monitors. 'Here it is. First draft ...'

The song came out in lush stereo through the speakers spaced all over the room. Everyone shut up.

Jimmy went red. He was embarrassed and delighted. It didn't even sound like his playing or his singing. It could have been something he bought on CD. Or heard on the radio. It sounded brilliant. Jimmy Collins. Rockstar.

At the end of it, Sparky came out with five plastic cups on a tray.

'What's the girl's name?' he said.

'Kayleigh,' answered Jimmy.

He handed round the cups.

'To Kayleigh,' he said, raising his own.

'To Kayleigh,' said everyone else.

Jimmy smiled to himself, looking at his little cup. She had her own song now. And a guy who spent hours gazing through the dark at his bedroom ceiling because he couldn't sleep for thinking of her. This had to work.

'Fucking water?!' spluttered Aesop, choking.

'Yeah. We don't have drink in the studio any more,' said Donal.

'Why not?' said Aesop. 'I thought it was a rock and roll thing.'

'Well it used to be, but let's put it this way ...' said Donal. 'Phil wasn't the only one that Sparky here had a go at.'

'Ah, hang on a minute now Donal,' said Sparky. 'Sid Vicious started that and you fucking know it. And anyway, you were the one who decided to give his mot a wedgie.'

They all laughed, Jimmy happier than he'd been in ages. Sparky liked the song. Really liked it. He looked at the plastic cup in his hand again. The only toast Beano had gotten was a slice of wholemeal in the ear. If Sparky liked it, Donal would like it. They'd do a good job on it for him.

Donal looked up at the clock.

'Well, it's a quarter past three. The others will be back in fifteen minutes, right? After that we've got half an hour to finish up with The Grove and then I get to find out whether or not Lavender's Teardrop is going to scandalise the family.

I've been listening to their tapes out there while you were recording. God ...'

Sparky stood up.

'Jimmy, I know you're probably bollixed after all that, but will you do me a favour?'

'Of course I will, Sparky. No problem. What?' said Jimmy immediately. He would have painted Sparky's house for him if he'd asked.

'Well, we've had Beano's folk bleedin' fusion and your song, but I was hoping to really test spillage and the damping in here. Do yiz do any, y'know, loud stuff?'

'Yeah. We could do Sabbath or something. That all right?'

'Perfect,' said Sparky. 'Sabbath. Or even one of your own songs if you want. Might as well get something else on tape while we're here, y'know? We don't have time for loads of takes or anything, so you'd have to just play it live, like. And loud. We might get two takes down. Hang on a minute.' He ran off quickly to get Gunther and put him back in his box. Songs that were too loud could upset him.

Jimmy had his back to Aesop, but could practically hear his eyes popping open.

'No Aesop,' he said, without even turning around.

'Ah come on Jimmy, ye bollocks. You had your go. Come on. Give me a chance. When will I ever get to do this again? Please? Please? Please?'

'What's this?' said Donal, looking between Aesop and Jimmy.

'You want noise?' Jimmy said to Sparky, who'd come back.

'Yeah. Really loud. Guitars, drums, the works. Something really fucking horrible. Do you have a song like that?'

Jimmy finally looked around at a beaming, nodding Aesop and then turned back around to Sparky.

'A horrible song? Oh yeah. I think we have one of them ...'

Half an hour later, Beano and Sandra walked into the sound room and stood rooted behind Donal and Sparky who hadn't even heard them come in. Through the window they saw the lads screaming, jumping and yelling in the other room, making the most horrendous racket they'd ever heard. They could barely make out the lyrics, although the general theme seemed to revolve around food and underwear.

'Oh God,' Beano whispered to Sandra. 'This is so embarrassing. I'll have to apologise to Donal. They're fucking crap!'

Twenty-three

Jimmy was on a high all week. Everyone in the office thought he was after scoring big-time at the weekend, the head on him. He wasn't normally one for standing in the corridors with his colleagues, having a chat about the weather and the game in Anfield, but this week people kept finding themselves cornered by a very different Jimmy to the quiet, studious, competent middle-manager that they knew. Now they were being grilled about family members and their general state of health. It was all a bit eerie, and by Wednesday more than one victim had taken to putting on their harried, busy, can't-stop-to-chat face as soon as they saw Jimmy Collins round a corner in front of them, armed with wide grin and bouncy stride.

What they didn't know was that Jimmy had gotten a call from Sparky on Monday morning, asking him did he want to sit in on the mixdown.

'Does a bear shite in the woods, Sparky?' he said. 'And wipe his arse with a white furry rabbit? Bloody right I'd like to sit in! But, I'm in work, y'know? I can come in in the evenings ...'

'That's grand, Jimmy. It takes all day to work out how I'm going to do it anyway. Except for Beano's songs. That doesn't take so long on account of me not being able to do much with them. I'm good, Jimmy, but I'm not bleedin' Wonder Woman. Even Donal here is wondering if he's really family. You want to come in around seven? We can do a couple of hours every night this week, if you're free. We got a booking for next Saturday, some Westlife shite, so that'll be it. This place has to start paying for itself then, or I'll be back to rubbing Van Morrison's bunions for him.'

Jimmy hung up and smiled. It was the only expression he was able to manage until the following Friday night, except for about five minutes on Wednesday morning, when he stubbed his toe on Shiggy's keg of lager on his way into the kitchen. It had been delivered on Tuesday and he'd forgotten all about it, it being early and a large metal barrel full of beer just inside the kitchen door not being something he was used to stumbling across. It had been a very curious Mr McGrath from next door that had rung his bell at ten o'clock on Tuesday night, with the keg at his feet and a delivery notice in his hand.

'You're not planning any silliness now, are you Jimmy?'

'Not at all, Mr McGrath. This is for someone else. Thanks for taking it in for me. I'm just minding it. He won it in a raffle.'

'Well, that's okay, Jimmy. Because we don't want a repeat of what happened the last time you had a party, do we?'

'Eh no,' said Jimmy. 'But I swear, Mr McGrath, I know nothing about your plants. I think it was some kids from the road did that.'

'Kids on this road, Jimmy, have toilets in their houses. They don't need to go weeing over the wall on people's strawberries.'

'Right. Well, I'm not having a party anyway, Mr McGrath, so there's nothing to worry about.'

Bloody Aesop and his Who Can Piss The Furthest competition. He even had Norman doing it, although the fact that it was Jennifer's friend Michelle who had actually won in the end, had added a subdued note to the evening. Everyone, with the notable exception of Mr McGrath, had done their best to put the whole disquieting incident out of their minds. Especially Michelle, around whom guys had since become very guarded.

For the first couple of nights in the studio with Sparky, a lot of the time ended up being spent on Beano's stuff. There were four songs and Sparky had committed to finishing them. He wasn't one to go back on his word, Jimmy saw, and he honestly did his best to give them a professional treatment, adding some digital effects and generally spicing things up a bit. It gave the gear a bit of a workout and also meant that Donal could put his hand on his heart at the family Christmas party and say he did his best by his nephew, or 'the little fecker', as he had taken to calling him after countless hours spent listening to his songs. He'd actually offered to let Beano sit in on the mix, the way Jimmy was now doing, but Beano had declined, saying he was too knackered after the weekend. Donal and Sparky couldn't believe that Beano would give up a chance like that. Jimmy could.

On Tuesday night they'd listened non-stop to *Red Rage* for about two hours, just trying to give it some life. By nine o'clock, the three of them were sitting in the control room with tired eyes and stiff necks. The relentlessly boring tune was now echoing cruelly around in their heads. And the lyrics. Jesus, the lyrics ...

> It's an outrage, we gotta turn the page,
> Live in a new age, get out of this cage,
> Get off the stage, disengage,
> Cos I'm in a red rage, a red, red, red, red rage.

It was painful enough after one listen. Twenty times later, you found you were in quite the red fucking rage yourself. They were getting desperate.

Donal stopped the music and they all sat in silence for about five minutes, trying to think. Eventually Donal took Jimmy's arm and sat him down next to him.

'Jimmy. My sister Joan is a great girl. Her husband Danny is a good mate of mine. I introduced them and me and Danny go for pints, y'know? I don't see too much of Joan or the kids any more. They're all grown up now anyway and everyone's too busy. Y'know the way. Christmas, maybe, or a wedding or something, is all. But we're still family, Jimmy. We'll always be family. You know Beano better than I do. Tell me, Jimmy. What's he taking?'

He sat back and watched Jimmy carefully, one hand on the arm of his chair like he was holding himself up, the fingers of the other quickly stroking his chin.

'Nothing,' said Jimmy, surprised. 'He's not on anything.'

Donal stood up.

'Shit!' he shouted. 'Shit, piss and corruption!' He turned back to Jimmy. 'Are you sure, Jimmy? You're positive, now?'

'Yeah, pretty much.'

'Ah ... feckin' ... bugger it,' said Donal, sitting down again and cupping his face with his hands. He looked heart-broken.

'Sorry Donal,' said Sparky.

'Thanks Sparky,' said Donal.

'We could've done something if it was drugs.'

'I know, I know. But it's not. He's just like that. Bollocks. Poor Joan.'

They did what they could with the song, adding some keyboard sounds and doing a job on it with what Sparky called the 'aural exciter'.

'I don't like using too much of these effects, Jimmy, but me hands are tied. There's nothing I can do,' he said. He looked embarrassed.

All this took up a lot of the time that they could've spent on Jimmy's song, but he didn't mind. He got to watch how all the editing and mixing equipment worked. There was a lot of computer work involved, which surprised Jimmy but didn't disappoint him. It was about time his intuitive grasp of technology was good for something, other than selling software solutions to poor bastards who didn't even realise that they had software problems until Jimmy started finding some for them. He sat and watched Sparky at work. It was truly a strange sensation to realise that this guy was closer to his Dad's age than his own, and yet was so utterly cool. His Dad's idea of cool was the silver chain he now used to hang his glasses around his neck so that he wouldn't keep losing them. The last album he'd brought into the house was some Perry Como abomination about fifteen years earlier and he'd won that in golf for coming last.

They pretty much finished up with Lavender's Teardrop early on Wednesday night, and then it was time for *Caillte*.

'Okay Jimmy,' said Sparky. 'Remember what I told you about this software?'

Jimmy closed his eyes.

'Eh, Protools. On a Mac G5. Mix Plus, 3 x 888/24, USD, Motor Mix, Autotune ... eh ... Retrospect, DDS4 tape back-up,' he said.

'You see that, Donal? Jimmy here is like meself when I was his age. I was the very same. Except for the hair,' said Sparky. He looked at Jimmy's blonde streaked hair like it might be contagious.

'What's wrong with me hair?' said Jimmy, combing one hand through it. The roots were coming out nicely now and he thought it was getting cooler by the day.

'Jimmy. You don't need that, right?' said Sparky, pointing with his coffee mug at Jimmy's head. 'You have talent. Don't think you have to have a crutch like blondy hair or black nail varnish or mad fucking colourdy pants to get the message across when you're making your music. That's only bollocks. A gimmick. Don't go for gimmicks or fads. It's all in there.' He pointed at Jimmy's groin. 'D'ye know what I mean? Jimmy, I've been in this business for thirty years. More. I've seen the shite people do get up to when they're on the stage, dressing like clowns or acting the maggot or having lasers and mirrors and fucking big balloons all over the place, to distract the audience from their crap music. Don't do that. Promise me you won't do that, Jimmy.' He was getting excited.

'Jesus, Sparky, it's only a haircut.'

'No Jimmy! No. It's not just a haircut. It's where it all starts.' He started waving his hands about the place. 'Jimmy, man, be true. Feel it. It's all around ye. Tap into it, man. Live it. Grab it and keep it.'

'Eh, relax the head Sparky,' said Donal, carefully.

Sparky ignored him.

'I've seen it all, Jimmy. Don't mind your hair or your clothes or what people think. You're better than that. You're alive, for fuck sake. Alive! Love every second of it, Jimmy. Don't just do it. Be it! Wake up. You don't want to just be in a band, Jim, you want to plug your face into the wall and play the electricity with your tongue, y'know? I did it, Jimmy. It woke me up, I can fucking tell you that for nothing. Those few seconds, before I went into a coma, were the most alive I've ever felt.' He stopped talking and turned back around to the console, breathing heavily and sweating.

'Donal?' said Jimmy, nervously. 'Is Sparky all right?'

'Eh, yeah. I think Beano's songs are giving him a flash-back. Sparky, pal, just relax. It's all right. Everything's grand. We're all grand, okay? Look, finish your coffee. It's getting cold on you.'

'He didn't really do that, did he? With his tongue?' said Jimmy.

'Yeah,' said Donal, rubbing his eyes. 'Fuck, that was a long day.'

'He said he'd been electrocuted. Jesus, I thought it was a dodgy amp or something.'

'No. Wasn't an amp, Jimmy. He was trying to kiss the little goblin that made the lights work. Nearly bloody killed him. Don't you try it, you hear me?'

'Right, yeah. I'll try and remember that,' said Jimmy, looking at Sparky, who had now calmed down and was drinking his coffee.

'Sparky?' said Donal. 'You okay?'

'What? Yeah, yeah. Grand. Where were we?'

'Eh, Protools ...' said Jimmy.

'Oh yeah. Good man Jimmy,' Sparky said. 'Right, we're using Protools. Let's see what we can make of this crap song of yours, right? Time to have a bit of fun.'

You've had quite enough fun for one lifetime, Sparky, thought Jimmy.

'You're the man, Sparky,' he said. 'I'm all ears.'

'Oh, just one thing, Jimmy ...' said Donal.

'Yeah?'

'Before we start, I just wanted to let you know that I know a couple of people in RTE. On the radio side. I think I can get *Caillte* some airtime, if it turns out well. I'm not promising anything, now. I never do that, so you might as well get used to it, but I'll put in a word and see if I can get you on a playlist.'

'Jesus, Donal, that'd be cool! Anything you can do, like ...'

'Yeah. Well, like I said, I'm not promising anything. If I do get something, it'll probably be late night or whatever. It's in Irish and all, y'know? Anyway, we'll see, right?'

'Thanks, Donal. I really appreciate it.'

'No problem. Maybe you can help me out with something, too.'

'What?'

'Well, you know computers, right?'

'Yeah ...'

'Yeah, well I want a Web page for this place and the bastards are quoting me thousands. Can you do it? We could come to an arrangement, y'know? Maybe you could use the place the odd time when there's nothing on, or whatever.'

'Brilliant! No problem, Donal. I'll make you the best Website in Dublin! God, if I could use this place ...'

'Good. Right. Come on, then. Let's make a song out of this nonsense you're after recording,' Donal smiled.

Sparky was grinning at the two of them, ready to go. He looked, relatively speaking, sane again.

On Friday night, Jimmy met the lads in the pub in time for last orders.

'Pint?' said Aesop, getting up with a groan as soon as Jimmy reached the table.

'Yeah. Good man,' said Jimmy.

They pushed up to let him sit down and, when Aesop arrived back with the beer, Jimmy smiled at them around the table and opened his bag.

'A toast lads,' he said, lifting up his glass.

They all raised theirs as well, looking at each other.

'To Sparky and Donal,' he said.

'To Sparky and Donal,' they repeated. Then they looked at Jimmy's other hand, which rose to take the place of the pint that was now pouring down his throat. It was clutching a shiny new CD in a clear plastic case. He put his glass down and looked around again.

'This is it,' he said simply and then yelled, 'Ye hay!! We fucking did it lads! We have a CD!!'

They cheered and passed the CD around, each of them feeling it and holding it up to the light, as if to make sure it wasn't a fake.

'Congratulations,' said Norman, beaming. 'Can't wait to hear it.'

'Well, why don't we go back to my place now and listen to it?' said Jimmy, moving to stand up.

'Yeah cool,' said Aesop. 'But hang on 'til I finish me pint here, will ye? Relax a minute. The CD isn't going anywhere.'

'Oh yeah, Shiggy, I forgot to tell you,' said Jimmy. 'Your beer arrived in my gaff the other day. I have it in me kitchen. The tap is there as well and they gave you six free glasses to ...'

'C'mon, y'right?' said Aesop, who had suddenly drained his glass and was standing up.

'Jaysis, Aesop, what happened to "relax a minute"?' said Jimmy, looking up at him.

'Fuck that. Let's go. C'mon,' said Aesop, picking up the

coats from the back of the bench and handing them around. 'We've a CD to listen to.'

'And beer to drink?' said Jimmy.

'Oh yeah. And that. Come on, Jimmy, hurry up with that. Marco, there's only a squirt in that glass; down it and let's go.'

Aesop practically bundled them out the door and down the street, in the direction of Jimmy's house.

'Hang on Aesop,' said Norman. 'I want to get chips.'

'I'll bleedin' make you chips when we get there,' said Aesop, breaking into a gentle trot.

'Aesop rike beer,' observed Shiggy.

'Yeah,' said Jimmy, watching Aesop slow to a walk after just fifty yards and bend over, gasping. 'I think it's the only thing left in his life that he hasn't become disillusioned about.'

They reached the house and Jimmy let them all in. Aesop ran straight into the kitchen and turned on the light, falling to his knees at the side of the keg.

'Look at it Jimmy,' he whispered. 'Look at it.'

'I don't need to look at it, Aesop. I've been fucking falling over it all week. It weighs a bloody ton.'

'We can fix that, Jimmy. There's no problem there. I know just how to make it lighter. Now. Hand me that pump yoke over there and let's get the party going.'

'Wait a minute, Aesop. The last time I had a party in here, I had a very irate neighbour around the next day, complaining about the smell of piss off his rhubarb. Take it easy, all right? There's enough beer in there to do us for a month. Anyway, it's Shiggy's beer.'

'My hole it's Shiggy's beer,' said Aesop. He stood up and pointed a finger at Jimmy. 'No one's worked harder for this than me,' he said, fiercely. 'Do you hear me? Fucking no one. Shiggy sang a song. One poxy song. Look at me. Look at me, Jimmy! I'm destroyed! I haven't slept for weeks. Even when I'm on me own I can't sleep, 'cos I'm expecting her to jump out of me wardrobe or something. I couldn't even run twenty feet down the road earlier and I nearly threw up. This is my beer, Jimmy.' He pointed at the red logo on the top of the keg. 'These people have taken enough from me. It's payback time.'

Twenty minutes later, they were all sitting in Jimmy's lounge with pints of beer. Jimmy had the remote for his stereo in his hand and looked at them all.

'Ready?' he said, and pushed play.

They sat and listened, shocked. They didn't know what they were expecting, but the song coming out of Jimmy's speakers had them wowing and whistling and cursing softly. It was amazing.

Jimmy sounded like himself, but different. The guitars were almost ethereal. Aesop cocked his head and took in the drums, while Shiggy was doing the same with the bass. Norman and Marco both sat with their mouths half open, looking from the stereo to the speakers to Jimmy and back to the stereo again. The song ended and they all looked at each other. Jimmy pressed stop.

'Fucking *hell*,' said Aesop.

The others nodded agreement.

'Wotcha think?' said Jimmy, grinning his head off.

'Jimmy ... Good God,' was all Norman could say.

Marco muttered something in Italian.

Shiggy pointed at the stereo.

'Pray again, Jimmy.'

Jimmy played it again. The reaction was almost exactly the same, but with more cursing.

'That's not all lads. Through the miracles of modern science, here's the dance version.'

'The what?' said Aesop.

'Shush,' said Jimmy. 'Listen ...'

He pressed play again and forwarded to track two. Immediately a drum and bass beat kicked in with some weird scratching noises. The song seemed to be much faster.

'Who's playing the drums?' said Aesop.

'You are,' said Jimmy.

'I fucking am not! I mightn't be a hundred percent this weather, Jimmy, but I know what I played.'

'We sampled it. And the bass. We sampled it and then looped it back over the track. It's about three seconds of a take, played over and over through the song.'

Aesop sat back, stunned.

'You mean ... they can *do* that? They can make me play dance music?'

He curled up on the couch, hugging his knees.

'Jesus, Aesop, it's not like some dirty old man dropped the hand on you. Look at you! You'd swear you'd been violated,' said Jimmy.

'Ah Jimmy, there's violation and there's violation. I'm not sure how I feel about all this. If they can do that, what else can they do?'

'Here. This'll make you feel better,' said Jimmy. He pressed play again.

Aesop heard himself say 'One, two, three, four ...' and then the rest of the band crashed in. Only one song sounded that good to Aesop's ears.

'Jesus, Jimmy. It's ... it's ...'

'Yeah, I know. And if this song ever gets played on the radio, then you'll be having a very fat and pissed off American rock star come around to sit on your face until you die.'

'It'd be worth it, Jimmy. God, it'd be worth it,' said Aesop, softly, as the first chorus roared in and the knocking on Jimmy's side wall started.

Twenty-four

Jimmy kept waiting for a call from Donal, but it never came. Donal didn't actually say he'd call, but Jimmy was hoping for that one magical conversation where Donal told him that his song was on Dave Fanning's playlist on 2FM. That thousands of people were hearing it every night, calling up the station to demand that they be allowed to buy a copy for themselves and inquiring about where they might do this. One particularly insistent caller would be a babe from Clontarf, who'd insist that she be put in touch with the composer. Jimmy rang the studio once that week, but Donal wasn't there and Sparky was too busy to talk for long.

'Boy band Jimmy,' said Sparky, as if this explained it all.

'Is that bad?' asked Jimmy.

'Not so much bad, as a bit depressing. I remember when you could have a face on you like a plate of stew and still make it in this business. There's five of them. Two can sing and the rest of them are like yer man out of *Frankie Goes to Hollywood*. They dance. Dance, dance, dance. That's all they do. They're even bleedin' dancing in here and no one's here to watch them only me, and I keep telling them to fucking give over. They're leaving scuffmarks on me lovely new wooden floor, the bastards. I had to tell them to take off their shoes. Jaysis. Ye'd think they were in a Michael Jackson video, the state of them. The oldest one is about twelve and they ask their manager before they go to the toilet. What's happening, Jimmy, y'know? They don't shave yet and they'll probably be on *Top of the Pops* in a month. Ah bollocks, look, Jimmy, I've to go. One of them's after going on his snot and knocking over the mike stands. I'll get the blame for that, watch, 'cos he only had his socks on. Jesus. Do I look like a bleedin' babysitter?'

'Oh God no,' said Jimmy, a small shiver running through him at the idea.

'Right,' said Sparky. 'Talk to you later, okay? Look at him, the bleedin' eejit. Knocks a thousand quid worth of gear onto the floor, then gets up and checks his hair in the mirror. I'll batter him, the fuckin' little ...'

Jimmy said goodbye and hung up, laughing. A twelve-year-old budding superstar was about to get an almighty bollocking from Sparky. He might need their business, but Jimmy suspected that Sparky would only put up with so much before he started terrorising them.

For a week Jimmy did as much work as he could on the two Websites, updating The Grove's one and building a new one for the studio. He was actually having a laugh with it. The band's site was bright and funky and the most important thing of all – a link to *Caillte* so that people could download a copy for themselves – took pride of place, under a big green banner. There were photos of the band on the stage, or just around the place, and lyrics to some of their other songs. *Caillte* was translated too. There was no mistaking the intent. Songwriter looking for a girl called Kayleigh. Not the subtlest of poetic devices, but Jimmy hadn't been in a subtle humour when he wrote it. There'd be no misunderstandings. If she heard it, she'd know.

The best photo on the site was of Shiggy, wearing all black leather and standing outside some temple thing in Japan. Gave the band a cool international look, Jimmy thought. Shiggy gave him the picture and explained that it was taken when he was seventeen. That didn't matter. Shiggy didn't seem to have changed since he was about twelve. Aesop's picture had him behind a drum kit during a gig they'd done in Waterford, a couple of years ago. It was a brilliant shot, his face down, arms flying, hair and sweat making a break from his head. His own picture was mid-solo, eyes closed and guitar strings held in a big bend. He looked like a guitar hero, except guitar heroes aren't usually pictured with their Mammies sitting on the couch behind them, drinking a cup of tea. It had been taken by Liz in the living-room, on the day Jimmy bought his new guitar. The whole portfolio was of a band who didn't take itself too seriously, and that was fine.

Getting photos of Donal and Sparky for their site proved a little more difficult. He'd brought Shiggy's digital camera into the studio to get some shots, and while Donal could be relied upon to stand still and look at the camera, Sparky was having trouble making eye contact with the lens.

'Just look at the camera, Sparky, and smile, okay?'

'I'm trying, Jimmy. It's just a bit freaky.'

'How is it freaky? It's just a camera, Sparky ...'

'To you maybe.'

Jimmy asked Donal about it later.

'Ah. It's an acid thing,' said Donal, looking away and pretending to be interested in whatever was in his breast pocket. 'Never take acid Jimmy,' he said absently, over his shoulder.

He eventually got Sparky from the side, working at the console and Donal said that was good enough. The Website was fairly simple; location map, phone numbers, Donal and Sparky's client list – including The Grove – the equipment available in the studio. It would do for starters and if Donal wanted more, they could talk about it afterwards.

While all this, and the small matter of his job, was keeping Jimmy busy, it wasn't doing anything for his nerves. Recording the song and getting the CD was all brilliant of course, but throughout the following week he was finding himself thinking more and more about Kayleigh. Now that his big clever idea was actually taking place, he was starting to get impatient. It had been weeks. She could be with some other bloke by now. A girl like that doesn't hang about waiting for bastards who don't call when they say they will, does she? He rang the nightclub and the restaurant another couple of times, but then gave up on the idea that she'd go back there looking for him. Anyway, it was getting embarrassing.

'Hello, La Parisienne. This is Jean. How can I help you?'

'Ah, hello Jean. My name is Jimmy Collins. I called last week ... eh, I think I was talking to a Dave? Is Dave there?'

'Dave Harrison or Dave Wright?'

'Eh, I don't know. Are either of them there?'

'Hang on. Jimmy Collins, was it?'

'Yeah.'

'Just a minute, Mr Collins.'

Well, they were polite enough. Dinner in there would probably be lovely.

'Hello?'

'Dave?'

'Dave Wright, yes. How can I help you?'

'Eh, this is Jimmy Collins. Was I talking to you about a girl called Kayleigh? Last week, like ...'

'I'm sorry. I don't know anyone called Kayleigh ...'

'Ah, right. Must have been the other Dave. Is he there?'

'No. He doesn't work on Wednesdays. Can I help you?'

'Well, maybe. Y'see, the thing is, I met this girl, right? And ...'

It went on like that, the silences from Dave becoming longer and longer as he began toying with the idea of just hanging up on the weirdo with the missing girlfriend. Eventually Jimmy thanked him, apologised for bothering him and said goodbye with the distinct feeling that the next time he called he'd be reported to the police for sounding far too peculiar. The nightclub was no better. He'd tried being more direct, to no avail.

'Hello?'

'Hello. My name is Jimmy Collins. I'm looking for a girl that I met in there a few weeks ago. Name of Kayleigh. We won a Karaoke competition. I lost her number, y'see? Did she leave a message for me, or anything?'

'No.'

'Eh, are you sure?'

'Yeah.'

'Absolutely?'

'Yeah.'

'Right. Okay. Well, thanks for the chat anyway. Jesus.'

'No problem.'

Click.

Bollocks to this, thought Jimmy. He was never going to find her that way, and one CD wasn't going to change the musical face of Ireland, was it?

There was nothing else for it. Little and all as he knew about the business, and loathe though he was to use the term, it was time to be pro-active about putting his song out there. Donal was busy. Fair enough. He'd get *Caillte* on the radio himself.

Two weeks later he had three hundred copies of his CD, and the Website was live. He felt a bit guilty about the CDs. He'd done most of them in work. His computer at home could make copies for him, but only one at a time. There was an industrial CD burner in work and he could do about thirty a day without being too obvious about it, but he felt so bad about having to hang around the media room for an hour every day, instead of being at his desk where he should have been, that he actually went out and bought three hundred blank CDs when he was done to replace the ones he'd used. God Jimmy, he said to himself, you'd make a bloody awful thief.

He did up some artwork on his computer at home and printed it out at work. More guilt. He had his own printer by his desk, but it took a long time to print one hundred and fifty colour sheets and every hum and click from the machine had him cringing that his boss would walk over in the middle of it and ask him what the hell he was up to with all the printing. It felt like when he called in sick with a hangover because Aesop had him out on the piss on a work night. It had only happened once or twice, but Jimmy hated himself for it. It was fine up until about lunchtime, but once he'd had a bucket of coffee and chewed a handful of tablets to make the pain go away, he'd sit there all afternoon feeling like a waster.

But he eventually got it all done. Three hundred CDs and three hundred inserts. It was time to get the lads around to help him put them all together.

'Ah Jimmy,' moaned Aesop. 'I'm bleedin' knackered.'

'There's still about twenty pints left in Shiggy's keg,' Jimmy pointed out.

'Right. I'll seeya about seven.'

It wasn't their usual venue for Friday night drinking, but Shiggy, Aesop, Marco and Norman all crowded around his coffee table, pints of beer nearby, and started cutting, folding and stacking. Free lager. It was like they'd be betraying themselves in a profoundly deep and personal way if they didn't go to Jimmy's to drink it. Of course, once they got there, they tried to make out like they were doing him a favour, but Jimmy wasn't fooled.

'Anyway,' he said, 'Piss off, Aesop. This is your CD as well, right?'

'I know it is. Amn't I here helping you?'

'And the fact that you're stuck into pints, and Sharon is nowhere near the place, has nothing to do with it?'

'Stop, Jimmy. Don't even mention her name.'

'Why not?'

'We had a row.'

'You had a row with a girl, Aesop?' Norman didn't believe it.

'Yes, Norman. A row. A disagreement.'

'Over what?'

'Nothing,' said Aesop, and started into a new pile of CDs.

The lads all looked at each other. Aesop was losing it. His hands were shaking and his hair was dank and tangled. There were tiny red veins squirming their way across his eyeballs and he kept sniffling.

'I think you're run down,' said Jimmy.

'Probably,' said Aesop.

'So, when you say you had a row, does that mean it's all over?'

'I didn't say that, Jimmy. We just need to work some things out.'

'Like what?'

'Ah Jesus, Jimmy, leave it, will you? Here, gimme up that scissors there and some of those sleeves. And will you change the music? It's a nice song and all, but I'm getting a pain in me hole listening to it over and over. Have you no AC/DC, or something? It's Friday night on the beer for fuck sake, not bleedin' Sunday afternoon on the couch.'

They finished the CDs by half ten. Marco went off to meet Jennifer in the pub with Shiggy, and Norman wanted to go home and check on his Mam, who hadn't been feeling well.

'Maybe someone put a clove of garlic in her knicker drawer,' said Aesop, once he heard the front door close behind Norman.

'I wouldn't say that out loud Aesop,' said Jimmy. 'Norman has very good ears when it comes to his Ma.'

'Best ears in the army,' said Aesop. 'Mind you, with the Irish army, that's not saying a lot, is it?'

'Are you going to tell me what's wrong with you and Sharon? There's still a couple of pints left. We might as well get plastered and moan about shite.'

'Ah Jaysis, Jimmy. Ye'd only laugh.'

'I won't laugh. C'mon to fuck. What's up with ye?'

'No, Jimmy. It's, eh ... it's a bit embarrassing.'

'Aesop, you're incapable of being embarrassed. Just tell me what happened, will ye?'

'She's ... she just ... Jimmy, she has no fucking respect, y'know?'

Jimmy put down his glass. This was a new one. He bit down on his lip and tried to swallow the giggle that was making its merry way up his throat.

'Respect?'

'Yeah. I mean, she calls me up whenever she feels like it, we do a bit of riding, sometimes she has a mate with her or something ... and then I don't hear from her again 'til she wants another jant a couple of days later. No phone calls from Athlone or Cork just to say "Hello", or "Howarya Aesop, how's your Granny" or fuck all, y'know? This has been going on for ages. I mean, it's not like I'm looking for a best mate or anything, but ... I don't know. It's like she's just using me.'

Jimmy couldn't take it any more. He broke his bollocks laughing.

'Ye bastard!' said Aesop. 'You said you wouldn't laugh.'

Jimmy was still laughing, but tried to stop so he could speak.

'Aesop. For fuck sake. What are you like? Respect? Using you? Can you cast your mind back over the last fifteen years? Before you met Sharon? Aesop, you spent all that time being the biggest using, disrespectful bastard in Dublin, and now you're giving out about Sharon? You're a cheeky bollocks, so you are.'

'Ah, hang on a minute, Jimmy. It's not the same thing.'

'It bloody is the same thing. The exact same thing!'

'It isn't. I've been honest with Sharon, right? I haven't done the dirt on her. I'm doing me best to ... y'know ... be a boyfriend.' He went red at that. 'But she pisses off down the country for work, or turns up at my gaff whenever she feels like it. Half the time, I don't even know who's going to be in her gaff when I get there. She has me up all night and then I have to piss off at seven in the morning and go home, 'cos she's got to drive to bleedin' Galway or something. She treats me like I'm just some poor bastard that's there whenever she wants me, but she doesn't put in any effort for *me*, y'know?'

'Aesop, you're getting mixed up. I know *you're* different with Sharon. My point is that what Sharon's doing is exactly what you've always done. How many birds did you have to get out of the house before your Dad woke up on a Sunday morning? How many lies have you told so you could get a portion? How many times did you treat a girl like shite once you've cleaned your pipes? Sharon is exactly the same. You are unbelievable, Aesop. You avoid getting close to any woman for years, and then the one woman you think you're actually into turns out to be a mad tart who no more wants to settle down with you than I fucking do! Can you not see it, Aesop? Come on, you dozy bastard. It's obvious.'

'What is?'

'Aesop. You want a real girlfriend but you're afraid. That's why you picked a girl that it would never work out with. That's what's obvious.'

'Bollocks, Jimmy. That's crap. You've been reading Sandra's books again, haven't you?'

'Sandra took all her books, Aesop. I'm serious. You're trying to grow up and be a bit normal, but you haven't got the balls for it.'

'Fuck off I haven't got the balls! Amn't I trying to make this work with Sharon?'

'That's my point, you fool. It'll never work with Sharon! She's a fucking spacer. She's having a laugh, doing her own thing. Leave her to it and get the fuck out, before you catch the pox off her or one of her mates. You're out of your depth.'

'She hasn't got the pox.'

'Sooner or later, Aesop, if you're getting involved in all

that scene, you'll be coming home with more than just aches and pains, right? These aren't shy little girls that you're picking up in the pub because you play the drums. Sharon and her buddies are way past that and you'd be better off staying the fuck away from them.'

'Actually, that's what the row was about.'

'What?'

'She wanted to go for four in the bed.'

'I thought yiz did that already?'

'Yeah. But not this way. Two blokes, two women.'

'Fuck.'

'Yeah.'

'And what did you say?'

'I told her to fuck off!'

'And what did she say?'

'Ah, she got all pissed off and said it was grand with women and all, so what's the difference.'

'And what did you say?'

'Will you stop saying that?'

'Well, tell me the fucking story then!'

'I am! She wanted some couple she knows to come along tomorrow night, right? I said what do you mean couple? She said Bob and Mary or fuckin' whatever. I said me bollocks. Who the fuck is Bob? Ah, says she, Bob is grand. Nice bloke. Likes a bit of fun, she says. Likes a bit of fun, y'know, winking at me. Right? Likes a bit of fun, she says, like I'm the Pope with a dose of the trots all of a sudden. What do you mean fun, says I? Ah, y'know, she says. No, I says, I don't bleedin' know. What kind of fun? You and me, she says, Bob and Mary, you and Mary, me and Bob, me and Mary ... Yeah, says I. You and Mary? Sharon, you and Mary and what? Well, Bob's into anything, she says. Well he's not into me, I says! Why not Aesop? 'Cos I'm not like that, I says. I mean, Jaysis, y'know Jimmy? It doesn't mean anything, she says. It's just between us. You never know 'til you try it. All that. Are you off your bleedin' trolley, I says to her. What, she says. You never know. Yiz might hit it off. The only thing I'll be hitting, Sharon, I says to her, is Bob's bollocks with a baseball bat if he fucking comes anywhere near me with it, right? Then we had a row.'

Jimmy sat and looked at him for a minute.

'That's a good story Aesop,' he said.

'Thanks.'

'You'll have to put that one in your repertoire.'

'Yeah. Need to spice it up a bit, but.'

They both laughed.

'So what now?' said Jimmy.

'I don't know. She said if I really cared about her, I'd do it.'

'Jaysis.'

'I know.'

'That's like "If you really loved me, you'd give me a blow-job".'

'I know.'

'Except for the bit about Bob's mickey up yer arse I s'pose.'

'Yeah. I told her no bleedin' way. So she just hung up. I think that's it, Jimmy. I found Superchick and she slipped through my fingers.'

'Ah, well. At least you have your pride. That's the main thing.'

'Yeah. And me cherry.'

'She wasn't really Superchick, though, was she Aesop?'

'I thought she was, Jimmy. Really. For a while there, I thought so.'

'How long?'

'A couple of nights anyway.'

'Yeah. Aesop, the whole Superchick thing was meant to be long-term, but, y'know?'

'Long-term? When was the last time I spent two nights

in a row with one bird, Jimmy?'

'Never.'

'Right. Well, that's long term then, isn't it?'

'And you really weren't tempted?'

'By what?'

'Bob.'

'Jimmy, I always said that if I ever turned homo, then I'd want you to be my first.'

'Wow. I feel so special when you get romantic like that.'

'Well then, stop asking me stupid questions, right? I have me principles, y'know?'

'Well, I'm glad to hear it, Aesop. I was having doubts there, for a while. For about twenty years, to be honest.'

'Yeah. Well I do.'

'So, you're not going to call her?'

'Nah. No point.'

'And you're still looking for Superchick?'

'We'll see, Jimmy. I'll get me hole tomorrow night – y'know, off some nice girl, like – to get Sharon out of me system and see how I feel then.'

'A nice girl, right. 'Cos you have your principles, yeah?'

'Exactly.'

Twenty-five

The door to the pub opened and a guy about the right age came in, but it wasn't who Jimmy was looking for. He turned back around to the bar and took another sup of his pint. It was only half past five, but the after-work crowd was starting to filter in for a quick scoop before heading home, and there were more people in the place than Jimmy would have liked. He told himself that if it was too noisy his plan would never work but in fact the problem was that he was starting to feel like an awful gobshite, creeping around like the place and asking questions like he was David Jason all of a sudden.

He was waiting for Tony King to arrive. King was a DJ on Rock FM and was one of the few people on the radio in Dublin who didn't play shite. His show was from seven to ten each weeknight and it was the only place to go if you were in the mood for some Frames, Jane's Addiction, Belle and Sebastian, Joy Division, Snow Patrol or even Neil Young. He played a lot of album tracks that you wouldn't know so well, songs by younger Indie bands and, most importantly, he also liked to sprinkle new songs around his playlist by up-and-coming Irish bands. Jimmy thought he was brilliant. Just the man.

He'd tried calling the station but the one time he'd gotten through, he managed to find himself actually on air.

'We have a caller from North Dublin. Hi caller. What's your name?'

'What? Oh bolloc ... eh, Jimmy. Jimmy Collins.'

'Hi Jimmy. What can we play for you?'

That was the point where Jimmy, if he'd been thinking instead of looking at his radio on the kitchen windowsill in horror and going red, could have asked Tony right there and then would he play his song if he sent it in? Maybe even mention that it was for Kayleigh, if she was listening. But Jimmy had expected to get a secretary, or whoever answered the phones in radio stations, and his mind went blank.

'I love the show, Mr King,' he said, and immediately punched himself in his free ear for being a prat.

'Glad to hear it, Jimmy. Thanks very much. What song would you like to hear?'

Christ, everyone he knew listened to this show. Mr King, he'd said.

'Eh, do you have any Jam?'

'Absolutely, Jimmy. Any favourite track?'

'*Eton Rifles?*'

'*Eton Rifles*. Great choice. From the late Seventies I think, right Jimmy? And anyone special you'd like to play that for?'

'Eh ... Aesop.'

'Aesop. Great. Well, thanks Jimmy. I'll go and find The Jam for you, and in the meantime here's The Cult and *She Sells Sanctuary* ...'

Jimmy hung up and looked at the fridge miserably.

Four minutes later Tony was back, talking to him from the windowsill again.

'Great. And here's The Jam with *Eton Rifles*. Going out to the special person in Jimmy's life. This one's for Aesop ...'

The phone rang almost immediately.

'You geebag.'

'Howya Aesop.'

'What the bleedin' hell are you doing?!'

'Look, I got a bit caught off guard, right? I was only looking for an address to post the bloody CD, and the next thing I'm talking to him on the radio. What was I s'posed to do?'

'"This one's for Aesop." I'm bleedin' mortified!'

'I know. I'm sorry, right?'

'Jesus. And *Eton Rifles*. Why didn't you get him to play *Tube Station* or *Modern World*?'

'Aesop, will you piss off? I wasn't thinking, okay? Look, I'll talk to you tomorrow, right?'

'I was only after having a smoke, Jimmy. I thought I was tripping, y'know? Lying on the bed watching me cloud and you coming out of the radio like it was bleedin' possessed. Me fuckin' heart ...'

'Okay, Aesop. Seeya, right?'

He eventually got the address for Rock FM and sent the CD, but that was over a week ago and he'd heard nothing. He decided to move the mountain to Mohammed. The radio station was just off Capel Street and he knew from his column in the Sunday Post that King liked to go to Nealon's the odd time for a pint before work. That's what he was doing there, looking around at the door every two minutes and checking his pocket again and again to make sure the CD was safe. It was the third time he'd come and the barman actually gave him a friendly nod this time when he pushed the door open. The tenner Jimmy had given him the last two nights for having a copy of the CD ready to play was the easiest twenty euro he'd ever earned and another ten tonight would be worth the smile.

Jimmy went for a quick piss and when he came back Tony King was sitting two seats down from his own, reading the newspaper and eating a ham and cheese sandwich. He sat down and nervously drank half his pint, calling for another. He stole a sideways glance. Tony looked cooler in his Sunday Post picture, but it was definitely him. The ears gave it away. Maybe that's why he got into being a DJ? Massive big ears like that must be deadly for listening to music.

'Tony King?' he said.

Tony looked around.

'Yeah?'

'Howya. I'm Jimmy Collins.'

Tony said nothing. Just nodded slightly.

'Eh, I called you on the radio last week. You played The

Jam for me ...'

'Oh yeah. For your girlfriend ... em ... Aesop, right?'

'Eh ... he's not me girlfriend. He's me drummer.'

Tony just nodded again, turning slightly in the chair to get a better look at Jimmy and peeking quickly to see where the barman was. Being in the public ear like he was, you had to be careful. It was amazing the things people took exception to. Having a caller show up uninvited next to you in the pub was about as welcome as seeing a red laser dot creep along the floor, up your leg and stop on your left nipple.

'Eh, the thing is, I'm in a band, and ... I was hoping you'd play a song of ours on the show. That's why I called last week, but I didn't expect to be talking to you on air and I kind of forgot to ask you.'

'Ah, right. Listen, Jimmy, I get a lot of songs, y'know? I'm sure yours is very good and all, but I can't play everything I get. Do you have a tape of it? I'll give it a listen and ...'

Jimmy nodded at the barman, who stopped the INXS album that was playing and put on *Caillte* instead.

'I've only got it on CD. And this is it,' he said, pointing at the ceiling, from where the music started to come.

Tony King listened for a minute, saying nothing, and then started to look like he just might be impressed. He was. The song sounded good. It didn't exactly thunder along, but it was obviously professionally put together, although it was hard to hear above the hum of pub conversation. Also, Jimmy Collins didn't appear to be a psychopath and that was always good for the digestion he thought, looking at the second half of his sandwich.

'Did you produce this yourself?' he asked.

'No. Donal Steele did it. You know Donal?'

'Yeah, I know Donal Steele. Or know of him, anyway. Isn't he setting up some new studio over in Temple Bar?'

'That's where we recorded it,' said Jimmy. He was starting to relax now. He could see by Tony's face that he was interested. Maybe he wouldn't play the song, but at least he'd listen to it properly before he chucked it in the bin.

'All right, Jimmy. I'll see what I can do. No promises, though, right? It's good to see you putting in the effort to get the song played. That counts for a lot.'

'Thanks Tony. Here's the CD.' He handed him a copy. 'There's three songs on it. That one, a dance version and another song we just put down for a laugh. Eh, don't play that last one on the radio or we'll all get sued.'

He nodded at the barman again who stopped the CD playing on the house system and gave it back to Jimmy with a thirty-euro grin.

'All right,' said Jimmy. 'Listen I have to go, right? I hope you like the song. If you could play it, that'd be brilliant. Say it's for Kayleigh, will you? Like Marillion? And I love your show, by the way. The only thing on the radio worth listening to unless you're eleven years old or me Da.'

Tony smiled and nodded.

'Right, Jimmy. Seeya then.'

'Seeya. Oh, one more thing. If you do play it, and Kayleigh calls the station looking for me, will you give her my number? I wrote it on the sleeve there.'

'Who's this Kayleigh?'

'Ah. Long story. Some bird. I lost her number. That's why I wrote the song ... to find her. Do you speak Irish? Listen to the lyrics and you'll get the idea.'

'Are you serious?'

'Yeah. Mad, isn't it?'

'Well, I s'pose there's worse reasons for writing a song.'

'I know. Wait'll you hear track three on that CD I just gave you. Seeya Tony, right? And thanks.'

'No problem. And Jimmy, it's Mr King if you don't mind ...'

Jimmy went red, gave him a grin and walked out. Slagging bastard. But he felt good. Tony looked like he might actually give it a twirl. Donal Steele. There was a name he'd have to start using more often around the place.

Jimmy got the bus back out to his folks' place. He hadn't been around there much lately and his Mam's tone was becoming more and more clipped on the phone. He couldn't afford to piss her off. The resulting guilt trip would be too long and painful to even think about. The last time he left it a month before calling around, all his bun privileges had been revoked. He decided to take the moral high ground and pretend that he was too old for such a ridiculous punishment to affect him, but it was Aesop who tormented him into apologising properly in the end. He bugged him and bugged him about what a bastard he was to his poor mother, and him with none, and eventually Jimmy relented and called around with flowers and a big kiss. He left two hours later with lipstick on his nose, shepherd's pie in his belly and a small football bag full of coconut slices in his hand, which was what Aesop had been after all along.

'Jimmy!' called his Mam from the sink, and tore through the kitchen and down the hall to give him a hug before he even had the door shut behind him.

'Howya Ma,' said Jimmy, smiling.

'Look, Seán. Jimmy's here. How are you, love? Seán, look.'

'I see him, yeah,' said Seán, his head buried in the sports pages.

'Howya Da.'

'Howya.'

'Jimmy, love, we haven't seen you in ages.'

'Yeah, I know. Sorry. I've been mad busy, y'know?'

'Ah, of course you have, chicken. Seán, put down that paper. And c'mere, how's everything? Work's going well?'

'Grand Ma. I've been doing a lot of work in a studio as well. Recording a few songs for a CD.'

'God. Did you hear that Seán? A CD. Seán, did you hear that?' said Peggy, poking him in the back.

'Amn't I feckin' sitting here next to him?' said Seán.

'Will you put down that paper before I burn it and say hello to your son?'

'I said hello to him. Didn't I?'

'Yeah you did, Da. That was great. Thanks.'

'Now. Can I just finish this little section about Celtic and then we can all sit down and talk about Jimmy until the dinner's ready? Then we can start talking about him again, while we're eating.'

'Don't mind him love,' said Peggy, leading Jimmy to his usual seat at the table. 'He was at Doctor Brady's again with his bowel.'

'In the name of jaysis, Peggy, he doesn't need the details. Tell the neighbours and all, why don't you?'

'Sure, I'm after telling Gertie already, Seán. She can let the rest of them know.'

Jimmy and his Mam laughed and his Dad just grumbled back to his paper.

'Anyway pet, before I forget, a fella called Donal called for you.'

'Did he? What did he say?'

'He just wants you to call him back. He said he'd be at work this evening. He didn't leave a number, though.'

'That's okay. Thanks. I'll call him now.'

'I don't know why he called here,' said Peggy, frowning.

'Ah, I gave him all my numbers. Just in case,' said Jimmy, backing towards the kitchen door and into the hall.

'Is it for work? Is something wrong?' said Peggy, following him.

'No, Ma. It's the music stuff I was talking about. Donal helped me make the CD, that's all.' He started closing the door.

'Oh, you've made it? Do you have it? Can I have a listen? Seán, do you hear this?' Her foot was stuck in the doorjamb.

'Just a second, Ma. I'll call Donal and come back, okay? Talk to Mr Chatterbox there for a minute. Ask him what he thinks of Rangers.' That always got his Dad's attention.

'What? Rangers? What's that? The feckin ... ng ... fgh ...'

Jimmy finally managed to ease the door closed and went down to the phone near the front door to ring Donal.

'Donal?'

'Jimmy? How're things?'

'Grand. I got a message from me Mam. Said you were looking for me.'

'Yeah. Eh, your Mam ... she likes a bit of a chat, doesn't she?'

'Yeah. Sorry. Did it take long?'

'To leave the message? Ah, about ten minutes. It was grand. I didn't realise you had elocution, Jimmy. That's why you're such a good singer. It gave you confidence. Did you know that?'

'Oh God ...'

'Yeah. And listen, when you're talking to Liz, will you make sure and give her my best for the wedding, right? That bloke from Donegal sounds lovely as well.'

'She likes to talk about us.'

'Nah. Really? Anyway Jimmy, the reason I called ... I think I might have gotten you a bit of airtime.'

'Yeah? Jaysis, Donal, that's brilliant. Where?'

'You remember I had this mate in RTE?'

'Course I do. It's not Dave Fanning's show, is it? Oh God ...'

'No Jimmy. Actually, it's not 2FM at all.'

'Well, what then? Radio One? Do they even play music?'

'No, Jimmy. I mean yeah, they do, but it's not them either. It's *Raidió na Gaeltachta*. Dara Beag Ó hUiginn. He's got a show for contemporary music in Irish, or as much of it as he can find, on Tuesdays and Thursdays. That's why I was trying to get you tonight. He said he'd try and play it at about half seven or eight.'

'*Raidió na Gaeltachta*?' said Jimmy.

That was the Irish language radio station. On the one hand it was a nationwide station, so everyone in the country could pick it up, but on the other hand Jimmy didn't know anyone who did. RTE, the national radio and television broadcaster, had four main radio stations. You had Radio One for the old fogies, 2FM for the younger crowd, Lyric for the Arts lot and *Raidio na Gaeltachta* for ... well, for whoever listened to the radio in Irish.

'I know it's not Dave Fanning, Jimmy, but it's a start, right? Never turn your nose up at publicity.'

'Jesus, I'm not, Donal. Not at all. It's great news. Really. Thanks a lot. God, I never even thought about the whole Irish angle. I only wrote the song like that 'cos it was easier.'

'Whatever, Jimmy. If Dara likes it, someone else in RTE might get to hear it. And anyway, there's more than just RTE, right? We'll see if we can get it into a few other stations as well.'

'Actually, Donal, I just had a pint with Tony King over at Rock FM. I gave him a copy and mentioned your name. I think he might play it.'

'Tony King? He's a good DJ, but I don't think I've met him.'

'Ah, he knows you by reputation. That was enough.'

'Well, I hope it's the new reputation he knows me by, Jimmy. Because there were a few years there, in the 1980s, when my reputation had a few stains on it, y'know? Jack Daniels, mostly. Maybe some dribble ...'

'Well, I think he might play it. He took the disc with him anyway, so we'll see.'

'Brilliant. And how did you manage to have a pint with him?'

'Well, it wasn't really with him. I just went into the pub the last few nights, 'til he showed up. Then I had the barman play it on the house system and gave him a copy.'

'Cheeky bastard, Jimmy! That's good stuff. Y'know, with that attitude, you can make it in this business, Jimmy. Never too late!'

'Ah, I don't know about that. Let's see if I get the Christmas Number One first, out of this one.'

'All right. Listen I've to go, right? Tell your Mammy it was lovely talking to her and I'm looking forward to the scones. Oh yeah, you've to bring me in some of her scones, by the way. When she brought them up I tried to explain to her that I didn't eat cakes, but after a while it just seemed easier to take them. I was dying to go to the jacks and there was no getting her off the phone.'

'Who are you telling? All right, seeya Donal. And thanks, right?'

'No problem. I'll call you if I've any other news.'

'Cool.'

Jimmy walked back in to the kitchen.

'Everything all right, love?' said Peggy.

'Grand, yeah. Donal was just telling me that they're going to try and play a song of mine on the radio tonight.'

His Mam squealed.

'Jimmy!! Oh, Jimmy that's brilliant. Where? What station?' she said, running to the radio in the corner. 'Seán help me with this thing.' She was banging at all the buttons and dials with her dishcloth.

'Here Ma, I'll do it. The song is in Irish, so it's on *Raidio na Gaeltachta* in the next hour, sometime.' Jimmy went to the radio and found the station. He listened carefully, his ear up to the speaker and his Mam at his shoulder.

'What's happening?' she whispered to him after a while. His folks didn't speak Irish very well.

'Eh, I think petrol's going up seven cent,' said Jimmy.

'No, your song I mean.'

'This is just the news, Ma. The DJ won't be on for another while yet.'

'Well, let's sit down then and eat,' said Peggy. 'We'll hear it if it comes on, won't we?'

'Yeah,' said Jimmy. 'Listen, I'm just going to call Aesop

and Shiggy, okay?' He checked the frequency of the station and ran back down the hall again. There was absolutely no chance of Aesop knowing where to find *Raidió na Gaeltachta* on his radio. There was more chance of Shiggy knowing where it was.

Seán and Jimmy sat for the next twenty minutes, being talked at. His normally garrulous mother had by now cast off any semblance of restraint with the excitement of it all, and seemed to be having about three conversations with herself at the same time. The lads weren't nearly fast enough with their contributions, so they just gave up after a while and sat there, nodding at her every now and again.

They were on their Angel Delight when Jimmy cocked his head and raised his hand, causing Peggy to shriek and smack Seán, who hadn't opened his mouth in at least fifteen minutes, on the side of the head with an oven glove to shut him up. She ran to the radio and turned it up.

'What's he saying, Jimmy? What's he saying?'

'Eh, this is a new song, by a Dublin band, The Grove, not released yet. Song called *Caillte*,' Jimmy said. He was frowning and grinning at the same time.

His mother squealed and started poking Seán again.

'Did you hear that, Seán?'

'Yes, Peggy, I heard it,' said Seán, rubbing his ear and cleaning Angel Delight off his forehead. 'Now will you sit down woman and relax, before you give yourself another fecking hernia?'

The three of them sat and listened. One minute into it, Peggy started to cry.

'Oh Jimmy,' she said, wiping her eyes with her apron.

'Oh Christ,' said Seán, shaking his head.

The song finished and Peggy started clapping.

Jimmy didn't move. He just sat there, grinning. He'd gotten the song on the radio. He'd done it!

Peggy ran out to the phone to call everyone she knew,

but it rang before she had a chance.

Back in the kitchen, Jimmy's Dad looked up at him.

'That was a good song, Jimmy. Fair play to you.'

Jimmy nearly choked on his dessert. He didn't know what to say. His father hadn't complimented him on his music since he'd sung *Away in a Manger*, in the school Nativity, when he was six.

His Mam, who called out from the hall, spared him any further embarrassment.

'Jimmy, love, it's Aesop.'

'Thanks Da,' he said, and stood up.

His Dad nodded, picked up the paper from the floor and got back to his Celtic story, while Jimmy trotted down the hall to the phone.

Peggy wouldn't give him the receiver.

'What's that, Aesop? Oh, the drums? Of course I did, love. I thought you played them lovely. Yes, love, you were easily the best out of everyone. Yes, best looking too. But Jimmy's got the voice. He gets that from his Mam, says you. All that talking. Ha!'

'Will you give me the phone Ma, please?' said Jimmy. This would go on all night if he didn't make her stop.

'Sorry love, Jimmy's here grabbing the phone off me. Seeya now. And congratulations. Tell your Dad I said hello. And Jennifer. Okay, love. Okay. Bye now.'

She handed the phone to Jimmy.

'Oh,' she said. 'Tell him I have an apple tart for him.'

'Okay Ma, thanks ... Aesop?'

'Jimmy!'

'What do you think?'

'Fucking deadly, Jimmy.'

'Yeah. And that's only the start, right? Yer man, Tony King, gets about ten thousand listeners every night. Imagine if he played it too! Jaysis ...'

'Jaysis, with both of them, Tony King and Dara Beag Ó

hUiginn, that'll make ten thousand and seven altogether.'

'I can't believe you're taking the piss out of it, Aesop. We were just on the radio! When was the last time you were on the radio, ye bollocks?'

'I know. I'm only messing. Really. It's deadly. So, anyway Jimmy, I think we should start talking about what to wear on *Top of the Pops*. I presume we'll be flying to London first class, yeah? Oh, and I'll be needing a new drumkit, for when we're on tour. A blue one. And a dirty big bag of gange for the hotel room, and some extra towels ...'

Jimmy just sat on the stairs and smiled. He was excited too.

Twenty-six

Tony King was a bastard. That was the only explanation Aesop could think of. Jimmy, Aesop and Shiggy all sat glued to the radio every night for days and there wasn't a sign of them becoming famous.

'Jimmy, I think he was just pulling your pud so you'd go away,' said Aesop. 'I've heard him play about five songs by new Irish bands and none of them were ours, the bollocks.'

'Relax, Aesop. I was talking to Donal the other day and he said that DJs don't just sit about in their radio stations, in the middle of all their records, and play them randomly. They plan it all out. Maybe Tony likes to plan further than most of them. He'll get around to it.'

'Come on, Jimmy. Admit it. He thought you were a stalker and just pretended to like it so you wouldn't follow him home and start going through his bins.'

'Nah, I don't think so, Aesop. He really didn't look like he was acting the bollocks. Anyway, why should he? It's a fucking good song, right? He's just waiting until he's got a space and then he'll put it in. Maybe he played it already? We might have missed it.'

'Jimmy, I've been lying on me bed for the last four nights, listening to him. I'm telling you, there's no way I missed me playing the drums on the radio.'

'Ah, my arse Aesop. The state you get yourself into when you're lying on that bed, you wouldn't have noticed if the radio had hopped off the shelf and ran out the door. Anyway, where are we on the CDs?'

'I sold seven,' said Aesop.

'Thirty-two,' said Shiggy, handing Jimmy a wad of money.

'Good man, Shiggy. Seven?' said Jimmy to Aesop. 'That's

not very many, is it?'

'Who am I s'posed to sell them to? Me Da took one, Jennifer took three, and me granny has one. Oh, and I sold two to your Ma.'

'What?! You cheeky bastard! I already gave my Ma one.'

'Well, she took two off me. Here's a tenner, look.'

'Aesop, she was only trying to help out. For fuck sake, could you not sell them to people you don't know?'

'But I never see people I don't know, Jimmy, do I?'

'But ... you could ... ah, forget about it. Shiggy, where did you sell yours?'

'Tokyo,' said Shiggy. 'My friends in Japan buy flom my Website. Then I mail them.'

'Tokyo. Well, at least we're going international, I s'pose, but it's not really putting a dent in the local market, is it?' He looked down at the money on the coffee table. 'So, that's nearly a hundred copies altogether, including the ones we sold at the gig on Saturday and the ones we gave to DJs and mates.'

That easily covered the blank CDs he bought and they'd agreed that they'd split anything that was left over three ways. Donal had started to explain all about royalty splits to him, but Jimmy wasn't really interested in getting into all that. Who wrote what lyric and who played what bit. They were still just mates in a band and pricking around with money like that, at this stage, would only start causing trouble. Three ways even. It was easier and no one would feel hard done by.

'Right,' said Jimmy. 'We had a couple of hundred hits on the Website, with the song being downloaded fifteen times by different people. About thirty people signed the guest book since it's gone up. Over a hundred heard the song at the gig and then Dara's played it on *Raidio na Gaeltachta* a few times, so however many listen to that ...'

'That'll be me, you, Brother James from school and one baldy oul' fella in Kerry who picks it up in his teeth when the weather's on the turn,' said Aesop.

'Aesop ...'

'All right, all right. All the Irish-speaking people in the country, who listen to Dara religiously every night because they've no friends.'

'Well, it's getting out there. We only recorded it, what, three weeks ago? The word will get around. It just needs some time, y'know, just ...' Jimmy broke off into silence and sat chewing his thumbnail.

'How will she get in touch with you?' said Aesop, watching him.

'What? Who?' said Jimmy, looking up.

'C'mon, ye spa. Kayleigh. That's what this is all about, right? If she hears the song, how is she s'posed to let you know? Have you thought about that?'

'I have a little bit, I s'pose. The guest book on the Website. Or hopefully someone she knows will know where the band plays. McGuigans Gig Guide is in most of the papers, so she'll know if she looks. Me email address and all is on the site too, and a link to the studio with their number. I asked Tony to play it as a request for her, if he plays it at all. Me Mam plays golf in Dollymount. That's near Clontarf, so I asked her to keep an ear to the ground. Told her I was looking for someone called Kayleigh, for a school reunion thing. Had to be careful with that one. Asking my Ma for help is dangerous. If you don't phrase it right, me poor Da will be eating beans on toast 'til the job is done. Besides that, I mentioned Kayleigh before we played the song on Saturday. And I've been doing searches on the Web for schools around here where she might teach. I'm telling you Aesop, if there's no joy in another couple of weeks, then she's either living in a cave or she's not interested.'

'Jesus. That's putting a *little* bit of thought into it? You're getting good at this stalking thing, aren't you? They should have had you looking for Shergar.'

'Yeah, well, this is it, isn't it? If she doesn't hear the song and I don't hear from her any other way soon, then I'll just forget about it. I tried, right? No point in being a stupid wanker about it.'

'Yeah. Ah, I'd say you'll be grand. She likes Frank Sinatra, doesn't she? So, she can't have that many friends herself. She probably tunes into Dara for a little pick-me-up when she gets depressed and wants to hear someone who's an even sadder bastard than she is.'

'Thanks for the encouragement, Aesop.'

'No problem.'

'I take it you're over Sharon?'

'Ah, yeah. Called her up and told her that was it. Another heart for me trophy room. Devastated so she was.'

'Yeah, I'd say.'

'Sure, it's not the quantity, Jimmy, it's the quality. She can ride all the blokes she wants, but where is she going to find someone else that can do the Wheelbarrow the way I can? We don't grow on trees, y'know?'

'Thank God.'

'I talk to Katie on Saturday,' said Shiggy.

'Yeah?' said Aesop.

'She ask about you, Aesop. Say you rook sick.'

'Yeah. Well, tell Katie I'm getting better. Much better.'

'And you haven't learnt any lessons from all this?' said Jimmy, looking at Aesop.

'Course I have, Jimmy. I've learnt that it's okay to take a break from it every now and again but, at the end of the day, the Murray goes round. Works better that way,' said Aesop, grinning.

But Jimmy knew him better than that. He'd changed. He was still all shiny white teeth, cracking his fingers and doing the cool bastard, but his eyes weren't in it. He was certainly looking better, but that was just the extra sleep he was getting. There was definitely a new Aesop underneath it all, desperately trying to beat the old Aesop back into puberty where he belonged. Sharon must have, literally, scared the fuck out of him. Well, thought Jimmy, there's no point in trying to rush him. It'll happen when he's ready. He was like a butterfly, Jimmy decided, about to emerge from a silken chrysalis. Then he looked over at the couch, where Aesop was explaining to Shiggy how to modify the Wheelbarrow so that it would work with two women, and realised that, no, he was nothing like that at all.

'Oh, here, I've a joke,' said Aesop, putting down the telly remote and the cup he'd been using as Wheelbarrow props. 'You'll like this one Shiggy ... these three lads are on a building site, right? An Irishman, an Italian and a Japanese bloke, y'see? So anyway, the gaffer comes up to them and says to the Irish bloke "I want you to knock down this wall." And he goes up to the Italian bloke, and says "I want you to shovel all this sand from here to over there," right? And the Japanese bloke says, "What do I do?" so yer man says "You're in charge of supplies." Then he says, "Right, I'm going off for two hours and when I come back, I want all that done or there'll be bleedin' trouble, okay?" So yer man goes off for two hours and comes back. The wall's still there. Sand hasn't moved. No sign of the lads. Eventually he finds the Italian and the Irish bloke in the hut, drinking tea. "What the fuck are yiz up to?" he roars at them. "What's that bleedin' wall still doing there?" And the Irish bloke says "Listen boss, you put the Japanese bloke in charge of supplies, right? Well he fecked off as soon as you did, and I had no sledgehammer to knock down the wall. What was I s'posed to do?" So the gaffer turns to the Italian, "Why didn't you move the bleedin' sand?" And the Italian bloke says "Hey, the Japanese guy, he piss off. No supplies, no? No shovel, no? Mama mia, what can I do, eh?" So yer man storms off out of the hut to find the Japanese bloke. He's raging. Yelling all over the place trying to find yer man. No sign of him. "I'll bleedin' batter him," he's thinking, and he goes over to the wall to sit down for a minute and cool down. The next thing the Japanese bloke hops over the wall, lands on the ground in front of him and smacks him in the mouth ... "Supplies!!"'

Jimmy and Aesop cracked up laughing. Shiggy just looked between the two of them, puzzled.

'Eh? Supplies? Eh?'

Aesop was laughing too hard to say anything, but Jimmy managed to hold up one hand. 'I'll tell you later, Shiggy. Give me a minute, will you?'

Before he had a chance to explain, the phone rang and Jimmy went out to the kitchen where he'd left it.

'Jimmy?'

'Donal. How're things?'

'Grand. You weren't in bed, were you?'

Jimmy checked his watch and couldn't believe that it was nearly midnight.

'No Donal, you're grand. Just having a chat with Aesop and Shiggy.'

'They're there? That's good, 'cos I've got a bit of news for you.'

Jimmy sat down.

'Yeah?'

'Are you sitting down, Jimmy?'

'Yeah. Why?'

'Guess.'

'Ah fuckin' hell Donal, what's up?'

'Okay, okay,' laughed Donal. 'Dara's pal, Oisín Mac-Donnacha – you heard of him?'

'No.'

'Right. Well, he has a show on TG4. Wants you to come in and play *Caillte*. And do an interview. Telly, Jimmy. You're hitting the big time!'

Jimmy's vision swam.

'Fuck,' he managed. 'Oh fuck oh fuck oh fuck ...'

'God. I thought you'd be happy Jimmy,' said Donal. Jimmy could hear the grin in his voice.

'Donal, if you were here I'd bleedin' kiss you. Oh God, Donal, that's fucking *brilliant*. I can't believe it! You're not bloody winding me up now, are you?'

'No messing, Jimmy. Dara and Oisín are good mates. Oisín's always looking for something new on his show. Not too many bands do songs like that in Irish. They both like your stuff apparently and since you can speak Irish, he thought it would be cool to have you on. A Dublin band with a song in Irish, y'know? They're usually from the country ...'

'Jaysis, Donal. I can't really speak Irish. I haven't spoken Irish properly in fifteen years. I'm bloody crap!'

'Well, you have five days to practise. They're taping the show on Sunday night. It's going out next Thursday. So. Are you busy Sunday? Aesop? Shiggy?'

'I'm not busy no, Donal, and the others will be there as well, don't you worry about that. This is unbelievable! Oh, man, I owe you big time.'

'Nah,' said Donal. 'You're a good lad, Jimmy. You deserve it. Oh, you'll probably have to mime the song, right? You don't have any artistic issues with that, do you?'

'Artistic issues me bollocks, Donal.'

'Glad to hear it. Listen, I've to go, right? Sparky here is going to murder one of these young fellas if I don't keep an eye on him. I'll talk to you tomorrow with the details.'

'Grand. Thanks again, Donal. Jesus, I don't believe it.'

'No problem, Jimmy.'

He went back inside. The lads were back to the Wheelbarrow, along with something Shiggy was calling a *Todai* which seemed just as complicated but with more spinning. Shiggy didn't know the English word, but Jimmy was guessing 'lighthouse'.

Aesop looked up.

'Who was that?'

'Donal.'

'Yeah? Any news?'

'Eh, you could say that, yeah. Lads ... we're going on the telly!'

Jimmy told them everything that Donal had said. They howled and cheered and yelled for about five minutes, jumping around the living room and punching the air. Only Mr McGrath next door seemed less than enthused with the news, as evidenced by his muffled promise, through the wall, that he'd beat the living snot out of Jimmy if he didn't shut the hell up in there. They sat down and looked at each other, beaming.

'Jaysis Jimmy,' said Aesop. 'That's a terrible grumpy neighbour you have there. Is he still into his gardening?'

'Don't even think about it Aesop,' said Jimmy.

Aesop grinned and stood up.

'Back in a minute lads,' he said. 'Just getting some air ...'

Shiggy and Aesop didn't leave until after two in the morning They talked about everything – what they would wear, the kinds of things they'd say in the interview, what this could do for the song and the band in general.

'It's only TG4 though,' said Aesop.

'Ah, don't fucking start that again Aesop,' said Jimmy.

'What is TG4?' said Shiggy.

'It's the Irish language TV station Shiggy,' said Jimmy. 'It's only been going a few years. Everyone thought it would be shite, but it's actually not that bad. It's mostly in Irish, though, so obviously not as many people watch it as we'd like. But it's the telly, lads. It's the fucking telly! More people will be watching it than listen to Dara on the radio. And stop trying to put a downer on it, Aesop. We can do *Top of the Pops* the week after, okay?'

'I'm only messing, Jimmy. It's brilliant. Jaysis, we might get to meet Twink.'

'Shut up, ye spa,' laughed Jimmy.

'*Anno*, Jimmy ...' said Shiggy.

'Yeah?'

'*Anno*, I cannot speak in Irish, *ne*?'

'Ah, don't worry about it Shiggy. I'll teach you a few basics so you can say hello. Anyway, you'll probably be better than this dozy bastard here. He had Brother James on Prozac halfway through Second Year. Munching the things he'd be, at the top of the class, and Aesop breaking his shite laughing at him and calling him *Séamusín Bocht*. I'll tell you Aesop, it's a wonder he never fucking killed you.'

'Ah Jimmy, I was only having a laugh with him. Anyway, it was his own fault. He should never have gone back to teaching after the stroke.'

It went on for another few hours and when they left Jimmy lay on his bed, looking at the ceiling. It was becoming a habit. God, things were going well. How long had he and Aesop being playing music? On and off for over fifteen years, anyway. He had about twenty songs of his own, that he reckoned were fairly okay, but he hadn't seriously thought of all this – a CD, radio, telly – since he'd gone to college. Once he started getting that Education his Dad was always on at him about, he pretty much saw his life stretching out before him. Rock-stardom wasn't part of it. There would always be the music and gigs and all that, but if all this was going to happen to him, it was supposed to happen when he was eighteen, not thirty.

Ah, cop on Jimmy, he said to himself. It's one song. It's been on a radio station that no one listens to and next week it'll be on a TV show that no one will watch if *The Sopranos* are on at the same time. It was the coolest thing that would probably ever happen to him, but Aesop was at least partly right. It wasn't exactly the Elvis Comeback Special, was it? No, he decided, it wasn't that, but it was still important.

Even if he ended up being a fat fifty-year-old, with three kids and the same job he'd always had, at least he could look back at the last few months and say that, for a little while, he was living life instead of just being carried along by it. TG4 or *Top of the Pops*, Jimmy wasn't going to kid himself. This was cool and he was going to enjoy every single minute of it. If he was going to be an embarrassment to his kids, like every good father should, then he might as well do it properly. Whatever this show on TG4 turned out like, and however cool Jimmy and the lads thought they looked and sounded, Jimmy knew that in twenty years he could bring out the video of the event and horrify his children in front of their friends. A fat fifty-year-old had to get his giggles somewhere, right?

Thoughts of children gave way to thoughts of Kayleigh. I wonder what she'd say about that, thought Jimmy, smiling? Is she lying in bed, wondering where I am? Wondering why I didn't call? Does she even wonder about me at all? That was the big question, of course. All this was for her. It had taken on a life of its own and everyone else – Shiggy and Aesop, Donal and Sparky, even his Mam – was excited about it for its own sake, but Jimmy hadn't forgotten how it all started. How sure he had been that there was a girl out there some-where just for him. And how he had managed to find her and lose her in the space of just a few hours. The song, and everything that had come from it, were for Kayleigh. Making the CD, working with real pros in the music industry, getting on the radio and telly, doing up the Website, writing such a great song – he'd always have all that. But he wanted more. He wanted her. He wasn't a completely useless bastard when it came to women. The story of the song was as good as the song. Come on, it didn't get much more romantic, did it? She'd have to be a real cow not to be gagging for him after all this.

As he dozed off to sleep, he thought about her seeing him on the telly, or hearing him on the radio, singing to her.

He took it further. The two of them holding hands, kissing, making love. Her friends jealous as hell that she had her own song, being played to lovers all over the world. Telling her how lucky she was to meet a guy like Jimmy Collins. A nice guy. A good catch. Anyone who could write a song like that was worth hanging on to. She'd just smile at them and squeeze his hand. A beautiful wedding, with *Caillte* being played by a string quartet as she glided up the aisle. Just before sleep finally took him, he saw her face and startling eyes. She'd come to him. Jimmy didn't know if he was going to be a rich and famous rock star and he didn't really care. He'd have Kayleigh. He was sure about that. From her perfect lips, he heard her last words to him on that night.

'I'll be waiting Rockstar,' she'd said.

He smiled and fell asleep.

Twenty-seven

The trouble with the Irish language, Jimmy had long since decided, wasn't in the language itself. For starters, Irish people, even kids, don't like being told what to do. When the Department of Education demands that Irish be a compulsory subject right up until the end of second-level schooling, then that alone is a reason to hate it. What use is Irish to someone who wants to get a job other than teaching Irish? The fact that being able to perform integral calculus, or quote Shakespeare, is at least equally pointless if you want to be, say, a chef, is usually lost and so the other two compulsory subjects, Maths and English, don't get anything like the same stick. Besides, the reasoning continues, being good at Maths or English doesn't make you sound like a complete farmer. It just wasn't sexy.

Jimmy had never particularly minded it. For starters, he could speak the language thanks to those summers spent in Connemara. He didn't pick it up immediately, but it was amazing how quickly you started using what you had, when the only way to ask that cute chick from Mayo up for a dance was through Irish. Going back to school every September and learning the poems and prose, and even the grammar, hadn't been too much of a problem after that kind of pressure.

He looked over at Aesop now, who was frowning at some of Jimmy's old school books. They were in his living room.

'How's it going?' he said.

'Jaysis, Jimmy, I can't remember anything!'

'Well, to remember it, Aesop, you'd kind of have to have known it in the first place.'

'Ah, come on. I wasn't that bad, was I?'

'Eh, yeah. You were shite. Look, what about the set pieces Brother James used to make us learn? You must remember them. The oul' bollocks would go over them again and again.'

'Ah, I wasn't listening to him, Jimmy. Who has conversations about farm equipment and how nice the flowers look? Besides Norman, I mean.'

'Come on. Look, if we just start talking in Irish, then maybe some of it will come back to you. And me.'

'Why doesn't Shiggy have to learn it?'

'Because, Aesop, Shiggy is Japanese, yeah? Can you see how it might be a bit difficult for him? Christ, if you can't do it after being in school for thirteen years, how is Shiggy going to pick it up in an afternoon? Anyway, I taught him how to say hello and goodbye, and a few other bits and pieces. He's practising at home.'

They started doing drills. It was all simple stuff; what's your name, how did you meet, how old are you, what kind of music do you like. Aesop was hopeless. All he could remember were the descriptive phrases that they'd had to learn to put in essays. 'As sweet as honey' or 'as sly as a fox' or 'as black as the night'. None of it was likely to come in handy in an interview. From Jimmy's point of view it was a useless exercise anyway. They'd try to have a conversation but he'd have to translate everything into English so that Aesop could answer him, and then he'd have to translate those answers into Irish so Aesop could try and learn them. It didn't make for a riveting listen.

At six on Saturday evening they called it a day and went to the pub to meet Shiggy, Norman and Marco. Jimmy tried to join in the slagging and laughs with everyone, but he was a bit nervous about going to Donnybrook the next day to record the show. TG4 were actually based in West Galway, but they recorded a lot of stuff in their studios in Dublin. Apparently there would be an audience, but it would only be about fifty or a hundred people. They were to get there at around two in the afternoon, to meet Oisín and go through the questions. They'd also practise doing the song. It wasn't exactly a sound check, since they'd be miming, but Jimmy had never lip-sync'd before and Aesop wasn't sure how to hit a drum kit without it making any noise. The very idea of it seemed to unsettle him.

They got the bus to Donnybrook the next day, and went into the main lobby, explaining to the security guy who they were. They were shown to a dressing room, where a business-like woman with a stern face, Pam, told them to change. They looked down at themselves and at each other.

'Change what?' said Aesop.

'Your clothes,' said Pam.

'What's wrong with these ones?' said Aesop. He was wearing black jeans, a black Megadeth T-shirt with a charming cracked, flaming skull motif, black socks and black runners. Pretty cool for a Sunday afternoon.

Pam just looked him up and down and sighed.

'Whatever. I'll talk to Barry from Lighting,' she said, and walked out without another word.

'Do you think she likes me?' said Aesop to Jimmy.

'No. And from the sounds of it, I don't think Barry from Lighting is going to think much of you, either.'

'Fuck him and all Barrys from Lighting, Jimmy. I won't be a pawn to the capitalist machine that's represented by these grey walls and their grey opinions of my art.' He was waving a finger in the air. 'My voice will be heard, Jimmy, and how I choose to express my individuality won't be dictated to me by so-called professionals that clamour frantically at the edges of their own anonymity. Y'know?'

'Good man. Now shut the fuck up and help Shiggy with his bass. We need to tune up.'

'But we're miming ...'

'So what? Doesn't mean we can be sloppy. Just 'cos nothing's plugged in, we still play it just like the CD, right?'

'Ooh, look Shiggy,' said Aesop. 'Jimmy the rock star's in charge now. Make sure and do what he says or he'll throw a tantrum and leave the band. Which drumsticks will I use Jimmy? I wouldn't want to cramp your style out there. Hey, they left sandwiches ...' He stopped talking abruptly and started tucking in. Shiggy joined him. Jimmy watched them, but he couldn't eat. He was starting to get seriously jittery.

Oisín came in after about half an hour and introduced himself. Jimmy and Aesop were immediately impressed. They were half expecting a fat oul' fella that looked like a pig farmer and smelled of vegetables, but Oisín wasn't much older than they were and looked like he could have been in a boy band himself a few years ago. What's more, he was speaking English and was telling them he loved the song and how he hoped it would be a big hit for them. It was hard not to relax around him, which is probably why he had his own chat show on the telly and they didn't. They went out to the studio itself and practised playing the song along with the CD a couple of times. Jimmy felt like a bit of a prat, just mouthing the words, and decided to sing out loud instead. His mike was only for show, so it wasn't like he could be heard. It wasn't even plugged in. He looked around at one stage and saw Aesop frowning and shifting in his seat.

'What's up with you?' he said.

'There's things on the drum skins,' said Aesop.

'What things?'

'These black fucking rubber things. They dull the sound.'

'So what? They're s'posed to do that.'

'I don't like them.'

'I don't care, Aesop. Just pretend they're not there.'

'But they sound shite!'

'It doesn't matter, Aesop. Just stop frowning, will you? You look like a sulky bollocks sitting back there.'

'Well, what do you want me to do?'

'Jesus, Aesop, smile, will you? Or just look cool or something.'

Aesop crossed his eyes and opened his mouth wide in a huge and grotesque grin, cocking his head to one side.

'How's this?'

'Is that the smile or the cool?'

'Both.'

'Right. Well, go back to the frown, then. Makes you look less like a wanker.'

The grim-faced Pam came back to them.

'Make-up,' she clipped, beckoning them absently after her like they were schoolchildren.

'Make-up?' said Aesop, putting down his drumsticks and folding his arms.

'Yes dear,' she said, without looking back. 'You have to wear make-up.'

'Why?'

'Because of the lights.'

'Jaysis. Is that your excuse for everything?' said Aesop.

'Aesop, shut bleedin' up, will you?' whispered Jimmy. Then he turned to Pam. 'Don't mind him, Pam. He's afraid someone will think he's gay. Right. Grand, yeah, no problem. Let's go lads.'

Aesop caught up to Jimmy and started whispering.

'Her and her bleedin' lights. If I looked like her, I'd make sure they were all turned off, the fuckin' head on her.'

'Aesop, give over will you? Don't go annoying anyone today, or they'll tell us to piss off home.'

'Ah, me bollocks they will, Jimmy. Don't mind Pam. She's just upset 'cos they won't let her read the news on account of the armpit she uses for a face.'

They went back to the dressing room, where a younger woman came in with a plastic toolbox full of smelly stuff.

'Hi,' said the girl, smiling. 'I'm Chrissie.'

Aesop eyed her box of tricks.

'Eh, sorry Chrissie, but do we have to do this?'

'Oh, don't worry. It's just a little dab around the cheeks. Takes the shine off.'

'But I'm not shiny,' said Aesop. 'Look,' he said, turning his face up to the light and pointing at it.

'Oh, under the lights out there everyone is shiny. Come on. Won't take a minute.' She was perky and very pretty and Aesop was very nervous. Jimmy knew this because he wasn't trying to get her to go into one of the wardrobes with him.

'Look, just don't make me look like Dame Edna, all right?'

'Listen petal, I couldn't make you look like Dame Edna if I took to your head with trowel and a bucket of plaster.'

'What? Why?' said Aesop, looking around at her. 'What's wrong with my head?'

'God,' said Chrissie to Jimmy. 'He's never happy is he?'

Jimmy just shook his head and Chrissie sat in front of a very fidgety Aesop, humming an old Carly Simon tune.

Aesop's edgy demeanour wasn't helped by the fact that Shiggy had brought his own make-up.

'Fuckin' hell, Shiggy, what do you have make-up for?'

'My face,' said Shiggy, puzzled.

'But ... but ... you're a bloke!'

'Yes,' nodded Shiggy. 'You too.' He pointed at Aesop, who was now having brown powder sponged onto his cheeks.

'Yeah, but at least I didn't bring me own.'

Shiggy turned to Chrissie, winking at Jimmy on the way.

'Chrissie-san, can I borrow mascara prease? I forget. Oh. And ripstick.'

'Ah Jaysis. Jimmy?' said Aesop, trying to look at Jimmy behind him without moving his head.

'Stop frowning,' said Chrissie, grabbing his chin. 'You'll get wrinkles in your powder and then you'll look silly, won't you?'

'Silly? And what do I look like now? You don't think I look silly now?'

'No,' said Chrissie, grinning. 'But you do look a bit gay ...'

'Ah, bleedin' hell ... Jimmy ...'

The last part of the preparation was to go over the questions that Oisín would ask. It was pretty basic. Stuff about the band and the song. Where they gig and how long they've been playing. Jimmy started to struggle with the vocabulary, but Oisín was really cool about it.

'Look Jimmy, if you can't think of the word, just use the English one, okay? This isn't a test or anything. I know it's TG4, but we're not mad zealots. You don't get kicked out for speaking English. Anyway, I'll talk to Shiggy there in English, so he can say a few words. And Aesop, I can talk to you in English as well if you like ...'

'Ah no. No, I'll give it a lash,' said Aesop, looking at Jimmy who was shaking his head furiously. 'Sure, it's only for a few minutes anyway, right? Just don't ask me anything hard.'

'No problem,' said Oisín, smiling. 'Okay, are we all set?'

The lads nodded.

'Right. Pam will be in to get you when we're ready to go. It'll be about an hour. And just relax, okay? This isn't *Today Tonight*. Young people watch this show – just have a laugh.' He winked at them and strolled out.

'Howyiz feeling?' said Jimmy, when the door closed.

'Me face is sticky,' said Aesop, the ends of his mouth turned down. He looked like a sad clown.

'Grand,' said Shiggy, grinning.

'Right,' said Jimmy. He started pacing and rubbing his hands on his leather-clad bum to try and wipe the sweat off them. He made a mental note. Leather is crap for wiping the sweat off your hands just before you go on the telly.

They did the song first.

It felt weird. Jimmy had his eyes closed for most of it, pretending he was in McGuigans, so that everything that was going on in the studio wouldn't distract him. When he did open them, he saw Shiggy doing his patented bass-player-with-bowel-disorder boogie next to him and closed them again before he started to laugh. He was afraid to look around at Aesop, who had slipped on a pair of black Bono shades at the last minute just to annoy Pam. She'd specifically asked them if they'd be wearing glasses, on account of the lights. At one stage, Jimmy heard a small clatter and a drumstick came scooting across the floor in front of him, but he tried to ignore it. At least it wasn't a broken one. Pam had asked Aesop not to hit the drums too hard either.

'Okay Pam,' he'd said. 'Or I could just go home altogether. Would that make things easier for you?' Aesop had always had this thing about authority. Jimmy's face was starting to hurt from the disapproving looks he'd been firing at him all afternoon.

When they finished the song, Oisín stood up clapping, spoke a few words into the camera and then gestured for them to come over. They walked to the couch, the audience still clapping, and sat down, Jimmy nearest him, then Shiggy and then Aesop. Jimmy tried wiping his hands on the couch, but that was made of some kind of leathery stuff as well. They were all smiling, red-faced and self-conscious, but somehow Oisín put them at ease in no time at all; quite an accomplishment considering that neither Aesop nor Shiggy had a bloody clue what he was saying. Jimmy watched him and decided to study the tape carefully when he got it. This was a completely different type of stage presence to the one he was used to, but Oisín was good at it whatever it was. While he was considering this, he noticed that Oisín had stopped talking and was looking at him in expectation.

'Eh ...'

Oisín didn't miss a beat. He just rephrased the question, smiling.

Ah right. How did the band start ...

There were about six or seven questions like this. No

sweat. Jimmy sailed through it, the Irish streaming out of him before he even had a chance to check that it made sense. It seemed to make sense to Oisín. He laughed and joked and smiled all through it, giving Jimmy little encouraging winks and nods when he knew that the camera was on Jimmy and not himself. He even got a cool bit in about Kayleigh.

'And it's a true story, right? The song, I mean ...' asked Oisín.

'That's right. I met this girl, Kayleigh, at a disco. We got on really well, but I lost her phone number that same night. That's why I wrote *Caillte*. I'm hoping she'll hear it and get in touch.'

'Wow. That's a really beautiful idea, Jimmy. I hope she does. But, it's a lot of trouble to go to for a girl you only just met the once, isn't it?'

Jimmy looked into his lap for a second, and then back up at Oisín.

'Not really, Oisín. Sometimes you just know ...'

The audience gave a delighted little murmur and Jimmy went red.

'And your friends won't give you a hard time for saying that on national TV?' said Oisín, laughing and gesturing to the other end of the couch.

Jimmy laughed and nodded sideways at Aesop.

'This fella? Well, he might if he could understand a word we're saying!'

The camera switched to Aesop, who was checking the bounciness of the couch and not paying attention. The audience laughed again.

The questions went on. Jimmy told Oisín that they were gigging in McGuigans on Saturday night, and that everyone was welcome.

'Especially this special girl you lost?' said Oisín.

'Yeah. That'd be great,' said Jimmy, stealing a quick glance at the camera. Okay Jimmy. Enough is enough. Don't go mad.

323

Then Oisín switched to the rest of the band, asking Jimmy to introduce Shiggy. Jimmy did, glad to be moving on. He didn't want to sound too pathetic. Oisín welcomed a beaming Shiggy, who immediately thanked him in perfect Irish, adding that it was a soft day thanks be to God. Oisín agreed that it was, laughing, and then asked him a few questions, in English, about how a Japanese guy ended up in Dublin, playing bass in a band and singing songs in Irish.

Shiggy summarised his life story in about ten faltering English sentences and, sitting there with his legs crossed but not quite reaching the floor and his dark eyes looking into the camera every now and again, proceeded to charm every single Irish-speaking girl in the country. He was so small on the couch, perched between Jimmy and Aesop, that he was practically screaming out to be cuddled. He finished by saying he loved Ireland (swoon), thought that the weather took a bit of getting used to (understanding nods) and that he thought Irish girls were very pretty (swoon, swoon, I must have him). He even managed a little blush and giggle as he said that, looking at Jimmy like he'd just made a fool of himself. Jimmy had to consciously close his mouth. Shiggy had done it again. It was like there was nothing he wasn't good at. The scary thing was that Jimmy knew the little coquettish glances at the camera and the shy eyes were all a bloody big act! Shiggy wasn't a bit shy. How did ... but he didn't get a chance to reflect much more on it, because Oisín had turned to Aesop and, after saying hello, asked him in Irish what kind of music he liked.

Aesop cleared his throat. Jimmy's went dry.

'Michael had never seen a combine harvester before,' said Aesop, nonchalantly, in Irish. Jimmy looked around at him, his mouth falling open again and his face going purple.

'Really?' said Oisín, laughing, still speaking Irish.

'Yes,' said Aesop, nodding and keeping up the Old Tongue. 'I ran as fast as the wind, because I like cake.'

'I see,' said Oisín. 'And what kind of cake do you like, Aesop?' Oisín was nothing if not a pro.

'Big cake,' said Aesop, smiling. He'd understood that one.

'I see. And what kind of music do you like?' Oisín tried once more, figuring that the pattern of the question had now been established in Aesop's mind.

'Eh ... big music.'

Oisín was laughing again. Jimmy was sure it was forced. Oisín was going to scrap the show. Aesop's arse would be getting the kicking of a lifetime as soon as this was over.

'Big music. Right. Very good. Okay Aesop, and you play the drums in the band. Is that difficult? You know, it seems to me that you have to have very strong arms to be able to play a whole concert, banging away like that. Do you ever get tired?'

'My brother lives in a swimming pool,' said Aesop.

'Does he?' said Oisín. He put his hand to his mouth and nodded. Jimmy thought he could see his eyes glistening. 'Does he really? Well, that's great. Good for your brother. I hope that he enjoyed *Caillte* as much as we all did here. It's been a real pleasure talking to you. Really. Thank you very much Aesop,' he said, with a small bow.

'I have a hole in my trousers,' said Aesop, nodding back.

Oisín took a drink of water.

'I'm afraid that's all we have time for this evening,' he said, at last. He was holding a handkerchief now, Jimmy saw, twisting it into a tight knot out of camera shot. It was obviously a device he used to focus. 'Thanks, guys, for coming in and playing for us and best of luck with the song. Ladies and gentlemen, can you all please give a big round of applause to The Grove and their new song, *Caillte*.'

The crowd applauded loudly. There were even a few whistles. Pam nodded at Oisín, who then turned around to the lads. He started speaking English again.

'Well done, guys, that's it. All finished. I'll wrap it up

325

myself later on this evening.'

Everyone in the studio was now laughing.

'Jesus Oisín,' said Jimmy, shaking his head miserably. 'I am so, so sorry about that.' He turned around to Aesop, pointing at him. 'I'm going to fucking kill you.'

'What?' said Aesop.

'Jimmy, Jimmy,' said Oisín. 'It's grand. Really. It was a bit of a laugh. Believe me, I haven't enjoyed an interview that much in years. I swear, all those boyos down in the *Gaeltacht* will just laugh at the thick Dubliner who can't speak Irish. Really. They'll get a kick out of it.'

'You're just trying to make me feel better, Oisín. Aesop, you are a complete arsehole. What did you think you were doing?'

'Ah, I didn't want to be the only one not able to say a few words, Jimmy. I just remembered some phrases from school, so I thought I'd throw them in, y'know?'

'But they were random phrases! They didn't mean anything! A combine harvester? Aesop. A combine bleedin' harvester?'

'Yeah. That was one of Brother James's drills. Do you remember it? God, that must be fifteen years ago. Do you think he'll be impressed? Do you think he'll forgive me now? For the stroke, like ...'

'Forgive you? If he watches that at all, Aesop, it'll probably fucking finish him off! How can you know the Irish for combine harvester, and not know the Irish for music? And you a drummer. And since when does Andy live in a bloody swimming pool?'

'Andy? He doesn't,' said Aesop, frowning at him. 'He lives on a barge. Oh God, I didn't say swimming pool, did I? Oh no, I'm mortified.'

'You're mortified now?! After the interview you just did, you're mortified because you mixed up swimming pool and barge? Aesop, you fucking big ...'

'Jimmy,' Oisín interrupted. 'Really, it doesn't matter. You all came across very well, and the song was great. It was a big hit. Relax. Look, go on up to the bar and I'll see you up there in about an hour, okay? The beer is on me. Go mad.' He was still laughing, as were most of the camera crew, the guy with the big mike and half the audience.

'Can you cut him out?' asked Jimmy, standing up.

'No need, Jimmy. It was perfect. Wait and see.'

They went back to the dressing-room first, because Aesop refused to go anywhere without taking off his make-up.

'I'd look stupid,' he said to Jimmy, smiling.

Chrissie popped her head in the door, with a big grin.

'Great stuff, guys. That got a giggle all over the building.'

'Thanks,' said Jimmy, glaring at Aesop.

'You need anything?' asked Chrissie.

'Do you have any cakes?' said Aesop.

'Big ones?' said Chrissie.

'Well, they're the ones I like, right?' said Aesop, turning it on again in a flash. He grinned at her.

'So I've heard,' she smiled back, all eyes and lips.

Jimmy looked at the two of them, and at Shiggy who had a huge bottle of Ponds Cold Cream out, and was dabbing it on his face. What looked like a rolled-up pair of tights was keeping his hair up and out of his eyes. Then Jimmy looked in the mirror, and saw that his face was all streaks from the sweat and his rubbing it. Shite. Was it like that all through the interview? He sat down on a stool with a big sigh and hung his head. God, that was a bloody disaster.

Shiggy handed him a small sponge.

'Jimmy, wipe away flom eyes,' he said, demonstrating with his own sponge.

Jimmy nodded and started wiping. So this was feckin' show business, was it?

Twenty-eight

Peggy hadn't enjoyed herself this much since Jimmy's twelfth birthday party. The house was packed. Of course, Jimmy and the rest of the band were there. So were Norman, Marco, Jennifer, Katie, Maeve, Michelle the Amazing Piss Monster, as Aesop and Norman privately called her, Sparky, Gertie from down the road, Peggy's sister and her husband, Seán's sister Madge, Nuala from next door and Father Paddy, the parish priest, who didn't even know why he was there. Peggy had called down to him the day before to get him to sign a Mass card and, before he knew what was happening, his Thursday night snooker game with Father Tom Dowling was out the window and he'd paid a fiver for a CD by a band he'd never heard of. Jimmy's Dad was there too somewhere, but he was mostly keeping out of the way. Peggy kept getting him to fetch buns and top up drinks and he was getting a pain in his arse with the whole thing. He wasn't even allowed near his own telly and Juventus were playing Inter on Sky Sports tonight.

Peggy herself was flying about the place like a demented dervish, doling out sausage rolls faster than anyone could eat them and pulling full cheesecakes and apple tarts out of thin air, to place them on steadily diminishing surfaces. The whole thing was a dry run for her Christmas baking spree, which would be starting in earnest the following week. Eggs all over the city were shitting themselves.

Oisín's show, *Cé Hé*, wasn't on until eight, but the party started as soon as people started to arrive, just after six. Luckily the priest didn't come until half past six, so Jimmy and the lads were spared the Angelus.

Father Paddy was now perched on the end of Seán's arm-chair, his feet jumping and his head nodding uncontrollably from the six cups of tea he'd had in the last hour. He tried drinking slowly so that his cup stayed half full for as long as possible, but Peggy spotted that manoeuvre straight away. She told him that his poor tea was gone stone cold and had it replaced in seconds with a fresh cup. He was starting to get a headache and there were spots dancing at the edges of his vision. The sugar-blasted profiteroles weren't helping, and he realised he'd made a terrible mistake in coming here first. He had to go out to Bayview after this to comfort poor Mrs Smith, recently bereaved, and he'd be no use at all to her in this state, jigging about on her sofa and spilling fucking sherry everywhere.

Sparky, on the other hand, was thoroughly enjoying his caffeine buzz. The fact that he'd refused a beer in favour of a cup of tea had immediately endeared him to Peggy, who thought him a fine sensible man with a nice smile and lovely manners, leaving Jimmy to wonder who the hell she was talking about. Sparky kept his stories limited to those concerning his own dear Mammy, whom Holy God had taken on him, and steered well clear of anything involving drugs, alcohol, sex and/or vomit – which for Sparky meant not talking very much about the years between 1973 and 1987. He hadn't had so much attention in years and kept grinning at Jimmy when he caught his eye and raising whatever bun he was currently munching in a toast.

Eventually it was five to eight and Jimmy turned on the telly. The ads were on. Everyone crowded around the set in the corner and the conversations died down, except for that of Norman and Seán, who were having a quiet discussion on the whole Soccer-in-Croke-Park thing. They'd been having it on and off since Euro '88 and neither one of them had budged an inch in all that time. Put the two of them in a room together and it was only a matter of when they'd start up. Entire Christmas parties had been devoted to the subject over the years.

The announcer came on and introduced *Cé Hé*. Everyone in the room cheered and Jimmy pounced on the video, pressing record. All over Dublin, his relations and friends who weren't in the house were doing the same thing. Jimmy didn't want to take any chances with a wonky tape or anything. And then Oisín was on the telly and Peggy fired a glance across at Seán that any man who's been married for thirty-five years would recognise. He shut up.

Only Jimmy, his Aunty Madge, Father Paddy and Michelle the Amazing Piss Monster were able to follow the show properly. Michelle had been to an all-Irish school, so her Irish was probably the best in the house. The others in the room were able to pick up enough bits and pieces to get a general idea of what was going on, with only Aesop, Marco, Shiggy and Seán left completely clueless. A whispering started up around the room as everyone translated what they could for his or her neighbour.

As it happened, Jimmy and the lads were the last guests the way the show had been edited. First up was a sixteen-year-old girl from Clare who'd won some poetry competition, followed by a feature on the depletion of the Bog of Allen. Then came the ads again and Oisín was back in the studio with a guy from University College Galway, who was explaining what student life was like (study, drink and mince for dinner) and mentioning every fifteen seconds that if any of the viewers were thinking of attending UCG, they should be sure and join the Irish Society. Jimmy checked his watch. There were only about ten minutes left in the show and Oisín hadn't mentioned them. He had a horrible feeling that Aesop's messing around had caused the slot to be pulled, and stared over at him to give him a dirty look. Aesop didn't notice. He was frowning down at a pamphlet that Father Paddy had slipped him, called *Respect and Love*. It was about not riding all the time. What troubled Aesop was that no one else in the room had gotten one. Did Father Paddy know something? Priests made him nervous. He stuffed the pamphlet into his pocket and looked at the man in black on the armchair out of the corner of his eye. He'd have to be careful. Father Paddy already looked pretty agitated sitting there, frowning intently at the telly and swiping in the air at something Aesop couldn't see.

Just when Jimmy was sure it was too late, Oisín finally introduced the band. Everyone in the room started cheering and clapping the lads on the back, and Jimmy went bright red. Then the camera switched to the three of them with their instruments, and everyone erupted again. The view panned across in front of Jimmy and around to where Aesop was twirling his drumsticks over his head, like he was trying to take off. More cheering. Shiggy, Aesop and Jimmy just grinned, glued to the screen. This was mad. They were on the telly! By the second verse the room had quietened down a bit and people actually started to listen to the song. Jimmy wasn't grinning anymore. He was staring hard and chewing his bottom lip. He caught a couple of timing slips where his hands on the guitar weren't following the song exactly. He knew no one else had noticed, but that wasn't the point. He'd have to be more careful the next time. The next time?! Yeah, right. He grinned again and stopped worrying about it. What next time would that be, Jimmy?

Everyone laughed when one of Aesop's sticks went flying, and then again when he immediately pulled another one out of a pouch by his leg and kept playing without missing a beat. He looked into the camera, raised one eyebrow above the shades, stuck his tongue into his cheek and wobbled his head from side to side. Jimmy could hear Peggy squeal in delight behind him. He looked around and saw that her face was all teary. She was wringing her hands on Seán's jumper beside her and giggling like a schoolgirl. Beside them, Norman looked like an eleven-year-old who'd just met his hero. He winked over at Jimmy. Marco and Jennifer had their arms around each other, next to him. Jennifer gave Jimmy a big thumbs up. Jimmy felt good.

Then the song was over and everyone cheered again. Next came the bit that Jimmy was dreading.

The camera view switched back to Oisín standing up and clapping, and then widened to take in the lads shaking his hand and sitting on the couch. The interview started and Jimmy could hear the impressed murmuring from everyone as he started talking in Irish on the telly. He looked around and saw that even Seán was impressed. The ones who could follow it looked over at Jimmy when he started talking about Kayleigh. Luckily, his Mam didn't seem to get it. If she had, then Jimmy would have been in for a very long night of explanations. Then it was Shiggy and the room started whistling again. It was the first time Jimmy had ever seen Shiggy go red without suspecting that he was faking it. And then Aesop. Jimmy grimaced and looked sideways at the telly through half closed eyes. Two seconds later, Michelle and Father Paddy were laughing their heads off. Michelle had one hand to her mouth, trying to keep it quiet, but Father Paddy was clearly having trouble controlling himself. He was thumping the arm of the chair, his head thrown back and his mouth stretched open like he was having his teeth scraped. There was a brief silence as he ran out of breath and then a huge donkey-like howl as his lungs filled up again. His cup was empty for the first time all night, the contents having slopped all over his trousers, and his bloodshot eyes streamed tears. He knew he was making a show of himself, but there was nothing he could do about it. The tea had him fucked.

This started everyone else laughing, too. Aesop's Irish was easy to understand, except for the combine harvester bit, and his cool delivery and Oisín's professionalism in the face of it just made the whole thing funnier, with Father Paddy's screeching adding to the mood. Eventually Jimmy started laughing too. Bloody Aesop. What could you do with him?

All too soon it was over and the credits were rolling up. Jimmy pressed stop on the video recorder and looked around. Everyone started clapping again and then chatting excitedly amongst themselves. Peggy was beaming at him and everyone else was telling the lads they did a great job. The party atmosphere lasted for about another half-hour, at which time Father Paddy announced that he'd have to be getting across to Bayview. His giggle fit seemed to have calmed him down somewhat. A lot of pent-up energy had come out in those thirty seconds and he felt that he'd probably be okay to drive now.

That started a small exodus, and by half nine the only people left were the band, Jimmy's folks, Jennifer, Katie, Marco and Norman. Only Peggy was sober at this stage, the younger ones having polished off the rest of the beer and Seán having long since decided that he might as well get stuck into his bottle of Paddy, seeing as there was no way he was going to get to see the soccer tonight. They all sat around laughing about the whole thing, with Peggy jumping up every ten minutes to answer the phone. Just about anyone who'd ever known Jimmy was calling, with the notable exception of Brother James who was probably stretched out somewhere having oxygen administered.

Donal called at about ten.

'Donal!'

'Jimmy! Great stuff. I didn't see it myself, but Sparky's here and he told me it went well. Fair play to you.'

'Ah stop. Did he tell you what that gobshite Aesop did?'

'Yeah. Don't mind that, Jimmy. A bit of a laugh, that's all. It's a good thing, believe me. Most bands these days are so far up their own arses, they can brush their teeth from the inside. A bit of a sense of humour is important. Anyway, besides all that, I just rang to tell you that I got a call from Tony King this evening.'

'Jesus! Yeah?'

'Yeah.'

'Is he going to play *Caillte*?'

'He's played it, Jimmy. It went out about half an hour ago. I was trying to ring you before, but it was engaged.'

'Ah shite. Yeah. That was me Mam talking to everyone. But that's cool! Did you hear it? What did he say about it?'

'I didn't hear it, Jimmy, but I'm sure he gave you a good word. Sounds like a nice bloke. We know a few of the same people. Anyway, there you go. Oh, he told me he'd play it tomorrow night as well. About the same time. And he said he'd give it a mention in his column in the *Sunday Post* this week.'

'Fucking hell!' said Jimmy

'Yeah. Listen, I have to rock and roll here. Deadlines, y'know?'

'Yeah. That's brilliant Donal. Thanks a lot. I'll talk to you tomorrow, all right? If you're talking to Oisín and Dara, will you tell them I said thanks as well?'

'Yeah, no problem. Seeya Jimmy. And congratulations. I think you might be a bit late for the Christmas Number One, but you never know. Maybe Valentine's Day ...'

'Yeah, or Paddy's Day,' said Jimmy, laughing. 'Seeya.'

'Right. Oh, am I s'posed to eat all these scones, by the way? Sparky brought them over from your Mam. I thought I was getting a few to go with a cup of tea, not enough to go into business.'

'You got off lightly, Donal, believe me. Father Paddy had to make two trips out to the car.'

Jimmy went back inside and told everyone that the song had gone out on Tony King's show. That called for another round of clapping, cheering and beer and Seán sloshed another couple of fingers of Paddy into his glass when he was sure that Peggy wasn't watching. Everyone was thrilled, but they were still more excited about the lads being on the telly. Jimmy knew better. Ten times more people heard the song on the radio than would have been watching Oisín's show. If it were to happen, it would happen because of Rock FM, not TG4, but Jimmy wasn't complaining. He'd learnt more about the music business in the last month or so, than he had in the previous fifteen years. He looked around the room and felt better than he could ever remember feeling. He was pissed, pleased, proud of himself and for the first time he knew – really knew – that he'd find Kayleigh again. With everything going this well, there just wasn't any doubt about it any more. She'd call, or turn up, or something. Jimmy looked at his Dad, who now had his arm around an equally plastered Norman, saying something about Lansdowne Road, and realised that nothing would ever be the same again. From now on, he'd always divide his life into 'before I was on the telly' and 'after I was on the telly'. He thought that the only thing that could make the night any better, would be for Kayleigh to come knocking on the front door. He was wrong.

'Jimmy, Mr and Mrs Collins, ah, everyone ...' said Marco, with a small burp. He was standing up against the sliding doors, with Jennifer linking his arm.

They all looked at him.

'My beautiful girlfriend, Jennifer, has agreed to become my beautiful fiancée,' he said.

Everyone gasped.

'This is such a happy night, we wanted to share the news with you now,' said Marco. Jennifer was blushing furiously and it was Jimmy's Dad that finally broke the spell.

'That's fuckin' brilliant!' he yelled, and danced over to give them both a hug, getting a massive clip on the ear from Peggy on the way for language.

Everyone crowded around them, hugging and kissing and wishing them well. Peggy dashed into the kitchen in a frenzied attempt to put the kettle on quickly so she wouldn't miss anything, and when she came back she was crying again.

This was all too much for her. Jimmy had a lump in his throat as well. There it was. He found himself looking at Jennifer and wondering … but then he just gave her another squeeze and said 'Brilliant', smiling at her. She looked so happy. Jimmy could wonder and wish all he wanted, but he doubted if he'd ever have been able to make Jen that happy. When he pulled away from her, she was crying as well. As were Marco and Katie. Aesop still looked completely stunned, and Norman was grinning like the blowjob goblin had just paid him a quick and furtive visit. Shiggy just grinned at everybody. He'd reached his limit about an hour ago.

'Eh, Paul,' said Jennifer. 'Don't mention it to Dad, will you? We weren't going to say anything until tomorrow, so he doesn't know. I'll tell him in the morning, okay? Hush hush.'

'Don't tell him?' said Aesop. 'Yeah, right. I usually pop into his room and sit on his bed for a chat when I come home. He can't sleep otherwise.'

Then they hugged, laughing, and Jimmy heard Aesop whisper into her ear.

'Mam would have loved him, Jen.'

There was a small glistening in Aesop's eye. Bloody hell, thought Jimmy. That was a new one too. Katie came over to them then and joined in the hug. Aesop looked up and got a kiss on the cheek from her for his trouble. Another axe buried. It was one of those nights.

Jimmy plonked down on the couch next to Shiggy and clapped him on the leg. Shiggy looked up with his huge blood-shot eyes and smiled.

'Jimmy-san. I'm borroxed,' he said, pointing to his nose.

'Me too, Shiggy,' said Jimmy, yawning. 'Me too.'

Jimmy strolled into McGuigans on Saturday evening, with a feeling he hadn't had since he was about seven-years-old and the Santy in Clery's told him that bringing him Kerplunk *and* Buckeroo would be no problem. He didn't even know why. There was just something in the air. Something was happening, or about to happen. It was all the excitement of being on the radio and telly, he reckoned. The lads had sat in his living room the night before, skulling cans of Kirin and listening to Tony King's show. Eventually there it was. Tony delivered as promised.

'And here's a new song. I played this one last night but it's so good, I thought I'd give it another spin. This is *Caillte*, by a band you may have seen gigging around Dublin called The Grove. They're playing McGuigans in Drumcondra tomorrow night, by the way. Watch out for these guys. This is something a bit special ... and hey Kayleigh, if you're listening, this is from Jimmy ...'

'Fuck me!' said Jimmy, looking around at the others in astonishment.

'Bloody hell,' said Norman. 'That'll do it!'

They listened to the song, all of them smiling their heads off. And then Tony went one better. He played *Kayleigh* by Marillion straight afterwards. Jimmy dropped his can when he heard it. Norman had to mop up the mess because Jimmy couldn't move. The whole thing was becoming surreal.

They headed out to the pub, where just about everyone seemed to know who they were. Not only that, they knew about the song, the TV appearance, Tony King's show, the works. Jimmy and Kayleigh were turning into the Love Story of the Year. To hear one girl in the pub tell it, half of Dublin was waiting to see what would happen next.   .

'Here he comes!' said John, from the bar of the Sound Cellar in McGuigans when he saw Jimmy coming down the stairs with his guitar case on Saturday evening.

'Howya John,' said Jimmy.

'Ooh. He remembers me name! Can I have an autograph, Jimmy? For the wife, like.'

'Yeah, no problem,' said Jimmy. 'Give us a pint though, will ye?' He sat up at the bar and took off his jacket.

'Would that be Guinness or would Sir perhaps like Champagne now that he's famous, like?'

'Do you have Champagne, John?' said Jimmy.

'Eh, no.'

'Well then.'

'I have white wine. I could shake up the bottle if you like. For the bubbles ...'

'Nah, Guinness is fine.'

'Grand so.'

He served it up when it was ready.

'This round's on the house, Jimmy.'

'Thanks John,' said Jimmy. 'Have one yourself so.'

John grinned.

'So, is this your last gig in McGuigans? We don't get too many people from the telly playing here, y'know?'

'Well, I'm not going to call you a mean bastard to your face, if that's what you mean. Not just yet. We'll wait for the Unplugged album before we start burning bridges.'

'Very sensible, Jimmy. Oh, Beano called earlier. He missed you at home and wanted a chat.'

'Beano? About what?'

'Eh, I think he wants to play here again. Tonight.'

'My arse, John.'

'Oh, thank God for that. I was afraid you'd let him. God, he was painful the last time. I haven't seen anyone bomb like that since *Saving Private Ryan*. I'd have been closing up early, only for Aesop.'

Jimmy laughed, took his pint to the stage and started to set up. The place was completely deserted still, only John pottering about with his cloth. Jimmy called to him to turn on the stage lights and stood there for a while, just looking out at the empty tables and chairs and smelling the Pledge. Neil Diamond was playing softly over the house system. How many times had Jimmy stood up here, giving it loads and wondering if he was actually any good or just a jammy bastard? He didn't even know. He looked into one of the red spotlights and suddenly felt more nervous than he could ever remember feeling before. This had been a psycho week. Telly, radio, Marco and Jennifer. He had butterflies all the way down his legs. It was as if he was suddenly at the end of something. Or the beginning. He told himself to stop being a spa, but it was no good. He couldn't help it.

The roar was the loudest Jimmy had ever heard. As soon as the house music went down and they stepped up onto the stage, the place started screaming and yelling. The word was out. There were a lot of regulars in the crowd. He knew the faces. Some of them had seen The Grove playing dozens of times. Most of them had seen them on *Cé Hé* and listened to Tony King's show, and they knew what was happening. In a week of firsts, this was another one. The Grove wasn't just his band any more; it was theirs too. He'd never thought of it like that before. The band's success was also theirs. They were part of it, and as proud of it as he was himself. It took a couple of minutes for them to shut up, with Shiggy, Aesop and himself just standing there, staring out at them, bewildered. Finally Jimmy waved them down and the three of them took up their instruments. He looked out into the crowd. God, he felt humble.

'Eh, thanks very much.' More cheering. He went on quickly, before they had a chance to go spare again. 'This has been a bit of a mad week. The last time I was on the telly was when me Mam was in *The Late Late Show* audience, pregnant with me.' Laughing. 'I didn't have much to say for meself that night, so I kept fairly quiet. Not like some people do. Some people don't know when to shut bleedin' up, y'know?' He looked around at Aesop, who gave a big thumbs up, and the crowd starting laughing and cheering again. 'Anyway, thanks for coming along tonight. John up there asked me to remind yiz all how important it is to drink in moderation.' Booing and John shaking his head vigorously behind the bar. 'But, he's only a grumpy oul' bastard, so bollocks to that!' They kicked off with *The Boys are Back in Town* and the place erupted.

An hour later, he looked around and swept the sweat from his head with a quick flick. They'd played mostly thumping rock songs. This wasn't a night for *Still in Love With You*. Shiggy and Aesop were on form tonight as well, playing out of their skins and throwing all the shapes. He was at it himself too, strutting and turning like he hadn't done in ages. The only thing wrong was in his stomach. The tingling was still there. Every now and again he peered against the lights to see if she'd turned up, but he couldn't see much in the glare. He did make out Sparky and Donal though, who came in halfway through the set and stood at the bar. Sparky gave a small wave and then got stuck into what looked like a pint of milk.

They broke it up after another half an hour and went down to the table, where Norman, Marco, Jennifer and the rest of the gang were sitting. After a quick half pint, Jimmy went up to the bar, to talk to Sparky and Donal. He didn't even know they were going to be there.

'Great gig Jimmy,' said Sparky, his milk moustache making him look like an evil, wrinkly child.

'Thanks, Sparky. Should you two not be working tonight?'

'Ah,' said Donal. 'We're celebrating. The end of our first recording session. All done.'

'First?' said Jimmy, pretending to be hurt.

'First one we got paid for Jimmy,' said Donal. 'Money, y'know? Pays the rent and keeps Sparky here in clean underpants and tablets for his liver. Listen, I don't want to distract you, but do you have a minute?'

Jimmy looked around. He'd planned on doing a quick search around the venue to see if she'd slipped in, but there wasn't much point. It wasn't the bloody Albert Hall, was it? If she was here, he'd see her. He looked at the clock over the bar.

'I've about five minutes,' he said.

'Grand.'

They walked over to the cigarette machine, where things were a bit quieter.

'Listen, I've a bit of news.'

'You always have a bit of news Donal,' said Jimmy.

'Yeah. Well, listen to this. Two things. First of all, Rocktopus want to cover *Meatloaf's Underpants.*'

'What?!' shouted Jimmy.

'You know Rocktopus?'

'Yeah. They're fucking terrible. Aesop likes them, so you know they're brutal. But ... how ... ?'

'Mate of mine is working on their new album. They're Welsh, right? He was over for the rugby a few weeks ago and dropped in to say hello. I gave him your CD and ... well, that's how things happen, y'know?'

'Fucking hell! Aesop will freak!'

'Yeah. And the other thing. I've got a DJ from Israel who wants to sample the dance version of *Caillte.*'

'A DJ from bleedin' Israel?! What the fuck are you talking about, Donal? What does that mean? He wants to sample it. What does that mean? Israel..?'

'Shush, Jimmy. It means two things. One, you're going to make a bit of dosh. And two, you're going to need a manager.' Donal took a piece a paper out of his pocket. 'My card,' he said, smiling.

'But ... but ...' said Jimmy.

'I'll talk to you later, Jimmy. There's more, but I just thought I'd mention that much to you. Look, you'd better go back up there. Aesop is looking for you. Break a leg.'

'Yeah,' said Jimmy, looking at the card in his hand. 'Oh, and thanks for not fucking distracting me by the way. Jesus ...'

Aesop came over the loudspeakers.

'Eh, if anyone can sing and play the guitar, will they come up here, please? We're after losing one of the junior members of the band. Doesn't matter if you're crap. Me and Shiggy are used to it ...'

Jimmy looked up at Donal again, still in shock, and ran back to the stage with his heart pounding. This was getting mental.

It got worse.

Of all the mad things that could have happened that night – and in this Jimmy included an army of penguins walking through the door and demanding that they play *Freebird* – the spectacle of his parents jiving on the dance floor in front of him was easily the most insane. But it was happening. Right there, in gloriously embarrassing technicolour, Peggy was twirling around Seán, who stood almost rooted to the spot, watching her. They even had a circle around them, clapping. Jimmy had no idea how his mother had managed to get his father to leave the house on a Saturday night and come here of all places, but he suspected that there wasn't much left in that bottle of Paddy in the sideboard. Eventually his father was released and practically ran to the bar to join Donal and Sparky, to whom he hadn't really spoken the other night but with whom he was about to forge a determined friendship. It was either that or be made dance again.

'Thanks very much,' said Jimmy, after the song. He was still stunned. He'd never seen anyone jive to a Prodigy song before and it hadn't been pretty. 'And my mother is here tonight, in case you hadn't guessed, so please watch what you say about me if you like your ears attached to your head. Right. Here's an oldie called *Unchained Melody* for me Mam, and Sparky up there at the bar. And Ma, I'm thirty years old. There is absolutely nothing you could do that would embarrass me.'

Three and a half minutes later he stepped to the mike again.

'I stand corrected.'

The rest of the set was as normal as anything was going to be that night. The band was on fire, the crowd was hopping and dancing and cheering. Marco and Jennifer were going for some kind of snog record and Norman had finally found someone that danced like he did in Jimmy's Mam. Everyone was in a real party mood, with Christmas coming on and with everything that had happened for the band that week. Even Beano and Sandra, who had come in quietly, were up dancing.

Sandra had given Jimmy a quick congratulatory kiss on the cheek earlier, and handed him a CD while Beano was at the bar.

'What's this?' he asked.

'It's Lavender's Teardrop. I know it's a big secret and all, you playing on it, but I thought you might like it for your scrapbook. Five songs you probably wish you'd never heard,' she said, grinning.

'Thanks Sandra,' he said. Then he looked at her. 'Five songs?'

'Oh yeah. Sparky's little joke. Track five is Beano doing the twelve times tables,' she laughed. 'It even has you doing twelve times eleven! Beano hit the roof when he heard it. He's making copies but without that one. What you have there is a collector's item, Jimmy. It'll be worth a fortune one day. Anyway, best of luck with everything. It's a beautiful song. I hope she appreciates it.' She gave his arm a squeeze and then went off to find Beano.

Now it was coming up to midnight and Jimmy knew that there was only time for three or four more songs. He was in some kind of zone and he didn't want the gig to ever end. No one had dropped a note all night and he felt like he belonged on the stage more than ever before. But the stomach thing was still there and Kayleigh still wasn't. Shit, he thought. This week was straight out of a bloody fairytale. Who ever heard of a fairytale that didn't have a happy ending? She had to be there! They played another two songs, and then John started signalling from the bar. That was it.

Superchick, thought Jimmy. My arse.

He introduced *Meatloaf's Underpants* as the last song, turning around to Aesop who stood up and bowed, pumping the air with his fists, and then they played it. Jimmy had finally managed to put some pleasant melody lines running through it so it didn't sound too bad any more. The crowd went crazy at the end and the band all came to the front of the stage and bowed. Then the chants for 'One More Song!' started up and Jimmy frowned theatrically and looked at his watch.

Then he smiled and started into *Caillte*.

The crowd hushed. There was an almost reverential silence.

Last chance, he thought, looking through the lights towards the door. If you were going to make a grand entrance and finish this thing Hollywood style, Kayleigh, then right about now would be a good time to do it. He closed his eyes and started to sing.

As he went on, he realised that some people in the crowd were singing in harmony with him. It sounded beautiful, but he didn't open his eyes. She'd be coming down the stairs now. The chorus filled the whole venue and he felt the tightness in his middle begin to ease, but he didn't open his eyes. Now she'd be gliding towards the stage, towards him. The last verse came straight from his soul, but it seemed like he wasn't even singing any more. Some kind of magic had filled the room, but he didn't open his eyes. The crowd would be parting for her, as she finally reached the front. The ringing notes at the end of the song died away and he knew it was time to look. She'd be there, standing right in front of him and looking up, tears coursing down her cheeks. He opened his eyes and looked down. And there she was – his mother.

So much for bloody fairytales.

Jimmy smiled weakly at the thundering applause that had every beam in the ceiling rattling and looked out. No. She wasn't there. Get real, Jimmy, she was never going to be there, was she? The cheering went on for ages, with shouts for more, but Jimmy and the lads just bowed again and again and eventually got off the stage. John turned up the house music and the stage lights went off.

Jimmy went straight to the toilet, to wash his face and change his shirt. He was drenched. He stood at the mirror for a minute, leaning on the sink, just looking. Best gig of his life. Best week of his life. All for her. God, where was she?

He cleaned himself up and went outside, stopping by the table to say hello to everyone.

'Go on up to your father love,' said Peggy, who was badgering Jennifer and Marco about the big day. 'He's dying to talk to you.'

Jimmy went up to the bar and stood with Sparky, Donal and his Dad.

'Pint?' said his Dad, looking around.

'Cheers,' said Jimmy.

By half past one, the place was cleared of punters. Jimmy's folks had gone home and only Jimmy and the gang were there, along with Donal and Sparky. John told them they could stay, but that he wasn't serving them any more beer.

'Ah, John. What's the fucking point then?' moaned Aesop.

'You can serve yourselves. Only this one time, though! To celebrate being on the telly and all,' said John. The world was gone mad.

Aesop jumped up and tried to kiss him, but John was armed with a mop and wasn't having any of it.

Later, they were all fairly pissed again. Donal and Jimmy had told Aesop about Rocktopus covering his song and it had taken ten minutes to calm him down. Then Donal said that they could easily make fifty grand from it, maybe more, depending on how Rocktopus's album went, and Aesop nearly fainted.

'Fif ... fifty ... fifty ...?' he said, his voice quavering. 'For that song?'

'Yep. That's the way it works Aesop,' said Donal.

'Fuck me. I could ... I could retire ...' said Aesop, looking around at everyone.

Jimmy just laughed at that, shaking his head.

Donal started into all the ways that royalties were split and the tax considerations and commissions and everything. It all sounded like a lot of work.

'You have to decide who wrote what as well,' he said. 'Tune, lyrics ...'

'Let's talk about it tomorrow,' said Jimmy. 'Right now I just want to drink pints while John is suffering from temporary insanity over there.'

They put on some CDs and started dancing around and messing. Then a slow Phil Collins song came on and Marco and Jennifer got up to dance. The rest of them watched for a minute, smiling as they gazed at each other and turned around and around. Then Katie grabbed Aesop's arm and pulled him onto the floor. Jimmy saw panic in Aesop's face and laughed. Aesop and Katie? Stranger things had happened. Most of this week, for instance, could put the prospect of Aesop and Katie to shame. Well, she'd put manners on him anyway, there was no doubt about that. Then Shiggy and Maeve got up, followed by Norman and Michelle the Amazing Piss Monster. The floor was full of couples now. Jimmy took a smoke from Donal and the two of them and Sparky sat back and watched, trying to ignore John noisily squeezing the last of the Parazone around the Gents.

Phil wasn't finished having a whinge, so Jimmy got up with Jennifer next and everyone else switched around, except for Aesop. Katie wasn't letting him go anywhere.

'How are you feeling?' said Jennifer, close to Jimmy's cheek.

'Ah, grand Jen. It's been some bloody week, hasn't it?'

She laughed.

'Yeah, it has. Eh, Jimmy ... ?' She paused.

'Yeah?'

'Just ... look ... I'm sorry she didn't show up.'

'Yeah ... thanks. You know the whole story, then?'

'Ah, of course I do, Jimmy. I've known for months. The whole Superchick thing? Marco couldn't keep a secret to save his life. Not if I wanted to be in on it anyway. I knew something was up when he started printing out pasta recipes from the web, the eejit. I got it out of him then. I even sent him out to his poker night with a bag of stale buns, for the craic. You should have seen the face on him when he tasted one. Myself and Katie were laughing all night, thinking of you lot trying to eat them, and the onion salt and everything.' She paused. 'But this Kayleigh from the song was your Superchick, wasn't she? It wasn't just a song or just some girl, was it? And I was watching you tonight. You wanted her to be here. I'm sorry she wasn't.'

'That's okay, Jen. I mean, look at all the stuff that's happened for the band. Y'know? You can't have everything, can you?'

'I don't know. Sometimes you can. I have,' she said, looking over at Marco and Maeve and smiling.

'Yeah. And you deserve it Jen,' said Jimmy.

She looked up at him.

'So do you, Jimmy.'

He shrugged. This was starting to get heavy. He felt a bit too fragile after the week he'd just had to keep talking about it. To Jen, of all people. His crying over Kayleigh was the last thing anyone needed tonight. Except him, maybe.

'So, did my brother find his Superchick?' said Jennifer.

'Eh, well he thought he did there for a while. Turned out to be more of a Superslag, though.'

'Yeah. That sounds about right. You think himself and Katie ... ?'

Jimmy looked over.

'Well, does it count if one partner is afraid of the other partner?' he said.

'Why not?'

'Yeah. Worked for my folks, didn't it?' said Jimmy, smiling.

She squeezed his shoulder.

'You'll keep an eye on him, won't you, Jimmy? When Marco and me ...'

'Don't worry, Jen. I think Aesop is turning a corner. Really. I know it sounds mad, but I think it's happening. He'll be fine.'

'God, I hope so. And Norman?'

'Ah, Norman's his own man. He'll find a woman when the time is right.'

'He's a really nice guy,' said Jennifer.

'The best, Jen. He's brilliant. She'll be lucky.'

After another while, Phil ran out of things to be sad about and they all sat down again and got stuck into the beer while it was going. The joking and slagging started up again, as it always did, but with a subdued Aesop being at the end of a lot of it for holding Katie's hand. He didn't bother explaining to Norman that he'd bloody let go if he could.

Shiggy slipped away to the bar to perform a special ritual. Something that would ensconce him into the group in a way that no amount of bass playing would ever be able to do. He pulled four pints of Guinness and started to watch them set. He'd been waiting for weeks to do this; practising at home every day with pint glasses of water the way Marco had shown him. This was his big moment. His coming of age.

There was a thump from the top of the stairs. The Sunday papers.

Jimmy suddenly remembered that Tony's column would be out. He ran up and grabbed the *Sunday Post*. There it was, on page eighteen.

They all crowded around the paper and scanned the column quickly. It was only two sentences, but they were good:

> ... Also making waves this week is a band from Drumcondra called The Grove. Look out for their excellent new single *Caillte*, which should be hitting the streets next week, just in time for Christmas ...

'Brilliant!' said Jimmy. 'But ... hang on ... what does he mean about a single hitting the streets?'

'Actually Jimmy,' said Donal, 'I took a couple of liberties, I'm afraid. You want to talk tonight or tomorrow?'

'Bloody hell ...' said Jimmy, wearily shaking his head. 'Tomorrow, Donal. I think I've had enough surprises for one night, y'know?'

Sparky stood up suddenly and they all looked at him. He had the paper in his hand and was trying to say something, but he couldn't. He just pointed to the bottom of the front page. Eventually he gave it to Aesop next to him and pointed at the small article. Everyone was looking at Aesop now, curiously.

'What is it, Aesop?' said Jimmy.

Aesop just shook his head, frowning and reading. Then he looked up. He was pale and staring at Jimmy.

'Aesop, what the fuck is it?'

'Eh, you know what you just said? About not wanting any more surprises?'

Jimmy nodded.

He handed Jimmy the paper and pointed.

Jimmy started reading. He seemed to shrink as he did.

'This isn't fucking happening,' he said, when he looked up. His face was burning.

They were all staring at him. Norman grabbed the paper and read it out loud, his eyes gradually turning into dinner plates.

GUILTY VERDICT RETURNED ON SCAM ARTISTS

At a special sitting of Dublin's Criminal Court yesterday, two women were found guilty of a series of crimes relating to a scam that has been operating in the city for at least six months. Ms Kayleigh Laird (28) of Fairview and Ms Leslie O'Connor (27) of Killester were arrested last week in connection with the scam.

A search of Ms Laird's home, on Thursday evening, revealed over two hundred mobile phones, all allegedly stolen from young men on the North Side of the city ...

There was stunned silence, everyone looking at Jimmy open-mouthed. He was holding his scarlet face in his hands, the wind sucked out of him and his skin tingling.

Then Shiggy made his grand entrance. Four perfect pints in two tiny hands, and not a drop spilt. He was beaming.

'Supplies!'

CRÍOCH
(The End)

Go raibh míle ...

The list of people who helped make this book a reality is a long and bendy one. First up, it goes without saying that the people who were around when I was starting out deserve even more thanks now that the book is actually sitting here in readers' hands. Ruth Kelly, Joe Burke, Angelika Burke, Seán Burke, Brian Dolan, Rie Dolan, Colm Steele and Fiona Lodge helped get it off the ground. Julia Klett and Christian Buchkremer gave it some very sexy wings. Jonie Hell, Niall McCarthy and Fiona MacDonnell were on hand to make sure that what I wrote about the recording and broadcasting industries wasn't completely devoid of the truth, although I think I managed to sneak a few clangers past them to suit myself when they weren't looking. Any beautifully and comprehensively researched verifiable facts are probably theirs. Any bloody awful rubbish is undoubtedly mine.

Before the fictional 'The Grove' was the very real 'Yer Mot's a Dog' and I'd like to thank Eric, Jonie and Brian (and Regina and Brian J.) for some great gig(gle)s. Not to mention the germ of an idea.

The book you're holding now would never have become a reality without those people who read an earlier version and took the time to write and tell me they enjoyed it. That made a huge difference to everything that happened afterwards. Thanks heaps. And to the many friends and my family who went above and beyond the call of duty to do what they could to help it all happen, I definitely owe you a pint as well (between yiz).

And, talking of going above and beyond, my publisher has been nothing short of exceptional and I'd like to thank everyone at Mercier Press for the incredible amount of work that they've put into *Superchick* and the faith they've shown in its author. It's a real privilege to work with such skilled and dedicated professionals.

Thanks to my parents, whose every bun and clip on the ear over the years – both dispensed with an even hand as deserved – are greatly appreciated now that I'm all grown up and mature.

Above all, by loads, thanks and much love to Ruth for putting up with both of us (me and the book) for this long. *Caillte a bheinn* ...

SJM
Sydney, 2005